ALSO BY ANGIE CRUZ

Soledad

Let It Rain Coffee

Angie Cruz

Simon & Schuster
New York London Toronto Sydney

SIMON & SCHUSTER
Rockefeller Center
1230 Avenue of the Americas
New York, NY 10020

SIMON & SCHUSTER and colophon are registered trademarks of Simon & Schuster, Inc.

For information about special discounts for bulk purchases,
please contact Simon & Schuster Special Sales:
1-800-456-6798 or business@simonandschuster.com.

Manufactured in the United States of America

10 9 8 7 6 5 4 3 2 1

Library of Congress Cataloging-in-Publication Data

Cruz, Angie.
    Let it rain coffee : a novel / Angie Cruz.
      p. cm.
      1. Washington Heights (New York, N.Y.)—Fiction. 2. Dominican Americans—Fiction.
    3. Immigrants—Fiction. I. Title.

    PS3603.R89L47 2005
    813'.6—dc22

                                                            2004065329

    ISBN 0-7432-1203-7

The author and the publisher gratefully acknowledge permission from the following source:
From "Guantanamera"; musical adaptation by Pete Seeger and Julian Orbon. Lyric adaptation by Julian Orbon, based on a poem by José Martí. Lyric editor: Hector Angulo. Original music and lyrics by José Fernandez Diaz. Copyright © 1963 (renewed) by Fall River Music, Inc. All rights reserved. Used by permission.

For the men, women, and children who died in the struggle against imperialism during the U.S. occupation in Dominican Republic in the early 1900s and in 1965.

En la lucha siempre, pa'lante.

When it's truly alive, memory doesn't contemplate history, it invites us to make it. More than in museums, where its poor old soul gets bored, memory is the air we breathe, and from the air, it breathes us.

—EDUARDO GALEANO, *UPSIDE DOWN*

Author's Note

The title of this book, *Let It Rain Coffee,* was inspired by the song "Ojalá que llueva café en el campo," by Juan Luis Guerra.

Los Llanos
1991

Don Chan Lee Colón de Juan Dolio ignored the stench that wafted through the valleys of Los Llanos. From the outside of his humble wooden house nothing seemed out of the ordinary. The passion fruit and mango trees were lush, shaking their leaves with the mildest of sea breezes, gossiping stories to the birds about Don Chan's strange old-man ways. The pigeons lifted their beaks, concerned that Doña Caridad hadn't left rice for them to feast on. It had been three days. No rice. No Doña Caridad. Only the strange smell from the small house where the Colón family had lived for three generations.

The house sat in an abandoned landscape. Its faded rose-colored paint peeled off. The train stocked with cane stalks woke the lazy goats in the yard where they lay, as if to guard the aging couple who refused to leave Los Llanos. The hungry pigs roaming his land turned their noses away. Many from the valley had taken off to live in the developing cities in search of jobs, but Don Chan and Doña Caridad stayed behind.

—I can't close my eyes without the city coming back and spitting on me, he said to the younger folk who accused him of being afraid of change.

Miraluz Altagracia Natera asked the driver to park far enough away from the house so as to not jolt Don Chan. There was a stillness in

Los Llanos that crept under her skin. The young man with a cleft lip who assisted Don Chan and tended to the land rich with mangoes, plátanos, cacao, and lechosas had called Miraluz weeks before.

—I don't think it's right for the old lady to be so far away from a doctor, the caretaker had said. —By the time anyone gets help, it'll be too late to save her. I don't mean to disrespect, but nothing anyone says to the old man sinks into that hard head of his.

—I'll do my best, Miraluz said, knowing very well that she was the daughter Don Chan had always wanted, the woman he had hoped his son, Santo, would marry. It had been a few months since she'd last taken a trip to Los Llanos. She often called or sent word to Don Chan, but the trip from San Pedro de Macorís to Los Llanos was long enough for her to keep postponing it.

Miraluz held her breath and pounded on the makeshift door. The flamboyan tree, rich with yellow flowers, bent over the porch and shaded the house from the harsh midday sun. The sky, a brilliant blue, made the cane fields iridescent.

—Anyone home? she yelled, contemplating whether she should pull the door open or wait.

—Open the door. It's me, Miraluz. She pushed against the latch. She had hired the driver for two hours and didn't have time for Don Chan's stubbornness. As she marched inside the little house, it trembled from her haste. That damn house, over seventy years old, the only one in the area to survive numerous hurricanes, revolutions, dictatorships, and wars.

—Don't fall apart on me now.

The house was in complete order: the cement floors freshly mopped, the wood for the kitchen stove piled up neatly into a small pyramid, the cans of water filled to the brim; the furniture propped against the walls, leaving the room spare, as if waiting for a gathering. Not much had changed in the eight years since she'd moved to the city. If it hadn't been for the strange odor that permeated every room, she would've thought it was 1965 and that any minute, Santo would burst through the door with some news about the Yanquis, or Doña Caridad would have piled up the víveres in the kitchen, freshly plucked from Los Llanos's communal garden, filling up the bellies of anyone who entered the Colón household. And Don Chan would be smoking his cigar, sitting alone somewhere, close enough to look over everyone, but far enough to gather courage for the battle.

Miraluz noticed the photographs she had sent Don Chan of her children, taped on the walls next to la Virgen de Altagracia. The door to the old couple's bedroom was partly opened. Miraluz caught a glimpse of Doña Caridad on her bed, behind the mosquito net. She covered her nose with her hands and her throat swelled from holding back tears.

Don Chan watched over Doña Caridad, who lay peacefully on worn yellow sheets, her brown skin turned ashen, her full lips dry and cracked. The relentless sun poured in through the window over her. The small wooden cross over the bed tipped over. His cigars rested beside a small glass of rum and a red candle lit to keep them company. A cassava shell filled with water and a yucca root placed on her nightstand for her journey.

—She said it was her time. Don Chan's voice cracked from disuse.

Miraluz put her hand on his bony shoulders. If she let go of him, Don Chan would fall apart, he was sure of it. He had spent hours sitting by the bed, watching over his wife. He tended to the house, returning to her side, tucking her arms over and under the sheets, changing the dial of the small radio, opening and closing the shutters, batting away the flies that sat on her face.

Miraluz pressed herself against his back, and bent down to kiss his head. Her hands were warm on his neck. How long had it been since someone had touched him? Her touch awakened his body. He hadn't died with his wife. He had waited for Doña Caridad to say something to make sense of her departure. Seventy years with his old lady, and she took part of his mind with her. Don't, he wanted to tell Miraluz, whose fingers lifted away from him. Don't move. I can't bear the absence.

...

Miraluz let go of Don Chan and saw his body fold over. She listened to his soft exhale, and walked away to allow him privacy. She asked the driver to take her to the nearest phone to call Don Chan's son, Santo, who had moved to the United States almost a decade ago. He would know what to do. She hoped that his wife, Esperanza, wouldn't pick up the phone.

1

Boarding, Sto. Dgo. to NYC
1991

Months after his wife passed away, Don Chan found himself at Las Américas Airport in the city of Santo Domingo. He didn't trust man-made machines, but he boarded the airplane to New York City anyway. And for most of the trip, he pretended that he wasn't afraid of it crashing. He closed his eyes and leaned back. Periodically, he checked his shirt pocket for his passport, pen, and visa. Every few minutes he shifted in his seat in fear of numbness.

—Desea café? the young flight attendant asked with a big smile.

—No, gracias, he replied. While the coffee could've settled his nerves, he didn't want to experience the awkwardness of finding the bathroom, only to obsess over the possibility that his waste would be spat into the sky. He knew the world was built in such a way that some got to piss in toilets high above everyone else while the less privileged sat at home thinking the piss was rain. He'd rather wait until his arrival. His son, Santo, had insisted he come to New York. And while Don Chan resisted at first, the invitation came as a blessing. Now that his wife had passed, their small house in Los Llanos felt too large for him, and the coffee he made for himself was always bitter.

—Let me go, Viejo. It's my time, were Doña Caridad's last words. They rattled around Don Chan's head like pennies in a tin cup. Was she trying to tell him that there is a better time to die? Is that why she died so peacefully? What if he didn't recognize his time? What if his life was taken from him? Would his restless soul torture the living until he found peace? The end was near for Don Chan. He knew that much. But to think that he would have to walk into death at any moment without resistance preoccupied him.

When the wheels of the plane touched the ground, the passengers burst into applause. He felt relief in the pit of his stomach. He took a deep breath. He focused on seeing his son, Santo, and his grandchildren, one of whom had been born American and he had yet to meet. He tried to imagine what he would find outside that plane. He touched the woolen fabric of the seat in front of him to assure himself that it was real.

In the immigration line, he pretended to understand English, nodding when the woman directed him to the longer line filled with anxious passengers. Don Chan looked over to the other line, for U.S. citizens, and sucked his teeth over the way the passengers with blue passports rushed through; a little girl, sunburned, head full of tiny braids, waved at him.

Don Chan walked up to the immigration desk.

—What were you doing in the Dominican Republic? the officer asked with a question mark on his brow line. He repeated himself in broken Spanish. His cheeks were pink, like the tops of his ears.

—I was born there.

The officer eyed him.

For the first time in a long time, Don Chan caught a glimpse of his own reflection. He never cared to look into a mirror back home, but from the quick look he caught of himself in the officer's eyes, Don Chan realized that his Chinese face was confusing the officer holding the Dominican passport.

—I can tell you a story, Don Chan said.

—Excuse me?

—My wife found me on the beach when she was four years old. And as if I was some kind of alien, she poked at my hair and said . . . —*Who are you?* And I said, —*Chan Lee, yo soy Chan Lee.* I couldn't remember anything but my name. It was 1916. I was six years old, washed up on the shores of Juan Dolio. If my wife were alive, she could prove it to you.

The officer behind the desk took Don Chan's passport and left him waiting. After he went through the trouble of getting his papers straight, Don Chan didn't understand why all the inquiry. He searched the line, noticing the worried, anxious, wound-up faces of the other passengers who were about to embark on a new life. It saddened him to think that after living almost his entire life on that small island, there was no one in that room who could explain to the officer who he was. The officer returned. He carefully checked the photograph and pecked at the computer. Don Chan wanted nothing more than to return home where no one scrutinized him.

—Are you here for business or pleasure?

—I'm here to see my son.

—Welcome to the United States, the officer said as he waved over the next person in line.

Don Chan's suitcases were already waiting for him at the baggage claim. To his surprise, the customs officer allowed him to exit the airport without asking for a tip for his hospitality. He hesitantly walked out of the airport into a cold that exposed a decaying sky and made his balls shrink. He didn't see Santo anywhere. He waited on the curb by the taxi stand.

—Taxi, you need a taxi. Men hovered around him showing him their business cards. —Thirty dollar. Forty dollar. Taxi. Taxi.

His bare ankles found no refuge. He pretended the cold didn't bother him and that he had been in an airport many times, that the snow piled by the curb was not a novelty. He stood against a wall for protection and felt himself contract into something small and hard. He held his bag near his legs, regretting the trip to New York City, wondering why no one was at the airport to pick him up. Crossing guards whistled so that cars could hurry along. Buses yielding, airplanes landing and taking off. Luggage crashing against the ground. Everything was so loud, he didn't hear Esperanza.

—Hey, Don Chan! A redheaded, full-figured woman in high heels hopped over the snow piles toward him and planted a wet kiss on his cheek. —Don't tell me it's been that long, she said and waved Santo's car over and pulled Don Chan's suitcases across the slush with one arm.

—What happened to your hair? he asked, marveling at the bright red that stood out among all the gray that made up the city. Esperanza was full of color: bright lips, cheeks, eyes, hair. A voluminous green full-length coat hid the weight she'd gained in the States.

—Qué loco eres, Viejo.

Esperanza rushed Don Chan across the street before the traffic light changed. People bumped against each other's bodies, without apologizing. She wrapped her scarf around his neck.—They still haven't invented the cure for the cold. With all the great things America has done, they still haven't figured that out, Esperanza said.

—If they invent the cure for the cold, who'd they sell all their medicines to? He had forgotten how naive she was.

—We have to hurry or they will give Santo a ticket.

Santo Colón. His only son. Suddenly, the violent cold weather and noise became a secondary concern for Don Chan. He patted down his hair and his stomach fluttered with anticipation.

Esperanza pushed the grocery bags from the backseat to one side to make room for herself. She watched Santo and Don Chan embrace outside the car before they put his things in the trunk. She made a promise to herself that she'd be optimistic. Don Chan was too old to be much trouble anymore. Maybe in Dominican Republic, he had Santo carrying out his every whim, but Santo was no longer a boy. He was a man with his own family, and Esperanza was his wife. Besides, he was living in her home now, and if he gave her a hard time, she'd send him back to live out his last days alone in his miserable campo.

—Coño, Santo, you're all bones, son. Is this woman feeding you? Don Chan asked as he climbed into the front seat.

Santo laughed. Esperanza bit her tongue.

—Or did the cold eat away at your meat?

—How was the flight? Santo asked, keeping his eye on the road.

—Slept through it.

Esperanza took care of plenty of old people and could tell that he hadn't slept a wink.

—Feels like a long way from home, doesn't it? Santo asked.

From the sea, to Juan Dolio, to Los Llanos, to Nueva York.

Not far enough, Esperanza thought.

Picking up Don Chan at the airport reminded Esperanza of how eager she had been to arrive in Nueva York. To Esperanza, New York City had always been Nueva York—an oasis of opportunity. And when she first saw all the trees in the distance, she had imagined that the Southfork Ranch in Dallas, Texas, was not too far off.

When she first arrived, many of the businesses on Broadway changed hands. She could only catch the tail end of the mom-and-pop sandwich shop specializing in deli meats, the specialty children's clothing store owned by a Cuban lady, who kept saying, —These Dominicans are making a mess around here. She didn't have time to get attached to, let alone miss, the neighborhood it once was before it became Nueva York. A neighborhood filled with fruit markets, a corner bookstore, the small photo shop that stank of unwashed scalp and damp wool, the five-and-dime that didn't sell anything for less than a quarter, or the bakery display cases of rugelach and babka. Of course, there were still traces of what the neighborhood had once been in the seventies, but the relics of time that belonged to older immigrants much like herself were quickly disappearing. She walked into a neighborhood in the early eighties celebrating the grand openings of freshly painted bodegas, travel agencies, botánicas, liquor and discount stores.

Back then she didn't see the buildings as gray, or the city as grimy; or mind the crowds of people sitting on the front stoops catching a cold on a sunny day. The police might have called it loitering, but Esperanza called it community. She didn't think twice about the threat of nuclear war, the stock market crashing, the lack of trees, or the fact that the streets had the smell of an impossible dream. The sidewalks had given her a bounce that lifted her up above everyone else's head, despite the faces of the old black couple, looking out their window, who had survived the sixties only to find that their children still couldn't get a decent education, and that cops sat in their cars, perched like hawks seeking out prey. She didn't notice how her moving in was inspiring an exodus so great that the apartment prices had dropped and the Sanitation Department stopped making daily visits. All that didn't matter to her. The novel sights of the city were filled with a beauty only the unknown could hold.

Had it been almost ten years since their arrival? Back then, Bobby was stuttering words, Dallas a newborn, Santo with a full head of hair, black and thick. She was thirty and could easily fit into a size-six pair of jeans. She still had those jeans in her closet. We were so young, Esperanza thought, and remembered how all four of them, wearing thin sweaters, had huddled toward their new home on Quepasó Street.

And much like they had, Don Chan arrived in Nueva York on one of the coldest days of the season.

—It's to thicken the blood, Santo said buttoning up his coat as they quickly made their way to their building.

The postal worker pushed his cart and waved.

—Hola, Esperanza said, waving to him as if she were on a float in a parade. And Esperanza was in a parade. The whole world walked beside her, cheering her on. If she had heard music, she would've started shaking her hips, bumping them into the Nueva York air.

—Look, Don Chan, we could send letters here.

In D.R., Esperanza had never sent a letter, because they never arrived. —That's when you know you're in civilization, she said, pointing to the man holding bushels of mail. —He has something to deliver.

—Is this it? Don Chan asked, looking at the impressive building that was bigger than what he had imagined. So this is brick, and stoops, fire escapes and lampposts. All things he had read about but had never seen. So this is a tree in a city: anemic, naked and alone among all the concrete. Music bounced inside apartments against the closed windows. Some neighbors pulled open their curtains to see who was entering the building. Cars honked their way up Quepasó Street, through the boys playing stickball.

Santo awkwardly opened the door's busted lock, and the building's lobby light twitched.

—¿Aquí se va la luz? Don Chan asked, noting how dark everything was.

—Never, Esperanza chirped with pride. —We always have lights.

Esperanza distracted Don Chan's attention away from the cigarette butts pushed up against the walls and the graffiti in the lobby. She hurried Don Chan along to escape the smell of pot and piss in the elevator.

—Doesn't anyone clean here? Don Chan asked.

—The super's off on the weekends, Esperanza said, frustrated that they still couldn't afford to move into a nicer building. —Don Chan, don't be ungrateful, Esperanza said as she walked slightly ahead of them. —He went from pissing in the dirt, with a house with no roof and he's complaining.

Esperanza threw her bags on the small yellow velvet sofa that was reupholstered in clear plastic. She opened the window. —It's either too hot or too cold, she said and moved about nervously to make room for Don Chan's things.

Don Chan held his face in his hands. The pressure against his cheeks reassured him. He looked out the window to see the Dominican flag waving from a corner lamppost. Some boys stood on the corners with hoods protecting their faces from the cold; fruit vendors rubbed their hands between serving customers; ambulance sirens wailed from a distance, cars double-parked all along the street; salsa blared from the back of one car and merengue from the other. He felt a headache coming.

—And where are my grandchildren? Don Chan asked, looking around at the cramped living room.

—La maldita televisión has them. Muchachos, your grandfather's home, Santo yelled. Slowly, they piled out of the dark bedroom.

—Roberto, come over here and kiss your grandfather. You might not remember me, but as a kid you followed me around all over Los Llanos.

Don Chan reached his arms out to Bobby and grabbed him. Bobby stared at his sneakers when he said hello and quickly pulled away. Look up, boy, Don Chan wanted to say.

—Call him Bobby. In America, he's Bobby, Esperanza said.

—Bobbi?

Don Chan pronounced an *o* sound versus an *a* sound.

—No, it's Bobby.

—Bobbi, he said again, Bobbi, Bobbi, struggling with his tongue to get it right. Upset that Esperanza changed Roberto María's name, when he was named after his great uncle, who had saved twenty-two people from drowning in a flood after a hurricane.

—Damn, boy, you're the spitting image of your father. My goodness, the same caramelo skin, shy eyes, a strong nose. That means you'll be able to make decisions. And tall too. What are you now, thirteen years old? Isn't that true, Esperanza?

—He has his father's attitude too.

Esperanza pulled Bobby away from him.

—And you, Dallas—is that how you say it? Come over here. I came all the way from Dominican Republic to meet you.

Don Chan wondered if his all-American granddaughter, born in Puerto Rico, understood a word he said. She was ten years old, still allowing her mother to comb her hair and put it in pigtails.

—Bendición, Abuelo. She gave him a kiss. She had the face of Doña Caridad. Round cheeks with dimples. Almond-shaped eyes and pink, full lips. —Hit me again.

He bent down to fetch Dallas's kiss, feeling a sudden pang of loss for his wife.

—Don Chan, you'll sleep in Dallas's room, and Dallas will be sharing a room with Bobby.

—I don't want to share with Bobby!

Bobby pulled Dallas's hair. Dallas shoved Bobby.

—Mami, Bobby yelled. —Tell her to leave me alone.

—Have some respect for your grandfather.

Santo rubbed his hand on his belt. They quickly composed themselves, stepping away from each other.

—You hungry? Santo asked, nudging Esperanza away so he could be alone with his father.

—Am I gonna have to change my name too? Don Chan joked. But he wasn't joking. What did they expect of him? He was too old to change anything. His name was Chan Lee Colón de Juan Dolio. He wasn't about to change his name.

—Dallas reminds me of *alas*, Esperanza said in her defense. —I called her that because I want her to fly.

—Fly where?

Don Chan regretted asking. He didn't want to know what Esperanza had up her sleeve. And the way she flitted about the room like a butterfly made him overly anxious. No, a butterfly was too beautiful. Esperanza was nothing like Las Mariposas, synonymous with the Mirabal sisters. Esperanza wouldn't have risked her life to save her country from Trujillo. No, no, Esperanza was more like a moth. Attracted to the lightbulb, plain and pesty.

—Fly in life. That's what all mothers want for their children.

Dallas did remind him of something. Don Chan placed his finger on his top lip. And in the same way he remembered certain dreams, or different moments in his life, he remembered the man in the cowboy hat inside la Loca's television, the first television in Los Llanos. Every Monday and Thursday night, the neighbors gathered around la Loca's TV.

—Dallas. Sí, sí. It's the novela with the cowboys.

Don Chan clapped when he made the connection. Ever since Doña Caridad's departure, he was forgetting many things. —Sí, sí, it was the only time you gave my son peace, when you went off to watch that show, Don Chan said, patting Santo on the back.

—And the next thing you knew, every woman in Los Llanos had the same haircut, Santo said and started to hum the *Dallas* theme song and wave his hands in the air playing conductor.

—You're exaggerating, Esperanza said, defending herself. —What's wrong with wanting things to change?

—Did you ever! Santo exclaimed.

—What does that mean? Esperanza tried to forget the arguments they'd had back in Los Llanos. On the nights she watched the show *Dallas*, she retired home to complain of the low ceilings she had to live under and the lopsided holes in the walls they called windows.

—Santo, why do you always hunch over like that? she'd say and go toward him to fix his shirt collar. She became annoyed by how shabby he looked in his loose *guayaberas*. She wanted him to tuck in his shirts. She patted pomade on her hands and pushed his hair away from his face to mimic Bobby Ewing's.

—*Mujer,* what is that stuff you put in my hair?

—I'm trying to fix it.

—You never complained about it before, Santo snapped back.

She hummed the *Dallas* theme song as she went about her days. Mouthing Pamela's dialogue when she became discouraged. *The important thing is to live each day to the fullest and as long as you do, they'll be the happiest in your life.* But no matter how much Esperanza polished her utensils, mirrors, the glass figurines on the shelves, they never shone for long. The dust was persistent. The condensation, salt, and heat made a coat of dirt on everything. The more the elements fought with her, the harder she tried to deceive them. And the short, feathered bangs that looked so great on Pamela didn't survive the humidity of D.R. No matter how much lye Esperanza combed through her hair, it curled and crimped and fanned out like an old broom.

—No más! Esperanza yelled at her own reflection in the blotchy mirror that made her brown skin look as if she was riddled with beauty marks. —*Maldita vida mía,* I'm going to Dallas, she had whispered to herself, afraid that if someone heard her, they'd convince her to stay in Los Llanos. She'd heard of people who made their way to Nueva York. Dallas couldn't be far off. She imagined herself working for a rich family. Just like Raul and Teresa, the Ewings' housekeepers. If only Teresa would have said something on that show but no, she just stood there in the background waiting to serve. Esperanza was tired of waiting.

She couldn't bear to see Santo work the land of Los Llanos every day so that her lazy neighbors, who got blisters from thinking about harvesting a crop, could eat off his sweat. Especially when all that time, she could've been living like a queen. Her father had warned her that if she left the capital where she was born, to live in Los Llanos with Santo, she would regret it. But all Santo had to do was take his share of the land away from Don Chan and breed cattle and cultivate rice like the Spaniards did back in the days. Or sell the land to some foreigners like other people had already done. But Don

Chan refused to sell the land and insisted on sharing the little that they had. And if Esperanza had learned anything from watching the Ewings, it was that no one becomes a millionaire by sharing.

She shouldn't have listened to Santo. She should've gone to Dallas as soon as she stepped on American soil. Esperanza saw Don Chan sitting in the big chair, his pants high up on his legs. He looked frail. His hair cut short, spiked up, despite the pomade he favored. The dark brown of his skin from years of being in the sun. The yellowed teeth from all the cigars and rolled tobacco. That was not what she had planned for her life at all. Having to wipe Don Chan's ass when he lost all his faculties. It was bound to happen.

—Dallas should've been named after her grandmother Caridad, Don Chan insisted.

Santo nodded along.

Just like Don Chan to talk a subject dry.

—If people could name their children after saints, why not after the Ewings? Esperanza interjected from the kitchen. —If it was up to you two, nothing would change. All the children would be named after family members, and we'd still be living in the boonies.

—Do you see how ungrateful she is? Don Chan nudged Santo. —She forgets everything. She should be happy that you weren't pushed into hiding, like our friend Ernesto Santo María Delosquesaben.

—Ay, Papá, I haven't thought of Ernesto in years. He took too many risks. That trip to Cuba was his biggest mistake. He was very kind to let us live in his house in Los Llanos, Santo said. —Have you heard from Ernesto, Papá?

—Miraluz told me she saw him pass through town not so long ago, he teaches in the university.

—Miraluz? What about her? Esperanza rushed out of the kitchen, hands wet, knife in one, a sponge in the other.

—Cálmate, mujer. We're talking about Ernesto.

Santo waved Esperanza to go back into the kitchen. Santo leaned over to his side to turn on the lamps. The night announced itself with the dark sky, the store gates closing and mothers calling their children in for dinner.

—We had some good times back in the day.

Santo used to meet with four guys at the local colmado and they would riff off songs that complained about the price of the plátano being too high or of the wind that blew the roof off their heads.

—I haven't played music since Aire Libre, Santo said.

—I still have your small keyboard in the house, Don Chan said.

—But it doesn't work.

—It's for the history books, Don Chan said and started playing air piano, humming a few notes, showing off to Santo how much he remembered.

—Damn, Papá, it's good to see you. It's really great to have you here.

Esperanza cleared up the sink and slapped the uncooked chicken as if it were Santo's face, regretting the idea of having Don Chan live with them. And why were they talking about Miraluz, anyway? That damn woman hanging out with them day and night as if she didn't have anything better to do. Miraluz's child running about like a savage while she spoke stupidities. —Revolución this, el pueblo that. Already Don Chan started with his back-in-the-day songs as if there was something romantic about living in a small cement house with a zinc roof, no running water, an outhouse in the back, and an iron stove fueled with coal. Esperanza was the one who fetched the water and heated the iron over the coal, and not once did she escape burning her skin from the endless piles of ironing. Feed the chickens, sweep the yard, wash the rice twice, three times over, so they wouldn't bite into a pebble.

—Talk all you want, Esperanza mumbled under her breath, angry that Santo turned a blind eye on how hard their lives were in Los Llanos. She had left her life in the city, her family, for Santo. She did it for love. —I was so naive. Esperanza thought back to her young self who had yet to learn that once the stomach was empty, love went out the window.

And when her stomach was empty, unlike her neighbors back home who spent afternoons in their patios waiting for the electricity to come back on, embellishing stories about absent neighbors, with the air always smelling of sweat, rum, and frankincense, Esperanza had her eye on more glamorous things, like champagne glasses, and low-cut dresses, weekly visits to the salon, and using words like *buying, selling, profit, inheritance.* She knew that the rich only made the rich richer and the poor were doomed by association.

You've got to take chances in life, if you want to make anything of it, Cliff Barnes told his sister Pamela Ewing one night, and Esperanza watched la Loca's TV as if she had just been touched by gospel.

In desperation, behind Santo's back, Esperanza saved up penny by penny for her trip to Dallas. She skimped on the sugar in his coffee and reduced the portions of bacalao served at dinner.

—Where's the meat, woman? You trying to starve me?

—Cariño, eat more rice to fill yourself. It's not my problem that your appetite has grown.

The day Esperanza counted enough money in her nylon stocking buried in the top drawer of her bureau, she made her way to the small town of Los Desesperados, where the yolas dispatched, a town that was once no more than a dirt road and a few shacks, until word got around that it was the closest way to launch out to Puerto Rico without getting caught by the coastal guards. In no time, the few shacks transformed into makeshift colmados, carrying last-minute necessities to take to the States and efficient motels for lovers to bid their last farewells. Soon, local entrepreneurs found a way to make good money off the secret port. Literates became letter writers, so campesinos could send word to their loved ones. Last wishes were sealed in bottles, then buried in the sand. Beggars, priests, and prostitutes made themselves available to feed last urges, just in case death awaited the brave passengers who dared to cross the ravenous Mona Passage, filled with sharks and angry waves.

Esperanza hid out in the bushes, fending off mosquitoes, befriending the other passengers who shared their food with her: crackers, salchichón, Malta Morena. No one whispered words of fear. They knew there was no turning back. All seventy-eight travelers took the journey into the unknown. Back then, the yola trips were less frequent, the raftsmen had little experience, few had lived and returned to tell the story. Esperanza didn't think about how her departure would make Santo feel, or that she might never see her son again. She looked at the horizon, a thin line of midnight that divided the sky and sea.

> Querido Santo,
> I left for Puerto Rico. As soon as I can, I will send word.
> Pray for me, Santo.
> Te amo,
> Esperanza

Santo had walked into his two-room house to find that Esperanza was gone. Quickly, he ran to Don Chan's.

—Y qué pasó con esa mujer? She's gone.

—I told you, that woman was trouble. You should've tied her foot to the almond tree in the backyard, Don Chan said. Esperanza was from the de los Santos clan. Many of the men in her family worked for Trujillo, and throughout the years supported his predecessor, Balaguer. —What else do you expect from the daughter of a man who protected Trujillo?

Santo kicked the chair and broke its last good leg. He threw the lamp with the missing bulb and punched the mattress. He tossed the pillow, still warm with Esperanza's breath, against the wall, tipping over the painting of Jesus. He didn't know how to face his son, Roberto María. How would he explain that his mother had left him? That she didn't trust her husband enough to help her. He would've taken that yola if it had meant that much to her. Better him than her. Santo racked his brain, wondering how he had failed Esperanza. Yes, their lives were simple, but they had a roof over their heads, food on the table. Wasn't that enough?

Doña Caridad let Santo sulk, and after a few days, slapped him across the face when Don Chan wasn't looking.

—Hijo, stop walking around like she cut off your dick. If you love her, go after her. You find a way to get to wherever she is and be with her. Following her doesn't make you less of a man. It makes you a devoted father who cares for his family. Don't worry about us. We're not going anywhere. Believe me, I've lived long enough to know that in one's lifetime, very little changes.

Santo applied for a visa at the embassy and waited, while Esperanza worked as a housekeeper in Puerto Rico. He counted the days until he would see her again. He wanted to be present when their daughter was born.

And when Santo insisted they meet in Nueva York, where he had already lined up a job driving a taxi, she couldn't help but be disappointed.

—Who cares if it's Dallas or the moon? What matters is that we'll be together. How are we going to live without papers? We have no family in Dallas. At least in Nueva York, I already have a job lined up. Mujer, ten paciencia. You'll see, amor. It'll all work out, Santo insisted.

Ten years later, Esperanza stood in the kitchen in New York City. She was much older, heavier, and tired. She scrubbed the chicken, chopped its limbs, gutted its belly, and damned those men who were too content spending all their hours talking políticas. Just like they did in Los Llanos, sitting in the backyard with friends, carrying out Don Chan's every whim, because among the campesinos, Don Chan was the only one who had traveled as far as China.

—You're all fools for listening to his stories, she mumbled under her breath. And in a campo like the one they lived in, stories had a way of catching on. Even the same fruit could acquire multiple names, creating an illusion of an agricultural variety in their town that existed nowhere else in the world. It didn't matter that Don Chan had no recollection of ever living in China; among the people of Los Llanos, he was the only one who looked Chinese, and nothing could take that away from him.

—Esos chinos sí saben, many said, as if being born in China granted Don Chan a gift for knowing things. She didn't care if he was once Jesus, she was sick of people telling her how great Don Chan was.

He was no longer in D.R. He had no followers in her house, so he better stop talking about the good old days or he'd wake up in the morning with his bed floating down the Hudson River.

Esperanza looked at the slaughter in her sink. Santo came up from behind her to get some ice from the fridge.

—What the hell is going on in here? Santo asked Esperanza. The water was boiling on the stove. The green peppers cracked open. The refrigerator door open.

—I'm making dinner.

She gathered the pieces of chicken and piled them on one plate. Hadn't he noticed how every day without fail she made dinner?

Don Chan looked at the walls, crowded with gold-framed mirrors and paint-by-number paintings of horses. The air was thick with cinnamon air freshener. The furniture too big for the size of the room. Don Chan's knees knocked against Bobby's bicycle. There was no place for him in all that clutter.

—Santo, tell your father to take a shower before we eat, Esperanza yelled from the kitchen.

—What if I don't want to? Don Chan whispered to Santo.

—Don't give her a hard time.

Santo handed him a fresh towel from the hallway closet. He showed him Dallas's bedroom and where he could put his things in the bathroom.

—This is your home now, Santo said to his father, who seemed a little lost. —I have to move my car. I'll be right back.

—I should go with you, Don Chan said.

—It's too cold outside. Wait for me here, Papá.

—Sí, sí, no hay problema.

Don Chan walked into the bathroom. He latched the lock and sat on the rim of the tub. He noticed the bulk of toilet paper, the peeling tub, and the spotted mirror. He turned the faucet on and off. How clear the water was. He cupped some in his hands. It was sweet. He was relieved to be alone. The radiator was clanking and hissing. What am I doing here? he asked.

In the mornings, Don Chan reached across his bed for Doña Caridad and waited to listen to the small gasps she made when she slept. The mild shock of forgetting she was gone, that he was no longer in D.R., caused such confusion, he bolted out of his bed to turn on the lights in the bedroom. —Sí, sí, he reminded himself, checking off his mental list of the things that were no longer true and the things he was set to do each day. He glanced over at the calendar given to him from the bodega owner up the street. One month had passed since his arrival.

Routine was his savior. He hadn't realized how much he had depended on Doña Caridad to remember things. Without her, it was a chore to maintain an organized closet. He made great efforts to line up in the closet his short-sleeved guayabera for warmer days and long-sleeved ones for winter. Three wool cardigans, a pile of freshly ironed boxer shorts, and a number of white short-sleeve undershirts were folded on a shelf. Black and navy straight-legged pants hung beside each other. A crate filled with dark-colored, thin, polyester dress socks. Two wide-brim felt hats, one black, the other navy, to protect his aging eyes from the sun. Order prevented him from forgetting things. With contempt, he checked the weather by placing his hand against the windowpane. In the Dominican Republic, Don Chan never had to check the weather. It was always predictably hot.

Don Chan arose before the sun. At his age, he didn't need much sleep. In Nueva York, the streets remained dark and impenetrable until much later than he liked. If he were in Los Llanos, he would've walked out of his house and seen the stars, or the cobalt sky, or the pink emerging from the horizon. The roosters would accompany him, along with the dogs that never went too far. He would relish the sound of the dried leaves that crunched under his feet, and sit on the old rocking chair that no longer rocked because the salt air had rusted off the back end.

It was a warm day for winter. As he left the apartment to buy his daily newspapers, he damned people for global warming. He tried not to think of the inevitable: a future where people would have to walk underground to protect themselves from the sun and pollution. —We're burying ourselves alive, he said to the nosy old woman who always opened the door to survey the hallways. And then he got angry at himself: After so many years of living, he still got hung up on something he couldn't do anything about, especially since any day could be the last day of his life. Ever since his wife died, he couldn't stop thinking about the statistics. Most widowers don't make it a year after their partners die. Not at his age. And while the actual days felt long in Nueva York, it felt as if it was just yesterday that he was sitting by his wife's bedside, four months ago.

Don Chan looked up and down Quepasó Street before he stepped out of the building. And although he had lived on the street for only one month, he knew its rhythms. When the cars were double-parked on the left side of the street, it was Monday, Wednesday, or Friday. On Tuesday and Thursday, they were parked on the right. Styrofoam trays peeked out of the garbage cans from last night's dinner specials. Arroz, habichuelas, and tostones if it was Monday. Tuesday, moro and steak. Wednesday, chicken and gandules. On the days the sanitation trucks came by, Don Chan greeted the super who piled up the garbage bags for the trucks to pick up. On Saturday mornings, the streets were a potpourri of cigarettes and beer bottles propped up against buildings.

It was Monday. The van driver headed to the factory in New Jersey was already warming up his car, waiting for his passengers on the corner. The music blasted against his fogged-up windowpanes as he woke himself up with a cup of coffee. Don Chan liked Mondays much better than Sundays. Sunday always felt like the end of something.

¿Hola, Chino? the man at the newsstand said as he pulled up his gates to open for business. —When will I beat your arrival? He shook Don Chan's hand.

—When I'm dead. And that could happen any minute now.

Don Chan paid him with the exact change and carefully folded the papers in half, tucked them underneath his arm, and headed over to the corner luncheonette to order his second cafecito of the day. The first café he drank at home before Esperanza woke up. He liked the second coffee to be served at the luncheonette, that way he could be away from home when she was putting on her face for work and Santo slept in.

Every day, Don Chan read three newspapers. It didn't matter which three. He liked being surprised. In the end, the news summed up to be the same. History repeated itself, and somehow, no matter how much people knew about the causes and effects of their actions, the patterns of current events didn't change. Throughout his life, this fact had baffled him.

Don Chan breathed in the absence of chaos that filled the streets during the day, imagining that behind all the windows, the children were getting ready to go to school, people were preparing to leave their houses to go to work, and his day was one blank canvas. He walked over to the luncheonette across the street, up the block, on the corner of his house, and noticed that a young girl was sitting in his favorite booth by the window.

Don Chan hesitated for a moment. He was often forgetting things. Some days, he spent hours trying to finish one task and remembering he had forgotten what he was looking for and then having to get up to search, only to forget again.

—Let the old man sit down.

Oswaldo, the counterman who was wearing a cheap tuxlike uniform and a name clip, directed the young girl to sit on one of the stools.

—No, no, let her sit. We can share this big booth. Don't people share in this country?

The young girl, who seemed to be about Dallas's age but much smaller in size, giggled at Don Chan, who now sat across from her.

—What's so funny? Don Chan teased her.

The young girl pulled the corner of her eyes and started moving her head like an Egyptian.

—You're mixing up your continents, Don Chan said.

The girl reminded him of Miraluz. Same straight black hair, flat nose, brown skin, heart-shaped lips, an indigenous quality to her face that assumed a trace of South America. Don Chan pulled his own eyes. —This is Asia. He moved his arms like an Egyptian image on a fresco, his hands and face going against each other in opposite directions. —And this is Egypt, which is in Africa. Ask your teacher to show you a globe and maybe you'll learn something.

The young girl immediately liked Don Chan. She was tempted to pull his shiny black hair that stuck out in all directions.

—What's your name?

—Hush, she whispered.

—You want to help me? Don Chan asked and pulled out his small pair of scissors from his guayabera pocket. He neatly unfolded the newspapers and piled them at the corner of the table.

—I cut and then you read them to me.

The young girl nodded.

He clipped the headlines. After many years of reading lies, he didn't have to read the articles to get at the truth. He stacked all the headlines on the coffee-shop table and, like a puzzle, started forming paragraphs with the headlines. The real news was in between the words, what was not being said.

—What you doing, Viejo? The counterman asked. Don Chan had been frequenting the luncheonette for weeks and the counterman had never asked him anything before.

—Do you really want to know? Don Chan didn't like to talk just to talk.

—I'm asking, ain't I?

The counterman with one lazy eye looked over at the mess Don Chan was making.

—This I learned from the CIA, Don Chan said with a laugh, wishing Miraluz was around so she could laugh along with him. Anyone who knew Don Chan would find it hilarious to hear his name and CIA in the same sentence.

—You were really CIA, Viejo?

—If I tell you, I'd have to kill you, Don Chan said with a serious face and then he relaxed him with a smile. By the gleam in the man's eye, Don Chan could tell the counter guy had seen one too many movies.

The little girl giggled some more while she diligently read out loud the headlines in her elementary Spanish.

—Forget the CIA, let me show you how you could find out how to predict the future, Don Chan said as he put together his paragraphs made up of headlines.

U.S. LURES DOMINICANS TO THE CRUEL SEA
DOMINICANS FIND BACK DOOR TO NEW YORK IN
PUERTO RICO
ANOTHER NATIVE GOES HOME TO DOMINICAN REPUBLIC
IN COFFIN
GYPSY CABS: A HARD, CHANCY LIFE ON THE SIDE STREETS
OF NYC

Oswaldo took a drag from his cigarette and walked over to be closer to them.

—This some crazy stuff, old man.

HOW THE SAUDIS AND KUWAITIS COULD GIVE BUSH A
$300 BILLION TAX CUT
BUSH SAYS IRAQI AGGRESSION THREATENS "OUR WAY OF
LIFE."
IRAQIS ARE STUNNED BY FEROCIOUS ASSAULT: DEATH
SUDDENLY RAINS DOWN THROUGH BLACK CLOUDS;
TANKS POP LIKE POPCORN
POSTWAR BOOM IN SAUDI STOCKS INFLAMES FUNDA-
MENTALISTS

—It's better not to know sometimes, Don Chan said, moving the headlines around.

—Viejo, live your life. That's the world. We're here. You can't be thinking about those things. Right, kiddo?

The young girl didn't respond, and ducked under and away from Oswaldo's grasp, moving to the other end of the booth, closer to the window.

—But everything that happens in the world affects you and your family. Doesn't it worry you?

Oswaldo adjusted his small bow tie. —Why you being mean to your daddy?

He pulled the young girl over to him.

Don Chan noticed her bite her upper lip and cringe when Oswaldo patted her head. She quickly broke away from him and busied herself with the clippings.

—You want a cigarette? Oswaldo asked Don Chan.

—No. I have to preserve as much of myself as I can.

—Ain't you tired of living yet? What are you, about seventy, eighty?

Don Chan looked over at the young girl.

—Hey, Chino, I'm talking to you?

—I bet she cares, Don Chan said. —Do you care, little girl? He pointed to the headlines. —Will you fight for your life, little girl?

Don Chan wanted her to look up at him. Suddenly, she became shy and withdrawn.

—Don't give her any ideas. She's already mad at me because I don't let her get her way. That's what happens to girls at her age, they turn against their parents. We might not share blood, but she knows that I love her like she was one of my own.

—So she's not your daughter?

—She's more my daughter than the two I left behind in El Salvador. After all the stinky diapers I had to buy for her.

Oswaldo pinched the young girl's cheek with his short stubby fingers and turned back to attend the early morning crowd.

It didn't take long before Don Chan claimed the head of the dinner table and torched cigars in front of Santo in temptation. To smell one brought back the dick-whipping, loud-talking, and backyard spitting of the men-only circles in the fields of Los Llanos; they sat around campfires, not shaving for days to show their solidarity to *los barbudos,* those bearded men, who seemed to have done the impossible by overthrowing Batista and pushing out the Americans from Cuban soil. *Los barbudos,* who in 1959 organized a group of Dominican exiles and Cubans and landed in D.R., to find that peasants turned them in; rural farmers decapitated *los barbudos,* handing over the heads in burlap bags to Trujillo in exchange for a bounty of a thousand dollars.

—It's a scar on my heart, Don Chan told Santo as they sat at the kitchen table waiting for Esperanza to return from the bodega so she could serve them dinner. —A hungry man will sell his mother if you give him the right price for her. —*We Live in Happiness Thanks to Trujillo?* You think people believed that bullshit?

—Remember *God Is in Heaven—Trujillo Is on Earth?* Santo added.

—Be careful. You say it too much, even you'll start believing it.

—Don't worry, Papá, he's been dead for over thirty years. The worms got him now.

—You ever wonder, what if? Don Chan asked Santo.

—What if what?

—What if that group of Cubans would've succeeded in overthrowing Trujillo in forty-seven? Castro was part of that group. What

if Castro met us in Los Llanos before he had met Che, then maybe
Cuba's history would've been ours.

—I wasn't even born then, Santo said, and leaned his chair back
to check the clock. He was late for work. He was hungry.

—What if those men would've come to us in Los Llanos, for help.
We would've protected *los barbudos* from all those crazy farmers who
were ready to chop their heads off. Wouldn't we?

—Yeah, and then years later, we'd have Castro running our shit.
Big improvement for sure.

—I'm serious, Santo. Try and imagine for a minute, us with Castro, working together. We'd have taken Trujillo's fortune and given it
back to the people. Just like in Cuba—we'd have access to doctors,
to the university, to the beaches.

—Oh yeah, public beaches in Cuba. Great idea. Makes it easier
for Cubans to escape by swimming to Miami. You can't change history, Papá.

Don Chan never got tired of talking about *what if* over dinner. Esperanza cringed when Santo leaned forward to listen to Don Chan's
every word. Don Chan tapped against the dinner table's edge,
singing the notes of familiar songs out loud.

—¡Ay, Papá! Santo responded to every detail Don Chan handed
over. And always the name Miraluz. There was never a story told
without Miraluz.

Santo picked up where Don Chan left off as if it was just yesterday that Santo was holding his beloved battery-operated keyboard,
bought used from a dead músico. Esperanza remembered the long
hours Santo put in to find notes that turned into music; when he
stayed up late nights looking for the keys, singing highs and lows,
until his composition caught a melody. In D.R., he played his piano
even when it had run out of batteries, despite Esperanza telling him
that he played it badly. He played after she had blown out the candles, pulled down the sheets, and padlocked all the doors. He played
as if he had found religion, trying to memorize his short composi-

tions so he could continue when he had another minute to do so.

Santo started to hum in the apartment just like he did back in D.R. Don Chan hummed along with him. Esperanza turned on the radio and played the easy-listening station so that they would lose all the nostalgic rhythm. She was losing Santo to the island. He went from drinking Budweiser to Presidente. He was driving his taxi less and spending more time at home. The men leaned back on their chairs, gnawing at toothpicks and spitting jokes.

—Remember Caamaño, Don Chan said, inhaling his cigar as he thought about el Coronel Francisco Alberto Caamaño Deñó, who'd spent years training a guerrilla army in Cuba to liberate Dominican Republic, and once he arrived in '73, he found that his comrades who stayed behind were missing fingers or were standing in line to make money off the new government.

—Who gives a shit anymore, Esperanza interrupted them, handing Santo the electric bill that needed to be paid in person because it was already one month late.

—A lot of people give a shit. You don't give a shit, Don Chan said, and then told Santo, —and you stopped giving a shit when you came here. You're so busy trying to pay the bills, there's no time to think in this country.

—And that isn't true in D.R.? Esperanza challenged him. —People are so hungry, they think the stars are UFOs.

—It's different in D.R. We have our tongue. Our peace of mind. Something beautiful to look at when we walk out of our house.

—What's so beautiful about Los Llanos? There's nothing left but trees.

—The flamboyan trees would be offended by that comment.

—Even the flamboyan tree knows that at first everything is full of flowers, but then it all goes to shit.

—And what about the hibiscus flowers that always rage with color? The brilliant sky that mimics the ocean, the fresh fruit at our disposal, free from all those chemicals you consume, that are turning your body into a breeding ground for cancer.

—Now come on, Papá, there's no point in getting all worked up,

Santo said, taking the bill and putting it in his pocket. —Can you both agree that both places have their good and bad? We should be happy we're alive.

—That's what has us all living in this shit hole. When Trujillo was in power, people said, At least we have roads now. People without cars loved Trujillo for the road they were never going to drive on.

Don Chan got up and paced. At least we are alive? Bullshit. He paced and couldn't stand his old body that wasn't at the speed of his mind. Santo had lost his cojones when he married Esperanza. He warned him about her kind. Humans, like dogs, came in types. Some were humbler than others, others more violent, and Esperanza was descended from a clan of opportunists. Her father waved Trujillo's flag as long as it bought them a house in the capital. And when Trujillo murdered innocent people, Esperanza's family looked away. Esperanza had money-grubbing blood in her, and Santo was forever doomed because of it.

—No te alteres, Viejo. Your heart is not what it used to be, Esperanza said. She noticed that Don Chan's hand had a slight tremor. There were moments when she felt sorry for him. A man with an un-lived dream was a restless man. The least she could do was let him talk himself into his grave.

—She's right, Papá, best not to get upset.

—At least things are better in D.R., Esperanza said.

—The U.S. invaded us in sixty-five so that D.R. wouldn't turn into another Cuba. And look at it, D.R. is another Cuba, it's Batista's Cuba. We've become whores for the tourists and U.S. aid.

Esperanza helped Don Chan sit down on the chair. He was an old man and frustrated, that's all. She could only imagine the torture if all her life she had worked for something and she didn't live her dream of buying her house, having her ranch, growing old with Santo beside her. What's the point of becoming upset with him? His days were numbered.

—I don't need your help, woman. I'm not an invalid yet, Don Chan said, moving away from them, making his way into his bedroom.

—Look at you two. It's not so bad. You live like rats. Twenty-five locks on the maldita door, afraid someone is going to break in. Spending your days and nights sheltered from the cold, hoarding things in closets. Goddamn rats.

Was the life they lived so miserable looking to Don Chan? thought Esperanza. Couldn't he see how far they had come? Maybe there were things they could do to make the apartment more pleasant. Santo had yet to fix the crack on the tiles by the refrigerator. None of her cabinets closed because the paint was so thick. Maybe she could do some things to make the house less dark, less cavelike. She had wanted to get some brocade fabric to make curtains like the ones she had seen on *Dallas*. And some gold paint to paint over all the wood frames and old lamps. She loved gold. If done right, no one would know the difference. With a few repairs, her home could look like the display in the store windows she often admired.

The more the men sat around the living room discussing política, the more sugar Esperanza added in the desserts. She sewed draperies of lace, bought pink toilet paper, and added frills to the shower curtains.

But like rats, her family was beginning to turn against each other. They were fine when they were four, but now that they were five in one apartment, it was happening. —Don't slam the door! Who left the toilet seat up! What am I going to do with all of you? Esperanza yelled, knowing very well no one in the Colón household was listening to her. While the men talked about the past, Esperanza thought about the future. Her children like little mice, endlessly screaming, —It's mine, —I want, —Give me.

Esperanza escaped to her room to watch *Dallas* reruns even though she had seen most episodes; she memorized the way Pamela Ewing wore her hair, feathered up front and tied in the back in a French twist. She envied Pamela. Why couldn't Esperanza have all the things she wanted? It wasn't fair. Esperanza needed a new look.

In the campo, the women would say it's not the dress, it's the hanger that makes the dress, but in America, that wasn't true. To be important, one has to look important.

—Do you really need another coat? Santo asked.

—I'm tired of always wearing the same thing all the time. Esperanza had already picked out the coat. It was midcalf length, with a fake-fur collar, the coat had darts around the waist so that she could hide all the weight she was gaining.

—What's wrong with the one you bought last year?

—Pamela never says, I love this necklace, but because I don't need it, I won't buy it.

—Who's Pamela?

—You don't know anything, do you?

Santo seemed small in the living-room recliner. He looked tired and hungry, and yet he never wanted to eat unless he was famished, as if he were always on some diet. Forget him, she thought, hugging herself, feeling the rolls of fat around her waist, accentuated by the cinched belt.

—You've become so cheap, she said.

—I'm not cheap. I'm an antimaterialist.

—Since when?

—Why do you always fight me, Esperanza?

—Don't raise your voice at me just because your father's here. Ever since he got here six months ago, you talk to me like I'm deaf.

—I'm not raising my voice, he said in a whisper. —And don't call me cheap.

—Go to Cuba if you want to live like un miserable. Damn you, Santo.

Esperanza hid away the store catalogs where she had circled all the things she wanted.

The more Don Chan preached, the more obsessed Esperanza became with acquiring things.

Esperanza saved her own pennies, just as she had for her trip on the yola a decade ago. She scrimped at every opportunity, while Santo tirelessly worked to save for the house she begged for. Half of her paycheck went to rent, but she cut corners on the groceries. Every minute she had alone, she counted the dollars and cents that added up to the new blouse she had seen at her neighbor's basement apartment. A real Chanel, which fell off a truck, in bright red, for only forty dollars; and the Gucci bag, just like the one in the magazine ad, the one that the guy who lived across the street stole when he worked at the high-end department store as a security guard. Santo could continue to wear his shoes with holes in the soles because he found them comfortable, but she much preferred to hike in the Fendi strappy sandals, one size too small, because when one gets stuff cheap, one has to expect a bit of discomfort. She liked to feel her shoes on her feet, silk on her skin, the weight of jewelry around her neck. The more she bought, the more insatiable she became. —God, can you help me out here? she asked, hoping he'd help her win the lottery she played on Sundays.

Within days of her prayers, she found a letter in the mail. *Esperanza Colón: You have been preapproved.* After working as a home attendant for five years, Esperanza was eligible for a credit card, her very own five-hundred-dollar credit card. It was better than winning the lottery because this she earned from her sweat. Days later another letter arrived. *You have been preapproved for up to 1,000 dollars.* Preapproved. Esperanza mouthed the words in front of the mirror, licking her lips in anticipation of her first credit-card purchase. It felt good to get some approval for once.

Once she filled out the applications, the cards arrived. With anticipation and naughtiness, Esperanza locked herself in her room while the men talked in the living room about the union breakers at the free-trade zones in D.R. While they argued about the consequences of foreign investors invading their island, Esperanza turned up the television to drown out their voices as she watched *Buy TV,* and salivated over the pearl necklace that regularly cost $250, but if she bought it within the next ten minutes, she could have it in three installments of $29.99. She watched the corner of the screen, seeing the numbers go up as hundreds of people called in, taking advantage of this once-in-a-lifetime offer. How could she resist picking up the phone and charging the pearl necklace that would look so lovely with her off-the-truck Chanel blouse? She bought nonstick baking pans, a cordless hairdryer, a Walkman for her commute to work. She was careful not to charge any of her cards all at once. Instead she spread out her purchases and had them delivered to the super, on the first floor.

When the bills came, Esperanza put them in a drawer. She planned to pay them when she had extra money. Every first of the month, the bills continued to come. Responsibly, she put them in the top drawer of her bureau, filed them with her panties and bras. Santo would never bother to look. She filed them without opening the envelopes. Those generous credit-card companies would have to wait. And when she reached the credit card's limit—which she only knew about because her cards no longer went through—she filed the credit card itself in the drawer, expecting to pay it all one day, little by little.

Nueva York to Los Llanos
1992   1961

When Don Chan wanted to escape Esperanza, he went to the bathroom. In Nueva York, there was no backyard, no colmado to hang around in. Not one fertile tree to lean back on and take an afternoon nap. He took his time when he showered in the evenings while she prepared dinner. The bathroom was crammed with her things: stockings hanging from the shower curtains, laundry baskets toppling over with dirty clothes, cosmetics bags, toiletries, soaps piled up on the shelves over the sink.

—¡Maldita sea! He had accidentally knocked over a small nylon makeup bag, spreading an assortment of lipsticks and cotton swabs. He picked them up. A loud, sharp sound went off outside the bathroom window. He covered his head with his arms and ducked low, away from the window. Where were his fatigues and boots? He waited for a few minutes, then pried open the small translucent window to see if anyone was waiting for him outside as he dressed himself. He tore open the hamper looking for his weapon. He recognized the pressed wool pants and button-down shirts of an old man, neatly hung on a hanger on the door. The steam fogged the mirrors. He pressed his finger against the mirror and made a line revealing part of his face. He startled himself. The man looking back at him was much older than he remembered.

He sat on the toilet seat and studied his arms under the fluorescent lights and wondered when exactly did his skin start to wrinkle, when was the first time he could see his bones so clearly, his veins like rivers on a map? Time was slipping, and his memories were slipping even faster. He became faint from the smell of talc, the humidity from the hot shower, the hiss and clank of the radiator like the crackle and pop of the wood chunks in the campfires back in Los Llanos.

When the boys in the back alley playing basketball yelled to celebrate their score, Don Chan longed to see his friends who gathered in the fields of Los Llanos, who after a long day of labor sat around the campfire in anticipation of his telling a story.

—Tell us a story so the heat becomes bearable, the crowd shouted at him.

—Are you ready? Don Chan teased.

—Like a dog in heat.

Don Chan took his cigar, clipped the end, lit it in the blazing fire, and cleared his throat. The only competing sounds were the howling dogs and the rustling of all the surrounding cane fields.

—My friends, I'm invisible.

—Invisible?

—Invisible! Don Chan insisted. —Invisible enough that I'll walk into the president's palace and bring back a souvenir for all of you to see.

The crowd laughed and cringed. It was a time when Dominicans were too afraid to say Trujillo's name out loud without looking over their shoulders. When Trujillo's men ransacked their homes looking for counterrevolutionaries and shook up their sisters without any warning. For a poor man from Los Llanos to steal a souvenir from under the president's nose was a death sentence, as far as they were concerned.

—We dare you, some yelled out.

The day Don Chan took the dare, he'd had a few too many drinks. But no amount of drinking could excuse him from keeping his word.

· · ·

Don Chan borrowed a suit from a dead man in a mortuary. The suit pants were an inch too long and the shirtsleeves an inch too short, but Don Chan wore it with confidence. Even the women gossiped, how for a Chino, he was quite handsome when he shaved. Don Chan made the arrangements with the Trucker in Los Llanos who often traveled to Ciudad Trujillo for business and was familiar with the soldiers who guarded the edge of each small village. If anyone could get Don Chan out of Los Llanos without getting arrested, it was the Trucker. Others had tried to leave Los Llanos, but the harassment by the soldiers discouraged many. Trujillo's soldiers flagged down all cars, documented the passengers' names, the villages they were from, and their destinations. If they didn't reach it within a certain time, they would be hunted down and arrested. No one wanted their names on any of his lists or linked to the groups that were planning to overthrow him. Especially after the Mirabal sisters, who risked their lives in the name of freedom, were clubbed to death by Trujillo's men months before.

Don Chan spat at those people who called him crazy for risking his life to prove a point.

—If all over the world there are men who walk through fire, feet over coals, by concentrating on their destination and not on the path, why can't I do the same? All of Trujillo's guards and their guns aren't stronger than my will, said Don Chan.

—Why start trouble for ourselves now? We've managed fine enough all these years. Doña Caridad tried reasoning with him while she pressed his shirt to wear on his mission. —We ain't going anywhere but old.

—No one leaves this town, because they're afraid. My father fled Juan Dolio because he feared the city. I'm tired of hiding. But worse, we don't even know what we're hiding from. We can't rely on the newspapers. They tell us nothing about what's happening in this country. We need to find out for ourselves.

—Take me to the palace, Don Chan told the Trucker, pointing toward the road.

The Trucker didn't talk while he drove on the narrow roads leading to the capital. Don Chan was too busy seeing Ciudad Trujillo for
the first time to care for a conversation. Manicured trees, mansion-
style homes, traffic jams, cars parked in driveways. The city dense
with people, wearing freshly shined shoes and dressed in their best.

—No one seems to give a shit, Don Chan said to the Trucker.
—These city folk don't look scared to me.

Women hid from the sun under umbrellas. Men sported white
hats and suits.

—Half of the city works for el Jefe. You don't bite the hand that
feeds you.

The sight of it all made Don Chan nervous. It was all too big, too
much, too loud.

—We're here. The Trucker pointed to the palatial building with
two guards standing upright on each side of the entrance.

—Are you sure? The palace looks smaller than I imagined it.

—Everything looks bigger in pictures, the Trucker reassured Don
Chan and pointed to the corner where he would wait for him.

Don Chan stood across the street surveying the entrance. He
watched a few people walk through the gates and noticed that the
guards hadn't asked them any questions. Don Chan held his empty
briefcase close to him. When he started walking toward the palace,
he hoped the guards couldn't smell the stench of death in the suit he
was wearing. Twenty, maybe thirty, men had already worn that dark
blue pin-striped suit on their funeral day before they were buried.
He bowed his head to them, but the young men wearing military
uniforms stayed in position and faced forward, unconcerned with
Don Chan's entry. It troubled Don Chan. He had anticipated more
resistance.

He climbed the gray marble steps leading up to the palace's entrance. There was no time to ask questions. He relied on his intu-
ition, which had proved to be a trustworthy compass. All his life,
people had asked him where he was from. The truth was that he
didn't know, so if he were caught, he'd pretend to be lost. Besides, he
was already up the steps. There was no turning back.

Don Chan walked into the president's palace, raising his leather briefcase as if he was carrying an important foreign message that needed to be delivered to the president at once. The older man behind the desk called out to him. Don Chan nodded in recognition and walked up the two flights of stairs and onto the crimson rug that softened his steps, making his entrance a silent one.

—Those guards thought I was the president of Japan, Don Chan said in a whisper so that the crowd in Los Llanos would lean into the fire and listen to every detail he fed them.

—How about the ambassador of China? one man said.

—Or the owner of Mitsubishi?

—Sí, sí, now you understand what I'm trying to tell you.

There was a door leading to an unguarded office filled with old paintings, leather-bound books, imported rugs, and armchairs upholstered in the finest Italian fabrics. The room had an aftertaste of gunpowder and metal. The shutters were partly closed, adding a mystery to the room, which nearly unhinged him. Don Chan assumed he was inside Trujillo's office. And if not, how would his neighbors in Los Llanos know different? He was in the palace. That was a feat in itself. Now he only had to get out. The desk was wiped clean, except for the leather desk mat, the fine pens, and other unidentifiable objects he knew were of no consequence. The entry was too easy. The office too quiet. Maybe he had fallen into a trap. For years he'd studied the sea and when it looked most peaceful, when the sky was at its bluest, the storm was about to come. Often the quieter the day, the more violent the storm. The guards were waiting for him to make a move. The butchers would pounce on him. They wouldn't kill him. That he was sure of. They'd chop off his hands, or maybe his ear, or pull out an eye, torturing him until he disclosed names. They would want to know who sent him.

Don Chan stood in the office, recalling stories of eyes poked out with pencils, charred skin, toes chopped, shards of glass shoved inside penises. His body tightened, his jaw locked, his bladder loosened. Suddenly the palace and all its opulence terrified him. Every part of his body was vulnerable to being punctured, tortured, cut off.

Would he survive to see Caridad again? Don Chan surveyed the room for a place to hide. Feeling death so close to his skin rattled him, excited him, made him leap out of his body and watch himself. Why had he taken such a risk?

Don Chan touched the thick linens in the windows, the silks of the pillows on the chairs. The ceiling three, four times his height, with gold moldings all around the wall edges. This is why people were assassinated? Why they go hungry? Don Chan almost yelled, Murderer, for the three sisters who were killed because they spoke up against the dictatorship. They were young women. Women! He wanted to scream for their husbands, and every other courageous person who dared to speak up and who lost his life because of it. What had he done with his own life but tell cowardly stories in his little village, waiting for things to change? It wasn't enough to talk. It was time for him to act. But first he had to show the people of Los Llanos that Trujillo could die like any other man. That while Trujillo's government had punished the east for their history of rebellions, and rumors of his latest victim ran rampant, Don Chan had to convince them that if they lived in fear, they would never be free.

He swiped a shiny object off the president's desk, slipping it inside his shirtsleeve. The cold metal accompanied him. It could serve as a weapon. He was ready and walked away from the guards who were busy flirting with one of the trabajadoras. He walked out, focusing on the exit. He bent over a blossoming hibiscus plant and took in its smell to throw off the guards at the kiosk. His will was stronger than their duty to work. They cannot see me, I am invisible, Don Chan thought and walked by them, focusing on the gates to exit the palace. And when they called out to him, he bowed as if he didn't understand a word.

Don Chan returned to the circle and sat at the campfire. The crowd, twice the size. The air, thick with mosquitoes from the afternoon rainfall. The stars hovered over their heads as if waiting to be plucked. Hairy spiders scurried away in fear of the flames. People hadn't seen Don Chan in days. They had thought him dead. Taken away by Trujillo. They looked for his hands, his fingers. Nothing seemed to be missing. There were no scars to speak of. In fact, Don Chan appeared bigger in size.

—Don't keep us waiting, tell us what happened to you, hombre.

—Do I have a story to tell you, he said, and clapped his hands to clear the air.

He noticed the crowd lean forward and gather closer around him, hushing each other from whispering remarks, wanting to catch every detail that came out of his mouth. He realized the power of his words and enjoyed the attention. So much so that he already missed the crowd while they were still before him. It wasn't enough that they were listening to him. He wanted the power to pull the moon closer toward them. To wave away the bugs that riddled the night. To dampen the fire so that only his voice could be heard. His thoughts scared him. The people of Los Llanos were hungry. Yes, he had told many stories before, but he too had never entered Ciudad Trujillo. He had traveled around the world through books, newspapers, other people's stories, but to leave his small town and return, he had yet to do that. He was no longer one of them. His journey had changed him.

He pulled out a shiny object that looked like a dull knife, with the words CIUDAD TRUJILLO carved on the handle. Without it he would think that his journey had been a dream.

—What the hell is it? another asked. He tried to cut his hand with it.

—I don't know what it is, but I know it's his, Don Chan said, looking over his trophy.

—And no one gave you any trouble?

—I was like a ghost, Don Chan continued.

—To the Invisible Man, cheered one, falling over the bucket he used as a chair.

—No, my friends, to the Invisible Ones.

Don Chan passed his hands over the crowd and raised his beer for a group cheer. —To those hijos de la gran puta, we're all invisible. We must use our invisibility against them. If we fight alone, we're invisible, but if we rise together, we won't be ignored, he said, riling up the crowd.

Don Chan passed his trophy around with pride. The flames bounced off the shiny object, blinding the men from the stars.

—It's for letters, a young woman yelled from the back of the circle. Don Chan couldn't see her in the dark.

—What did you say? Don Chan yelled over the crowd.

—People use it to open letters, she said.

—Why can't they use their hands? one man said, and they all laughed at her.

—Go home to your parents, little girl. You have no business here, one said as he took another swig of his beer.

Miraluz got up and exposed her long legs and tall build. Her body was pear shaped. Her long hair was tied back in a bun. She walked away. Santo stood and stretched his neck to take a closer look at her. Miraluz had outgrown the dress that rose above her knees. She was new in Los Llanos.

—Quiet! Don Chan yelled to the crowd. —What's your name?

—I'm the granddaughter of María Magdalena Natera. I'm here to watch over her until she feels better.

—How do you know about this opener for letters? Don Chan asked.

The men howled and barked and laughed at each other, unsure where Don Chan was going with all the questions.

—I read about them in a book, she said, coming in closer, the flames lighting up her brown skin.

—It's late for you to be out like this at night. You know what Trujillo does to young women, Don Chan said. —He'll take you away.

—He'll die tomorrow. She said it like a gamble. —I saw it in a dream.

—And if he doesn't die tomorrow? Don Chan was amused by her spunk.

—Then I won't return to your circle again. And allow you men to think that you know everything.

—What a mouth on that woman, one man said, chugging more beer. He spilled it over himself and demanded Don Chan's attention.

She walked away.

—Señorita Natera. What's your name?

—Miraluz Altagracia. But you can call me Miraluz when you see me tomorrow.

Don Chan laughed to indulge the girl.

Santo at thirteen had recently discovered his erection and secretly hoped she was right about Trujillo so he could see her again.

The next day, on May 30, 1961, El Generalísimo Dr. Rafael Leónidas Trujillo Molina Benefactor de la Patria y Padre de la Patria Nueva was assassinated.

LA NACION
DIARIO DE LA TARDE
CIUDAD TRUJILLO R.D.

12 Páginas   5 Centavos

AÑO XXII - NUMERO ##   JUEVES 1 DE JUNIO DE 1961   AÑO 31 DE LA ERA DE TRUJILLO

REVELAN DETALLES MUERTE DE TRUJILLO
Generalísimo Muere Como Un Valiente

According to official reports released today by the Dominican armed forces, El Generalísimo Doctor Rafael Leónidas Trujillo Molina exchanged gunshots with the assailants who killed him two nights ago . . . According to the driver, Trujillo said, "I am wounded, but stop the car so we can fight." . . .

HEROE Y MARTIR NACIONAL . . . who performed the miracle of turning chaos into order, and nothing into wealth. TRUJILLO HA CAIDO, PERO SU OBRA NO PERECERA . . . Trujillo the great, the authentic pioneer of the Dominican consciousness . . . TRUJILLO: SU NOMBRE PERTENECE. A LA HISTORIA, SU OBRA A LOS DOMINICANOS . . . They have left the Dominican Republic orphaned . . . LA MUERTE DE TRUJILLO SIEMBRA EL DOLOR EN EL HOGAR DOMINICANO . . . in all the Dominican homes reigns sadness and pain.

At three in the morning, Santo dropped his last customer home from a night of dancing at El Volcán. Every night since his father's arrival, his shifts in the taxi seemed longer. Eight long months.

—You should've been there, man. Ahí estaba Fernandito doing his shit. The walls were sweating, it was so good, his passenger said as he stumbled out of the car and kissed his girlfriend. From the length of their kiss, Santo could tell they had recently met each other. She giggled after each of his sentences. She squealed as he pulled her into the building.

Nights like that, Santo felt an extra pang to return to Los Llanos. To go back to a time when music blared from radios even when the stars were out and it didn't cost him a day's wage to take his wife out to a club with live music. He stepped out of the car to stretch his legs and smoke a cigarette before he headed home. Esperanza didn't know he was smoking again. Santo lit up and looked around the quiet street of Los Desamparados, which was nothing like the loud and busy street of Quepasó. His father was right. What were they doing living in the freezing weather? Santo tossed the cigarette to the stacks of garbage bags on the side street. He heard the ting of a piano. He opened the door of his car and the sound went off again in the desolate streets. When he stayed still, it was silent. When he moved, he heard music.

He looked up at the building windows. Some insomniac was playing a joke on him. There could be no other explanation. There were no lights on except for a lone kitchen window. He laughed out loud and waved his hands to all the dark windows, at the joker who was playing tricks on him.

He opened the car door again and noticed the heavy wooden legs and three thick planks of wood patched up together like a lopsided dining table. Anyone passing by would've assumed it was broken, but Santo had an eye for these things because he had been to many thrift shops looking for one in case he won the Dominican lottery. Any Sunday, he was planning to hit the numbers with Dallas's birthday date.

The table was a sealed piano. Inside it he was sure to find keys and strings. He tried to budge it out from under the garbage bags. It had been a slow night. He was hungry, tired, he must've been hearing things. He wiped his eyes. He searched for a witness.

When he pulled it out from under the garbage, and positioned it in the middle of the sidewalk, it looked out of place. The piano was out of its element, like Santo felt out of his element. —Who threw you out? he asked as he slid his fingers on the aging wood and played on the keys that had once been there. The streets were very quiet that night. Not a single car came by. When Santo tapped his fingers against the dark and damp wood, he was serenaded with a selection of random melancholic notes.

—Get that thing out of here, Esperanza said when she saw the size of it.

—Estás loca mujer, after everything I went through to get it here. No way.

In order to get it into their apartment, Santo needed the help of two men.

—What if someone pissed on it? What if someone died on it? What if the person who owned it was miserable and cursed it? You ever think of that? Besides, where do you think we're gonna put this monstrosity? On the top of my head? Esperanza asked, flinging her arms up to the heavens.

—We can put it in the kids' room, Santo pleaded.

• • •

Dallas heard him say it, but she couldn't believe it. The dead person's piano, which someone had pissed on, with a curse, no less, in her room?

—It won't fit, Dallas said to whoever listened. Santo's eyes pleaded with Dallas to help him out. After all, she knew she was his favorite, his little girl, his princess. They were supposed to be allies.

—I don't want that table in my room, Dallas said, storming out, not making eye contact with either of them. She couldn't stand to see her father hurt. He had never asked for anything from her before, and the one thing he did ask for, she refused him. She had already given up her room so Don Chan could have a place to sleep. As it was, her bed and Bobby's were close enough to each other that when Bobby tossed around and flung his arm in his sleep he sometimes slapped her face. She didn't want that ghost of a piano inside her itty-bitty room that only had a small window facing the alley.

—No, she cried. No way.

Esperanza refused to let him bring the table past the foyer. It stood on its side in their skinny hallway for weeks. Neither of them gave in. Dallas climbed around the enormous wooden legs, wondering when Santo and Esperanza would make up. It was easy for them to stay angry at each other, when Santo worked nights and Esperanza worked days. If they stayed on schedule, they could spend weeks without having to talk much at all.

Don Chan didn't like Sundays because everyone was home. The luncheonette didn't open until noon. The streets were filled with churchgoing women and their children, stopping and starting as they made their way up the street. Everyone wanted to have a conversation. —Hey, Viejo, how are things going? How you feeling? Where you heading?

—Estamos vivo, was his reply as he concentrated on his routine, because if he broke it, he inevitably would forget something he wanted to do and then the entire day would be thrown off. It was easier to stay home and not leave his room on Sundays and wait until Monday when everything went back on schedule.

On Sundays, Esperanza insisted that they all sit around the dinner table like a family because it would save their children from a life of delinquency on the streets. That was the rule. And even though their fights allowed Don Chan to have Santo to himself and Esperanza's silent treatment was a holiday for the ears, the tense silence between them at the dinner table stole away his appetite.

—Maybe it's time I fly back home, Santo said as he served himself a generous helping of rice. —It's been too long.

—¿Qué qué? Esperanza looked mortified.

Esperanza was convinced that it was Don Chan who'd put him up to it. Santo had never mentioned the topic before. The dinner table was crowded with dishes: red beans, a pile of maduros, a bowl of rice, a stack of pork chops, a small salad, and two glasses of milk for the children.

—But your father just got here and you want to leave now?

—We can all go together. Santo ignored Esperanza. —The entire family. A vacation.

—We don't have money for that, Esperanza said, and served Bobby and Dallas.

—I think it's a great idea, Don Chan said, pushing the issue. —Don't you, kids?

—Will we see horses? Dallas asked. Much like her mother, she loved horses and had never seen one in real life.

—And goats, cows, chickens, pigs, and lizards, Don Chan added, wondering if a ten-year-old cared for such things. Dallas was growing up so fast. —I'll take you to Los Llanos so you can see the house your father was born in.

—I don't like lizards, Dallas said.

—Pass the water, Esperanza said. She tossed around the chunks of avocado, picked at the pork chop.

—Are you on a diet? Santo noticed Esperanza wasn't eating.

—Bobby, hurry up and eat, you have homework to do. And you, Dallas, hurry up too so you can help me in the kitchen.

—She doesn't want you to go, Don Chan said.

Esperanza stabbed the flesh with her fork. It was none of his business. Why couldn't he have grown old and catatonic? Just sit there and say nothing like one of the clients she took care of. It's much easier when old people don't talk.

—Don't be ridiculous, Papá. She worries about money. But if we always worry about money, when will we live life?

—That's right, son. You want to live to work or work to live? From what I can see, both of you live to work. What's the point to live at all?

—Easy for you to say, you never worked a day of your life, Esperanza snapped.

—Now, Esperanza . . . Santo warned her not to disrespect his father. It would only make the situation worse.

—I was working the land since the day I was born. How do you think we put food on the table in Los Llanos? You're so ungrateful.

—How else would you have survived in that campo without us sending checks back home every month? Esperanza stood up and started putting dishes away. —Dallas, help me, por dios. Someone help me.

Dallas took the dishes to the kitchen.

—Sit, Dallas. We haven't finished eating, Santo said.

—All I said is maybe we should take a trip as a family. We've been in New York over ten years. We never go anywhere.

—Please, Santo, not in front of the children.

—Then when? I only see you while you sleep, if that. We never talk anymore.

—You can blame your father for that. There's a lot of things we don't do anymore. Esperanza glanced down at his crotch to make her point.

Santo stood up and pushed the table with his knees. Esperanza grabbed the jug of water to keep it from tipping. Dallas and Bobby didn't move.

—One maldito trip to see our old friends. Can a man at least dream?

Los Llanos
1961

Back in Los Llanos, when Don Chan looked at Miraluz, it made him forget the blanket of stars above them. Her black eyes and reddish brown coloring that blended in with the fire aroused his body. He returned home to Doña Caridad at night and searched inside his wife's skirt for Miraluz's wisdom. He kneaded her thick thighs and full ass, trying to understand how Miraluz knew about Trujillo's death. It couldn't have been a dream. He had heard of people who dreamed the future, but so accurately, as if she had the power to make things happen?

—Get out from under there, Doña Caridad said, pulling down her skirt. —Don't you see I'm trying to get things done?

Doña Caridad wasn't ready for Don Chan's new affection. He wasn't one to touch her, let alone kiss, lick, suck the juices from inside her. Their intimacy was simply him entering her and her relaxing into him, until he was ready to climax. First, he took that crazy trip into the capital, then he suddenly became fascinated with her body. She had heard that, like women, men go through a change of life. Did Don Chan want another child? She was too old to have children. Would he abandon her because of it? She spread her legs and allowed him to look inside her vagina so he could hopefully find what he was searching for.

He stretched her lips, feeling her insides, so warm, him wondering what did Miraluz taste like. He kissed Doña Caridad's inner thighs, trying to push the desire for Miraluz away, focusing on his wife, who had given him his son. To feel the inside of her walls tense up around his tongue and fingers excited him. How deep could he have gone inside her without losing himself completely? Maybe if he tried hard enough, he could slip into Caridad and be reborn again.

Doña Caridad didn't know what made her body shake and release with such joy when Don Chan dug his fingers and tongue inside her, but she too had become filled with passion, sometimes finding herself touching her own body and riding the waves of highs and lows that often brought her to ecstasy. She perfumed her body daily with rose petals from her garden, just in case Don Chan returned home with desire. She added rum to her hot chocolates and always shaved her legs in anticipation of his return.

Meanwhile, as Doña Caridad raged with desire, Don Chan became more worried over his newfound passion for Miraluz. She showed up every night at the campfire, asking Don Chan to impart a story that provided inspiration. Even though the men respected her, and some even feared her when she spoke her mind, she in turn waited to hear from Don Chan. Her presence brought on such frustration in him that he drank to forget, and soon the gatherings in the fields of Los Llanos were filled with slanderous stories that mimicked the popular merengue songs about women who betrayed men.

—What are we going to do now that Trujillo is dead? Miraluz asked after attending a few of the meetings and listening to the men talk nonsense.

Trujillo was dead and the restlessness was everywhere. Even in the trees. People didn't know who to trust or what to believe. It took two days for the newspapers to announce the assassination.

—Do? Didn't you dream the answer last night? Don Chan teased her.

—Go home, little girl. We're doing what we gonna do, one man said as he passed around the tub of ice.

—We have enough to worry about, said another man. —I say Trujillo is dead, let's be grateful for our blessings and hope that the next government is kinder to us.

—Do you agree with him? Miraluz asked Don Chan directly. She was wearing the yellow dress. The hem went up high on her thigh. Don Chan wanted her to stop talking. He wanted to tell her to go home. But she wasn't a little girl. She wore the breasts and curves of a woman.

When he didn't answer, she walked away. Santo followed behind her so she wouldn't walk alone in the night. The flames did a different dance that night. One of hope, fear, excitement.

—Come back, little girl! Don Chan sobered up. —Didn't your family teach you to respect your elders?

—There's no time for respect. Unless you have something to say, I have better things to do.

Don Chan didn't know if he should be insulted or inspired. When Trujillo was alive, it was easy to discern who the enemy was and gather the people of Los Llanos to spit at the dictatorship. Even easier to learn about the atrocities and know who to punch at. But now that Trujillo was dead, where would they start? The government was in flux. The people confused. Don Chan saw the flames grow with the evening breeze. Miraluz was waiting for an answer. He didn't want to disappoint her.

—Haven't you read the news? Trujillo's men are taking over the office without asking the people what they want, Miraluz said.

—Yes I know, but what can we do?

—We can't just sit here, Miraluz urged.

—But we're not politicians.

—Who cares about politics? All over the world, people are fighting and we sit here and do nothing.

—And you think it's so easy?

—Then why do you bother and tell us stories about Toussaint, who fought for the freedom of his people, or Martí, who died in battle for Cuba? If you want us to sit here and do nothing, then talk about flowers and the stars that serve as an escape.

—What do you want us to do? he said, struggling to hold himself back from wiping the dust off her cheeks. She was beautiful when she was angry.

—Let's storm the palace. There are more of us than there are of them. Let's . . . well, I don't know, you're the one who has to tell us what to do. What do we do if we have another Trujillo? And that dictator decides to sell what's left of Los Llanos to some foreigners and we are forced to leave our land? —Do you have a title to your land? Miraluz asked and pointed to different people in the circle. All of them shook their heads.

—I don't know what we'll do.

—Well, then, we need a leader who does.

Don Chan didn't want Miraluz to abandon the circle.

—Wait, he said, not sure what he could offer her.

—I heard that people in the capital are organizing for the next election. Our first since 1930. Maybe that's something we can do. We can get the people of Los Llanos to vote, Don Chan said, wondering if it was his idea or Miraluz's.

She was trembling. She hadn't been prepared for her own outburst or for a response from him. She didn't know she had so much to say.

—Do you all agree? Don Chan asked the crowd, who didn't want to think about the possibility of losing their land. They already had too many worries.

—Whatever you say, Don Chan. Now hand me over a beer, one man said. —Who has a dirty joke to sweeten this night?

Nueva York
1992

Bobby arrived home barefoot on a Sunday. Esperanza and Santo were still not speaking to each other. It was impossible for Don Chan to find a place in the apartment where he didn't feel like he was in the way. So when the door bell rang, he went to answer it because it offered him something to do.

—You okay, Bobby?

Some kids from two blocks over Quepasó Street had stolen Bobby's sneakers and leather jacket.

—What happened to you? Santo asked, rushing at Bobby. His son had walked in socks on the cold winter streets.

—You just let them take your things? Santo took a pretend jab at him, to wake him up and get a reaction. Bobby didn't flinch. He fell back against the wall. He was still in shock from the robbery and angry with his father for pushing him around. Santo wasn't there. He hadn't seen the three guys, bigger and faster than Bobby, the way they had surrounded him and thrown him off his own feet. Before he could blink, they had his stuff and there was nothing he could do about it.

—Fuck you, he wanted to say to his father. —I ain't like you and I won't ever be like you.

—Santo, take it easy on the kid, Don Chan said, putting his hand on Santo's shoulder.

—You're the one who said we have to fight for what's ours. I'm killing myself every day so some punk can steal from you and you don't fight back? Look at you, I could tell by your clean face that you handed it over to them. Santo inspected Bobby's face. Bobby held back tears while his father pushed him against the wall.

—It's a pair of sneakers, Don Chan said. —No, no, Santo, let the kid be.

Esperanza pulled Bobby toward her and held him. —Don't listen to him. He's a brute.

—Why is it that everyone thinks they can tell me what to do? Am I not the man of this house? He's my son and I do with him what I want.

When he was in Los Llanos, it was the way of Don Chan, and now in Nueva York, Esperanza watched his every move, telling him what to do and not to do. On the streets, he got crap from the cops, at the taxi base they kept upping the fees without warning, so Santo had to work more hours to make his weekly goal. All because he let people push him around.

—You're going to learn how to fight, Santo said and dragged Bobby into the imaginary boxing ring in the living room. The entertainment center and sofa were the ropes. Santo let Dallas play referee.

—You, Dallas, watch and learn. I don't want any sleazy guy messing with a daughter of mine.

—Okay, Bobby, hit me.

—Santo, he's a child, Don Chan said, sitting in the corner.

—So was I, Papá, and that never stopped you.

—What are you talking about? Don Chan tried to hold Santo back. Santo pulled away from Don Chan and started to hop around like a boxer.

—C'mon, kid, show me what you got, Santo said, bouncing around him.

—Don't punk out in front of your abuelo. Tell him, Papá, what you did to me when I arrived home with the empty buckets of water because I dropped them on the way.

—That was a long time ago, I don't know what you're talking about. Don Chan fidgeted in his chair. His face gathered into a tight map of wrinkles as his hands pushed up against his face, trying to remember.

—Back in the day, punks like you would have calluses on their knees from kneeling on rice.

—Remember that, Papá. Every time I messed up, you made me kneel until my knees bled, so I didn't mess up again.

—Leave him alone, Esperanza yelled at Santo.

—When you going to become a man, Bobby? Eh? If you had earned those sneakers, you wouldn't let someone take your stuff right off your feet.

Bobby was barely thirteen years old. He wasn't going to hit his father. Santo kicked Bobby on the leg and then tried to jab him in the gut and before Bobby knew what was going on, he was down.

—Ten, nine, eight, seven, six . . . That was Dallas's favorite part. And when Bobby was down on the floor, Dallas counted; pounding her fist on the floor next to his face like she had seen it many times during the boxing matches.

—You gonna let your father beat you up? Don't be a pendejo, Bobby, only because you're smaller doesn't mean you can't win. Isn't that what you taught me, Papá? That we could win no matter how many bombs they throw at us, that a machete in the hand of a smart man is more dangerous than a gun in the hand of a stupid man. Wasn't that what you said?

—Santo, why don't we all sit down and talk.

—Look who the punks are now, Papá. After all that bullshit we went through, look at us.

—Leave the kid alone, Don Chan pleaded.

—C'mon, Bobby, show me what kind of son I raised. Get up, Santo said, pulling Bobby up from the ground. Dallas laughed, calling Bobby a wuss.

Bobby didn't fight back. He didn't want to hit anyone. He was more afraid of the anger he kept tucked deep down inside him. What if he let it all out, could he kill someone? Could something happen between him and his father that he would regret? He didn't want to go there, and because he didn't want to go there, he tried to block Santo's badgering from his mind. Bobby had his head tipped low, flared his nose as if smoke was coming out of him.

—Yeah, c'mon, Bobby, I'll be easy on you, Dallas said. She was bouncing around like the boxers do on TV. —C'mon, wuss, she yelled to rile up a real fight. Rooting for a bigger battle, another knockout, so she could count backward again. But before Bobby could be knocked out again, Esperanza started yelling.

—What did I say about fighting in the house? You, Santo, are raising our children to be barbarians.

—I'm teaching them to defend themselves.

—I'm so sorry, mijo, Don Chan said, looking at Bobby, a younger version of Santo. What did I do to you?

—You stay out of it, Santo yelled back at his father. Santo had found a numbness to get through his thirteen-hour workdays before his father's arrival. He had shut down all the longing for a different life. He accepted the sacrifice to work for his children. But then his father was making it difficult for Santo to do his shifts day after day. How did ten years go by and he still didn't own much more than his old beat-up car? And then Esperanza gave him a hard time about the piano. What had he asked from her? Damn her, damn his father. Damn his ungrateful children.

—Vete a la mierda, Don Chan said, hurt and confused. He didn't ask to come to Nueva York. He left for the bedroom and slammed the door behind him.

—If I left them up to you, they'd still be sucking on your tit, Santo told Esperanza.

—Ay, Santo, don't go there in front of the children, please.

—How is he going to survive in this city if he lets some punk take his shoes?

Bobby leaned against the shelves stuffed with magazines and the television, stereo, and speakers.

—Look what you did to pobre Bobby. He returns home from violence on the street and you have violence in this house. Do you think that's good for the boy, Santo? What have we talked about? To be different, to be decent, to have children who will grow up to be good people and get good jobs. We don't want them to become tigres, fighting like cats on the street. No, Santo. Not my Bobby.

—We might want something, Esperanza, but the world wants something else. I'm just saying that it don't matter how good we are, you go out in the world and people will try to beat you up and take everything you got. I want them to learn how to defend themselves.

—Since when? Esperanza asked.

—What do you mean?

—You never stood up for anything. Always hiding behind your father's big mouth.

—I should've stayed in D.R. and let you fend for yourself. You'd probably still be stuck in Puerto Rico.

He looked over at Bobby and hated Bobby for taking on the things Santo hated about himself. Don't end up like me, Santo thought.

Bobby glared at Santo and then Dallas and ran out of the room and locked himself in the bathroom. Dallas giggled on the sofa, waiting to see what was going to happen next.

Santo had gone too far. He knew it. And when he looked over at Esperanza, he wanted to take it all back. He was tired of being so angry. He missed her. What had happened to them? To the woman he'd fallen in love with?

Esperanza noticed a fierceness in Santo's eyes. It excited her. Since Don Chan's arrival, Santo and Esperanza had stopped talking like they used to. She was also tired of fighting with him. They were drifting apart while living under the same roof.

Santo's arms and shoulders collapsed. His eyes drooped in sadness. He let out a deep sigh.

—Come here, Santo said to Esperanza.

Looking at him, his tall, slender build, his full and well-defined lips reminded her that this was the same man who had followed her to the U.S., even after she had abandoned them. This was the same man who worked all day and night to take care of them. She walked toward him and said, —Ay, Santo, mi miel de abeja, honey from the bees, so sweet to lick, to eat, so sweet, she said while Dallas sat on the sofa and watched. Esperanza didn't like the ruthless Santo who was training her son to be a man, but his assertive tone made her soft for him. She walked up close to him, pulled into his warmth. And on that particular day, the radio was playing the old Dominican songs that reminded them of their youth.

The kind of songs where all the instruments had their moment and held their own: the *güiro*, the trumpet, the congas, the guitar. All playing a slow bolero, slow enough so Esperanza's thighs could nestle between Santo's legs. They moved three steps back, three steps forward; back and forth, trying not to trip over the coffee table, Bobby's bike and the chairs. As they danced, he dipped her. With each step his hands trailed farther down her back and her arms held him tighter around his neck. They forgot Dallas was watching. It was only when they kissed and she giggled that they woke up from the dream the song offered, the dream of remembering where it all began for them.

—So you think it's funny, huh? Santo winked at Dallas as he pulled away from Esperanza, who was flushed. She wanted to dance into the bedroom and make love. But as soon as Esperanza heard the sharp pitch of Dallas's voice, she remembered she was a mother and she hadn't made dinner for her children. So she kissed Santo lightly on the lips and went into the kitchen.

Dallas giggled some more and then sprang up to face her father.
—Dance with me, Papi?
Dallas stood on the sofa to be his height.
—Of course I'll dance with you.

He bowed like a gentleman, picked her up from the couch into his arms, and placed her firmly on the floor. He moved Dallas around the room faster than the rhythm of the music. And while they moved, the floor against their feet, Dallas was laughing so hard her stomach hurt and no sound was coming out of her mouth. But she wanted him to dance with her for real. To dance with her like he danced with her mother. So Dallas wiggled her way up his body, climbing him so she could look at him eye to eye and said, —For real this time.
—Very well.
And Dallas put her arms around his neck and brought her body close to his in a way so that she could smell his sweet breath, the

scent of minty toothpaste. She dug her nose in his neck, feeling his heart beat against her chest.

—Okay, Dallas, when you dance with a man you must always remember that where you place your hand will suggest what kind of girl you are. Since I'm your father, you could hold on to me around my neck. But for anyone else, you make sure you always place your left hand flat against his shoulder. Arms outstretched so he knows to keep his distance.

He pulled her away to show how much distance, making Dallas giggle with embarrassment.

—Don't let him put your hands on his heart. When a man does that, he's trying to seduce you. It's a trick. It'll make you think he really likes you, that he doesn't let all the girls touch his heart that way. But he does. He wants you to feel special so you'll fall for him. He knows that once you fall for him, and that can easily happen with one good dance, you'll let him touch you. You can never let any man touch you, not until you're old enough to get married. Never let his hand grab you low on your waist when you dance. Make him hold you loosely on your back, but nowhere near your bra. You hear me?

—Sí, Papi, I hear you.

Dallas held on to him tighter, wondering what if the men she met didn't dance? How would she find out their intentions? She held on to him as they moved around their crowded living room to merengue beats, shaking their hips from side to side, he digging his feet into the wooden floor, she floating on air as she danced with her father. Her beautiful father who was dark like her grandmother, with thick hair, whose lips were full and whose eyelashes curled up so long, they kissed his eyebrows.

Los Llanos
1962–1963

Every organization needs a name. Don Chan knew that much. People wouldn't know they belonged to something if they didn't have a name to call it by. And so the Invisible Ones were born. And with it, Don Chan's paranoia. If in the past, the people of Los Llanos innocently met around campfires to tell stories, now that Don Chan had an agenda, they had to be a lot more careful. All members of the Invisible Ones were to go by first name only, to avoid being put on any opposing parties' death list.

However, the first-name-only rule created myriad confusion when barking orders, because of mothers naming all their children by a patron saint or a soap star: Antonio, Martín, Altagracia, Octavio, María, José, and Jesús. People found themselves fighting over the car wheel or who would be the one to pick up the flyers that announced a "child's birthday party."

Robertico's cumpleaños. Come celebrate.

The meetings in the fields were filled with music. Disguised in songs were Don Chan's chants to inspire all the complacent to join the Invisible Ones.

—And who do the rich rely on?

—Nosotros! Don Chan said, responding to his own question, raising his hand to assert his point.

—Who do they leave their children with?

—Nosotros! the crowd responded, following his lead. Many banging on pots, others raising their hands in agreement. Drums picking up in beat.

—Who guards their house?

—Nosotros!

—Who chauffeurs their car?

—Nosotros!

—And they accuse us of stealing, they claim to pay us too much, they call us lazy when they talk to their friends, as if we don't have ears. We're not animals, we're not children, Don Chan chanted. As he watched the people dance until their feet were too tired to jump, to swing, to turn in the dirt, it was difficult for Don Chan to discern if the people attending the parties would vote at the elections.

—Now we only need to find someone for them to vote for, Santo said.

—Maybe Don Chan should run, Miraluz said, volunteering him.

—I'm not interested, Don Chan said but didn't mean it. The thought had crossed his mind. But he knew he wouldn't win. A Chinese-looking man as president. The people wouldn't be able to look past his face. —For now, mobilizing the people is most important.

And while the Invisible Ones scrubbed floors, poured drinks, chauffeured cars, trimmed gardens, shined shoes, painted walls, and more, they were taking notes, making maps, plans of streets and important estates. For what, they weren't sure, but Don Chan insisted they stayed alert and learn everything they could in preparation.

—For too long we've been working passively. Even in our smallest acts we need to right the wrongs.

Women were not sleeping with married men, in solidarity with other women; men were not talking to their friends who beat their wives, employers who abused their workers were finding centipedes in their shoes. Employers' gas tanks were emptied in the middle of the night, their electricity lines were being tapped into, their clothes were being burned with irons by workers.

The Invisible Ones multiplied, from Los Llanos to Dajabón. The people were restless, tired of bogus elections. Grandmothers prayed every Sunday morning for the return of the titles of land stolen from them. Santeras lit candles and sacrificed goats, asking the saints for employment. And children with hungry bellies danced in circles, hoping that when it rained, it would rain coffee, so that they could have something to sell on the streets.

Months later, a truck drove into Los Llanos. People gathered. Seldom did foreign trucks drive through their small town. A white skinned, blue-eyed man dressed in work pants and an open shirt stepped out.

—My name is Juan Bosch, he said, not fazed by the emaciated mule, the clotheslines, the chickens eating grain, the smell of manure, tobacco and burning wood. Like one of them, he wiped the sweat from his brow with his shirtsleeve and took an empty seat where the men were having a drink.

—You represent el pueblo, and this country should serve you, Bosch said, his accent affected from the years he lived in exile.

Don Chan listened to Bosch's ideas about cooperative stores, agrarian reform, ways to improve education and health facilities. Bosch denounced the Dominican rich who wore their Spanish ancestry like their true bandera and the gringos who wanted D.R. as their new stomping ground.

—I leave you this transistor radio so you can follow what is happening in the city. I will win the presidency because el pueblo will support me. And I will do right by you all. I promise.

—Everyone must vote. We'll vote twice if we have to, Don Chan told the crowds soon after Bosch's visit. This man would ensure their freedom.

Miraluz didn't trust a man whose hands looked like alabaster. And Juan Bosch, an intellectual, had lots of ideas, but what did he know about the way of the land?

—It's a terrible idea, Miraluz said. —Even if this so-called man is sympathetic to the needs of el pueblo, he won't risk his life for it.

Miraluz was surrounded by a group of spineless followers. She no longer wore the yellow dress, she wore jeans and a large T-shirt. Her hair was pulled back in a long braid. Don Chan could still see her small waist underneath the big clothes.

Don Chan glared at her. It was not the appropriate time for her smart mouth. They needed to appear united or they wouldn't progress at all.

—The goal is for him to enforce laws that protect us, Don Chan said.—The constitution won't allow for a dictatorship again.

—But we need someone like us, who knows what it's like to be poor, Miraluz insisted. —Someone like Toussaint. He wasn't afraid to die for his people's freedom.

—You want us to end up like Haiti? another called out. —Forget the Haitians.

—Speak for yourself. Many of us have Haiti in our blood. Santo stood close to Miraluz to show solidarity.

Miraluz held on to Santo's arms. Don Chan felt a twinge of jealousy. He had lost control of the crowd and was also losing the affections of Miraluz.

—Be careful what you wish for, Miraluz. Everything looks simple when you read it out of a book, but nothing that requires violence is heroic, Don Chan said and pulled Santo from her. —Trujillo wasn't only poor, but he had Haitian in him, and he ordered the murder of tens of thousands of Haitians. I've made up my mind. You want to go bomb the president's palace? Do as you will, but I'm voting for Bosch.

Months later, the people elected Juan Bosch, and Los Llanos gathered the distressed, the unemployed, the frustrated on Sundays. The music and the abundance of cane juice kept the spirits high. They were so filled with optimism, that even when a hurricane stormed through the valley and stole away the rooftops from over their heads, they said, —No hay nada mal que por bien no venga. And fell asleep in their homes with a view to the stars, wondering why they ever had a roof to begin with. They had chosen their own president for the first time in their lives. And the blessings in Los Llanos were abundant. A hurricane had ripped through town, unearthing a number of treasures on the land people squatted on.

Don Chan had found a sealed aluminum soup pot. The pot was sealed with cement. He looked for a machete and tried to pry it open, but the pot rolled around on the ground as if it had a mind of its own. Don Chan took the pot and held it between his feet. He pressed his body against the knife. Inside the pot was enough money to legalize the titles of the land that his family and many people of Los Llanos had worked on for so many years.

The stories about treasures so long forgotten even by those who had buried them made a gold digger of any hungry man or woman working the fields in Los Llanos. Soon, people all over D.R. talked about the rich land of Los Llanos, most assuming that the campesinos were making up lies and all that talk of richness was about the well-watered soil. No more money was ever to be found. But the people of Los Llanos dug up jewelry, silver, guns, grenades, bullets, knives. Materials left behind by past rebel groups and government officials who, while they smiled and ate dinner with Trujillo, stole from under his nose.

—Now that we legally own our land, who can stop us from doing as we want? Don Chan said to all those who joined him in his vision of a country that is owned by the people who work the land. —If we work the land, we should own the land.

The people planted seeds as they made wishes and watched the acres that were once cane fields turn into communal gardens filled with a variety of fruit and vegetables. And soon, people's bellies were so full, no longer did their employers' comments vex them or did their circumstances seem bleak. Now they had a country of their own, and when it came to the fruits in the trees, it was all for the taking.

Within three months, gossip about Los Llanos and Don Chan's storytelling hour went from kitchen to kitchen. Soon the Chino who lived in Los Llanos was known all over D.R. Fights broke out between drunkards over the name. Was it Invincible or Invisible? Don Chan himself was no longer invisible. And people were wise enough to keep him a secret because being the only Chino in Los Llanos made him vulnerable. Instead, they called him a medicine man to explain the crowds that sometimes gathered in the small town park filled with processions for saints and dances of palo. So popular had the parties of Los Llanos become, high government officials and television celebrities called on him to cure their ailments. Don Chan cured everything from bleeding rectums to impotence, and as a natural entertainer, he created a show for all to see and singled out the richest of his guests, placing his hand on their foreheads and saying words as if they were being fed to him from the heavens.

—Your problem is that you're too busy thinking about your pocketbook and don't spend enough time dancing with your wife. Go home, drink ginger tea with honey, give all the money you keep in your safe to the people who serve you, and make love to your wife. You'll see, you'll suffer no more pain.

The crowd laughed along with the patient, who admitted that it had been years since he had taken time off, that he never slept a full night because he feared someone was going to break into his house. And yes it was also true . . . he didn't remember the last time he'd danced with his wife.

In return, Don Chan and his family were gifted with sweet breads, rice puddings, goats raised on oregano, pigs and fruits from the other side of the island. Don Chan was afraid to admit that full bellies made the Invisible Ones as indifferent to the injustices of the world as the rich whom he often criticized. Now that they had their land, and grew enough food to feed themselves, people spent their days making love and dancing their nights away. Don Chan wondered how long they could isolate themselves from the calamities affecting the cities and campos surrounding them. The people of Los Llanos were too busy enjoying abundance to care about what was brewing in the cities of D.R.

Nueva York
1992

The Colón family were all home for the first time in a long while. Don Chan napped in his bedroom. Esperanza made dinner with Dallas in the kitchen. Santo lounged in the living room, reading, while Bobby slouched on the sofa and watched the baseball game. The small radio was on a news station in the kitchen. The house smelled of frying oil and boiling beans.

—Esperanza, did you hear about this woman? Santo yelled over to the kitchen.

—What woman? Esperanza yelled back, chopping the onions and peppers. Dallas was washing the lettuce and beating it against the sink to dry.

—She lived on Quepasó Street, Santo said, reading the article, but not believing the story could possibly be true. It was right around the corner. It could've been Esperanza or Dallas or him.

The phone rang and Esperanza picked it up, struggling to hold it with her neck. —Aló?

—May I speak to Miss Esperanza Colón, please?

—Sí, this is Esperanza.

—Miss Colón, this is a collection agency, and we're collecting a debt of yours for two thousand dollars.

Esperanza felt blood drain from her face, the room spin around. She smiled over at Santo, who looked up in curiosity. She shooed away Dallas, who repeated everything to her father.

In the bedroom, Don Chan picked up the other line, hoping it was a call from Miraluz. It had been weeks since he had last heard from her.

—This poor woman, Santo said, shaking his head. —She was walking on Quepasó and one of those potted plants, you know, the ones people keep on the fire escapes, fell on her head. Can you believe that?

—Just a second . . . , Esperanza yelled and then leaned out the window so her voice didn't carry over to Santo. —Two thousand dollars, what do you mean two thousand dollars? she told the man on the phone. —I haven't bought anything for that much. —Ay diosito, Esperanza whispered.

—You got to read this, Esperanza. Maybe you know her? Santo yelled into the kitchen.

—Sí, amor, I'll be with you in a minute!

Don Chan continued to listen in. Dollars he understood, and whispering could only mean that Esperanza wasn't happy with the news.

—You can work out a payment plan with us. If not, we'll be forced to go to court.

—Court? Corte? Cárcel? Aja, Esperanza is going to jail! Don Chan wondered what trouble she had gotten herself into now.

—Court? Esperanza didn't want to alarm Santo, so she held back any signs of emotion. Court! She didn't feel very well. Lightheadedness, nausea, everything she ever worked for was quickly slipping from her. She pictured herself in an orange jumpsuit behind a glass wall, begging Santo for forgiveness. In her head she went through the inventory of all her purchases. Two thousand dollars? Impossible! She touched the rim of the new ceramic bowls she had bought from *Buy TV*, trying to distract herself from what she was being told on the phone.

—Hello, Miss Colón, are you still there?

The voice was cold and calculated, as if he was reading from a sheet. —Hello.

—Yes, I'm here, but you'll have to call me next week. It's not a good time, she said and hung up before the man on the other end of the line could respond. She rushed over to her underwear drawer to look at the bills she had perfectly organized. She saw how month by month, her 100-dollar necklace had turned into a 220-dollar purchase. Interest. Eighteen percent interest adds up, plus late penalties. —Ay diosito, she said, sitting on the edge of her bed, feeling very disconnected to the woman who bought all those things. What am I going to do? Esperanza wondered if *Buy TV* would take it all back. The vegetable curler was still in its box. And the figurine that wound up and played the bells was stored away in the closet. She stored them so she could pace the appearance of her purchases. Santo didn't notice that the sheets were new, that their pillows were firmer. He enjoyed their luxuries, assuming his antimaterialist ways bought him such comfort.

Don Chan hurried out of the bedroom to catch Esperanza in her moment of doom. He had always known that she wasn't to be trusted and now Santo would see for himself. She had nowhere to hide.

—Papá, you must've heard the news? Santo looked very distressed.

—You already know? Don Chan said.

—That poor woman.

—Poor woman? What's wrong with you, Santo? Snap out of it, son. Was there not anything Esperanza could do that would make him see the truth?

—But she worked six days a week, overtime on many nights, and look what happened to her.

—I can't believe you feel sorry for her.

—I can't believe you're being so insensitive, Santo said. Especially when they were all still grieving for the loss of Doña Caridad. The poor woman's life was taken away from her just like that, and she was a young woman still. Couldn't be much older than Esperanza. —Look what it says here. Santo showed Don Chan the article. The cover story told by the sister of the woman who was killed by the terra-cotta pot.

—Oh my, Don Chan said as he read the first few lines. —Pobre mujer, he said, forgetting to tell Santo about Esperanza. The poor woman had missed her son's first steps because she desperately wanted to go back home to D.R. and buy a house in which to retire. She deprived herself of good, comfortable shoes to the point that her bunions forced her to double her shoe size. All this so she could save for the house she never got to live in. She had never taken a vacation to visit her family back home, because she didn't have the time, because she was trying to save money. Even when her homesickness brought her to tears. The vision of her life in the future kept her going. And now, she had nothing. She was dead without a future, and worse, without a present she could enjoy. The article ended with her son's quote, "Mami worked very hard."

—I think I knew this woman. Sí, sí, she frequented the luncheonette. For take-out coffee mostly. Brief hellos. Always in a hurry, Don Chan said, and the story saddened him so much his eyes watered. A terrible thing that happens with old age. He could no longer control certain things about his body, such as his tear ducts, the weakness of his knees, and losing his breath when climbing a few flights of stairs.

Santo took the paper away from Don Chan and sat in his usual corner to finish reading before he departed for work. To read the articles and feel informed made the day worthwhile. It also gave him something to talk about with his father and his passengers.

—You know that about twenty people a year die from something that falls out of a window? Santo said in disbelief.

Don Chan went to catch Esperanza. But when he saw Esperanza sitting at the edge of her bed, her head tucked into her shoulders, the way she hunched over the letters and gripped the envelopes, her knuckles swelling into a puffy red, he felt a deep sorrow for her. Or was he feeling sorrow for the woman who died? Poor woman, her life snatched by a stupid pot, an unexpected wind, a careless tenant who didn't take the precautions to secure the pot outside their window. Don Chan startled Esperanza as he hovered in front of her bedroom door. She stuffed the envelopes in her drawer and pressed down her shirt as if the wrinkles exposed her fears, her worries, her troubles.

—Do you need something? Esperanza's eyes were misty.

—Well, I wanted to . . . Don Chan had forgotten why he had rushed into her room. He was angry with her. Ah yes, she was in trouble.

—I was thinking of preparing you octopus tomorrow, she said as she picked up her clothes from the ironing board. —I heard they came in fresh at the fish market.

—Sí, sí, that sounds nice, Don Chan said, surprised by the gesture. How did she know he liked octopus?

—I'll pick them up on my way home from work.

—But I'll prepare them, you use too much oil for my taste, Don Chan said.

—As you wish. Esperanza walked back into the kitchen. He followed her because he wanted her to know that she couldn't hide from him. He was there to accuse her of something. Of what exactly, he didn't know. And she was making it difficult for him by being so nice.

Dancing around the living room with Esperanza convinced Santo that what they needed was a night alone where they could forget all their problems. And what better place than the Palladium?

—Esperanza, what if we go dancing tonight? Santo asked her as soon as she arrived home from work, before she could take off her work clothes and change into her housedress. That matronly house-dress that he disliked. It covered all her curves. Don't change, not yet, he wanted to say. He took a good look at her while she was dressed for the world. Makeup, hairdo, and all. Was there something for them to celebrate, an anniversary perhaps?

—I'm working tomorrow, early, she said. She tasted her lips. She played with her bangs covering her eyes.

—We'll order fried chicken for the kids. My father can watch them tonight.

Santo put one arm around her waist and kissed her on the lips. When was the last time they had kissed each other like that? He did it again, sucked her bottom lip and pressed her pelvis onto his. Yes, tonight he wanted to dance. And he wanted to fuck her. Not make love. No, he wanted to be with her as if he'd just met her in a club. To feel the heaviness of his wife over him and get lost in her flesh. He wanted them to sleep naked like they did before Bobby was born. They could lock their bedroom door for privacy.

—C'mon, amor. Let's break the routine for once.

—Maybe next week, she said, but didn't mean it. She had no time to dance. Or energy, for that matter.

What had gotten into him? Esperanza couldn't bear how loving he was, not after what she had done. Secrets were awful in that way. He was trying to get closer to her and all she could think about was the debt she was in, the trouble this was going to cause for them. She wanted to be left alone. She needed space to think. It had been a horrible day. Her client spent the entire day complaining. Her agency told her she could do overtime, which meant working nights. She had no choice. She had to tell Santo about the overtime. And then, of course, the debt.

—No no, Santo, not tonight, there's too much for me to do around the house. Besides, it's so cold out there. Don't you have to work? You know if you don't put in the hours . . .

—But it's our anniversary, Santo said, laying it on thick. Everything about Nueva York was about tomorrow. He wanted it to be about today. —You could wear one of the fancy dresses you have. I could wear one of my new shirts that still have the tags on. You always complain that you never have any place to wear your nice clothes.

—Our anniversary was six months ago, she snapped back. —Besides, we have no money to be going out like that.

—Today is the day I fell in love with you. Shouldn't we celebrate that?

—Estás loco. We never celebrated that before. Besides, how could you remember such a day?

Esperanza didn't understand why he was insisting. As if he knew. As if he wanted her to feel more ashamed over the debt she had acquired. If he looked at her for too long, he would know. She turned away from him.

—How could I forget? Santo said, grabbing on to her waist, pulling her in again. He thought back to the dreamer he once was, the kind of man who would give anything to mop the sweat off a stage after Tito Puente played the drums.

—I have to get up so early in the morning, Santo. We could go next week. We'll plan it better. But today is not a good day.

—Forget that I asked. Santo walked away, grabbed his car keys and coat, wondering what had happened to the woman he married.

The Esperanza he met back in 1965 would've joined him for a night of dancing and she would've been excited about it too.

But 1965 was another time. Everything about 1965 was about today or never. Do or die. Who could've thought of a tomorrow, when bullets were then showering the city of Santo Domingo? There was no time for contemplation, everything was urgent. And when Santo closed his eyes, the machine guns reminded him of the timbales and the cry of the women could've easily been La Lupe from the stage at the Palladium.

Santo had first heard of the Palladium in '65. On Saturday nights, the radio broadcast live bands and Tito Puente dueled it out with Tito Rodriguez, when Dizzy Gillespie, Celia Cruz, Mongo Santamaria bumped beats against each other until the sun came up. Santo planned on boogalooing his way to hanging out with the Bang Bang crowd. Oh yes, thought Santo. The music had helped him forget that he was in the middle of a war.

Santo remembered the way Don Chan had him hold the globe in his hands when he was still too small to grab a bottle. Don Chan would say, —This is the world. This is where we are. And D.R. looked so small in the context of the world. Even the United States looked small compared to China. —Every time you feel claustrophobic, mijo, remember we're but a grain of sand in the desert. Santo was his captive listener.

All that talk about the world, and his father never ventured far from his campo. What good were all those geography lessons when he hadn't even made the trip to the Palladium? Ten years. A hundred and fifty blocks away. A fifteen-dollar cab fare. Eight, maybe nine miles. Esperanza was right; if it weren't for her, Santo would've never left Los Llanos. But since their arrival in Nueva York, all she wanted to do was work.

He could use a little ear-splitting music, speakers banging against his heart. If he had his way, he would spend the rest of his life dancing up and against one of those girls in low-cut dresses, and maybe on a slow night, he'd get to play the keyboard onstage. Even if they never let him onstage, what if he could get a job there? Just so he could catch rehearsal sessions and stand by the speakers and let the vibrations lift him off the floor. It would beat driving a taxi. Maybe the musicians would let him join in and jam a little or maybe he could walk the city streets at night with neon flashing in his face. Slow his hips down, bop his head to the clave, and walk long strides with his hat tipped over one eye. And he could sit on street corners and share a smoke with another music lover.

And why not? Santo decided that for once he was living for today and taking control of his own destiny. Once he made enough money to cover his expenses, he would escape and go downtown. On Saturday nights, ladies got in free and men paid ten dollars to get into the Palladium. He had ten dollars in his pocket. He took his last fare for the night and slid into the highway heading south. So what if Esperanza didn't want to join him. He knew he should've waited until Esperanza had a night off from work so they could go out together. But after living in Nueva York for so many years, her *next weeks* were not enough. It wasn't enough to listen to live shows on the radio while he drove customers around, listening to passengers talk about Tito's drums or Gillespie's trumpet. He wanted to go inside a real New York City nightclub and feel it himself. Not one of those cheap discos that riddled uptown and which only played bad merengue and were filled with rowdy youngsters. No, Santo wanted to experience the real thing. He was tired of sitting in his taxi seven days a week, only stretching his legs to piss and get a quick bite. Could this be it to life? He didn't ask for all this responsibility. All he ever wanted was to live. Wake up to the sun and fall asleep, with the moon, like the old men in Los Llanos who couldn't care less if the PSP, or PRD, or ABC took power as long as they could sit under a tree with a cold beer and dance with their women. There had to be time in life for that.

He drove by the club and watched the crowd trying to enter. There was no parking. He drove around several times and the cars were double-parked. It was Saturday night. He needed a miracle to find a space. Santo made a promise to himself that if he found parking, he'd take the chance and go into the nightclub. Santo drove around the block, praying to the parking gods. As it was, he had very little time to return home before Esperanza would start to worry. Santo double-parked, thinking that if he stopped moving, maybe then someone would leave their parking spot. And as if the gods themselves wanted Santo to go to the club, a car pulled out and he eased in. Santo sweated with anticipation. It was too easy. Could he be so lucky? He took it as a sign that he was at the right place at the right time. And hadn't he endured a long enough wait? Didn't he deserve this blessing?

He slicked back his hair with some water he kept in a jug for when his car overheated. He checked his face in the rearview mirror, pressing down his eyebrows, making sure that everything was in place. He tucked in his shirt and brushed down his pants and noticed his shoes were a bit scuffed. Who would notice? Especially among a crowd. He left his coat opened. His chest exposed to the cold air.

—Palladium, here I come, he said and pushed up his chest and recalled John Travolta's strut in *Saturday Night Fever*. Santo felt the eyes of the women on him as he walked up ahead in the line. He felt good looking. He felt special. He had found parking on a Saturday night. Now all he had to do was get into the hardest club in New York City.

Nonchalantly, he perused the posters of the upcoming Marc Anthony concert. He casually smiled at a group of ladies waiting in the front of the line and walked right over to them as if they had been friends for years. In minutes, the bouncers opened the ropes and let them all in. For free. He walked in with the four ladies dressed in tight dresses and high heels and let them grab his arms. What an entrance, Santo thought.

—Hola, papi, you're new around here, one of them said. And he smiled back at them, loving the way the cluster of women's bodies felt against his. He gave them the Santo Colón Smile. It was the reason Esperanza fell in love with him and it was the reason the women grabbed him. For the first time since he had arrived in New York City, he felt like himself. Free. No one knew him there. He could be one of the musicians, one of the promoters of the party, or the biggest music producer in town. Who would know the difference? Santo had arrived with four beautiful ladies and was allowed past the red velvet ropes as if he owned the place. He walked through the dark passageway into the large doorway and into the bright red lights and enormous dance floor. He tried to appear indifferent to the high ceilings, the beautiful crowd, the half-naked women dancing on the small platforms around the dance floor. He walked up to the stage, and from the dance floor, the stage was meant to intimidate. He touched it, put his hands flat on it, and thought about all the people who had walked on it and all the songs they sang to him when he still lived back in the campo. He pressed his head against the front stage and didn't care if anyone was looking. Women and men were dancing around him to the DJ's salsa, pushing and shoving him closer against the speakers. He fought to keep himself from climbing onstage and playing the keyboard. And to avoid being kicked out of the club, he walked back and away. From a distance, he could see the stage more clearly. It was cluttered with drums, and the microphones were in the front line. He watched the bright skirts lift as women spun around. The music, the movement, the big, open smiles filled the place. And the smoke hanging over the crowd made the homeliest woman look as beautiful as the movie star Ava Gardner, who Santo so much loved.

Santo ordered a rum and Coke at the bar and sipped it slow, letting the alcohol penetrate his hungry stomach. He hadn't had dinner that night. He didn't care. He was feeding off the loud boom of the speakers and he stood by them and let the sounds hump his backside. He let the swelling of the singer's voice caress his face and throat and before he knew it, he was downing the rum and Coke. He put the glass down and grabbed one of the women he'd entered with and pulled her onto the dance floor. He spun her around until she was dizzy and he felt the drink swish in his head. He felt her hands around his neck and he moved with her, his legs between her thighs, one, two, three, back and forth, one, two, three, turn and turn, and she stayed close, and she laughed, and he smiled, and she breathed in his ear, and he felt the clasp of her bra and her breast pressed against his chest, and the music was pounding in his heart and he was singing the words out loud, and she put her hand in his hair, and all he could do was think of Esperanza. Why wasn't she there with him? Why was she so stubborn? He turned the young woman with soft skin, who looked eighteen, so lovely, so young. She felt good in his hands. And for a long moment, he indulged and grabbed her close and they danced to the DJ's mix until the band came on. Then the horns blared, and the drumming began and she jumped, clapping in anticipation of the live music. He jumped with her and in the midst of all the excitement, she grabbed his face and kissed him. The taste of pineapples and coconut hit him with a pang of nostalgia that made him dizzy with desire. It made him want to go back home. And why did he have to go all the way downtown to feel the heart of his country? And that's when he decided that somehow, he had to convince Esperanza that they didn't belong in Nueva York. That he wanted to go home. It wasn't his father's fault. She'd blame it on him. But he didn't do anything more than remind Santo of what he had forgotten about himself. That he hates the cold weather. That he had had enough. If he was going to waste away his life struggling in Nueva York, why not in Los Llanos, where at least people understood him when he spoke. And he caught his breath and wiped his mouth as if he could erase another woman's kiss. His cheeks were flushed from the heat and the desire to return home. I'm going home, he said to himself. I don't care how much Esperanza fights me, I'm going home.

When he exited the club and saw the crowd of young, sweaty faces, he felt old among the crowd. He got in his car and turned on the radio. —Live from the Palladium, the radio crooned. He blasted the music while he rode on the highway.

—I'm going home.

The Colón family was sleeping when the phone call came through. Esperanza burst into the children's bedroom, wearing slippers and a sweater over her nightgown.

—Get dressed, Dallas, get dressed. Esperanza turned on all the lights in the apartment, as if the lights themselves could alleviate the pain she was feeling. —Bobby, make sure Dallas wears her gloves and hat, and hurry, we have to go to the emergency room.

Bobby ran to the closets, pulling Dallas with him. He tucked their jeans inside their boots, and wrapped their necks and chins with loosely knitted scarves while Esperanza prayed Don Chan wouldn't wake up. He was too old to get such a scare.

—Andale! Let's go before your abuelo wakes up.

Santo's death had been a quick one. He was stabbed in the neck, right below his earlobe. The same pressure point that, if you press hard enough, you can give yourself a shot of pain that goes straight to the head, causing a headache that lasts hours if not days. The part of the neck that if kissed, licked, or touched softly would arouse desire. A steak knife cut through his flesh and tore into the artery, which stopped the blood from flowing to his brain. The thief knew to twist the knife and pull it out so that the blood gushed.

The police found Santo dead inside his black sedan, which had a thin red stripe all along the sides. He was wearing the heavy, acrylic brown coat Esperanza had bought him at a double-reduced sale at Macy's. He was wearing his gloves when he was stabbed, which hid the brand-new shiny silver watch Esperanza had given him for Christmas. The autopsy reports showed that the knife tore open the glove, cutting a vein on his wrist. They took his car radio, his gold necklace, the cash he earned that night, the rabbit's foot that hung from the rearview mirror.

The nurse who had called Esperanza was waiting with a pile of papers for Esperanza to sign. Esperanza shoved winter hats over the children's heads and pushed them out into the cold city air. Piled snow gathered on the sidewalk. They were all so quiet, Dallas wondered if they would ever speak again. Esperanza struggled to hold herself together as they walked up Broadway, deep into the night. The same street the children had walked up countless times with their father, to pick up bread for their mother at Greenbaum's, a Jewish bakery where they made fresh bread every day like they do downtown.

—Ya sabes, *don't be bringing me no bread from those bodegas around here. Every time I try and bite into the shit they sell, I lose a tooth.*

It was the same bustling Broadway the children had seen countless times from their father's shoulders, filled with people going to sneaker, stereo, and furniture stores. Beauty salons doubled as travel agencies, smoke shops doubled as arcades, bodegas that were plastered with stickers. Flower shops, botánicas, 99-cent stores. Street carts selling empanadas, helado de coco, habichuelas con dulce, pastelitos. Stores spilling out into the sidewalks with racks of plátanos, T-shirts, jeans, detergents, and plastic food containers. Spanish music blasted onto the street from stores, out of cars, from people's headphones.

There was no music the night Santo died. It was later than the children had ever been up and awake, outside in the streets Esperanza called unsafe. But despite the dealing, the occasional shootouts, the loud music they heard from their apartment windows, Broadway was asleep. They imagined everyone was sleeping, tucked away in their beds; and if people were outside, it was because they had an emergency. And the Colón family had an emergency that night, and to attend to that emergency they had to walk over to the emergency room.

The seats in the waiting room were filled with people who were trying to find refuge from the cold, people who smelled like dried piss, old wounds, and alcohol. People holding brown paper bags, hyperventilating, vomiting. Children crying, people slashed, with broken limbs, sneezing, coughing, waiting. Everyone was waiting.

—I don't care if there's a fucking line, let me see my husband, Esperanza screamed at anyone who would listen to her. She screamed louder than the babies crying, than the old man wailing, sitting by the wall, than the vacuum cleaner, than the lady screaming from withdrawal, louder than the ambulance siren.

—I want to see my husband!

The police officer guarding the entrance grabbed Esperanza and tried to wrestle her down. Bobby held on to Dallas. His skinny arms pressed up against her as strongly as his thirteen-year-old body could bear. That night, Bobby's lips quivered and his neck tightened up as he held back the tears. Dallas was too busy looking around to feel anything. Too busy looking at people waiting in line, sitting in the waiting area, banging on the soda machines, talking on the pay phone. She was looking at the lines of fluorescent lights that raced across the ceiling. She was listening to the ladies.

—Ay por Dios, why don't they let the poor woman see her husband? said a lady sitting in the waiting area.

Esperanza kicked and screamed, punched the cops, the janitor, a guy who was also waiting.

—Let me see my husband. Por favor!

Bobby and Dallas had never seen their mother cry. It made Dallas want to cry to see her cry. She prayed her mother would calm down so people could stop staring at them. Esperanza was wearing a scarf over her head. Not a scratch of makeup on her amber skin. Esperanza only screamed in Spanish, because that night, she didn't have the energy to translate herself. No one understood her pain. No one knew her husband, Santo, who was a good man, who didn't deserve this. Not Santo. Not her husband, not their father, not the man who worked his whole life for something better.

And then a nurse emerged from reception and said Esperanza's name in the most soothing voice she had ever heard. To Esperanza, the nurse, la morena americana, came to her like an angel.

—Mrs. Esperanza Colón, please come with me.

And this lady Esperanza didn't know looked at her as if she had lived many more years and seen many more things than Esperanza could've ever imagined. And the black nurse, who was wearing the white dress, the white stockings, the white shoes, opened her wings and Esperanza did quiet down, as babies do when someone holds them. The nurse opened her arms and Esperanza breathed in the scent of fresh-baked bread right out of the oven. She held the nurse as if walking into the light of heaven, as if through her she would see her Santo again.

—You children, stay here. Me and your mama have somewhere to go. Everything will be all right, Mrs. Esperanza Colón. The nurse walked Esperanza away from her children, who no longer looked like her children, but orphans.

—The lord tightens the rope sometimes, but he don't choke no one. Not good people like you and me, the nurse said.

Bobby made Dallas sit down.

—Come on, Dallas. He pulled at her scarf as if it were a leash.

Bobby held her tight for a little bit, and then when he finally let go of her, Bobby cried. And when Bobby started to cry, Dallas let all the pain trapped in her chest erupt from her eyes. And it felt good to let the tears come. It felt so good, she felt herself splash onto the floor, spread all over everyone's feet. She sank inside the crack of the tiles. Dallas and Bobby tried to keep themselves afloat, trying not to think that their father was dead. And if he was dead, it meant that now Bobby was the man of the house. Bobby wanted to call Don Chan. Let him take care of things. But Esperanza had said to wait. And they waited. And waited some more. They watched the doors, HOSPITAL STAFF ONLY, swing open and close. They waited for their mother to emerge, hoping that it was all a bad dream.

—We should call Abuelo, Dallas said, tugging at Bobby's shirt.

—We'll wait to see what Mami says first. Bobby held Dallas, who was still sniffling, in the crook of his arm.

CAB DRIVER ROBBED AND KILLED ON RIVERSIDE DRIVE

Don Chan read the headline the next morning at the luncheonette. He stared at the photo of Santo. It showed him spread out over the front seat, unconscious. Santo was number eleven. During that winter, eleven taxi drivers were held up and killed. But only the last one, who died was ever remembered. He searched between the lines for an explanation. Why hadn't Esperanza woken him? Don Chan held his head to keep it from breaking. A pain shot up into his forehead. He could not remember how he'd arrived at the luncheonette. What city was he in? What day of the week was it?

The newspapers didn't tell the story about the Colóns, how the other families who lost their fathers and husbands were coping, they didn't say if they would survive. They reported the cold facts. Santo was killed, Esperanza had lost the only love of her life, and the children, a father. When they watched the news that night on television, the reporters didn't send their condolences.

—Turn it off, Don Chan insisted when he saw the television on. —Look at me. Ask me about your father, he wanted to say to his grandchildren, but his voice was being held hostage by his heart.

Dallas wanted to scream like she saw people do on television. But after her flood of tears at the hospital, she felt nothing. She said nothing. She heard of people feeling numb after someone died. But she didn't feel right about it.

Bobby was on his best behavior, fetching all the things his mother demanded. She didn't have to beg Bobby to stay off the streets. He had already become afraid of the streets that took his father.

—I'll see you when I get back from school, Mami, Bobby said.

—It's test week, I have to go to class.

On many days, Bobby tried to break away from her grasp without making her cry. He covered her with a blanket, making sure the television was on for her to watch, placing a glass of water and a bottle of aspirin at her feet, just in case.

—You're so skinny, Bobby, she said, grabbing his arm. —How

you gonna take care of us if you don't start eating well? Esperanza held on to his bony hands.

Esperanza couldn't bear leaving the house to take care of people, when she desperately wanted to be taken care of. The neighbors brought over Tupperware filled with food she wouldn't eat. They offered to help her around the house if she needed something, but in ten years she had never made such an offer to anyone. She was always too busy, and the thought of owing someone more than she already did was too much. No thank you, she said to them, pretending to be fine.

Throughout the day, she left the television on. It made her feel less alone. She searched the television for something to tell her about her fate. How should she be acting? Her children fatherless. Esperanza a widow and a single mother. Dallas didn't own a black dress, or white satin ribbons for her hair. She wondered what all those grieving people on television were doing while the commercials were on. She watched the *Dallas* reruns and lost herself to their world.

If I had just stayed out of his life, Pamela Ewing said before Esperanza could turn off the TV. No, not Bobby; Esperanza reached out to the television. She had seen the episode before. Two, maybe three times. Bobby Ewing had died. She had forgotten that? *If I hadn't come here . . . He wouldn't have died.* Pamela cried and banged against the silk pillows on her bed. Esperanza had always loved the dress Pamela was wearing in that episode. *He was trying to save me,* Pamela cried, as her family tried to console her. *Oh my poor Bobby, he's dead, he's dead. And it was my fault.* —Oh no, Pamela, it's not your fault, Esperanza told her and came up close to the television.

What if she couldn't pay the rent? What if they were thrown out into the streets? If she worked more hours, she would never see her children. They would grow up delinquents, hating her, like all those children who hated their mamás on those talk shows. She sobbed and threw dishes against the wall and then sat at the kitchen table with the stillness of someone who had been defeated.

Without the TV, the silence drove her mad. The absence of Santo's whistling was about to drive her over the edge. The tail of the whistle was trapped in her ear, an incomplete melody.

That damn piano, their last fight. Even after they had made up and started talking again, they kept the piano in the doorway, tucked in the foyer, waiting to be thrown out or brought in. —Why did I give him such a hard time? It's a stupid table.

After Santo's death, Esperanza put his beloved table in the kids' room, as he had wished it to be. Dallas and her mother scrubbed the table with Comet, being careful not to scrape off the musical notes on the table's belly. She asked the man upstairs, who was into spiritual things, for help. —Cosas espirituales, Esperanza said, rubbing her fingertips as if the essence of the spiritual were garnered in her own hands.

—Your father loved this table, Dallas. I don't know why, but he loved it so.

Don Chan didn't want to go to the luncheonette in the mornings, as if his next walk up Quepasó Street would greet him with more bad news. If he had lost part of his mind when his wife, Caridad, died, he lost all his desire to live when Santo died. Something had gone wrong with the order of things. He had survived a year without his wife. How long could he live without his son? A parent was not supposed to grieve over a child's life. The spirit was not equipped for it. Don Chan's voice changed. It cracked, as if something was caught in his throat. His eyes became lazy, drooping in a half sleep. It wasn't Santo's time. It couldn't have been his time. Don Chan couldn't motivate himself to follow his daily routine. In the mornings, he sat at the kitchen table and Esperanza joined him. Pouring the café, no words passed between them, their anger with each other was a thread that kept them from falling over, a reminder that they were still alive.

Esperanza put sugar in the eggs, her socks didn't match, her dark roots were starting to show. She was like a chicken whose head was twisted and hung over onto its side, running around in circles, running from, running to, who knows where, but running. She was running them to school, running to work, running from the streets that terrified her. Everything seemed dangerous. Every sound jolted her from her sleep, forcing her to check if the doors were locked, that no one was lurking on her fire escape. She was running from the sound of the phone and the look in everyone's eyes. She didn't want to look at her children. Especially not at Don Chan, who must have blamed her for making Santo leave D.R. If he hadn't been wearing the watch, maybe he could've still been alive. Damn you, Santo. How many times did I tell him not to park the car around Riverside Drive? What was he thinking? She said it in the same tone she used when talking about the times he forgot to put down the toilet seat, or pick up the milk on his way home.

—It's so dark and desolate down there by the park. I never wanted him to drive a taxi, she said. —Why did I let him do it?

She retraced their last moments, his last desires, and hated herself all the more for it. I should've gone dancing with him. I should've asked him to stay home. There was no closure, no sign of the impending tragedy. It was as if he knew he needed to say good-bye to her. The way he pulled her body in. She remembered the swell in his pants.

Esperanza was running. When she looked at Dallas's and Bobby's faces, her babies, Bobby barely fourteen, already developing a protective shell and unforgiving eyes, she ran. And Dallas a smaller version of herself, round and soft features, except she had her father's hair, thick, wavy hair, and her father's lips, thick, full lips, and his color, a rich caramel; she couldn't look at her. No matter where she looked, Esperanza wanted to run.

She didn't want to be around friends and family who made her feel like a child for crying over her loss. Her best friend was her husband, Santo, and he was gone. Now she was partly gone.

She walked through her days numb. Nothing was clear. Not the sights before her eyes, not the sounds of the city or people's voices. Esperanza could no longer work without pauses. Her body and mind demanded the pauses. Often, she took a pause after work by sitting on the front stoop of her building before she walked inside to deal with her children. She noticed that the sun and moon were out at the same time. The sign of an angel coming. The thought gave her chills. She tugged her sweater around her chest.

—Miss Esperanza?

—Ay dios mío. Esperanza was startled by the soft voice coming from behind her ear. It was soft and clear, as if she was listening to it from inside herself.

—Are you okay? the young girl asked.

—Sí, sí. Do I know you? Esperanza recognized her from the neighborhood. She would sometimes hang out in the luncheonette with her stepfather in the mornings. She was the daughter of the lady across the street who worked double shifts at the hospital. Without invitation, the girl sat down next to Esperanza. She pulled out a pack of gum and offered one up to Esperanza, who took it. The gum was sweet and quickly lost its flavor.

She looked over at the girl. —What you doing outside alone? You can't be but ten years old.

—I'm eleven.

—What's your name again?

—Hush, she said and sat behind Esperanza on the higher step. She positioned one foot next to each of Esperanza's thighs and started undoing the combs in her hair.

—Mami loves when I comb her hair, especially when she comes home from work and she's had a bad day. She never asks me, I just do it.

Esperanza resisted at first. It was a strange sensation to have Hush's fingers undo her hair. Hush pulled and tugged her hair gently, nerve endings coming alive that Esperanza didn't know she had. With each tug she started to feel her forehead relax, her jaw drop, her body exhale and surrender to Hush's attention. Her tear ducts swelled, and like an explosion she caught herself crying into her hands as Hush patted down the curly tendrils on her head. Hush's small body, thin and frail, hugged the round Esperanza as the sky laid a blanket over the city. The desolate streets became a sanctuary for them, where Esperanza didn't have to care who walked by and if they stared at her. She didn't care about anything except that Hush with her soothing voice was keeping her from falling apart. How did she know not to move? How did Hush know to embrace Esperanza and tell her, —It's gonna be okay, Señora Esperanza. Everything will be fine.

—Ay, ay, ay, el dolor. It's killing me, Esperanza said, turning around into Hush's little body. Hush smelled like bread, sweet and spicy cloves.

Hush held Esperanza for a long time and said, —Mami says that the Lord lets the dead watch over us until we're ready to let go. And if he's watching, Miss Esperanza, I don't think your husband wants to see you in such a mess. I can tell you haven't combed your hair in days. Mami says that in this world, women with nappy heads don't got the luxury of not fixing their hair. Someone gonna think you a homeless or something.

Esperanza continued sobbing, hiding her face in Hush's jacket.

—Why don't we go inside, Miss Esperanza? It's dark out.

The Colón household had a white sheet thrown over it. The sunlight no longer came in. The phone hardly rang and no matter how high the stove was turned up, nothing boiled, fried, cooked quite right. Time moved slowly and wrapped itself around them, making it hard to walk through their days. Don Chan had no one to talk to, so he read the newspaper out loud, just so that he could listen to his voice. Esperanza was filled with Not now, Can it wait, I'm so tired, comments that encouraged Bobby to find comfort on street corners where his friends yessed him to numbness. Dallas didn't take off her headphones, except when she was on the phone or when she was about to fall asleep.

And then time played a trick on the Colón family. Up until Santo's burial, Don Chan was slightly built, spine erect, and with a head full of hair. There were no wrinkles to speak of, except for the few that went across on his forehead, alluding to all the thinking he'd done throughout the years. But overnight, he shriveled up into a prune. Esperanza was the first to notice the receding hairline and the bend to his back. At first, she looked away. She had enough to think about between running the house on her own, the bills, her children, without thinking about Don Chan's grief and deterioration.

Don Chan was ready to die alongside his son, and gravity was pulling him underground, skin, teeth, and all. His memories were starting to spin his head into a web, catching the beginnings and endings.

—Abuelo, what year is it?

—What kind of question is that, Dallas? Don't they teach you anything at school?

—C'mon, Abuelo, tell me what year it is?

Dallas wanted to prove how her grandfather was forgetting things. He had called her Caridad one time and Bobby, Santo. He ducked when he heard a plane fly above him and pulled Dallas away from the window when a car backfired. At night, more than once he checked that the doors were locked.

Don Chan slapped his knee and shook his head.

—Leave your grandfather alone, Esperanza said, shooing Dallas away. Don Chan's skin dragged around the eyes. She looked over at the family photograph they had taken a few months after his arrival. It was as if the years had fallen on him in one big heap. Aging is supposed to happen slowly and carefully so as not to shake up the psyche.

—Don Chan, I'm making an appointment so you can get a checkup, Esperanza said at dinner.

—So they can do experiments on me?

—There is this nice doctor who's willing to use my insurance to see you. His office is a few blocks away. If it won't cost us anything, it doesn't hurt to check. He might be able to prescribe a pill or something so you could feel better.

—I don't need no doctors giving me no pills.

How dare anyone suggest he put chemicals into his body? He didn't trust the pharmaceutical companies, the same companies who funded studies based on profits, not on people's well-being. The thought of swallowing a pill gave Don Chan indigestion.

For as long as he could remember, everything he ate was clean. Clean like the earth. Brown rice, steamed spinach, fresh beans without an ounce of seasoning except for fresh garlic, onions, and a dash of salt to awaken the nutrients. Fresh-squeezed juices. All from his backyard. He drank boiled water, which he put through a filter he changed every three months, and he never forgot to gulp a teaspoon of olive oil in the morning and cod-liver oil in the night to grease the bones.

Esperanza looked over at Bobby.

—Abuelo, if you go to the doctor, then we won't have to worry that something will happen to you.

Now that Bobby's voice had gone through the transition from being a boy to the voice of a young man, it was as if Santo was speaking from the grave. Don Chan saw all three faces around the table, anticipating his answer. It was the first time he saw them as his family. They were all he had left.

—Fine. But only because Santo asked me.

They didn't correct him, as he had made the mistake often. Esperanza nodded at Bobby. He was the man of the house now. And soon she was going to ask Bobby to help her with the bills.

Esperanza and Don Chan arrived at the clinic, and the doctor saw them immediately.

—This is your father? the doctor asked, surprised by there being no resemblance.

—I look like my mother, Esperanza said, afraid Don Chan wouldn't qualify for her insurance.

The doctor frowned. —I'm already breaking so many laws, and I try to keep within certain boundaries for my own integrity.

The office was small, on the first floor. The wall behind his desk was plastered with diplomas. Esperanza assumed he was an important man and then thought how great it would be to work in a doctor's office.

—What seems to be the problem, Don Chan?

Don Chan sat on the chair by the doctor's desk while Esperanza stood nearby to fill in the silences.

—I have no problems, Don Chan said, trying to stay in good humor while the doctor checked his blood pressure. The idea of being checked made him nervous. If something was wrong, he didn't want to know. What's the point at his age?

—So why are you here? The doctor looked into his ears, listened to his heart, opened his mouth wide with a wooden stick and asked Don Chan to say aaaah.

—Beats me, Don Chan said, and he folded his arms against his chest.

—Doctor, this man, I mean, my father, has never had a checkup in his life. And he came from D.R. a year ago after his wife died, and now my husband . . .

—My son . . . Don Chan attempted to fill in.

Esperanza was about to cry and Don Chan was fidgeting in the chair. What could anyone tell him about himself that he didn't already know? Time was catching up with him. It was inevitable. The end of the world was a sure thing. Why not his life? He wanted to go home. But now he was stuck here for the last of his days.

—Enough, Don Chan said and got up from the chair. —I'll wait for you outside.

Don Chan watched Esperanza talk to the doctor from the waiting room. Don Chan searched through the headlines in the newspaper.

NEW YORK OFFICER SAID TO BE CLEARED

IN FATAL SHOOTING

CAN IT BE? PROGRESS IN MIDEAST TALK?

CUBAN PILOT DIVERTS AIRLINER TO FLORIDA;

48 SEEK ASYLUM

—What do you think, Doctor? Should I worry? Esperanza asked.

—Everything looks fine to me. I'd like to get some urine samples, but he looks great. How old is he?

—No one knows for sure. He's always forgetting things. Like the year, our names, nothing major, I don't think.

—Here's a prescription that should help with his memory lapses. He might have had a mild stroke. Strong enough to cause some confusion. But I'm afraid aging is normal.

—But a month ago, he looked like this.

Esperanza held up the photograph of Don Chan from a few months before, to show a glowing Don Chan who raced Santo to the car. Not so long ago, he arm-wrestled two men and won himself a sack of rice at the bodega. She put the photograph so close to the doctor's face, he had to take two steps back.

—He was fine when my husband was alive. Esperanza's eyes teared up all over again. She looked around the doctor's tiny office in the clinic, wondering if the mind could make the body age so fast. —His wife died not even a year ago and now his son. Maybe it's too much for him, Esperanza said and wept softly, trying very hard to keep her composure in front of the generous doctor who now had many people waiting for him in the room outside.

—I can see why you're concerned. He certainly does not look like the same man in this photo.

The doctor scrunched up his face with curiosity. —Who can understand nature? he said with a tinge of curiosity in his voice. —Death provokes all sorts of enigmas.

—The trauma of death, Esperanza said aloud, checking in on Don Chan, whose hands trembled as he tried to hold the newspaper up.

—I knew of a young woman whose hair turned white overnight when she saw her husband kiss her daughter on the mouth.

Esperanza took a tissue from the doctor.

—And there was a man who molted when he found out he was adopted.

Esperanza gasped, combing through her hair, caressing her arms, taking a peek in the mirror to make sure she was intact.

—Relax, Miss Colón, these are rare instances. Flukes. Be assured that Don Chan's body is catching up with the time he has lived. You have to worry about yourself. He reached out to hold Esperanza.

She noticed the doctor's liver spots, his soft skin, and looked into his gray eyes for assurance.

—Maybe Don Chan realized that he's closer to dying than he thought. That always happens at funerals. We mourn as much for our last days as we do for the dead, he said. —You have a long life ahead of you, Esperanza. Live it fully. It looks like the old man can take care of himself.

Esperanza kissed the doctor on the cheek. She felt a wave of relief and walked with Don Chan back home thinking about the words: Live it fully.

While they walked, Esperanza looked over at the frail Don Chan and felt the burden of his skeleton on her back. She knew very well the smell of a human being who no longer cared to mask his scent with cologne and deodorant, who no longer had the energy to bathe and could only wash with the help of a home attendant and wet towels. Human shit and piss. Old piss on sheets, dead-skin flakes, crusty eyes, long nose hairs that would need to be trimmed, his beard would need to be shaved, his nails clipped.

Ay, ay, ay, thought Esperanza, remembering the old man she took care of in Queens who was eighty-eight years old. He didn't talk, eyes always wandering, holding on to any image that resembled something familiar. Who even after a bath and lots of baby powder reeked of decay.

—Ay, ay, ay, Esperanza sighed, breathing heavily, feeling her stomach stress the thin belt she bought on sale at Macy's; her favorite belt that she was able to purchase for an additional 15 percent deduction with the coupon she received in the mail.

—Ay diosito, why me? she said, starting to hyperventilate. What if Don Chan became bedridden? But the doctor told her she had to take care of herself, not worry about him. To live her life fully.

She walked into her apartment and sat on the plastic-covered sofa cushion and noticed how uncomfortable it was. She unzipped the plastic slipcover and plopped herself back on the pillow. She bounced lightly on the crushed velvet. It felt wonderful and soft. What was she preserving the furniture for anyway? Why hadn't she taken off the plastic sooner? It had covered the sofa for ten years. She had the right to sit on her own sofa and not have her thighs peel off some stupid plastic.

She looked around and realized that the entire apartment was covered in a thin film of dust. She was trying to preserve every little bit of Santo that was left behind. But if she didn't start cleaning, maybe she too would wake up with a face full of wrinkles and a life that showed nothing for it. Don Chan's days might be numbered, but not hers.

Esperanza wiped the dust off the television screen with a piece of tissue, off the figurines on the shelves, off the photographs of Dallas and Bobby. She thought about getting a cloth and cleaning spray from the kitchen, but she couldn't tear herself away from the dust.

Tissue would have to do. Her hands ached at the joints as she beat the curtains in the living room and lifted the shade. She turned on the lamps, and gathered the dust balls behind the reclining chair with her hands, looking forward to the moment she would be able to sit down so she could alleviate her tiredness with a glob of menthol spread around the back of her neck. She gathered the dust balls into one big mass of gray, and collapsed on the floor cross-legged, forming a small mountain of dirt with her hands. Her body felt heavy, her arms heavy, her legs, every inch of her collapsed into her body.

When the phone rang, she jumped. Every day, the collection agency called to harass her even after she explained that Santo had died. They threatened her with court, said that they could repossess everything in her home over a certain value if she didn't take immediate action.

Then the doorbell rang. Esperanza's heart skipped a beat again. Yes, lock me up and let me sleep. I don't care what you feed me, anything will be better than this life.

It was the postal worker with a box. It had been months since she'd received a package in the mail. The thrill of receiving anything was a thing of the past.

—Could you sign, please? he asked her. A smile curled up from her lip for the first time since Santo's death. —What could it be? she said, holding the unlabeled box, trying to remember what she could've ordered that had taken its time to reach her. The box was heavy enough to be substantial, but the weight didn't jar a memory.

—What did you get? Dallas climbed onto the chair at the kitchen table.

—Who knows? Esperanza felt a bit relieved that she didn't have to hide her purchases from Santo anymore.

Esperanza relished each tear of the box as if she was opening her last gift. From under the Styrofoam, she pulled out a dark gray clay urn. On it were the words:

Santo Colón de Juan Dolio,
Vaya con Dios.

2

Juan Dolio
1916–1922

Doña Caridad had spotted Don Chan washed up on shore in Juan Dolio.

—Where do you come from? She poked at little Chan's unfamiliar face, his hair so shiny it looked blue in the sun and his eyes small as the eye of a needle.

Little Chan pointed at the tiny bird flying behind her, leaping from tree to tree, chirping its monotonous song. The emerald bird lifted its head to expose its red throat and pink feathers as it prepared to mate.

—So you like birds, her father Don José Colón de Juan Dolio said, grateful that the young boy had survived his journey. —That's a tody bird. It never flies alone. Are you alone?

Little Chan stared back at him with blank eyes. Don José assumed he was about six years of age from the size of his head. After many years of watching the sea ebb and flow, the way the color of the water changed with the mood of the sky, it was the first time he didn't bury bones. Throughout his life, he saw the carcasses that washed up offshore from people who didn't survive their journeys to his land. And when time permitted, he gathered the bones and buried them in the sand to honor their arrival.

—Little Chan, it's an honor to have you, Don José said and bent down to take his hand. —Are you hungry?

Little Chan looked around. His eyelids and hair were full of sand and salt. His clothes damp with seawater.

At lunch, Don José served Little Chan first to show that he should feel at home with his new family. The young Caridad giggled as if she had found a treasure and it was for her to keep.

At first, little Chan didn't understand that he would never see his family again. He took the long journeys on the small fishing boat with Don José in the hope he'd find his mother and father. Although there was very little he understood, he knew there was something different about him, that he belonged somewhere else. No matter how hard he tried, he could not recollect one memory from the first years of his life. Traveling workers explained to Don José that Little Chan looked like the Chinos from Panamá. —Cuba, hombre. —You're a Chino from Cuba, said another. —There're a whole bunch of Chinos in Jamaica. That's where you're from. They had shiploads heading to Jamaica to work the cane.

But little Chan couldn't remember anything but his name.

From the edge of the sea, Don José's shack, in the thick of the bushes, was a small sanctuary that protected his wife and three daughters. Even when the bloody wars overturned his island, rulers emerging only to be humbled by yet another ruler, Don José relied on the sea, like his father and his grandfather, all of whom understood the language of the water.

Before little Chan's arrival, Don José had taken the fishing trips alone. For years he looked forward to being alone with the sea. At first, Don José resisted little Chan's persistence in joining him on the boat but soon found that he enjoyed little Chan's company. For hours the old man and little Chan sat on the boat waiting for the fish to bite. With his new friend, the sea took on a fresh palette and the clouds acquired a variety of names as little Chan tried to find the animals in nebulous shapes. It was the first time Don José shared the stories he had learned from the sea.

—You see, little Chan, the sea, as well as the trees, the rocks, the eyes of a child are the compass to the soul's journey.

Little Chan tried very hard to understand Don José and slowly picked up words, like *mar, sol, tierra, luna, pescado*. Together they'd laugh at their misunderstandings. Months and months passed and little Chan no longer looked for ships, in search of his parents. Don José was his new family.

Don José and little Chan saw the big American ships sail toward San Pedro de Macorís. And soon after, Don José had heard about the small insurrections around the country, that the peasants and landowners alike did not want the U.S. to put its nose in a matter they could take care of themselves. Everyone knew that to intervene on trouble in someone else's house was an insult. They were not children and felt capable of ruling themselves. They feared having to give up their freedom to the United States. Even the poorest peasants knew that when someone gave them a dollar, it was only because they could make two off their backs.

Don José could tell by the crashing of the waves and the restlessness of the animals on his land that there was about to be great trouble in D.R. Untrusting of the U.S. occupation, Don José cut his trips into the city and made his fishing voyages closer to shore. At night, the Colón de Juan Dolio family didn't light a fire because it was better not to be seen so that the military never questioned their existence.

—I go with you I want to see city, little Chan said.

—No, you protect the women while I go away, Don José said.

—I want to see city, little Chan said. He had spent a year listening to Don José tell the adventures of Martí, in Cuba, the Haitian revolution that Don José carried in his blood, the stories of all the ancestors who washed up onshore and who Don José buried so they could die with honor.

—When you're older, you can come. Now you stay with the women.

Little Chan looked straight at Don José. Every child knew that to look an elder in the eye was asking for cruel punishment. Don José's first impulse was to teach little Chan a lesson, but if Don José had learned anything from the hours he spent with nature it was that to abuse part of oneself didn't teach any lesson at all. If everything that was alive was a part of Don José, to hit little Chan would be to hit himself. If little Chan survived the sea, the city won't kill him, Don José thought.

—Put on some sandals. The journey is long and it will burn your feet.

Little Chan walked along with Don José through the thick of the trees in Juan Dolio, his head up high, excited that he would see the city he only knew in his imagination. The neighbors looked at them and whispered about the odd couple, a dark, tall man and a small Chinese boy.

—They laugh at me, little Chan said, wondering why people pointed.

—No, no, little Chan, they don't understand how special you are.

Don José had little Chan climb on his shoulders so he could rest his feet.

They walked into the opening of the city and stopped to look at all the vendors lining the streets. The marines pulled on the skirts of women who stared into their blue and green eyes. Crowds of people bumped against each other. Horses pushed people away as they charged through the city; pickpockets feasted on the oblivious crowd gathered around to listen to politicians who stood on small stages giving speeches. Newspaper vendors on bicycles and wagons shouted out headlines, hungry dogs sniffed the ground and around people's feet for scraps, the handicapped leaned against the rotunda begging for change. Fathers hid their daughters inside their arms as the malecón's tempestuous water splashed against the wall. Many rushed about through the crowds, praying that they could survive one more day without being asked for a bribe by a self-appointed official.

Little Chan gasped at the sight of all the bustling people, tugging at Don José's pants leg to show him the green parrot on the man's shoulder, the circus lady juggling limes, the ships that, up close, were the size of mountains. Maybe bigger, thought little Chan. He had never seen something as big as a ship, with such great presence.

—Hold on to my pants leg, Don José said, not swayed by little Chan's curiosity. All the excitement of the city was a breeding ground for trouble. If he spent one moment looking at the clown the marines had brought to entertain the crowds, thieves would steal the few pennies he had in his pocket to buy his supplies.

Little Chan held on to Don José's pants leg, and looked around trying to see as much as he could before they had to return to Juan Dolio. He tripped and splashed his feet in puddles, giggling and excited.

—Look where you're going. The city is not for playing, Don José said, more frustrated at how fast the city had grown. It was a sign of the beginning of the end for people like him who worked from the sea.

—Excuse me, sir.

A man, who Don José assumed was untrustworthy by the beard that hid his face, called out after them. Don José pretended not to hear him.

—Señor, excuse me, the man said again, reaching up to grab Don José's shoulder.

The man was small and round, red from too much sun.

Little Chan hid behind Don José, wrapping his arms around his leg.

—I offer you this pouch for the boy, the man said, showing Don José a glimpse of the coins inside the small red pouch.

—I'm sorry, but he's not for sale, Don José said and moved away from him in haste.

The man followed. Don José carried little Chan on his back so it would be easier for them to move about through the crowds. He slipped in behind the houses and crossed over to the street. All he needed was some fishing supplies and some herbs for his daughter who had stomach problems. Everything else could wait. It had been a bad idea to bring little Chan into the city. Don José did not know what was going on in the city with the occupation, but the selling of children?

The man persisted.

—Señor, you bargain hard. I'll give you my pouch and my horse for the China boy.

—He's not for sale.

—But I'm already overpaying you. Look at him, he needs to be fattened up. It is true my horse is old and doesn't do much anymore, but a man like yourself must need a horse.

Little Chan wrapped his arms around Don José's neck, not understanding what was happening. But he could tell Don José was scared by the quickening of his stride.

Don José continued to walk and the man chased after him. Why did he persist?

—You see, I had a China boy myself and he died. It was not the best investment I made, he only worked for me for six years. You see, the China boys have a special skill for work, and they're not lazy or cause trouble like the Haitians. No no, the China boys can go for hours and never say no to anything you ask. You should see what the China boys did in America. Built the railroad by hand practically. And when they're young like your China boy is, you can train them very well, the man said, waving his hands in the air as if he had told the story many times before.

Don José was shocked. It was too difficult to bear. He kept moving, holding on to little Chan's legs with all his might. But no matter how quickly Don José walked, the man chased him.

—So I said to myself that better a China boy than a horse for me. In my kind of work, a horse is not as necessary. I will throw in my watch as well. A man like yourself must need a watch. My own father made this watch. He gave it to me as a boy. So you see, I'm not trying to trick you here. A fair price I offer you for this boy who doesn't have any meat on his bones.

—He's not for sale. The boy is my son, Don José said, glaring at the man sternly, and for the first time in his life he could imagine killing a man.

That day, Don José understood that little Chan was not safe around people hungry enough to steal him away and sell him for a profit. The people of Juan Dolio were good people, but they also were too hungry to be trusted.

He had heard about the valley of Los Llanos. That the insurrections by the guerrillas were so bloody that the U.S. air-bombed the area and had recently incarcerated 112 men involved in the resistance against the U.S., leaving Los Llanos a valley of women and children.

—That will be a good place for us, Don José told his family at dinner.

—The women of Los Llanos will need some men to do the hard labor. For years, we have lived off the sea. Now we will learn to live off the land. We'll start our journey tomorrow.

3

Nueva York
1994

Two years had passed since the death of Santo. Don Chan looked over at his calendar and marked an X on the Monday. He pressed his hand against the window to learn that it was a short-sleeved guayabera day. The pile of freshly ironed boxer shorts and white short-sleeved undershirts wouldn't last him a week. He made a note on the pad he now kept in his pocket that he would do laundry before Esperanza came looking through his things and tried to do it for him. As it was, he felt like a burden, taking up space inside her apartment. The last thing he needed was for her to complain about how tired she was because she had to take care of him. When Santo was alive, Don Chan felt more comfortable speaking his mind and doing as he pleased around the house. Now Don Chan felt like a guest who had overstayed his welcome. He couldn't work at his age. At least in Los Llanos he spent his days in his garden and watched over the goats. How could he grow anything in all this concrete? Give me a plot of land, I'll get to work tomorrow, thought Don Chan. The thought of the city made Don Chan angry all over again. His son worked ten years in this stupid city and only left bills to show for it. Now Esperanza will work all her life and won't own a pot to piss in.

So in every way he could, he tried not to be a burden. He added a number of chores to his daily routine, like throwing out the garbage, doing his laundry, watering the plants, and watching over the children, who were hardly children anymore. Dallas had recently turned into a señorita, and Bobby was spending extra time in the bathroom. And all that activity required Don Chan to do more napping during the day.

Don Chan no longer had to avoid Esperanza in the morning because she was always working. Every other night she slept at her client's home.

—Watch those kids for me, Esperanza asked him. —I might have eyes on the back of my head for those children, but I need you to make sure they stay out of trouble.

—Seguro que sí, Don Chan said.

When he woke up to go to the bathroom in the middle of the night, he made sure to see if Bobby and Dallas were in their bedroom.

With time, he no longer minded the nosy old woman who popped open her door when he was at the elevator. He expected to see her so he could say, —Buenos días. And because he knew that she would open the door again upon his arrival, he would bring her fresh pan de agua from the bodega for her breakfast.

—You didn't have to do that, she said.

Don Chan was too busy to notice that she wasn't wearing her curlers anymore. He was thinking about what day it was, the newspaper he had to buy, if the elevator would take long that morning, and if it did, would he arrive at the luncheonette too late to occupy his favorite booth by the window?

Don Chan looked up and down Quepasó Street when he exited the building, as if there was traffic on the sidewalk. It was his way of making sure nothing had changed, and if it did, he would prepare for it. The cars were double-parked on the left side of the street, Styrofoam containers with pernil, arroz, habichuelas, and tostones leftovers. The van driver, heading to the factory across the river, waved over to him as he waited for his passengers on the corner. Monday morning. Everything was in its place.

—Hola, Chino.

The man at the newsstand was already behind his counter and had Don Chan's three newspapers ready for him.

—You beat me today, Don Chan said.

—And you're not dead yet, the man at the newsstand joked.

Don Chan had the exact change in his pocket. He headed over to the corner luncheonette. His booth was free. He had forgotten his scissors. Where had he placed them? He searched on the floor. In three years of living in Nueva York, he had never forgotten his scissors. Don Chan walked back to the apartment. He went back to his bed and lay down with his clothes and shoes still on. He looked over at his calendar. He was about to mark Tuesday but then remembered it was Monday and he had already put an X over the box that morning. He walked over to his closet. He stared at the neat closet of guayaberas, pants, and wool cardigans. He had forgotten something. His newspapers at the luncheonette. He'd left them on the table. Bobby and Dallas were up. The television was on. They were getting ready to go to school. Dallas had made herself cereal.

—Want some, Abuelo?

—Did you lose something? Bobby asked, wondering why he wasn't at the luncheonette.

—My scissors, he said, and surprised himself. —My scissors! That's right, he was looking for his scissors.

Bobby went to his grandfather's bedroom and saw the scissors on his nightstand.

—Here you go, Bobby said. —Are you sure you're okay?

—Sí, sí, Don Chan said and went back to the bedroom. Sitting on the bed, starting up again, walking out of the apartment. Looking east and west, the cars were no longer double-parked. The sanitation trucks had already emptied the garbage cans. —Monday, Monday, Monday, Don Chan said to not forget. His markers of the day were in the past. He walked over to the newsstand.

—The usual, he said to the man at the newsstand.

—What happened to the ones I sold you this morning?

—Oh yes . . . those . . . I left them at the luncheonette, I will see if they are still there.

Don Chan hurried over to the luncheonette. The three newspapers were waiting for him. The booth was empty. He ordered his café. He took out his scissors. He periodically looked up to make sure Bobby and Dallas left the apartment on time so they wouldn't be late for school.

Esperanza had worked for three different clients in an effort to make enough money to pay off her debt. The financial adviser from the local credit union sat down with her after Santo died and told her that if she couldn't afford to pay more than the minimum balance on her bills, she would have to pay the credit cards for at least thirty years.

That long? That's like la vida entera?

Esperanza didn't believe him. She had only bought a few things, and she would be happy to return it all if it meant that the creditors would leave her alone. Some of it was like new, in boxes. Besides, the financial adviser was too young to know all the answers. He was still in school and the grandson of her nosy neighbor next door, and if he knew so much about finance, why was his grandmother still living in that crappy building of theirs?

But two years did pass and no amount of working lowered the principal balances. What would the credit cards do when she couldn't work anymore? She didn't want to think about it. They couldn't put an old lady in jail. Could they? Bobby will have to get a job and help out.

—When I was a child back in D.R., children were expected to work as soon as they walked. These kids have it too easy, Esperanza said as she got ready to go to her new assignment where she would work a double overnight in the Bronx.

—You're working in the Bronx? Bobby asked. —Do we need money that bad?

—Well, the last lady I was working for didn't need me anymore.

Esperanza didn't want to tell him that her client had found certain things missing in her apartment. Her client had accused her without caring about hurting Esperanza's feelings. The client had a number of strokes that debilitated her legs and arms but didn't have any problems using her mouth. She was never kind to Esperanza. When she accused her of stealing, Esperanza asked the agency to switch her to someone else. She'd rather travel to the Bronx than be called a thief.

—Of course we need money, Esperanza said. She didn't bring up Santo's name because somehow to mention it still caused awkward silences and teary eyes. Bobby was fifteen; at fifteen Santo was studying and working the fields with his father, and Esperanza was gathering mangoes and selling them on the roads. Bobby should work and help out.

—I heard that the McDonald's in the neighborhood hires kids at your age. It wouldn't hurt if you got a job.

Bobby watched his mother get ready for work. The thought of a job had crossed his mind, but he didn't want to work as a delivery boy at a supermarket or at McD's. If he waited until he turned sixteen, he could get his working papers and work at a clothing store or Foot Locker. At least in a place like that, he could hook himself up with gear.

Damn, Bobby thought. He should've left the room before she mentioned working.

—The woman's son downstairs has a job working at Nuts for Donuts, by the hospital. They train you and everything. It's better than you spending all your time hanging out on the corner with those thugs.

—They ain't thugs.

—Well, they can't be up to no good standing outside in the cold all day, like they don't have family.

Esperanza gathered her things and hated that she had to stay overnight at her client's. She worked twenty-four hours, then had twenty-four hours off. It was the way the agency started breaking up the schedule. The agency's argument was, if you're sleeping, you're not really working. But Esperanza had still to meet an old person who slept through the night. Don Chan had few nights when he didn't walk around the apartment, opening and closing the refrigerator and doors. It annoyed her that he was so old. If he had been younger, she could've sent him to work or to live back in the campo. Old Señora María Magdalena lived by herself in Los Llanos. Why couldn't Don Chan? They could pay a relative a few dollars to watch over him. But then again, who would keep an eye on Dallas and Bobby at night? For better or for worse, Don Chan demanded a certain respect from the children.

—I'll get an application tomorrow, Bobby said to appease her as he flipped through television channels.

—Make sure you watch over Dallas and your grandfather. I count on you, she said and kissed him. —I don't know how I would get by without you, she said. He cringed when she rubbed her hand through his hair, when she pulled his head against her breast. She always held him a minute too long.

—Be careful, a'ight, he said, ducking under her arm to catch the score of the baseball game on TV.

—Don't worry, son, one day I'm getting that job at the hospital. You heard that the lady upstairs graduated with a nursing degree, taking one class a semester—it took her ten years, but she now works as a nurse, and with another five years of schooling, she's planning to work up to becoming a physician's assistant. And in some ways, my working as a home attendant is like being a nurse.

Esperanza took the train to the last stop, and when she got out of the train, she took a bus, to arrive on a block filled with trees. She wasn't expecting to see trees in the Bronx. She wasn't expecting to see strollers and carts selling helado de coco. Or fruit markets or grand prewar buildings and discount stores. This couldn't be the Bronx where all the gangs were, where she'd heard the buildings were burned down and the mice ruled.

She walked to the building address on her contract, following the directions carefully. When she arrived, she felt triumphant for not getting lost. Through the glass doors, she was surprised to see how shiny the floors of the lobby were. The new lobby doors and the stained glass that bordered the lobby windows gave her a pang of envy. She damned her super and all those families who destroyed everything in her building. For years, she had wanted to move far- ther north of Quepasó Street, where the Jewish families lived. Around los judíos is very decente, Esperanza thought. Unlike us Do- minicans who aren't decentes, we're so loud, we can't get off the streets. We want to make people deaf with all that merengue. Jewish people work hard and go to school. That's why they don't like when we move into their buildings, they're afraid we'll blast the music.

She rang the bell to Mr. Hernández's apartment. No one an- swered. She checked again the address on the form they had sent her. 4L. She rang it again, and when the lobby door buzzed, she ran into the building. The elevator had music. She recognized the melody and rocked her body to distract herself from the fact that she needed to go to the bathroom. Elevators motivated her bladder. She saw her reflection in the corner mirrors placed strategically to see muggers. She noticed how all the floors were freshly waxed. They smelled citrusy.

—So this is the Bronx, she said. Why would anyone be scared of this? She knocked on the door decorated with a dried flower wreath. A woman, hair set in curls all over her head, a starched bata barely covering her knees, opened the door.

—Hola, señora. Adelante, she said.

—Soy Esperanza.

—Good, because we need a lot of hope around here. Este viejo thinks he gonna die every time he hear the phone ring. As if God calls and warns folks of such a thing.

—Where can I put my things? Esperanza asked, searching for the bathroom, noting how different it was from her apartment, which was crowded with furniture and family. The Hernández apartment was a spacious two-bedroom. The windows overlooked Van Cort- landt Park. She had heard many stories about the park with the pub- lic swimming pool. There was plenty of room for Mr. Hernández to move around in his wheelchair. In the living room, there was a love seat with a cotton sheet draped on the cushions, a round glass end table, a dark wood dining table pressed against the window near the kitchen. A small stand with a thirteen-inch television, and a record player and a shelf filled with record albums. One long bookshelf occupied with books and the *Encyclopaedia Britannica,* which Esperanza recognized from the infomercials. No figurines or flowers. No pantry filled with dishes. No photographs, except for two frames hanging on the wall over the sofa, of Mr. and Mrs. Hernández, the other of their belated parrot, Cuca.

—Ven, ven, the woman said, walking Esperanza around, showing her the bathroom, the bedroom where Mr. Hernández slept and the twin bed Esperanza would sleep on. —Don't mind the mess. I hope you're not one of those stuffy workers who don't like to clean. I had this lady come here and she refused to cook or anything. She fed my husband his farina in the morning and his sopita at night, and never, not once, did she cook for me. Not once did she scrub the stove. And she was a young woman con twice the energía I had and she didn't help me around here. Are you gonna give me a hard time too?

—It says here Mr. Hernández doesn't have a wife, Esperanza reminded the lady. If Esperanza had wanted to be a trabajadora she would've stayed in Dominican Republic.

—I'm his mistress, she said, and gave Esperanza a devilish grin. She was obviously the woman in the picture. Thirty years might have passed, but she wore the same face.

—The state don't help no one, unless you're slitting your wrist. I make no money. I still work forty hours a week, paying my taxes, and when my husband fell in bed, 'cause his liver was out, then his heart slowed down, then he couldn't breathe right, little by little no le queda nada a ese hombre, I couldn't stay home; insurance pays for his doctors, but not his medicine. So who gonna pay for his medicine?

—Don't you have any kids? Esperanza asked.

—Got one son who moved to Russia and another son died in the army. They said it was an accident. Maldito Army ese.

—No me digas. I'm so sorry.

—It was a long time ago. He died during practice. My son was never too smart. That's why he went to the army. Didn't do well in school. Didn't like working too hard, and then I have my other son, who was the opposite. He was too smart for his own good. Wanted too much and he married una gringa who can't sit down long enough to warm her seat. But at least she speaks Spanish. Better a gringa who speak Spanish than a gringa who don't . . . Tienes hijos?

—Two.

—Still children?

—I have Bobby, who's practically a man, and Dallas, my only girl.

—Watch them, mija. The streets are a magnet for trouble.

—Yeah, but my kids don't get into trouble. They good all around.

—You say that now, but the next thing you know, you have a kid in prison and the other knocked up. It happens every day.

—But not my children. If you met them, you'd know. They know better than to get into trouble like that.

—You've been here long? Mrs. Hernández asked.

—Awhile now.

—You wanna go back like everybody else?

—To Dominican Republic? Oh no. I was thinking Dallas, Texas, would be a nice place to retire.

—Dallas. Why? It gets to be a hundred and ten over there in the summer.

—Oh, I like the idea of a ranch. You know, I always had an affinity for horses. Back in Los Llanos we had a horse. He was the boniest thing you'd ever seen, but give him a good kick and he'd give you a ride to remember.

—Is that right? But Dallas is a long ways from here.

—So was Nueva York and look at me now. Jock Ewing said that any man can win when things go his way, *it's the man who overcomes adversity who is the true champion.*

—I don't know Jock, but no truer words have been said, Mrs. Hernández said, nodding in agreement.

—And Jock's son Bobby, if you see this man, painted to perfection, I tell you. He said that nobody has it all, *you just have to play the hand you've been dealt.* And my husband and I were dealt a bad hand. We were born in the wrong place, planted in the wrong lot. We were born to be roses or gladiolus, but we were planted among a whole bunch of weeds in D.R. There really is nothing in D.R. for me. God got confused when he planted our seed.

—Gladiolus? I never liked the way they smelled much.

Esperanza pretended not to be offended. Everyone has a right to an opinion.

—Well, I ain't gonna die until I touch Cuba again. I don't care if I have to live till I'm a hundred. Maybe that's the difference between those of us whose land was taken from us and those who run away from it.

—And Mr. Hernández?

Mrs. Hernández looked over at Mr. Hernández, who was reading the paper. It was as if he wasn't in the room. She fixed her curl so it landed to the side and curled toward her ear. She pressed her lips together to spread the pink lip color.

—Me dió una pena, to divorce him. Of course it's only on paper, so the government could help us. I can't take care of him by myself anymore. I'm too tired. He's too heavy. And he's like a child now. Twenty-four hours he needs to be watched. When am I supposed to work? I might be sixty years old, but I'm not staying home all day with that crazy man. You know something, it's less work to go to my job every day and have you deal with him than me put up with his shit all day and night. All the time he complains. Tears the place apart looking for something he doesn't need. But after being married forty years, it still made me sad to write down in the application that he was abandoned and left alone. I would never do that. I just rather work a little, save up some money, so when I'm left alone, I can retire back home. Maybe by then, all of us could go back home.

Esperanza washed her hands in the kitchen sink.

—Un cafecito? Mrs. Hernández said.

—Sí, señora, Esperanza said, grateful for Mrs. Hernández's hospitality.

—Let's see if you can do that right. The other lady couldn't boil an egg.

Esperanza was taken aback. She wondered if she would even be allowed to have some. Back home, las trabajadoras weren't allowed to drink from the same cups as their employers. What if she didn't make the coffee, would she lose her job? Esperanza looked over at the stove and saw the percolator waiting. She excused herself to use the bathroom and then began to make the coffee, dark, the way she liked it.

She waited for the coffee to rise and listened to it purr on the stovetop. She served Mrs. Hernández and watched her take a sip. Mrs. Hernández smiled, drinking it all until she was done, and then abruptly got up and peeled off her bata, revealing a skirt and blouse that tugged around her breasts.

—Where are you going? Esperanza asked.

—To work. I told you that's why you're here, so that I can work the twenty-four-hour laundromat down the block. Don't give him any sugar, even if he begs for it, Mrs. Hernández said. —It makes him crazy.

—Sí, señora, Esperanza said, looking over at Mr. Hernández, who must've met many home attendants before. She was happy to be left alone with him. She was ready to curl up in bed and take a nap. But Mr. Hernández didn't look tired. He was on page three of the newspaper, reading every word, looking up on occasion.

While Don Chan napped, Dallas sneaked over to the luncheonette's basement to meet with Hush to play spin the bottle. She left the television on in her bedroom and opened the tap in the bathroom, just enough to make Don Chan assume she was in there. She left the lights on and closed the door. If Don Chan woke up, he wouldn't bother her in the bathroom. Ever since she became a señorita she was entitled to certain types of privacies to do *cosas de mujeres,* as her mother liked to say.

If the radio station played his old music, Don Chan would nap for two hours minimum. Before she left she sneaked into her mother's bedroom. Her mother didn't allow her to wear makeup. Not until she turned fifteen. And Dallas was twelve. Most of the girls in her school were already wearing makeup. —If your friend jumped off a bridge, would you do the same? was Esperanza's response. —We could only trust familia, Esperanza told her and would say nothing more about the subject.

Dallas applied the lipstick, blush, and mascara. She had enough time to take it off before her mother came home. She kissed her reflection and unbuttoned her shirt to show some of her new cleavage. One day she woke up and it was there. Two soft lumps budding out of her chest. Like the hair between her legs, every day there was more of it. Soft and straight, like her eyebrows.

If she timed it right, she could chill with Hush and make dinner before Esperanza returned home from work. Esperanza had warned her that if she ended up like the fulanita upstairs, who got pregnant and ruined her life, she would kill Dallas with her own two hands. She would send her straight to Dominican Republic. —Children don't have rights in D.R., she'd warn Dallas. And if Esperanza knew how many tap kisses she had already shared under the auspices of playing spin the bottle or seven minutes in heaven, Dallas was sure her mother would take away her favorite clothes and destroy her Madonna and Back Street Boys posters.

Dallas was careful. Her mother might not trust her, but she knew how to take care of herself. It wasn't as if she was going to let some stupid kid ruin her life. She was curious, that was all. And she still had to experience seven minutes in heaven. She made up stories in her head of what it would be like to stay inside a closet with a boy. Sometimes the boys took out their penises for the girls to see, but the girls never admitted to showing anything in return. Despite the beer smell and moldy boxes lined against the wall of the basement, Dallas looked forward to playing games in the dimmed lights with Hush, her best friend.

Hush was Salvadorian. Her name always came out soft, sparking a curiosity that made people cock their heads. Hush. Her name was a mistake. When she was born, her mother, Soraida, was hiding in the back of a truck under blankets. The man being smuggled into the U.S. with them kept saying hush every time Soraida cried. Hush was slipping out of Soraida like diarrhea. Hush like a rude comment, an onion burp. Hush, who used to go to the same elementary school as Dallas, until Soraida married Oswaldo, and he helped pay for Hush to attend St. Rose of Lima. For months, Dallas begged her mother to find the money so that she could also attend.

—You want to go to Catholic school when you complain about going to church with me on Sundays? Please, I was already coming home with the cheese when you were still milking the cow.

Hush practically lived in the luncheonette, along with three other kids from around the way, none of whom attended their school but who were cute enough to tap kiss and play spin the bottle.

Then Hush spun the bottle.

—I'll spin and it's a tongue-kiss game, Hush said.

They all nodded because no one—especially Dallas, who had

never kissed anyone—wanted to be called scared. She had practiced tongue kissing on the back of her hand for so long that she'd given herself black and blues. Esperanza called it a disgusting habit, much like the way Dallas bit her nails and liked to stick her hands inside her armpits when they were cold.

The first spin pointed to the staircase leading up to the luncheonette. Hush grabbed the bottle and spun it again, licking her lips, while Dallas hugged her knees. The three boys crouched on their feet as they waited for the bottle to stop. They sat waiting on milk crates in the dim basement, musty from the damp cardboard boxes and lack of windows. The green Presidente beer bottle spun past each of them, slowly slid toward the boys, and finally stopped in front of Dallas. They gasped. One boy fell back. Hush covered her mouth. —I ain't gonna kiss Hush, Dallas said with a face of disgust.

—'Cause she smell, one boy said.

—'Cause she eat cat food, another said.

Hush's lips puffed out into a pout and she ran away, hiding herself deeper in the storage space where the stacks of toilet paper and pancake mix were piled high to the ceiling.

Dallas went after her. And when she found Hush curled up, tucked in a sack of rice, she went to hug her. Hush, half the size of Dallas, felt very fragile in her arms. Dallas saw how hurt Hush was and that she could lose the only friend she had in the world, the only friend who was allowed to sleep over at her place.

—I'm so sorry, Dallas said.

Hush turned around and smiled.

—Those stupid boys, Hush said and grabbed Dallas's face and kissed her. Her pouty lips dug into hers, their tongues swapping spit, cold, tasting like cherry soda. Dallas sucked on her tongue, trying to taste every bit of her, her lips a little salty from the heat. Everything started to tingle. Her insides pulsating, contracting, even Hush's slight caress on her arms awoke desire she didn't know existed in her. And when Hush pushed herself on her, her thighs pushing between her legs, Dallas remembered her mother and father dancing bachata. She remembered the way they moved back and forth, forth and back and wondered if she and Hush could dance that way. She wanted her to keep her leg inside her thighs, although she was afraid of what was happening to her: the weakness in her knees, her arms trembling from not knowing what to do with them. Her heart beating rapidly, afraid someone would walk in and find them. When they parted, Dallas wanted to hide. What had she done? She had kissed Hush, whose lips were rosy and full. When she puckered them, they looked like a heart.

Dallas was careful to sneak back into the apartment. Don Chan wasn't napping on the recliner. She slipped into the kitchen and opened the fridge door as if she was looking for something to eat. Don Chan walked in.

—What are you doing here? he demanded, not recognizing Dallas right away.

—I live here.

—Oh, it's you, Dallas, he said. He could hardly see a thing without his glasses.

Dallas wanted to check her lips in the mirror to see if someone would be able to tell the difference she felt.

—Where were you?

—In the bedroom, Abuelo.

—But I looked and you weren't there.

—Abuelo, are you sure you're feeling all right? You look tired. She took his arm and walked him to the recliner chair that he didn't like to sit in because it was difficult for him to get out of it.

—Sí, sí, I feel fine. But I looked in your bedroom and you weren't there.

—C'mon, Abuelo, tell me the year. Dallas giggled to herself thinking about Hush, the cola taste. Her throat hurt from holding in all her emotions.

Esperanza had not caught on that Don Chan's memory lapses had gotten worse, because she was never home.

—Abuelo? Dallas pulled at his sleeve. She knew his time was coming up. They all knew. —Abuelo, say something, Dallas insisted.

Don Chan looked bewildered. He had forgotten something again.

Caridad would be mad at him. She always looked at him with disappointment.

—Caridad, why are you mad at me?

Dallas didn't respond. The way he said the name Caridad gave her goose bumps.

—Come sit on my lap, he said, reaching out to Dallas.

Dallas rested on his lap. If she put all her weight on him, she'd break his leg in half. She held his hand and smelled his pine scent with a dash of cigar; cigars he only smoked on rare occasions because the sweet smell gave Esperanza migraines. Caridad had been a woman of few words. But when she talked, her words were like bullets. A now-or-never way of talking that had earned her respect. Dallas had heard stories about her from Don Chan before. Dallas stroked her grandfather's hair and wondered what it must be like to be so old, to start forgetting the easiest things for her to remember. Like the year, her name.

—You know Graciela means nothing to me, Don Chan said.

—Graciela? Dallas was confused. It was the first time he'd mentioned her. She had heard many things about Miraluz, but Graciela?

—It's that maldito rum that messes with my head. I won't do it again. I promise, I'll never take a sip of that damn rum from Ramoncito's colmado again.

—Again? Dallas was seeing a side of Don Chan she hadn't imagined. He didn't seem like the kind of man who would have cheated on her grandmother.

The apartment door opened.

—Get off of him, Bobby said, pulling Dallas away from Don Chan.

—Bobby, what you doing home?

—I live here.

—Caridad, Don Chan called out to Dallas.

—There's no Caridad here, Bobby said, plopping himself on the sofa, turning on the TV.

—Of course not, Don Chan said, finding his wits again. —Why would you say such a thing?

—Dallas, aren't you supposed to make dinner? You know Abuelo got to eat.

Bobby was hungry and he was thinking about Dallas's pepper steak.

—Aren't you supposed to clean the bathroom? Dallas snapped back. Bobby never did anything and Esperanza let him get away with it. In the mornings, he barged in on her before she was done getting dressed. It was bad enough they shared a bedroom, but he never knocked on the door.

—Bitch!

—Asshole!

—Respect Abuelo, man. Bobby was pissed that he had to find a job when she could sit on her fat butt doing nothing.

Bobby decided he'd just do it. Walk into McDonald's and apply for a job and anyone who had a problem with it could go to hell. At least if he started making some money, he could take one of the girls from around the block to a movie. Not like all the punks up the street who were always mooching off the dealers to get something to eat and bumming cigarettes. He could buy himself clothes and hook himself up with some new sneakers. He could get his ear pierced and plug in the small zirconia he saw at the jewelry store. If his mother wanted him to act like the man of the house, then she had to stop mama-boying him, as if he was the poor kid who was left an orphan. That was two years ago.

Don Chan was sitting at the luncheonette and saw Santo exiting the building. What was he doing out at this time of day? Don Chan had not finished clipping his headlines. The traffic cops were at the end of the block, making their way up. Santo should've still been sleeping. But there was something different about Santo that day. Did he comb his hair? Don Chan paid his tab and went outside to catch up with him. He had wanted to talk to him about the meeting planned in the church in la capital. He had received word that from east to west, the people were planning to meet in la capital, to discuss how to dispose of Reid Cabral and his associates and bring back Juan Bosch.

Bobby saw Don Chan, shuffling out of the luncheonette, and tried to dodge him.

—Oye mijo, where you going? Don Chan shouted from across the street.

The guys were on the corner. Bobby stood silent for a moment, afraid that everyone already knew that he was about to try for a job at McDonald's.

—Not now, Abuelo. Bobby waved him good-bye.

—I'll walk with you, Don Chan said. It was a good day for it, a quiet Saturday morning and the sun was out. The guys on the corner yelled out, —Wassup, Bobby, and Bobby looked at his feet as he walked along with his grandfather.

—Where are you going? Don Chan asked again, nervous because he didn't often leave Quepasó Street. He looked at the street sign and then to the next block to make sure he didn't lose his way.

—Where you going so early on a Saturday, Abuelo?

—Against time if possible.

The answer threw Bobby off.

—You should walk west then, Bobby said, thinking that the football games in California were later than the games in New York City, which must mean that walking west was going against time. The west lagged behind, in the past. Bobby was heading east.

—Clever. Don Chan had never thought of Santo as clever. They crossed the street and turned on Broadway. Don Chan started to feel vulnerable. He didn't often walk on Broadway, unless he knew where he was going.

—Don't act so surprised.

Bobby wondered if Don Chan was planning to walk all fifteen blocks to the McDonald's with him.

—Well, can you blame me? You never say much these days. How was I supposed to know you're funny?

Don Chan allowed the silence between them as they walked on Broadway. He saw the police officer walking his beat on Quepasó Street and sucked his teeth. What right did they have to invade his country?

—Those Yanquis never get enough.

—So you saw how the Mets beat the hell out of those Yankees last game, Abuelo?

—We need to find a way to get the Yanquis out of here, Don Chan said, looking around to make sure no one was spying on their conversation. —If the Yanquis don't leave, we'll have another dictator for sure.

Bobby stopped and held his grandfather's shoulders.

—Abuelo? It's me, Bobby.

Suddenly the city of Nueva York revealed itself before Don Chan's eyes.

—Of course you are, Don Chan said and patted his grandson's face in recognition.

—You should go home, Abuelo. I have a ways to go.

—But I want to come with you.

—You can't come with me.

—Your father always let me go with him.

—I'm not my father, Bobby said, remembering how his father had called him pendejo when he got jumped. Bobby had wished him dead. Santo was not only robbed, he got killed. Damn you, Papi, Bobby said to himself. Bobby clenched his jaw.

Don Chan felt a chill in his bones. He was underdressed, yet refused to wear a coat. The streets were filling up with Saturday shoppers. The line for the million-dollar lotto drawing was forming around the block.

—Do you think about your father?

—Could we not talk about him please? Bobby didn't want to get worked up before McD's. —Look, Abuelo, no disrespect, you should go back home. I don't want you to get tired.

—I'm not tired.

—I'll see you at home, a'ight. Stay on Broadway until you hit Quepasó. I'll be home soon.

Bobby kissed Don Chan on the cheek and left before his grandfather could follow him. Don Chan stood on the corner and watched Bobby become smaller in the distance.

Bobby ordered large fries and a Coke at McDonald's and sat down in a booth near the register to watch. He was just waiting until the line cleared up, but with time it got longer and the girls behind the register looked stressed. Bobby scouted the place and couldn't imagine

himself in the brown-and-yellow uniform. He figured he could always change in the bathroom before he went home. The guys in the
kitchen were sweating over the grill, one of the managers was yelling
at them to move faster. The line was now a ten-minute wait. If it
reached fifteen minutes, then the promotion said the customers
would get 50 percent off their combo meal.

—Hurry up, the manager said, pushing them along, pulling out
the cooked fries and putting them into a tray under the heat lamp
and placing a new batch of frozen fries in the hot oil.

Bobby calculated the value of a combo meal. Was it really a value?
If he bought a small Coke, large fries, and a cheeseburger, it would
be about three-fourths of the price of the combo with the large Coke.
And did he want that much more Coke anyway? Bobby added up all
types of configurations, and at four dollars an hour, he would have
to work one hour after taxes, for a combo. But if he worked there, he
would never have to buy McDonald's again. So he would save money
because he ate there at least twice a week.

Time went by and Bobby didn't notice that the employees had
switched, from the breakfast/lunch shift to the dinner shift. He
picked at his fries until they were cold and tasted like cardboard.
The cola turned into sweet water. It was good to sit in the booth. He
had time to shake off all that talk he had with his grandfather about
a past he didn't want to think about. He made eyes at a girl sitting
across from him who was having lunch with her family. She smiled,
exposing her braces.

Bobby looked over at the counter. It was now or never. Ask for
the application and then walk away. Not a big deal. But he had a
problem with asking for things. It was what got him in trouble at
school. If he didn't understand, he didn't ask. To ask was admitting
he wasn't listening. But sometimes he was listening and still didn't
understand. But this wasn't school. There was a FOR HIRE sign. He
had a pen in his pocket. He could fill out the application and leave it
with the manager and then wait for them to call him. But what if
they didn't call? What kind of a loser would he be? His mother
would tell all her friends. Soon his friends would tease him that even
McD's had rejected his ass. All the girls from the block would see the

big L on his forehead. Bobby decided he wouldn't tell his mother he'd applied. Besides, he didn't want the job, so it didn't matter either way. Bobby walked over to the counter. The traffic was dying down. It was an hour of transition. If he waited any longer, it would get busy again with the dinner crowd.

The counter looked wider than he remembered it. The girl at the register eyed him. She had seen him sitting at the booth. She knew he had a question.

—Uh . . . can I uh speak with the manager?

—Joanne! the girl yelled out. "Marielys" was the name he read off her lapel. Also the "Employee of the Month." Her photo was up on the wall.

Bobby looked around to make sure he didn't know anyone.

Joanne emerged from behind the swinging doors.

—How can I help you? she asked and then stepped back to take a better look. —Oh shit, Bobby Colón?

Joanne de la Vega, who Bobby had gone to sixth grade with. For years they were tight because they lived in the same building. Together they locked themselves in Joanne's bedroom. When her mother was out working, they watched the nudie channel from the fixed cable box her father had installed, to laugh at how disgusting people were.

—Joanne? Bobby backed away.

Back when he was twelve, and she thirteen, and Bobby discovered that the slightest breeze prompted an erection, Joanne was there to witness it. The last time they were together was on the rooftop.

—Can I see it? she had asked and turned her head away.

—What? Bobby hadn't understood the question at first.

—I've never seen a real one. And we're like best friends. I won't tell anyone, I promise.

—But . . .

Bobby had hidden his growing erection. He wasn't ready to share it. He had just discovered it. It was bad enough he had to hide it from Dallas in the mornings. Or his mother, who didn't think twice about opening the bathroom door without knocking first.

—Real quick. You can take it out and put it back in and it will be like it never happened.

—And what do I get? Bobby asked, trying to stall. He hoped it could be like when he traded baseball cards. But Joanne was asking for more than just a card from his collection. She wanted to expose him.

—What you want? she said matter-of-factly.

—Maybe you can let me touch you, he said, licking his lips. Bobby thought about the guys at school who wore the smell of a girl on their fingers like a trophy.

—That's not fair, touching a girl is like third base. And seeing a guy's penis is like watching the game from the nosebleed seats. No way, Bobby.

Bobby was nervous. She was standing close enough that he could smell her ice-cream breath.

—It's not a big deal, Bobby. Look, it's dying to come out, Joanne said as his erection poked up against his pants. She went to unzip him. Awkwardly he pulled it out of his shorts. She went to touch it. Bobby couldn't hold it back. It exploded in her hand, on her jeans. She laughed. He turned around, pulling it back inside his pants.

Bobby had avoided Joanne ever since. Why had she laughed?

Bobby stood at the McDonald's counter for a minute, wondering how he could leave without making a scene. He didn't want to look at her face, but when he looked down, he noticed how big Joanne's breasts had gotten, which turned the top of his ears red.

—What you doing here? she asked.

—Getting some fries.

—Did you ask for the manager? Joanne looked hopeful.

—Nah, man, I was just . . . you know, forget it, I have to run. I got peeps waiting for me. But I see you around, a'ight?

Dallas was nervous about seeing Hush again after their kiss. Would they kiss again? Did she want to? Was it normal? These thoughts pre-occupied her so much, she had to double-check that she didn't forget to do anything before leaving the apartment. She forewent the lipstick and instead applied some cocoa-butter balm so her lips softened. She hurried over to the luncheonette. Her mother had been acting weird and protective since Dallas had gotten her period. She even gave her a hard time about using the telephone. She hadn't been able to call Hush since the kiss. At the luncheonette, Dallas slipped downstairs as if going to the bathroom and then opened the door to the storage/recreation room. During the day, it belonged to Hush and all her friends; at night it was where the men played poker and hid from their wives.

The lights were on, but no one was around in the basement. Dallas was about to go home when she heard a noise in the back. She should leave. If someone caught her and wanted to tell her mother about the afternoons she spent in the basement, they could ruin her life. But she sneaked over by the stacks of flour. It was Mario, the skinny, knock-kneed, eighteen-year-old high school dropout who worked with his uncle making deliveries to the luncheonette. He was pushing up on a girl.

—Please, Mario whispered. I promise, just once. Hush giggled from Mario's affections.

—Hush?

Dallas touched her lips with her fingertips, as if she could erase something. She wanted Hush to see her. The sounds went from the slurp and slime of gutting a chicken, to the plunging of a toilet bowl, wet, with a pull and push. Get out of here, Dallas told herself. It was too embarrassing to be caught watching. But she couldn't help staring. Her body filled with rage.

—Dallas? Hush said.

—Oh shit, Mario said, pulling away.

—Oh don't worry. It's just my friend, Hush said, tucked in her shirt, and giggled some more. Reaching her hand out to Dallas to kiss her hello on the cheek.

—Uh, I . . . Dallas became dizzy, losing her orientation.

—I uh . . . see you around, Dallas said, grateful for the exit sign.

—But wait, Hush said.

—Later, okay? Dallas felt as if she was looking through a broken piece of glass; everything before her moved away and expanded.

—Hola, Mrs. Colón, is Dallas home?

Dallas waved frantically at her mother.

—I'm sorry, Hush, she told me to tell you she's not home. I don't know what's wrong with her.

Hush yelled into Dallas's window and waited around the building hoping she would catch her exiting or entering.

—Y por qué you don't talk to Hush no more? Esperanza asked Dallas.—She's better to have as a friend than the fulanita upstairs who I see hanging out in the streets at night like un cuero.

Esperanza might not have approved that Soraida always left Hush with her stepfather, Oswaldo, at the luncheonette because it wasn't proper for a young girl to always be out like that without supervision—especially one who was now a señorita. But unlike Dallas, Hush always carried a book with her and made good grades. Esperanza's children didn't study, and that made her angry.

—I don't feel like talking to her.

But Dallas missed Hush so much, she thought she wouldn't be able to sleep through the night ever again. It was Hush who defended her when kids around the way teased her with her name: —Let's go visit Dallas. —Let's stomp on Dallas. —Stupid Dallas. —Fat-ass Dallas.

—May I leave a letter for Dallas? Hush asked Don Chan days later.
—Of course you can. You know you're always welcome here.
—Thank you, Don Chan. Make sure Dallas gets my letter.
Don Chan put Hush's letter among all of Esperanza's bills.

Dallas assumed Hush didn't care about her anymore. If she did, she would've kept persisting. Esperanza was right. Friends can't be trusted. But Dallas missed Hush. She missed hanging up on Hush when she called and pretending not to hear her name outside her window. And when she was stuck at home with nothing to do, the temptation to call Hush overwhelmed her. Every time she picked up the phone to call Hush, she remembered ugly-ass Mario all up in her shit, and hung up. I won't ever be your friend, Dallas said to herself but then leaped toward the phone when it rang, hoping it was Hush. But it never was. Months passed and Hush didn't call.

—Dallas, can you find the phone bill in that pile over there? I have to pay it in person or they're turning it off, Esperanza said, pointing to the stack of mail she had accumulated and hardly had the time to look through. The pile was filled with catalogs and notices: Lung Association. Bank of America. Chia Pet Catalog. For Dallas.

—It's not here, Dallas told her as she looked through each envelope carefully.

For Dallas written in red pen.

—What's this? Dallas asked her mother.

—How should I know?

—Mami, what if it's important?

—What could be so important at your age? Esperanza said as she prepared dinner and arranged the laundry on the kitchen table. Get over here and help your mother before I burn the house down.

Dallas kept the envelope in her jeans pocket and checked on occasion to see if it was still there. She waited until she was alone in her bedroom. She held the envelope to her nose. It didn't smell like Hush; it smelled like kitchen. How long had it been sitting there? Why was her mother so stupid?

Dear Dallas,

My teacher said that one letter has more power than 10,000 phone calls. If u want me to leave u alone I will. But I want u 2 know that u will always b my best friend. That I hope u call me 1 day so we could b friends again.

U R 2 Good 2 B 4got10.

Your best friend 4ever,
Hush

Best friend 4ever? Dallas wondered if anything lasted that long. She thought her father would be around forever and then he died. Nothing was forever, Hush. —So why are you trying so hard, Dallas said to the words on the page, filled with rage. In a few days, she'd call to tell Hush to her face that it was over between them, that they could never be friends again.

Bobby ran out of the apartment when his mother came home from work.

—Where you going?

—I'll be right back, he said before she could ask him again about the job he didn't have.

It was a summer day. Bobby played basketball with his friend Lalo; the hoop a jacked-up crate hanging from the fire-escape ladder. He didn't want to think about anything but the ball, Lalo's sloppy dribbling, and how easy it was to beat his ass. He was so caught up in victory, he didn't notice the arrival of White-boy Arnold. Arnold was thirteen and lived on another block, but wanted to fit in so bad, he walked with an extra bend to his knee and said everything in the past tense.

—Checked this out, he said, pulling out a .22 revolver, cracked open to show two bullets inside, ready for an assassination. But Arnold wasn't planning to assassinate anyone. The gun was his father's, a retired cop who collected guns and kept them in a leather case in his bedroom.

Bobby licked his lips over and over again, afraid of what trouble White-boy Arnold was bringing. Instinctively, he was thinking of ways to get away from there, out of the afternoon sun. For the first time ever, he was hoping that his mother would call him from the window. But everything got real tranquil and the gun on Arnold's hand was shooting off light beams in all directions, making itself larger than it was.

—That's a'ight, Lalo said as he looked around. He walked over to a parked car and slid his hand under it, tucking a package in his pocket.

White-boy Arnold had a nervous bounce to him.

—Let me hold it? Bobby said. Ever since the new precinct opened up, the number of cops had tripled on Quepasó Street. Didn't Arnold know that?

Bobby grabbed the gun by the handle, laid it flat on his palm. He hadn't realized how heavy they were. How dangerous they felt in the hand. The metal was cold, like a beer bottle just out of the fridge.

—Yo, son, my father got a case of them shit. You ever need to get strapped, you talk to me. White-boy Arnold hit his chest to show loyalty.

Dallas dialed Hush's number, and when she heard her voice, she was tempted to hang up.

—Hello, Hush said in a soft voice.

Dallas paused and regretted pausing, because then Hush would know she was nervous.

—Hello? Hush asked again.

—Hi, it's me, you wanna meet?

—Dallas?

—Yeah, it's me. You wanna meet at the park by the benches before my mother comes home from work?

—Sure, Hush said, breathing into the phone.

Dallas hung up. She was still angry. But she wasn't sure why anymore.

Dallas sneaked out of the apartment and walked toward the park benches down Quepasó Street. Hush was already there. Hush pulled out a cigarette from her pocket. It had been a few months since they'd seen each other. There was something different about Hush that Dallas couldn't place.

—You smoking now?

—Only when I'm nervous.

—What's making you so nervous? You trying to kill yourself?

—Lots of shit is going on, Hush said and wanted to tell Dallas about her stepfather, Oswaldo. The way he ogled her when she was sitting on the sofa watching television. Sometimes he sat next to her, close enough so his leg touched her foot. It was difficult to hide from him in their small one-bedroom apartment, where she slept in the living room without a door to lock at night. She knew the look he gave her. Mario looked at her in the same way, but Mario asked her permission and he never did anything to Hush she didn't feel comfortable with. Her mother didn't understand that. And when she caught Hush and Mario kissing in the lobby of her building, Soraida held up a Bible to her breast like an armor, and called Hush una mujer perdida.

—I gotta get out of my house. I can't wait till college, Dallas. I'm so outta here. You have no idea how ready I am.

—College? The way my grades are, I'll never make it to college. We're still in junior high, and you're thinking college. Damn, girl!

—Not only are you gonna go to college, we're going together, Hush said as she inhaled and exhaled away from Dallas.

—You're the nerd. No college that accepts you will accept me.

Hush was top of her class each semester. Dallas barely passed from grade to grade.

—Shut up. That's not true. You need to come with me. You're the only family I got, Hush said, looking away into the weeping willow tree that hung over them.

—But I'm still mad at you, Hush. I don't think I'll ever be okay with you again. You think I'll go to some college with you so you could diss me for a punk-ass guy like Mario? Hell no. For that, I stay here.

—I didn't diss you. I was going to tell you about Mario.

—But you didn't. I had to find out like some stranger. That's messed up.

—You can't be mad at me forever.

—You wanna bet?

—Well, then we'd be like real sisters. 'Cause family always mad at each other and love each other just the same.

—Let me try that, Dallas said and put her hand out toward the cigarette.

Dallas put it in her mouth and coughed.

—This shit is nastier than I thought.

—You get used to it, Hush said and moved around. Sitting on the bench, then getting up, then walking to hug the tree, then back toward Dallas.

—Why should I get used to something that's nasty? I don't get it.

—I'll stop smoking if you become my friend again.

—Hush, you crazy.

—It takes one to know one.

—Fuck you, bitch. Dallas got up to push her a little.

—You know I'd never fight you, Hush said. —You and your dirty skirt.

Dallas's new white denim skirt was now filthy from sitting on the bench.

—Look at this, Dallas said. They both checked out the streaks of dirt around Dallas's bottom. They didn't notice the two men who'd driven up in a van and parked by their bench. They were still looking at Dallas's skirt, contemplating whether the streaks were permanent or could be bleached out, when a sweaty, unshaven man grabbed Dallas from behind. She felt the cold metal against her neck; his clammy hands on her arms; his chest against her back; she saw his hair locked in gel, slicked back.

—Run, Hush! Dallas screamed. She went past fear altogether. She couldn't feel her body. She was ready to sacrifice her life for Hush; there was no point in both of them dying. She was going to be brave like she was sure her father was brave when the man put the knife to his neck. She didn't look down at her feet, just straight ahead and right at Hush, who said, —Let her go, take me.

Dallas watched Hush rocking from one foot to another as if she had to go to the bathroom. She was trying hard to be the strong one, waving her hands around and keeping a safe distance, looking around to see if anyone was coming. But the guy pressed the gun harder against Dallas's neck, behind her earlobe, digging into the dent there, the same place her father was stabbed. Her poor father; was that how he felt, his last few minutes in a dark car, with a stranger's smell as a last memory? Her father also died by a park. Her dear old father, Dallas thought, watching the weeping willow blow against them as her heart beat faster, popping out of her chest. Dallas didn't feel the tears come down her face. Only the metal on her skin, the fat, sweaty man against her back, up close, as if he was contemplating taking her with him. She should've never gone out to meet Hush. Where were the cops when she needed them? Her mother would never let her hang outside again. She wanted to see his face, but if she looked, he'd get angry. She hoped someone would walk by. No one was in the park at that hour. She watched Hush rocking, pacing, like a windup doll gone mad.

—Run, Hush, Dallas said in a low whisper. —Run.

—Hell no. You better let her go, Hush said with more determination, as if all the moving around was cranking up her power, as if she was contemplating a superhero move.

—Let her go, motherfucker, Hush said, on her tiptoes to make herself a bit taller, stretching her arms out to enlarge her presence.

Dallas tasted her tears on her lips. She missed her father. She felt her heart, and the back of her throat, and the pain in the arch of her back as she struggled to keep her body away from the man holding the gun.

—Don't mess with me, Hush said, threatening the sweaty man who was still laughing, grabbing at Dallas's breast, squeezing her breast with his hand, licking her neck as he pulled her chain with his teeth. The same necklace she had been wearing since the day she was born.

—Shut up, Dallas said, knowing that Hush's threats were making it worse.

—Help! Help! Police! Police! screamed the old German lady with the hairy upper lip.

Bobby, Arnold, and Lalo heard the scream.

—It's your sister, Lalo said as they approached the scene. He pulled a gun from his pants.

—What the fuck? Bobby didn't recognize Lalo for a minute.

Bobby had Arnold's gun in his hand. He followed Lalo's lead and between both of them, they surrounded the mugger holding Dallas with one arm and the gun with the other.

—Bobby! Dallas cried. The sight of him made her lose the feeling in her knees. She slipped from under the mugger's arms and ran toward Hush. —Bobby! They screamed in unison. The mugger pointed the gun at Bobby.

—Help! Help! Police! Police! continued the old German lady.

—Shut the fuck up, Bobby shouted, waving the gun at the old lady.

When they heard the sirens approaching, Lalo ran away and was chased, caught down the street, and thrown on the ground. The driver of the van pulled away, the mugger tried to escape toward the van's opened door, dropping the gun. There was a bang. The mugger, on the ground, held his leg. When Bobby opened his eyes, he found himself surrounded; the colorful lights from the cop cars danced about over his face.

—Where's my son? Esperanza charged into the precinct. She had watched *L.A. Law* for too many years and knew that they couldn't lock up her Bobby for no good reason.

—What do you mean, juvenile delinquent? Assault? Drugs? Possession of a deadly weapon? My Bobby?

The city was under new management and there was "zero tolerance" for juvenile offenders. Between Bobby's association with Lalo, who was on probation for drugs, the possession of a deadly weapon, and the gun wound inflicted on the mugger by Bobby, his case didn't look good.

—He saved my life, Dallas said as his corroborating witness. —We were getting mugged. That man was ready to kill me.

—But why did Bobby shoot after the mugger had already dropped the gun? Did Bobby have a history with the alleged mugger? the police officer asked.

—No. Of course not, Dallas said.

—It says here he threatened to shoot Ms. Schoberth, when she called out for the police.

—She's a liar. He told her to be quiet. That's all.

—Officer, can't you let my Bobby come home? Esperanza pleaded.

—What do you know about Lalo Martinez, Mrs. Esperanza?

—They played basketball together. His family lives on our street. They've been friends since they were children.

—Did you know that Lalo was on probation?

—I heard he got into some trouble. But my Bobby never did nothing wrong. He's a good kid. I swear to you.

—Where did Bobby get the gun? the police officer asked.

—That boy with all the freckles. I can't ever say his name right.

—Arnold Keener. He says Bobby stole the gun from his father's house when he went to visit him earlier, on the day the alleged crime was committed.

—Impossible. Bobby was home all morning.

Bobby was charged as a juvenile delinquent on two counts: possession of a deadly weapon and assault with a deadly weapon.

—But you can't take my Bobby away.

Esperanza pleaded with the public defender, but the judge feared that Bobby was one of those kids who had flown under the radar for a while and it had finally caught up with him. It was best for his own good to lock him up in a medium-security detention facility to scare him out of becoming a repeat offender.

That was the last time Esperanza saw the Bobby to whom she'd given birth. After only weeks at Spofford Juvenile Detention, the wall between her and Bobby grew thick.

—I'm just doing my time, he said every time she asked how he was feeling.

—Don't you need anything, Bobby? Is there anything I can bring you that will make it easier for you here? I mean, I'm so sorry, Bobby. You got to stay strong because your room at home is waiting for you. The counselor told me that if you keep your grades up in here, they will let you out early for good behavior. Gotta keep the mind going, Bobby. That's all we have, you hear me? Ignorance is expensive.

When she looked at him, he was her little boy; he didn't even have facial hair. He was thin and muscular from playing basketball with his friends. His hands and feet were disproportionate to the rest of his body, like a puppy. She couldn't stand seeing him in that stupid jumper, in that room so gray, so cold, so dark. And when Esperanza cried, Bobby did soften up some from the hardness he had to have around the other guys who were locked up for doing something stupid they didn't admit regretting.

—Mamá, stop crying. I'll be home soon. It's not as bad as it looks.

4

Spofford Juvenile Detention Center
1994–1997

Bobby's days ticktocked to lights on and lights out.

—Got a problem, son?

—What you looking at, motherfucker?

Voices rising, one on top of the other, spinning in his head. The clock in the playpen ticktocked, counting the days that went by. Bobby breathed. Just like the lady wearing the Buddha T-shirt had told him to do. She came once a week and gave a workshop on meditation.

—They might have you locked up in here, but you can set yourself free through enlightenment, she said as she lifted her arms into the air, stretching up into a sun salutation, pushing out her chest with each deep inhale.

Bobby couldn't hear himself breathe the first time he tried it. At the juvie detention, all day there was the blaring TV, the booming music, the laughter competing with the rattling of keys, the pounding of walls, fist up against cheeks.

—Yo yo, son, wassup? —What you in here for, son? —Why you always sitting in that corner like you praying? God don't come around here, son. —Off-the-boat, plátano-sucking motherfucker, what the fuck is your problem? —Punk-ass crooked-dick, maricón, your mama birthed you through her ass, nigga.

∙∙∙

Bobby listened and he didn't listen. He listened to his breath, four times. The Buddha lady said if he could think of nothing else for twelve breaths, he would see light, he would be free.

—Remember a place you felt safe, said the white lady, who once lived in the mountains in a monastery and didn't eat for eight days because she wanted to clean out all the toxins in her body. She hiked up the mountain for three days and stayed at the monastery for months, so she could find peace, so she would never be in anyone's prison.

—Go back to a time when you were far from these four walls.

With each breath, Bobby went back to the Sunday afternoons when he and his father stayed home and his mother attended Mass.

—Ven acá, Bobby. Take off those uncomfortable clothes your mama make you wear, make yourself a Coca-Cola straight up, and lay down with your father so we can watch the game.

And Bobby pared down to boxers and a white T-shirt with under-arm stains, just like his father. And Santo poured himself a rum on the rocks. And together, propped up on pillows, they lay back on hot summer days, the fan pushing warm air into their faces, the TV on the highest-volume setting so they could hear the game over the music playing out on the streets.

—As long as we can do this every once in a while, we'll be fine, Santo said as he ruffled Bobby's hair.

Bobby took in the warmth of his parents' bed, the softness of the comforter, smelling his mother's scent all over the sheet: lavender, comino, and corn oil.

—Get up, motherfucker. —I said that's my chair. —Yo, Bobby, you don't gotta move. He don't got his name on your chair. —Yeah, Bobby, don't got to be telling anybody anything. —If you wanna survive this place, you gotta look everyone in the eye, so they know you ain't afraid to fight. And if you fight, you gotta make sure you hurt the asshole who fucks with you 'cause then they know not to fuck with you again.

•••

—Breathe, Bobby. In and out of your belly. At first it will be difficult. But if you do it every day before you go to sleep, if you figure out how to get there, you will be able to do it anytime; in a crowded subway, in the middle of a riot. With your breath you can make everything stop. You have that power, Bobby.

Bobby never said much, he nodded as if he were listening, to satisfy the storytellers, the dreamers; the talkers who never finished a thought without being interrupted.

—*Yo, Bobby, when I get out of here, I'm gonna clean up my shit. I'm gonna get myself a real job and help my momma. —Hear this out, Bobby, I got myself a lady outside waiting for me. She waiting, so when I come out, I could hit that pussy. She my virgin queen. I'm gonna do right by her. I ain't gonna trip like these motherfuckers, talking about blazing the pussy when you know they had never seen one. I got myself the real thing. Pure shit, bro. —Bobby, don't listen to him. That cocksucker got his dog waiting for him. Poor thing walks with a limp from being fucked up the ass so much. —Man, Bobby, you saw the lady baking in the kitchen, who got the red hair and shit? I'm gonna take her and make her bleed like a fiending bitch. You know she like it like that. She hungry for some of this, bro.*

They talked and grabbed their balls, and scratched their bellies, and wiped their foreheads, and spat on the ground. They chewed on their lips and hangnails, waiting, for a trial, to get out, for a phone call, for a visitor, for a package, for another day to go by without too much pain, boredom, trouble.

Bobby listened, but he didn't really listen. He let the days pass, the weeks pass, the months pass and he heard a cacophony of words, same words from different guys, who were inside for selling weed, others for stealing cars. Others for beating up someone so bad, they sent him to the hospital. Faces changing, kids being moved to new facilities down the block, across town, upstate. And

Bobby tried to breathe deep, in and out, so nothing could touch him, like he imagined Bruce Lee inhaling and exhaling before he made his next move.

—Go to your core. Go to that place where nothing could touch you. The lady liked to stand on her tiptoes when she was trying to make a point. And all Bobby could do was think about his father. Hot, sweaty Sundays, when everyone left him and his father alone, so they could drink and watch the game: Bobby holding a cold Coca-Cola and his father holding rum. Why did his father have to die? Could Santo see him? Was he disappointed?

—My being here is a mistake, Bobby said to himself, but mostly to his father. —I don't belong here.

Nueva York
1995

Don Chan didn't remember leaving the apartment door open. He was sure he locked it. Or was that yesterday? All the lights were off.

Don Chan picked up his cane. It felt heavy in his hands, which trembled against his liking. He was in no condition to fight an intruder. Would that be the way he was going to die, with a gun pushed up against his ribs? No, he had survived too long to die that way. He had seen too many guns in his day.

Don Chan held his walking cane like a weapon, and with caution, moved into each room, drawing open the curtains, hoping there was someone outside who would hear him yell for help if needed.

—Qué estúpida. She'll be in debt forever, so a thief could take it. Don Chan talked to the windows, the walls riddled with old photographs, the velvety pillows that crowded the sofa bought on credit. He remembered his late wife's famous words, —Te dan un ala y te quitan el corazón. Banks gave people credit who then worked, to pay it back, their entire lives. The anger built up inside him and pushed back the fear propelled by the unlocked door of his apartment, the possible intruder. He would much rather be angry than scared. At least anger made him act.

He contemplated turning on the lights. But he would rather not see the clutter that filled the living room. The sound of the television in Dallas's room accompanied him. He was sitting in an apartment whose walls filled him with painful memories and fear of leaving the house, his fear that someone would break in to take what, his life? What leads a person to the kind of place where no matter how much he racked his brain, he had no answers? Don Chan wished he could run. In his mind, running was possible and more. But his body wouldn't let him. The walls he so much despised were the walls that protected him. He preferred the lock on the door.

—Goddamn it, he said. And stood still and listened. But nothing moved, except for the floorboards vibrating from the bass of the music playing downstairs. And the door? Could he have forgotten to lock it? He couldn't admit that to anyone, especially Esperanza. If he did, they wouldn't trust him to be alone, and he didn't need anyone watching over him.

He stood in the dark room wondering where Santo was. He had been missing for weeks. Don Chan trespassed into Esperanza's room and became nauseous with the smell of her perfume. A woman who wore that much perfume was hiding something.

Don Chan searched through Esperanza's drawers, pulling out her makeup, hair brushes, blouses. Her closet was bursting at the seams with her collection of clothes and shoes. Stacked up in piles were things she had ordered and still had not taken out of their boxes.

—How many things did she need? he said out loud. He found Santo's old wallet and took it with him. It contained a photograph of when he was a child. He looked over at Esperanza's small altar behind the door and wiped off the dust on the top of the white candle.

Don Chan found the newspaper clippings of Santo's murder. He reread them. He looked at the photo and didn't want to recognize him.

—No, no it can't be, Don Chan said, and sorrow came over him as if years hadn't passed.

—Damn you, for killing my son, he said, and wept, not knowing who to blame anymore. He rubbed the creases from the old newspaper. He staggered over to the hallway in the apartment entrance and replaced the photo of Jesus with the clipping.

—This way I won't forget.

•••

That night Esperanza arrived home from work and stripped out of her clothes, wanting nothing more than to sleep on her own sheets and pillows. At first, she wasn't sure about the Hernández job, but sleeping over there was an escape from the mess her apartment had become: piles of clothes in the hamper, mail to look through, vegetables going bad in the fridge, dust on the figurines on the shelves. She relied on Dallas for some things around the house, but child hands could keep order only to a point. In D.R., Dallas would've been ripe for training to have her own home, a husband, some children, but in Nueva York, Dallas was a child with breasts.

To her surprise, Dallas had left the dishes washed. The apartment was unusually calm. Dallas had even cleaned the bathroom. Esperanza could tell from the shine on the mirror. Seeing everything in order brought unexpected joy. Life wasn't so bad.

She opened the children's door to announce her arrival, and Dallas looked up and away from the television.

—I finished my homework, Dallas said before her mother asked.

—Did your grandfather eat dinner?

—Some.

—Where is he?

—Sleeping, I guess.

—So early?

—He looked tired.

—Was he not feeling well?

—I don't know.

Dallas didn't tear her eyes away from the television show. That damn Walkman and phone. Unless Esperanza called her out to do something, Dallas locked herself in her room. What could she be hiding in there? When she had been Dallas's age, her father wouldn't allow a door in Esperanza's bedroom. And still, even with all her father's supervision, Esperanza had run off with Santo.

Esperanza walked into her bedroom. Ever since Bobby went to prison, she felt as if she had forgotten something important. There was an emptiness in her house that couldn't be filled even after she rearranged the furniture. But that wasn't what was bothering her. There was something else that was different. She walked backward to retrace her steps. She looked around. She was too tired to try to make sense of it.

She peeked into Don Chan's room.

—Are you all right?

—Why wouldn't I be? Don Chan said and turned his back to be left alone.

Esperanza felt sorry for him. Don Chan reminded Esperanza of Mr. Hernández. They were about the same age, except Mr. Hernández had had a stroke and he slurred his words and couldn't stand listening to himself. Esperanza preferred it that way.

In the kitchen, she put away the pots. She wasn't hungry. It was as if Santo was on the other side of the wall. She batted away the buzzing around her ear, the tail of a whistle. A familiar tune. Santo's tune.

She took a shower and prepared herself for sleep. But she couldn't shake the feeling. Someone had definitely been in her bedroom, looking through her things. The top drawer was partly opened. In bed, her sheets felt heavy over her body. It was too early for sleep, but if she lay down, maybe the air pushing into her ears would cease. She spread her arms to feel that the other side of her bed was cold. She always slept on one side to keep from rumpling the sheets. It made it easier to make the bed in the morning. But then there was the emptiness. His side. As if it were waiting for him to appear.

He left for work the night he died. But he didn't want to work. He wanted to go dancing. He wanted to kiss. He had an erection that day. She missed his erection, holding it in her hand. The way heat came off it. How after they made love, he allowed her to hold it while they fell asleep. It had been months since they'd made love. There was never enough time. When they found each other in bed, they were so exhausted. But that night, before he died, he had wanted her. As if he knew it would be their last opportunity. He begged her to go dancing. Why couldn't she have supported him when he said he wanted to return to D.R.? Why had she been so afraid of the possibility? And that stupid table. She didn't need to fight him. With time, he would've gotten tired of it and she could've thrown it out and he wouldn't have noticed.

Esperanza moved to the middle of the bed. She spread her legs and arms, filling up the empty space. She had prayed for Santo to appear, just for his company, so she had someone to talk to. Esperanza kept his ashes on the altar in her room to keep his spirit close. She believed that if she concentrated hard enough, she could feel him press against her back while she slept; that she felt his caress like a warm breeze when she needed comfort. It had been over three years since his death. She had to move on. And if she ever were to return to D.R., she would spread Santo's ashes so he could rest in peace.

Why couldn't all of what had happened the past three years be a dream? Like it happened for Pamela when Bobby Ewing died in *Dallas*. After the fancy funeral and all that crying, after Pamela went off and got married to another man, one year later, it was the beginning of a new season, Pamela was in bed and heard the shower on. Startled, she walked into the bathroom.

Good morning, Bobby Ewing said, sporting that smile of his, as if he had never been gone all that time.

What if tomorrow morning Esperanza would wake up and find her Bobby sleeping in his bedroom? What if Santo would knock at her door, and say, Buenos días, corazón?

Los Llanos
1963

Juan Bosch had lasted seven months in office. The heirs of the former Trujillo government took over and soon after, a number of the Invisible Ones started to disappear.

—What's happening, Papá? Santo asked Don Chan.

—They want our land. Without Juan Bosch, the government will force us to sell it. They make more profit that way.

—Forget Juan Bosch! Miraluz was sick of the will of the politicians. —We can fight and protect Los Llanos ourselves, right, Santo?

—We would need to arm ourselves then, Santo said.

—Why do you think we found those guns buried under our feet? Don't you think our ancestors are telling us something? Miraluz said. —My grandfather fought for Los Llanos.

—And then the U.S. air-bombed them and it was over, Don Chan said.

Don Chan walked over to the garden. Miraluz and Santo walked after him. He looked at the size of it and was proud to see how it was flourishing. The sections were delineated by the size of each family. The fruits that were not eaten were sold and the money distributed among them. For seven months, the people of Los Llanos had lived harmoniously. Slowly, they were learning to trust each other, planning to set up cooperative schools, medical facilities, and a recreation center.

—We'll organize to bring Juan Bosch back into office. He can change the laws to protect us, Don Chan said.

—Nobody follows the law in this country, Santo said. —The law changes with the desires of the rich. The military acts as if the constitution doesn't exist.

—I say let's cage all of those people who make up the military, the politicians, and the rich—just like they did our ancestors—and then burn them alive. Maybe then they will let us live our lives in peace, Miraluz said.

—Are you serious? Santo was surprised by her aggression. But something had her worked up.

—Violence isn't necessary. If we kill, we're the same as the people we criticize. We can win by teaching the people and using the constitution, said Don Chan.

—And you think the military, Balaguer, and all the men who make money from the government, will allow for a fair reelection? Please, Don Chan, Miraluz said, rolling her eyes. —For someone so wise, it's crazy to think any government will look after the best interests of the people over their wallets. When in history have we seen people like us win their freedom without some bloodshed?

—Papá, it's true. They're already coming after us. Two of the Invisible Ones have disappeared for three days. Their wives are worried.

—You want us to wait here defenseless while they capture and torture each and every one of us, chop off our heads, and put them on a twenty-foot pole as an example? Miraluz's fists were clenched.

—Who would do that? Santo was disgusted.

—People don't do that anymore, Don Chan said with a sigh.

—If you get in their way, they will. Miraluz's face was lined with beads of sweat. —Explain to me why I don't sleep at night and can think of nothing else but ripping the tongues out of men who lie and cheat and steal, and rape. I'll make a necklace of tongues to wear around my neck, with every one of them.

Her voice cracked. She was out of breath. Words pumping out from within her belly. She was so angry and tired and didn't care if they thought she was crazy. She was tired of staying up at night listening to the cries of the dead of Los Llanos murmuring the stories of how they fought the Americans for seven years to keep their freedom and land. The men of Los Llanos had been caged like animals, taken away from their wives and children, to ensure that no one in Los Llanos dared to fight the government ever again. Forty-two years later, the dead were still pushing up against the earth in protest.

Santo was worried about Miraluz. He wanted to defend her, but she wasn't making sense.

—Santo, take Miraluz home.

—Explain to me, Don Chan, how is it that I believe in you, when you're such a coward?

She wanted him to hold her, help her sleep through the night, and be like other women her age, who thought about first kisses and their favorite shade of lipstick.

—Santo! Don Chan yelled. —Take Miraluz home. Your mouth will get you killed before you can do any good. How do you think we cultivated our garden? Con la mente. Don Chan pointed at his head. —By working together. He clasped his hands. —Now we're no longer hungry. That is something we can be proud of. The time will come when you can sacrifice your life, if that's your desire, but if you want to be one of us, then I suggest you do as I say. If not, go home and take care of your grandmother.

Miraluz refused to put up with Don Chan's condescending talk about her going to take care of her grandmother, as if she were a child. She walked away from him through the woods, toward her grandmother's house. Santo chased after her.

—Wait for me.

—Go be your father's pet. What's the point if I'm not allowed to disagree with him? He might as well be Trujillo, she said, pushing shrubbery aside, kicking the dirt, the dried branches scratching at her legs.

—That's not fair, Miraluz. My father has always encouraged you to speak your mind.

—As if I need his permission, she snapped back.

—Why are you so angry? What's going on with you?

Santo grabbed her shoulders, turning her around so he could get a better look at her. The fruits weren't being eaten fast enough. They were rotting at their feet. The soil was still damp from the recent rain. They could hear the faint music from a radio in one of the houses. She wasn't like any other woman he had ever met. She carried an impenetrable darkness, and yet she was fire that caught on and swelled, dangerous and beautiful at the same time.

—I hate him.

Miraluz pounded softly on Santo's chest, not understanding her fury.

—You're just anxious because so much is changing.

Santo caressed her face, lifting her head so he could look into her eyes. —But we must be patient.

—I never want to see him again.

—But what will he do without you? No one else talks to him the way you do. I think he likes it.

Miraluz pushed Santo against a tree. —Why do you follow me around all the time?

—I don't follow you. I walk with you because it's the decent thing for a man to do. Besides, I thought you liked my company. Why else would you kiss me good night the way you do?

Miraluz looked Santo over, his lean and tall build. His hair was long enough to tuck behind his ears. He was taller than his father, more handsome, a lot less balls. She grabbed them to see how big they were.

—What are you doing? Santo pulled away.

—You don't want me to touch you? she said, unbuckling his pants.

—Yes, but . . .

—Don't you want to touch me? she said, feeling inside his pants, his pubic hair dry and hot, her hands catching his balls and squeezing them gently. They were bigger than she'd imagined.

—Here? Now? Santo pulled up his pants and pushed her away.

—Don't you love me, Santo? Even if you don't mean it, will you say that you love me?

—But why do you say such things? I love you, Miraluz. I wanted to say it to you in so many different ways but I didn't want to scare you. I didn't know—

Miraluz shut him up by pushing her tongue inside his mouth, tasting the salt on his lips.

—Not here, not like this, Santo said.

Miraluz ignored him and pushed his fingers inside her, hoping he could fill the longing she was feeling for Don Chan. Santo didn't understand the fire in between Miraluz's legs.

—Someone might come, he said, looking through the cracks between the trees. She pressed her body against his and put his hand under her skirt again. She sucked on Santo's tongue, wondering why Don Chan patronized her in that way. Why didn't he want her the way she wanted him? She wasn't a little girl anymore. If only he'd given her the opportunity to please him, to stroke, kiss, and love him. Miraluz grabbed Santo's cock and pulled on it. He swelled in her hands and stumbled around her. She bit his ear, his lips. She dug his face into her neck, placing his hands on her breasts.

—I love you, Miraluz, Santo said into her ear as he thrust in and out of her wetness. He carried her in his arms, her back against the tree. Her ache didn't stop. The more he pushed in and out of her, the more emptiness she felt. She pulled him out before he came inside her. —I'm sorry, Santo, this is all wrong. She fixed her skirt, her hair, and then held in laughter, covering her mouth because of how strange she felt. —We can't do this anymore. She walked away from him.

—But what did I do wrong? Give me another chance, Miraluz.

—Leave me alone, okay?

—Can I at least walk you home? He asked, unclear about what had happened. He wondered if he was officially not a virgin, even though he didn't have an orgasm. He was mystified by the extraordinary and beautiful Miraluz who didn't make any sense.

Bronx
1996

Esperanza found Mrs. Hernández hunched over her husband, helping him reach over his spittoon.

—You gotta stop enabling him, Mrs. Hernández. He needs to exercise those arms or else the old man will lose his strength altogether.

—I can't stand to see him struggle. You don't know what it's like to feel like I do and watch him get weaker every day.

—Help him get stronger then.

Esperanza hung her sweater on the hook and pulled out her white blazer from her tote bag. It wasn't required, but she liked to wear it. It made her feel more professional.

—He ain't getting any stronger. But I ain't gonna let him take away the little I got left either. I have lots of things I still want to do in life. I was thinking that I wouldn't mind building something. You know, I have some money saved in the bank.

—I thought you didn't have any money. You can barely pay for medicine.

—Even when you don't got nothing, you have to save something.

Mrs. Hernández went about getting ready to go to work at the laundromat.

—On some days, I save two dollars, other days I save one dollar, but no matter what, I never touch it. I keep those dollars in the bank and pretend it's not even there. Let them accumulate and do what they will.

—Well, I don't know if you know anything about building, Mrs. Hernández. But you can't build much with a few dollars.

—You could if you've been saving a few dollars for as long as I've been here. Compound interest, it's called. You see, I wasn't lucky like those gusanos who got rich from the U.S. government. No, I came later, when the embargo had us all eating like we were on some low-protein diet.

Esperanza had always wanted to build something too. Nothing fancy. Just a white house, on a few acres, with three or four bedrooms. Elegant columns on the front porch. And some fireplaces. She had always liked the way they looked on television.

—If I told you how much money I've saved, you'd know how old I am. Mrs. Hernández started to laugh to herself as she pinned up her dyed black hair and pulled down the red sweater buttoned all the way to her neck.

—I got a lot of life in me yet, Mrs. Hernández said, sucking her teeth and pushing in her nose hairs before she applied her lipstick.

—I thought you were going to work.

Esperanza noticed she had more spunk than usual.

—I am. What exactly are you implying?

—You look very nice, that's all.

—You got to be ready for things in this world. Mrs. Hernández kissed Mr. Hernández good-bye on his forehead. —Now don't give Esperanza a hard time.

Esperanza took a deep breath, happy to be alone in the serenity the Hernández apartment offered. Mr. Hernández was reading the paper propped on his lap. She wheeled him over to the window so that he could seize the last bit of sunlight of the day. Then she rolled up her sleeves to do the dishes. It wasn't part of her job, but Mrs. Hernández expected her to do them, in the same way she expected Esperanza to prepare her breakfast. At first, it infuriated Esperanza. She pretended not to hear Mrs. Hernández when she asked her to make coffee or sweep the kitchen. But throughout the years, she began not to mind it. After all, she was practically living in the Hernández apartment. And she'd never gotten to see her own parents grow old. She never got to see Santo grow old. And when she grew old, would someone take care of her? She didn't want to think of it. She hadn't thought about meeting anyone new. When? How? Where? She didn't have the time. And the children, how would they accept such a thing, especially with Don Chan being alive? Besides, it's not like Bobby Ewing would be knocking on her door anytime soon, if ever.

All those hours she had spent with Mr. Hernández. Nearly four years. Longer than Bobby had been in juvie. Bobby would be returning home soon. How time flew by. All those years Mrs. Hernández had saved one dollar here . . . one dollar there . . . and now she had enough to build something. Esperanza knew that trick. That's how she'd saved the money to come to New York in the first place. But since her arrival, she couldn't accumulate a dime. Every dollar went to a plátano, a gallon of milk. And what was extra went to the bills. No matter what she did, she sank deeper in debt. She had only succeeded in accumulating days, months, years. If she could only sell all that time lost. Her time. Bobby's time in prison, Santo's unlived time. All lost. What would their lives have been like if they had stayed in Los Llanos? Or maybe if she would've stayed in D.R., and moved to la capital, maybe Bobby would've been enrolling himself in the university, like her sister's daughter, who was studying law. But if Esperanza had never left, she wouldn't have been able to send the twenty dollars here and the thirty dollars there that helped pay for her niece's books, paper, and pencils.

—At least we have each other, Esperanza told Mr. Hernández, who grunted when she said anything. She massaged Mr. Hernández's legs and feet. She read in a magazine that it was good for him. Maybe he didn't feel much, but it was good for his circulation. He still had strength in his legs though he refused to exercise on the walker.

—What's the point if I have nowhere to go? he slurred.

Esperanza combed his hair and trimmed his nails. She clipped his cuticles and pinched his cheeks for color. He didn't like that, but didn't fight her, either. She dabbed cologne behind his ears after she bathed him with a moist towel, and tried not to look at his privates when he went to the bathroom. He didn't say it, but she was sure he liked to have her around. Maybe even more than his wife.

Los Llanos
1964

It was the scent of burning cilantro that woke the people of Los Llanos. In the darkness of the night, they turned in their sleep, dreaming of stewed goat with onions and peppers. Fried tostones. Garlic and yucca. Roasted almonds. Grilled pineapples. —Is it morn-·ing? Don Chan asked Caridad, nudging her warm body, wondering why the chickens were awake.

Miraluz ran out of her house and saw them. The two men lighting the garden, their silhouettes a trace darker than the blackened sky, blending in and out of the dark shape of the trees and plants. Something went hot inside her, as if she were watching her own self lit on fire. She tried to find her voice to scream for help. She reached out her hand to stop them, as if they were close enough to get caught. —Don't, she wanted to say. Not the avocado tree, no, no, not that hibiscus she planted for her medicinal tea. And when she found her voice, when she realized that the burning garden was not a nightmare, she felt a callused hand against her mouth. A knife on her throat.

Caridad was the first to hear the shrill scream. —Wake up! Caridad yelled, wake up! Santo jumped out of his bed. And ran to find Don

Chan running out with buckets of water. The garden ablaze, as if the sun had dropped and was rolling in their direction. —They are trying to starve us to death, Santo told his mother as they ran after Don Chan. He had heard that the armed forces, under the present leadership of Reid Cabral, were on a mission to sabotage the lives of Bosch's supporters. —I saw him, Miraluz said about the man who scarred her arm with his knife as a warning. —His skin was like an alligator.

Don Chan walked toward the fire. Toward the people of Los Llanos, batting away the flames with damp palm leaves up and above the burning plants, to save the older trees that would take years to grow again. The children pulled from the earth the smaller plants that had not been hurt. The pomegranates had fallen, cracked open, exposing their bloody flesh. Don Chan took off his shirt and gathered mangoes, sour oranges, cherries, piling them up away from the fire and then running back again to salvage some more. He ordered the people to gather, to pluck, to harvest the last of their garden.

Weeks later, a car drove into Los Llanos with three men: a priest, a decorated military general, and a pale-faced man in a suit, ready to talk business. They were pointing to the acres of land. They were shaking hands.

—Don't look at me, he said to the foreigners and realized that, even when they looked over at his small wooden home, they didn't see it or him. They saw the well-watered soil, the acres and acres of fields that were suitable for cultivating cane and coffee to export abroad.

—Get off my land. Get out of my house, Don Chan said from his doorway. They were too far away to hear him. He recalled the fear he had felt during Trujillo's regime, when the thought of conspiring against the government was enough to get Don Chan killed.

Nueva York—Spofford
1996

Esperanza walked into the apartment loaded with bags of groceries. She had a full day. She was off duty for twenty-four hours before she had to return to Mr. Hernández's house. In that time, she planned to visit Bobby at Spofford. She dreaded taking that bus ride: all those sad-looking people on that bus going to that horrible place. If she'd beat him like she was beat by her parents, they would in turn put her in jail. But if the correctional officers whipped her Bobby, they called it "behavior management." Why was the law messing with things parents should be able to fix? She knew her child. He was no criminal.

—Hey, Viejo, you okay? Esperanza yelled over to Don Chan, napping in the living room, on the recliner. She placed the bags on the kitchen table. She peeled off her coat and turned on the overhead lights.

—How could you be in the dark all the time? It scares me.

—Can't a man have some peace?

—I don't have time for peace . . . I've two hours to get ready and catch the bus to see Bobby.

—I'm going with you.

—It's a long trip. It's better that you stay home.

—You can't keep me from him. Don Chan believed that Santo's incarceration was of Esperanza's making. How else was she able to wear all that gold around her neck? She was the one who was sup-

posed to be in jail, not Santo. How much money did she get for
turning him in?

—Fine, do as you will.

Esperanza slept on the long bus ride to Spofford. Don Chan couldn't
sleep on moving vehicles. Even when he was tired, he stayed on
guard. The bus stopped and started. Stopped and started. A man,
dressed in military gear, got up from his seat, leaving a large black
bag behind him. He stood in the narrow aisle and pumped his arms,
as if the pumping helped the bus move faster. The man returned to
his bag occasionally. His jerky movements made some of the passengers laugh. He wasn't trying to entertain. He looked inside the bag as
if it were filled with some unspoken treasure. He jerked his hands
up in the air when the driver talked through the intercom to warn
passengers of a delay due to a car accident ahead. His hands jerked
back down to cover his ears, as if the driver's voice caused him pain.

At first, Don Chan was amused. He assumed the man was a
Desert Storm veteran. He was young enough to have been part of
that war. Injected, perhaps, with the serum that protected healthy
young men from biological warfare but made them lose brain cells.
He had met some of those soldiers when they came back from the
Gulf, and saw how their hair had turned white from lack of sleep.
That their puppy eyes weren't from being in love, but from having
seen too much.

Don Chan watched the veteran and felt as if a coin in his hand
had flipped over and he could see the other side. Back in the inva-
sion of '65, he had spat at the young American boys who claimed
Santo Domingo. They appeared so arrogant. Invasive. But this man
caused something new to surge in Don Chan. Not anger, as he had
felt for the American soldiers who took the side of the corrupt military that overthrew Juan Bosch. No, he felt a profound sadness for
this soldier. What had been accomplished in his war? What had he
been forced to do and now could not sleep because of it.

When the bus moved, the veteran jumped up and chugged along
like a five-year-old, moving his arms like engine gears. The faster the

bus moved, the faster the veteran moved, and without realizing it, Don Chan moved his own arms. He too wore fatigues and held a gun. He too felt lost and scared and wanted to say "Fuck you" to everyone and chug along like a five-year-old. He moved his arms in sharp ups and downs, as if he was lifting something. People stared at Don Chan, but he didn't care. Maybe they should also join. Maybe if they all joined, the madman wouldn't look so crazy. Wasn't that how it worked? If you got lots of people to do a crazy thing, it became so normal that no one questioned it? Don Chan sneered straight at the woman holding a bag from Starbucks.

—Don't look at me like I'm crazy when you paid four dollars for café con leche. That's crazy. People back home make four dollars a day. You should give that money to someone who needs it.

He could already hear the resistance from people who felt they worked hard for their money and deserved little pleasures like whipped cream, cubed sugar, and double espresso. How could four dollars make a difference in anyone's life? Maybe buy some meat for dinner. Give them one day off to see their kids. Maybe the four dollars could give a person enough time to make a plan, to fight for better wages, to fall in love, to vote in a better administration. Just maybe, and then again, maybe not.

But why was Don Chan thinking of all those things as he moved his arms up and down. The man no longer chugged along with the bus. But Don Chan was caught up in his own movement. And what felt like big movements reflected off the glass windows as small movements. Maybe Don Chan wasn't moving much at all. He sat down and suddenly felt embarrassed for exposing himself like that in public.

At the juvenile detention facility, Esperanza couldn't sit with her Bobby without the armed guards watching over her. She cringed when she had to go through the metal detectors. They didn't allow her to bring him his favorite cookies or any good deodorant. They wouldn't let her hug him too long, because that was how the mothers passed things to their sons.

—Are you doing your homework? she asked Bobby.

Don Chan sat next to her and looked around at all the tables with parents visiting their children. The prison wasn't what he'd imagined it to be. The lights made everyone look green skinned and ill.

—Oh, you look so thin. Do they feed you okay? she asked. —I'm so sorry, Esperanza said, blaming herself for not being around enough. Esperanza's eyes watered, when she saw the coldness in Bobby. —My baby, she said. —You don't belong here with these tigres.

Bobby didn't understand what she was apologizing for. She must've aged at least ten years.

—C'mon, Mom, it's not as bad at it looks.

—Let her be sorry. She sold you out to save her ass, Don Chan said.

—You're such an evil old man. She wiped her nose, holding back tears.

—I want some time alone with him. Don Chan didn't like to talk to Santo while Esperanza was around. She was always interrupting him.

Esperanza wiped below her eyes to neaten up her eyeliner. She didn't protest. Don Chan couldn't visit Bobby as often because usually she traveled to Spofford directly from Mrs. Hernández's apartment. She excused herself to go to the bathroom.

Bobby knew what was coming from Don Chan.

—We're going to get you out of here, son. I don't know what deal you made to keep Esperanza out of jail, but we're getting you out.

—Abuelo, I'm not your son.

—No, son. They want to turn you against me. They want you to hate me. But hate is not born son, it's taught.

—Papi's dead, Abuelo.

—Dead? Santo, why you play games with me? They giving you something strange that's making you crazy? I'm trying to tell you I was wrong.

—Wrong about what?

—About everything. Don Chan looked around. He started to whisper. —It's my fault you're so angry. You were just a baby, you see, and I filled your brain with hate. You could barely say your name and I was asking you to say the word perejil. Perejil. Try and say that word, Santito. Try and say the word. See if you could roll your *r*'s or if your tongue betrays you.

—Calm down, Abuelo . . . that was a long time ago, Bobby said, reaching out to him.

—And I made you say the word perejil and you fumbled over the word, your tongue too short to roll yours *r*'s, and then . . .

Don Chan raised his arm, as if he were about to slap Bobby, but he was trying to use his arms as a machete. —Now, in the name of Trujillo, you die.

The guards approached him.

—Is everything okay? the guard asked.

Bobby looked over and nodded. Don Chan leaned closer to Bobby.

—Don't you think he deserves to die, Santo? Shouldn't we pray for his death before we go to bed? And you prayed out loud before bed, *Diosito, I ask you to take care of Mami and Papi and que se muera Trujillo también.* I'm so sorry, son, for pushing you so hard.

Another apology. Esperanza apologized, Don Chan apologized. But Bobby felt responsible for getting himself in his own mess. He shouldn't have taken the gun from White-boy Arnold. He shouldn't have shot the guy. What was he thinking? He wasn't thinking. He was trying to protect Dallas and Hush, but he wasn't thinking at all. Damn, Bobby said, getting angry at everyone. Angry at his father for dying on him. Because maybe if he would've still been around, he would've never left the apartment that day. Maybe if his mother hadn't asked him to get a job, he wouldn't have been dodging her and maybe he would've been home for ten more minutes, and White-boy Arnold wouldn't have seen him. —Fuck, Bobby said and slammed his fist against the table, forgetting where he was. Don Chan leaned back. The guards hovered over Bobby.

—Are you sure everything's okay? the guard asked Don Chan.

—You trying to protect me from my own son? Don Chan got up. To do what, he didn't know. But he didn't need protection. His son was no criminal. Why did they have him wear those clothes as if he were a criminal?

Esperanza returned, freshened up.

—Those guards must get something from feeling us up. I'm sure they don't need to be checking us so thoroughly.

Fifteen minutes: The loudspeaker announced that they were running out of visitation time.

—Can I hold his hand? Esperanza asked the guard, who looked away. —Don't worry, Bobby, I heard that if you behave in here and do well in your classes, they'll let you out early. That kid Arnold is supposed to confess that he stole the gun from his father. And when that confession is on record, it might help get you out of here sooner.

Don Chan became confused. Bobby?

—And Lalo continues to deny that you had anything to do with the deal. So that will help you a lot.

Sí, sí. Bobby was in trouble, Don Chan remembered. Why didn't Bobby say anything?

—Bobby, Don Chan said, as if seeing him for the first time.

—Hola, Abuelo. Bendición.

—Just like your father, Don Chan said, not believing how similar they were. —Makes it difficult for an old man to keep it straight.

—It's a'ight, Abuelo. I'm glad you came.

Los Llanos
1965

Miraluz was washing clothes by the river when Don Chan approached her. He waited before speaking to her. She had the head of a bull, the nature of a goat. She was still angry from their last conversation because Don Chan had sent her off to her grandmother. But she deserved it. She was wise for her age, but he was three times as old as she. She should know better than to talk to him with disrespect.

—What do you want? Miraluz turned around and spoke first. The words pierced him like a dagger.

—So that's how you greet an old friend?

Miraluz shaded her eyes from the sun. He had gained some weight, which he wore well. His hair was long, falling over his face. The unbuttoned blue guayabera exposed a thin undershirt.

—Don't you see I'm busy?

Miraluz had tried to avoid him. But there was nowhere to hide from Don Chan. His name lived in every kitchen.

—We miss you, Don Chan said.

—I want nothing to do with a movement of cowards.

—Did you not eat from the garden? Don Chan said. —The garden was part of the movement.

Miraluz gathered the clothing and sheets in her basket. Don Chan looked handsomer than she remembered. Her grandmother didn't understand why Miraluz refused to return to the fields, why the mere mention of Don Chan made her slam the tin dishes against the buckets of water.

—I saw you planting in the gardens today.

—With everyone leaving Los Llanos, I'm not sure if it will ever be the same. Maybe she too would have to leave Los Llanos to find work in the nearby cities.

—Of course it will. It's only the beginning, Don Chan said. You saw how people started to come together and make plans for developing Los Llanos when they saw the fruits of the garden. It's only the beginning toward realizing our independence. We can't lose hope.

—More than hope has been lost. People are afraid and hungry now.

—We're organizing to go into the capital to put Juan Bosch back into office. There are some rebel groups there we can align with. We found a place to work out of, in a clinic near the Ozama River.

—And what do I have to do with it?

Miraluz walked away. Don Chan followed her. She shook her hips because she felt his stare.

—You're one of the few in Los Llanos who knows how to read and write. We need you.

—I told you, I've no time to make a man with alabaster hands more powerful.

Miraluz hung the washed pieces on the line by her house. The sun poured over them. Her dress, drenched in river water, clung to her skin. Don Chan tried to help her. She looked over at him and lifted her chin. She stretched her lips to one side of her face in suspicion, biting her bottom lip, attempting to disguise her joy at his visit. He needed her. Why did it take him so long to figure that out? Besides, even if Don Chan was wrong about Bosch, she had always wanted to go to la capital and see for herself the energy of the city.

—I'll come. But you can't tell me what to do.

—Fine, Don Chan said. —As long as you don't put anyone in danger, you can do as you please.

—Will we bring the weapons we found?

—Yes, just in case. I hope we don't need them.

—And I don't want to be treated like a woman. I want you to treat me the way you treat Santo or any other man.

—As you wish.

Miraluz wiped her hands with her dress. She tucked the wisp of hair flying into her eyes behind her ear, and reached out to shake his hand.

—Very well then. We leave at the end of the week. Don Chan held her hand for a long while. Almost four years had passed since he had first met Miraluz. So much had happened in that time: Trujillo's death, Bosch's win, Los Llanos's independence. And now they were witnessing its fall unless they did something to change it. The laundry flapped against him. He moved away from it and held on to her hand. Her body moved toward him for an embrace. He held her. Felt her breasts press against him. He gently combed his fingers through her hair and placed her head against his chest for fear of what might happen between them. Señora María Magdalena's call for Miraluz from inside the house broke their trance. Miraluz unfolded herself from his arms and pressed her lips together, acknowledging that they shared a secret.

← STO. Domingo Libre 0.km
Ciudad Trujillo →
Sign posted on the border exiting Santo Domingo, 1965

In April 1965, before the U.S. occupation, Esperanza had first noticed Santo from the windows of her house. He was stationed over at
the clinic by the Ozama River.

—Get away from there, you'll get hurt, her father said, angry that
after all the progress the city had made under Trujillo's regime, it was
now being destroyed. Newly constructed buildings were riddled with
bullet holes.

Esperanza had no intention of living like her father, who lived in
fear when Trujillo was alive and had been even more afraid of him
since his death. She watched the unshaven men across the street
through her bedroom window when her father left the house. Her father thought it was a clinic, but through the curtains, she saw that
something more was going on inside that small house with the red
cross painted on it. She watched Santo stand in front of the clinic
smoking his cigar, wearing his pants low around his waist. She admired the way his arm muscles flexed when he pulled bloody men
into the clinic. He was so very brave, she thought as she watched the
chaotic streets teeming with torn limbs, children hiding under slabs
of wood, trying to stop the ding in their ears from the loud gunshots,
the flying dust, the burning tires that filled the streets with smoke.

At night, she listened to Los barbudos' laughter, and the boom of their voices filled her head with dreams about their adventures around the city, maybe even around the world. She wanted to travel. The study of maps was her favorite lesson in school, as well as the stories of people who took long journeys despite the odds. She fantasized about escaping from under the eyes of her father so she could learn Santo's name, but her father locked up the gates at night and kept the keys inside his trousers. During the day, her mother carried the keys in her housedress. Since the takeover of the presidential palace by civilians, school had been canceled. Her father insisted that they didn't leave the house unless he could ensure that they were safe.

—I have to go to your tía's and pick up some supplies, her mother said one day.

She handed over the keys to Esperanza. —Take care of each other.

Her mother made sure Esperanza locked the gates as she climbed into the car parked in front of the house.

—We don't have much time, Esperanza said to her sister and ran to the mirror to fix her hair. She put some cooking oil on her lips and pinched her cheeks. She told her sister to watch her back.

—Are you crazy? Pura said. —What if something happens to you?

—Nothing will happen to me. Haven't you noticed how tranquil the city is? Esperanza hurried across the street. There had been a cease-fire for two days, which gave the city a different kind of tension. The air was dusty, the sky a strange orange gray. Santo watched Esperanza peer into the clinic's window.

—Can I help you? he said from behind her.

Esperanza's eyes widened. She looked around, afraid her mother would catch her. Her sister waved for her to return from across the street.

—I have to go, she said, making sure Santo got a good look at her.

—Wait, what's your name? he asked, wondering how old she was. At least fifteen, he hoped.

Then she ran across the street, locking the gate behind her.

Esperanza continued to search for Santo out her window. Each time they caught each other's gaze, Santo casually walked by and slipped her notes. *What's your favorite color? Flower? Day?*

When he walked by her window, she would whisper the answer. *Esperanza. Azul. Rosas. Lunes.*

On Sundays, her father braved the trip to church, along with other faithful followers. Instead of taking Holy Communion, Esperanza lost herself in the crowd and sneaked away to meet Santo, who would wait in the small confession room in the back. When she stood, face-to-face with Santo, when she looked at his dark eyes, his tall, lean build, she forgot her father, she forgot they were hiding, she forgot that the city was in a civil war and that her father would never approve of him. Santo was a guerrilla, a rebel. Her father was working on Balaguer's campaign and yearned for the kind of stability Trujillo had offered the people. And Santo's beard was a sure indication that he could not care less about order.

For weeks he wrote her letters about the garden in Los Llanos, about La Lupe's melodic wail, which cracked ice with its purity and passion, about his father being from China, about Los barbudos in Cuba, all the things that made her think he was a man of the world. A learned man. Not like the boys she knew at school who couldn't carry on a conversation. So when Santo embraced her as if he had known her his entire life, she decided that he was going to be hers. And the thought brought on a perverse smile for stealing a kiss with her father's enemy, to be with a man who didn't care for laws, government, and order. She had had enough of such things under her father's roof. But she couldn't tell Santo about her father, who was a distant cousin to Emilio de los Santos, who, along with right-wing lawyers and businessmen, had deposed Juan Bosch in '63. No, she wouldn't tell him anything until she was sure he loved her.

Quepasó Street—Spofford Juvenile Detention

Each time Don Chan took the ride to Spofford Juvenile Detention, he hoped to see the veteran again. Esperanza grabbed the window seat and he took the aisle. She pulled out the cookies she'd brought Bobby and unwrapped them to offer some to Don Chan.

—I don't eat sugar, Don Chan said. —It's tragic how something so sweet killed so many.

—I could never do anything right by you. Esperanza took a bite from a cookie.

Don Chan didn't respond. He looked past her, out to the East River. She pulled a photo out of her wallet.

—He sure does look like him, doesn't he? she said, thinking about how much Bobby was changing and looking more like Santo, who was an indio version of Bobby Ewing. And when Santo wore that cowboy hat, ay papá, qué hombre! Esperanza buried Santo in the cowboy hat she had bought him for his birthday. —But my Bobby has a hardness to him that Santo never had. He hasn't learned to wipe his own ass yet, and he's already finding big trouble, spending the best years of his life locked up. It breaks my heart to think of it. Nothing like Santo, who wouldn't hold a loaded gun even if his life depended on it.

—What you talking about? Santo carried a gun around all the time. We all did, Don Chan corrected her.

—It wasn't loaded.

—It's because you made him soft.

—What?

—I don't know how you did it, woman, but you cut off Santo's balls, and I swear I've never recognized him since.

—Watch your mouth. Only 'cause you old don't mean you could be spitting nastiness like that.

—Before he met you, Santo was ready to die for his country. You can ask Miraluz—she was always by him.

—Don't talk to me about that woman. She acted like she had more rights over him than his own wife.

—But it's true. He would've never been in prison if you hadn't gotten yourself into trouble.

—You don't know what you're talking about. So please let's not fight. Not on this bus. People are staring at us.

Esperanza looked behind her and to the seat next to her and noticed that people were napping. She hadn't realized how bad Don Chan's memory lapses were. There was no point in fighting with a man who didn't make sense.

—You always care about what people think. Even in D.R., I remember you were so worried what the neighbors would say. That's what has us in this hole in the first place. We so worried about making a scene that we don't do anything at all.

—Por favor, not now. I'm tired. I have to work tonight. What do you have to do, eh?

—I've done plenty, Don Chan said.

—You live in your dreams, old man. You never knew Santo. All this time you talk about him as if you were of the same mind. But you didn't know him.

—What do you mean? Don Chan clenched his teeth. He wanted to get up to stretch his legs, to get away from Esperanza's flowery perfume. She was so thick she took up part of his seat and hogged the armrest.

—Nothing, forget it. It's not important.

—It's important enough, Don Chan said.

—Santo was living on borrowed time.

—What?

—He started working for Balaguer behind your back or else they were going to kill you both.

—Lies. You speak lies.

—Everyone knew. But no one said anything to you because they were afraid of what you might do. Esperanza was whispering.

—Do? What on earth does that mean?

—I'd rather not talk about it . . . I rather not. Esperanza went into her purse to do something with her hands. Anything. The bus wasn't moving fast enough. He wasn't going to let her sleep.

—You made him afraid? Don Chan said.

—He had reason to be afraid, Esperanza said.

—We were all afraid. But one can't live in fear.

—Jodio, Viejo . . . you don't remember anything like it was. You're rewriting history.

—But what do you mean? Don Chan couldn't rely on his own mind. What had he forgotten?

—It's the past. It doesn't matter.

—The past visits me every day. It matters to me, Don Chan said.

—Remember? We were at a bar?

—What bar? What night? You're making up lies, woman.

—There was a man. He came to sit at our table and said, —I'm looking for el chino de Los Llanos. And placed a machete to Santo's neck.

—You lie, woman. I don't want to know any more of your lies.

—And I saved your life, remember that? Esperanza said.

Don Chan turned his back on her and didn't know why she kept talking when he told her he wasn't interested in fiction.

—And I told him, buy me a drink first, so I can say farewell to my husband. I'll never forget his face, the executioner's jaw dropped, right on the floor. —Señorita, it's your lucky night, 'cause I could use a drink, but the Chino will buy it. The executioner waved over the bartender to serve us a round of drinks.

—When did you ever go to a bar with us? These are pure lies, Don Chan insisted.

Santo and I had just gotten married. I reached out to Santo, whose leg was banging against that table. I was so afraid for you both. So I told the executioner, —*My father is a de los Santos, from la capital.*

And he said, —*I loved a de los Santos girl once. She wouldn't date a gardener. So I got a job in the government and then she said she wouldn't date a man in politics.*

—And then you slammed your hand on the table and said, —*We had a garden, but bastards like you burned it.*

Don Chan had a faint memory of something, but no, Esperanza wasn't there. He didn't remember that.

—And Santo told the executioner, —*Tell Balaguer that he doesn't have to worry, there is nothing in Los Llanos but mosquitoes and weeds.*

—Woman, you speak lies, Don Chan said and was feeling his heart against his chest.

—How can you forget? You wear the scar from the machete on your hand. Look for yourself, Viejo.

Don Chan didn't want to open his palm. Esperanza struggled with him and then gave up.

—You promised him that night that it was over. You told him that it would take at least another forty years before Los Llanos could start trouble again and by then you'd be dead.

—But I'm not dead, am I? Don Chan said, banging his scarred palm against the armrest. —I'm still alive and now I can't do anything in this body. All I can do is watch people die. Everyone die. My wife, my son . . . Every day I see things fall apart and I can't do anything. Maldita sea! Why is this bus taking so long?

Esperanza handed over the water bottle to Don Chan, and some tissues. She looked over at him as he blew his nose and thought how any day that little engine of a man was bound to lose all his steam. There was no point in getting him worked up. He did a good enough job of that himself.

Nueva York to Santo Domingo
1996   1965

Don Chan couldn't get over how devious Esperanza had always been. Ever since Santo laid eyes on her, he had acquired a faraway look that meant he no longer belonged to him or the fight. But Santo was never a fighter. For his heart, perhaps, but for politics? Don Chan could not recall Santo ever holding a hand grenade. It was Miraluz who sat day in and day out beside Don Chan. Her fingers danced on the typewriter, her gun nestled between her legs, and bullets weighed down the pockets of her shirt. Miraluz was the son he'd wished Santo had become. If she suspected a traitor, she pulled a gun. She made sure to protect Don Chan, and fought the war he didn't like to admit was happening.

The past was in Don Chan's living room. Santo was in the living room. He was everywhere, in the odd pieces of junk he brought in when he scavenged streets late at night. Santo was in the echo of the songs he sang when he would get ready to leave for work.

—Esperanza wants me to think that because a hungry fool needed a fix, he killed you for a cheap car radio and a gold chain. But I know better, Don Chan said. —Don't worry, son, Don Chan told the photograph sitting on the shelf. —Miraluz and I will figure out how to bring you back home.

• • •

Santo was supposed to raid the president's palace, along with all the Invisible Ones, in 1965. But Santo didn't get farther than across the street before he was back in the headquarters. Santo had tripped over paint cans, spreading red paint over the concrete. The paint stuck to the soles of the guerrillas' shoes, marking their trails and endangering their hideout.

Soon after, Santo confessed, —Papá, I met this woman.

—A woman? There isn't time for such things. Don Chan slapped Santo over the head with his hat.

—Why didn't you take off your shoes? Better you sit and do nothing at all. With those troubled feet, the Yanquis and the military will be spanking our behinds before we gain control.

The marines had landed to ensure democracy, but immediately sided with the armed forces that were subscribers to Trujillo's politics.

—Why don't the Yanquis let us figure it out for ourselves? It's hardly democratic for the U.S. to impose democracy on another country! Don Chan yelled over to Santo and Miraluz.

—And Fidel and Ché eat like kings while their people fight over rationed eggs, Santo said.

—Don Chan, should we kill him for speaking against Ché? Miraluz said, pointing her pencil at Santo while he dramatically fell to the floor.

—Not today, I still need him for some errands. But tomorrow perhaps, Don Chan said with a fake laugh and thought how the politics of a person and the way they ruled a government were full of contradictions. Everyone's hearts jumped when they heard planes fly low over them.

—All that fighting, and for what? As if some rocks and machetes could put a dent on those airplanes flying above us, Santo said, thinking about Esperanza and the way she gazed at him, which made his body swell into manliness. Unlike Miraluz, who made Santo feel inadequate because nothing he did satisfied her.

A young woman ran into the headquarters. —They're giving away guns in el Parque Independencia.

—What are you all waiting for? Don Chan commanded the

young men taking afternoon naps on the floor, —Go get them.

—*Están ametrallando nuestra ciudad,* announced Radio Santo Domingo. The rebellion was multiplying.

—Look at this mess! Santo ran out to carry in a woman with a flesh wound on her thigh. —People are too greedy, and greed makes people violent. That's why the revolution will fail, Santo said to Miraluz, who ran for the disinfectant and cotton.

—Don't say that. We'll never win if you think like that. People are willing to sacrifice, right? Miraluz asked the wounded woman who cried over the pain in her leg.

Santo spent his days writing songs about the soot, the blood, the loud explosions, the rain of dirt and rocks, bloody eyes, the collection of fingers found in the rubble along with the used bullets and burned vegetation. He sang about the wallets looted from dead guerrillas, about the sneering U.S. Marines, and the savagery of the government's military being armed by them. The women raped on their way home and the gold teeth yanked out of soldiers' mouths. The more he witnessed, the harder it was for him to go outside and face any of it. He spent his time singing, encouraging the wounded to sing along so they would forget the pain they were feeling.

So while Don Chan geared up to walk his beat on the streets, making sure the younger members of the Invisible Ones stayed out of harm's way, Santo took a stroll across the street and leaned against the walls of Esperanza's house, pretending he was taking a smoke.

Santo's cockiness amused Esperanza. He held on to his cigarettes as if he were the classiest thing since champagne. His shirt clung to him; he smelled of petroleum, burned wood, like the wet earth and sea.

—Give me your handkerchief, she said, poking her fingers through the gates to touch a piece of him. She had no idea how afraid Santo was, just standing there, a clear shot, vulnerable against the military. Her smile burned a hole in his heart.

Santo sat by the light of the small window, facing the street, waiting until Esperanza gave him the signal, flashing her mirror into his eyes so he could visit with her again.

•••

At night, in the thick of the darkness, the scores of gunshots made Don Chan fear the numbers of the dead the next morning. He bought the newspapers, searching for names he recognized.

PATRIA
VOCERO DE LA DOMINICANIDAD

6 Páginas   10 Centavos

AÑO I   SANTO DOMINGO   17 DE JUNIO DE 1965

THE YANQUIS CAME TO "SAVE LIVES"
Civilians Assassinated by the Gringo gun on June 15 and 16 in the Tragic Massacre of Santo Domingo

—But they're just children, he said to anyone listening. He passed around the photos of the dead young men and women, half dressed, bandaged, waiting to be buried, to his compatriots and begged them to be careful and not to take careless risks. What had he gotten them all into?

He took a ride with Miraluz to the president's palace. Since his arrival he had yet to visit it because the days slipped through his fingers with the endless work at the headquarters.—I just want to see something, Don Chan told Miraluz, who chauffeured him in the borrowed car. An image he had seen in the papers had been itching away at him. It was a photograph of Caamaño with the palace as a backdrop.

—Must bring back memories, Miraluz said, looking at the palace, the iron gates, the pronounced dome, the four guards in front, the almond trees at the entrance. —You had some balls to sneak into that place while Trujillo was still alive.

—Let's get out of here before we get killed, Don Chan said.

He looked away from Miraluz, out the window, to hide the feelings of betrayal consuming him. In 1961, the Trucker drove him to a palace so Don Chan could prove his invisibility. But it wasn't the president's. And if he hadn't gone to the palace in 1961, what building had he stolen the letter opener from? Don Chan chewed the last of his cuticles wondering why had the Trucker misled him? To save Don Chan from killing himself? Who else knew the truth? The Trucker must have conspired with someone.

Don Chan returned to the headquarters suspect of all his comrades. The Trucker had fled in 1963 to Puerto Rico. Don Chan had no one to turn to, to be angry with, to blame. Suddenly he felt alone and vulnerable. Because of this he talked all the time, telling people what to do, uneasy when people sat around. —A movement requires movement, Don Chan said and then demanded that if they didn't have anything to do, they should walk in place to rile up some energy in the room. He feared that he had misled the Invisible Ones into a war that could never be won.

All those hungry, shirtless soldiers with sticks, rocks, guns, attacking planes and tanks, running for cover. People were holding up mirrors outside their windows to blind the pilots. Why are they attacking the women and children finding cover at home? The radio announced that the families of the pilots had been abducted and brought over to the Duarte Bridge to discourage the pilots from attacking the area. The casualties were many, many unidentified.

—Can we just stop everything so we could think for a minute? There has to be a better way than this mess.

—It's too late to think, Miraluz said. To think, to ask too many questions, would make it all too confusing, make a person way too sympathetic with the enemy.

—But people don't know what they're fighting for, Don Chan told Miraluz in dismay. The people were angry with their bosses, at the gasoline prices. They wanted a sure meal, a good roof over their heads, and access to good doctors and education. Women waved their babies outside their windows to discourage bombing. Everyone with a gripe was letting off steam on the streets. The poor were vandalizing, betrayed lovers were venting on merchants. Couples were fucking to prevent the extinction of the Dominican people. Don Chan wanted it to stop. But it was too late. To stop would make the deaths of many a waste. To continue meant that more would die without any certainty of freedom.

—We might not win this war, said Miraluz—but like my great-grandfather told me when he was still alive, if the Yanquis plan to take us over, they won't be able to do it without seeing some blood.

Don Chan stood on guard by the door. Miraluz stood close by him. They were on duty to guard the stockpiled ammunition. And to care for the wounded who were too weak to return to their houses. Santo was standing by Esperanza's window.

—He's asking for trouble, Miraluz said, disappointed by Santo's weakness with his heart. Don Chan wasn't weak. Miraluz pulled her body close to him, pressing herself slightly behind him. He hadn't bathed in days because there had been no water since the day the marines landed. He reeked of cigars, earth, damp leaves, and fresh meat.

A truck pulled up in front of Esperanza's house. Two men approached Santo.

—What the fuck is that boy doing? Don Chan said.

Miraluz picked up her gun from the floor.

Don Chan held her back.

—No, wait. Santo could talk his way out of it, Don Chan said. —Better not to expose ourselves unless necessary.

Don Chan checked for his gun. It was loaded. He had yet to use it. He refused to use it. Just carrying it around felt like too much power for a man. He would feel better if each and every gun around the world was destroyed. Why couldn't they return to the days when men fought with fists and knives? The killing was slower that way. The destruction reparable. Fighting with one's hand allowed more time for negotiation, for regret, for sorrow, for loss. But the gun was too fast for the spirit.

The men patted down Santo's body. He was taken inside the house. Miraluz and Don Chan waited by the door of the clinic.

—What do we do? Miraluz was ready to break into the house to save Santo.

Don Chan held her back and waited until one of the men walked out of the small house made of cement. It was the man with alligator skin.

—It's him, Miraluz said, pulling on Don Chan's arm.

—Him who?

—The man who burned our garden, she said, as if he were once again holding a knife to her throat. She touched the scar on her arm.

—Are you sure?

—Certain, she said.

Don Chan went toward the man. He felt like a ghost. No one could see him, or hear the yell that blew out of Don Chan when the man's body fell back with the blow of Don Chan's fire. As if the bullet had penetrated Don Chan, traveling through his own body. The rage in Don Chan found an unexpected peace and comfort. The perpetual cloud of dust and insistent heat that surrounded them held Don Chan up so he wouldn't fall. The gun gained the weight of another man. Too heavy to hold.

5

Quepasó Street
1997

Don Chan looked over at the pile of calendars on his nightstand. He had a calendar for every year since he moved to New York. There were six. He reached over and marked an X on Monday. *Bobby's coming home.* Who's Bobby? Don Chan juggled his brain, trying to remember why he would write such a thing on the calendar. He pressed his hand against the window. He needed a sweater. It was April. Had to buy the seeds for the beets, lettuce, and corn, get them all ready to plant. Before the tomatoes. That's next month. He pulled out his notepad and made a list of the things he would pick up at the store. Caridad loves the perennials, maybe he could plant some of them on the side of the house.

Don Chan got dressed and walked out of the apartment. He waited for the elevator. He had forgotten something. Something didn't seem right. He walked back into the apartment and into his bedroom. On his way out of the apartment, he remembered his coffee. But Esperanza was already in the kitchen. What was she doing there?

—I made some coffee. It's not as strong as the one you make.

—No, it's fine. Don Chan was confused but let her serve him a shot of espresso.

—I took off from work, because I'm picking up Bobby at the center. God, I miss him. It will be nice to have him back.

—I guess it would, Don Chan said. Determined to get to the nursery before it got crowded. There was nothing worse than a crowd of people trying to buy seeds.

Don Chan checked for his scissors and pad in his pocket before he exited.

The nosy old woman who popped open her door in the morning was waiting for him.

—Hola, Don Chan, she said, pushing her cat back inside.

—Buenos días, he said and remembered that he needed to buy his newspaper and arrive at the luncheonette before someone claimed his booth. And yes, Bobby was coming home. And things started to catch in Don Chan's mind, like a bobbin and thread, one stitch at a time. All his markers were falling into place. His newspapers were ready; the streets were waking up from their slumber; the sanitation trucks swept the gutters; the cop ticketed the late birds who didn't rise on time to move their cars; bodega owners pulled out benches to pile up crates of yuccas, greens, and onions; the gates from stores were halfway up as merchants set up for a day's business; the young men who crowded up against the walls, as if they were responsible for holding up the building throughout the day, were still asleep.

One youth staggered out of his building and sat on the front steps waiting for a car to pull up. When Don Chan's eyes met with the young man's, he recognized the look of despair in his eyes. After the U.S. occupation, many of the youth in the Invisibles Ones had that look. Lost. Wounded. Pissed. Unarmed. The youth hid his face farther into his hood.

Bobby. My grandson, Bobby, Don Chan thought. That's who's coming home.

—Well, that's good news, isn't it? he told the lady sitting at the booth next to his, who smiled back in agreement.

He checked his notepad. Tomatoes, corn, lettuce. What is this? It couldn't be that important if he didn't remember what it was.

Esperanza listened to Radio WADO while she readied herself to catch the bus to Spofford.

—Qué bonito día! The radio host dragged the last word up and over an old Johnny Ventura merengue.

—What a beautiful day, Esperanza repeated, slamming the snooze button. She often dreaded Mondays, but Bobby was coming home. And for the first time in a long time, she wasn't working on a Monday. Two days off in a row. It felt as if she were on vacation. She drew open the curtains and looked out to see the weather, delighted that it was warmer and that she didn't have to wear a heavy coat.

Esperanza ran over to the kitchen to boil a pot of water, so that by the time she showered, the water would be ready for the plátanos. After her shower, she ran back into the kitchen, trying not to wake Dallas. She peeled the plátanos, took out the eggs and the salchichón from the fridge, then threw the salchichón slices in hot oil, and while one side cooked, she ran back to her room to put on jeans, a blouse. She prided herself on her ability to multitask.

She opened the small tin on her dresser. It used to hold cookies, but now she puts in a few dollars every day, even if it's just one. She slips it in and pretends she lost that dollar, or played it on the lotto. If Mrs. Hernández could save enough to build something, maybe by the time she gets to be her age, Esperanza would have enough to build her house. Sometimes she put two dollars, other times she put five. She never counted how much, as if by looking at the money for too long it would make it disappear. Or by having the strength not to look at it would help it multiply.

She prepared Dallas and Don Chan's breakfast. He wouldn't eat it, but she didn't care. She had a day off. She could make her family breakfast. Then ran back into her room to do her makeup. After years of the same routine, Esperanza could put her makeup on blind. She powdered her skin, and lined her brows; she applied the lipstick in one stroke and patted on crème blush, which she spread with her fingers. She feathered her bangs and tied the rest of her hair back into a ponytail. She puckered her lips in the mirror and wondered: If she had been born in the States, would she have been an actress like Rita Hayworth or Raquel Welch? But she would've changed her name, maybe into Hope Saint or Saint Hope. Something American sounding.

—A woman could only dream, she said, playing with the cowboy hat she'd bought back when she still had credit cards, hoping to wear it when she finally took that plane to Texas and became a wife to a rancher. She turned around the portrait of Santo on her altar. He was always staring at her. He didn't need to know that she had such thoughts. She breathed in that unusual moment of complete privacy. —A woman's got to be ready. Mrs. Hernández was right. And this is the only life I know of, Esperanza said to the vibrant woman staring back at her, who was anxious to see her son come home so she could make him a real meal and put some meat back on him. She tied a silk scarf around her neck, finished buttoning up her blouse and lacing her black sneakers that had a small wedged heel to give her more height.

She ran around the apartment, turning on all the lights to wake up Dallas. —Wake up, you lazy bum, she said, breakfast is in the kitchen. Make sure you lock the door and close the windows before you leave for school. And change the sheets on Bobby's bed. My baby's coming home.

Juvie had Bobby on a clock, and when he returned home, he kept to that schedule to manage his days. On some nights, he'd wake up and forget where he was. When cars backfired, he threw himself against the floor and slid only his head under the bed, because his body no longer fit under it the way it did when he was a child. There were no guards to beat on him, no one to mess with him. He was home and the only other person in the room was Dallas, who was all grown. She felt like a stranger.

Esperanza put bunk beds in their room so that they had more privacy. But Bobby and Dallas were estranged enough to treat each other like an instrument. *Turn off the lights. Open the window. Can I change the channel?* Dallas no longer had her own room, and she resented his arrival. She moved some of her clothes into her mother's room to get ready for school in private. She sighed heavily when she realized the small inconveniences Bobby had brought on.

When Esperanza was home, she tried to have everyone eat dinner together, again like a family.

—You can register for community college, now that you earned your diploma, Bobby, Esperanza said as she served him dinner.

—Ma, I'm not ready. Can you give me a break?

—Why do you give him a break and not me? Maybe I should go to jail. Maybe that way you won't keep asking me about homework.

—Please, Dallas don't start with me, Esperanza said.

—I'm gonna get myself a GED.

—El GED? Esperanza pronounced it "head," and said it as if Dallas had announced that she wanted to join a cult and shave her head.

—Sí, Mami, a head.

—I did not sacrifice my life so you could get a GED. She wanted a real, certified diploma from her, one she could frame in the hallway among all the other accomplishments she hoped they would achieve.

Don Chan sat down and was surprised to see Bobby.

—Where've you been? Don Chan asked.

—Traveling, Abuelo. Seeing the world.

—That's good to travel. It's the best way to learn. I'm from China, you know.

Bobby sat on the front steps of his building. Overwhelmed, he tried to take in the world that he took for granted before juvie, in homeopathic doses. A few drops at a time. The questions: Why? How? Who? Where? The suggestions: Why don't you . . . Can you . . . Shouldn't you . . . The worrying: Why are you out so late . . . Why do you look so pale . . . Eat something . . . Drink something . . . The demands: You can't just stay home all day without working . . . Mami, aren't you going to make Bobby do shit around the house, too . . . Watch after your grandfather and sister. You're the man of the house now. The smells: burned sugar. If Esperanza was making flan, that meant she was in a good mood or she needed a favor from someone. Pepper steak. Grilled onions, bloody steak, tossed in a pan. All he could eat. Ice cream. Shot up to his forehead and coated his stomach, preparing him for a nap. Had it always been so sweet? Remote controls. Jeans. Choices. Girls. Quepasó Street was full of them. Winking, smiling, ignoring, flirting. Girls who had become women while he was gone. The new crop that was too young to know about what had happened to him. Beer. Weed. The nudie channel. The ability to go wherever he wanted, whenever he wanted. All his senses were tuning in, reminding him of the narratives tucked into his past. If he wasn't careful, all of it would come at him too fast. He wished he could put all of it inside a computer screen. Cut and paste everything he was rediscovering into one file, the way he had learned to organize his computer exercises from the tutorials he finished in juvie.

—Computers are not that difficult, the instructor at the detention center told him. —Not if you take your time with it.

When he first worked on a computer, every button opened up a file, a layer, erased something he had worked on, and then the lost file became a mystery. He didn't think he would ever figure it out. But when he started learning the computer programs, for the first time ever he felt he controlled something. He used to look forward to working on that keyboard. It was four hours a week. A reward for his good behavior. Four hours and Bobby's fingers searched for a way to *delete* the people who irritated him and *tab* forward into a better place. And now that he was on the outside, he felt *cap locked* and *bold*. Everyone could see him: **EX-CON**. They assumed he was dangerous. That he had messed up his life in some irreparable way. There were no *backspace* or *insert* options to fix what had happened three years before. He needed an *escape* button to start over.

Dallas turned fifteen and could finally wear makeup: black liquid eyeliner that had people around her way calling her China. Her hair slicked back tight around the temples added to the effect.

Instead of a quinceañera, Esperanza promised Dallas that she'd buy her a leather jacket when she had some extra money. Not some off-the-truck jacket from a local store, no, her mother was going to take her downtown, to Macy's, so she could get something nice. Dallas didn't need a big party like some of the girls in her school were having, with damas and caballeros and dresses, patchworked from images they found in magazines. She wasn't about to make herself up like Miss America as if she were some doll on a wedding cake. She'd rather have new clothes. A pair of jeans. Some cute sneakers like the ones she saw in the store the last time she cut school and went exploring downtown. That way, in the fall, when she started her junior year, she'd be ready.

She walked up Quepasó Street wearing her mother's perfume, leaving a trail of flowery scents behind her. It was eight AM and people were already out. Car stereos boomed against fogged-up windows. Mothers rushed their kids to day care. Grandmothers pushed wheeled carts heavy with their forty-year-old sons' dirty laundry. Boys posted on the street corners, in front of the buildings, running upstairs to work inside the neighborhood drug laboratories, concocting the next superdrug to be sold downtown on Wall Street.

—Hey, mami, what's your name? one of the guys at the corner yelled.

—Oh please, Dallas said. Like they didn't know that her big brother had shot a guy and was back home from jail. They better not even try messing with her.

But she liked their attention and swung her hips, implying that she could handle all of them though they weren't good enough for her. Dallas didn't want some loser punk hanging on the corner. She wanted a guy who made money. With a car. Not a drug dealer who wore gold like it was going out of style. She'd seen enough people die. She didn't need to be worried about her boyfriend getting shot or going to jail. And she wasn't about to wait two or three years for some guy who was stupid enough to get himself in trouble. She was tired of waiting for things, let alone a man. She especially didn't want no mama's boy who took his mother's money to take girls out. Who had his sisters doing all his shit just as she had to clean up after Bobby when he was around. Dallas had bigger plans. Like finding herself a guy with a future. Who knew how to take care of himself.

She took the train downtown, fantasizing about the boyfriend she would meet one day. She cut her eyes at girls who checked her out, and let an old lady sit in her seat so that she could lean against the doors and listen to new beats on her Walkman. Why couldn't she meet a guy with a two-seater convertible? They could cruise slowly up her block, and then peel off on Broadway so that everyone would know she was gone. Driving in a car low enough to the ground where she could feel the speed inside her thighs. Everyone would envy her. And if Hush wasn't acting stupid, Dallas would let her squeeze in the car with them: the two-seater convertible, boyfriend with the green eyes and dark, curly hair and a stomach like a washboard, because maybe he would be an athlete or something. And he would drive them to places like BBQ, Red Lobster, or IHOP. And they would bring back doggy bags and show off the logos and act like they had it like that and everyone around the way would know that Dallas had access to wheels.

Dallas was so not feeling school. But Bobby was home, and she didn't know if she could trust him yet. She'd hardly seen Bobby because they wouldn't let her visit juvie. So he felt like a stranger. The fact that they could incarcerate a juvenile but not let one visit was contradictory to Dallas. Whatever, Dallas didn't care to take some wack-ass bus to the Bronx anyway, when she could have the house to herself for like a minute.

She didn't want to go to school, but she knew she had to. There were only two months left and school would be over. She had already cut school on Friday, and if she cut a class back to back it most definitely would get a letter sent home, and what if she missed pulling out the letter before her mother got to it, like it almost happened the other day. Her mother was hemming a new pair of pants. She had asked Dallas to read her the mail.

Dallas divided the mail between junk, important, and unidentifiable.

Important. To Mr. and Mrs. Colón. Re: Dallas Colón.

—Speak up, I can't read your mind, Esperanza said, threading a needle under poor light conditions. —We need brighter bulbs in here. Maybe I'll put fluorescent lights in all the rooms.

—They want you to donate money, Dallas lied, slipping the letter on the junk pile with the other paper she intended to throw away.

—Me donate? What they think, I'm rich? I should be a charity. Forget them. Read me the other stuff. I don't have time for all this.

Dallas tried not to cut the same class two days in a row and always showed up for the tests. If it was a Thursday and she had missed Wednesday, then she tried not to miss Friday. If she had gone too far—which she sometimes did—Monday was a good day to start fresh and make a strong appearance in class, which meant she would have to ask a lot of questions and take notes. Teachers liked that. On the days she didn't go to school, she sometimes went back home and watched TV in her room. Don Chan couldn't remember when she was home or not. But now Bobby could. Most times, she'd chill with friends in Central Park or at someone's house. Or go shopping for things she didn't have the money to buy.

Anything was better than going to class. It was not like she needed a lot to entertain her, but the teachers were killing her with the monotony of their voices. She struggled to keep her eyes open.

To not yawn. To follow an idea. No one around her was paying any mind to the teachers either. They passed notes, they flirted, they fell asleep or were lulled by medication. Lots of kids at school had dead eyes from the meds. Their skin puffed up, making them look fragile, doll-like. Even if the teachers were nice and Dallas tried to learn, the announcements from the office went off on the intercom every few minutes. *Reminder that all seniors are expected to assemble in the auditorium, eighth period.* Loud, piercing sounds. Crash, boom, scratch on the mike. *For students attending Sunday's field trip, you will not be allowed to ride on the buses without a signed permission form from your parents.* Quiet for about ten minutes, until the intercom interrupted the lesson again. Kids loafing out in the hallways, banging on the door, starting fights. Dallas couldn't deal. She held her head with her hands, glancing periodically at the windows, praying for time to move faster so she could get on with her day.

B high school was supposed to be better than her zoned school, GW high school, but Dallas still felt that it was the biggest loser school on the planet. No one had chosen to be there. She got in through a lottery. Hush got into Bronx Science, the brain school, the specialized school. It changed her. She started on some punk shit Dallas didn't understand: heavy metal, black lipstick, blue streaks in her hair. She turned blanquita overnight. Hush also became secretive and didn't like to hang out on Quepasó Street.

—Can we just chill at your house? she would say.

—Who you hiding from? Dallas asked her.

—Everybody. Then Hush would change the subject. Snuggling up under Dallas's comforter, often staying the night and skipping out in the early morning to go to school.

Dallas struggled through her morning classes, and was proud of herself. She made it through lunch period without cutting out. She was running late to Mr. Estrella's math class because she stopped in the bathroom to reapply her lipstick. She hadn't done the homework. He assigned everyone a series of analytical questions to prepare them for the PSAT. The dingy hallways were lined with broken fluorescent lamps that blinked like strobe lights. The walls filled with the ghost of old graffiti. She noticed some kids were smoking in the stairwell, the vents exposed them. Freshmen often forgot to cover the vents.

At the end of the hallway, she also noticed that the emergency EXIT door, usually chained closed, was wide open, and no one was on guard. The open doors were like two arms. The sun poured in, blinding her. The doors wanted to hug her. They opened up so she could taste a little bit of the outside world.

Dallas made her exit unnoticed. Dropping her head, pulling her backpack off her shoulder, she concealed her face from the guards in the front of the school. It was almost summer, warm enough that she could take off her jacket and tie it around her waist. No one followed her out. She left seventh, eighth, and ninth periods behind.

She took the train to the end of the city, then hopped on the Staten Island ferry. It was a boat. It had a view. It was peaceful. Sometimes she took it twice, back and forth, because the movement was calming. When she did her homework, the ferry was a good place to concentrate. No one bothered her.

—She did not say that to you, the woman sitting behind Dallas said to another woman.

—You better believe she said that to me, said the other. —If I don't go to work tomorrow, she said I best not come back. After eleven years. White folk don't think we human. I swear they don't.

They were around her mother's age.

She wanted to be closer to her mother. But it was never the right time to talk with her. Her mother was always telling her what to do, giving her chores. Expecting her to listen, to agree with her. Esperanza complained. Dallas tuned out. —Can't you keep your eye on what you have to do? Esperanza would push her out of the way to do things herself, because Dallas burned the rice or left the bleach on the shirts for too long, or forgot to take the water out of the iron. Her mother worried about oxidation, the house catching on fire, thinning cotton. —If your father was here, Esperanza would say.

Dallas bounced out of the train on Thirty-fourth Street, walked into Macy's and through the coat section, which had shrunk to half its size to make room for the spring and summer collections. She found the jacket she had been eyeing throughout winter, which she was hoping her mother would buy for her. It was 50 percent off on the clearance rack, plus another 15 percent off with the coupon they sent in the mail. She tried it on. The smell was strong, pungent, new. It made her look sophisticated. Different. Like she belonged in a magazine ad, with some cute guy asking her for a cigarette. Except Dallas didn't care for cigarettes, maybe a martini with an olive. She had never tried one, but it looked good on TV. It had to be better than beer. The jacket was butter-soft leather, genuine, Italian, and would have to be taken care of. She would let no one else wear it. Maybe Hush. But only when they were together and she could watch over it.

—Can you put this jacket on hold for me? That way I can bring my mother to pay for it, she asked the short, stocky saleslady, who must've started working in Macy's when it first opened.

—Yes, dear. We hold merchandise for one week. What's your name?

Dallas felt very grown up when asked the question.

—Dallas Colón.

The woman stared at her, waiting for a real answer.

Dallas showed her the school ID card.

—Oh, the saleslady said and nodded and put Dallas's leather jacket on a special rack. —We'll see you soon, dear. Have a nice day.

With Esperanza working so many hours, Don Chan began to pick up the mail. He went through the mail as if expecting a letter. In the five years he had lived in Nueva York, no one had sent him anything. No one called, except for Miraluz from time to time. She'd call and tell him that she had checked up on his little house in Los Llanos, that the land had become quite savage since the death of Doña Caridad. But everything was fine. —You know how nothing changes here, she said. —En la lucha, como siempre. She told him about the nest of hummingbirds on a tree nearby and the wall of roses that was coming up on the side of his shack, which would please him. But it did worry Miraluz, because it meant bugs would start to eat up the wood beams. Unless she found someone to paint it.

—Is that it? he'd ask her, knowing that there had to be more. It was Los Llanos after all. What had happened to all the land? The people? The Invisible Ones?

—People are busy, Don Chan. —I lost my reception job at the hospital after the strike.

—There was a strike?

—Isn't there always? But don't you worry, I've been working in la Zona Franca, it's awful with this heat, but prices are going up here so fast, I had to do something. I said I never would go there, but, Don Chan, at my age . . . they don't hire women my age anymore. Those overseers want young girls to ogle. The only reason I got work at the factory was because, remember Ernesto Santa María Delosquesaben's uncle, Chucho?

—Yes, I remember.

—Well, his uncle's father's cousin oversees the place. Ay Viejo, no es fácil, the economy has us choked.

—Miraluz, you should be running the country by now.

—I ain't giving up, Miraluz said. —I've been organizing the women at the factory for a union. The owners have the gangs bullying us. But don't worry, they haven't gotten to me yet.

Don Chan sat at the kitchen table feeling alone. His grandchildren ignored him. Esperanza waited for him to die. No one cared about him anymore. Yes, he had the nosy neighbor next door who took to inviting him in the afternoons and preparing him soup. And she listened to Don Chan tell her stories, and there was the van driver who no longer waited in the van for his customers, but parked in front of the luncheonette to start off his day with Don Chan. And the bodeguero who counted on Don Chan to tell him the weather and watch the store when he needed to go to the bathroom. But when Don Chan died, would anyone really miss him?

Don Chan looked through the letters. Parents of Dallas Colón? He looked at the envelope up in the light. Precinct? Policía. He opened the envelope. Date and time. Truancy notice. Don Chan kept the letter.

—What does this say? Don Chan asked Bobby, who spent his days watching sports and his night out on the streets. —Is she in trouble?

—She's cutting school.

—Why would she do that?

—Beats me, Bobby said and wanted his grandfather to leave him alone so he could watch the last few minutes of his game.

—I'm supposed to be keeping an eye on you two. Now Esperanza's going to start on me over this.

—Don't get me involved, Bobby said. It was between Dallas and his mother. He had enough to think about.

•••

The next day, Don Chan drank his café at the luncheonette. He made a note on his pad. *Follow Dallas.* He waited for Dallas to leave the apartment.

—Where you going, Viejo? Oswaldo yelled over at him from behind the counter, pointing at the newspapers he had left at the booth.

Don Chan had gone to sit down and read the papers when he recognized Dallas, walking by the luncheonette. She waved at him.

Something told him he should go after her. He wanted to tell her something before it was too late. Soon, he would no longer be able to walk the streets of Nueva York without a companion. It was bad enough he had to use a cane. He never imagined this would happen to him. That he would have to rely on someone. That his body would no longer obey him. That morning, he almost couldn't hold his bladder long enough to piss in his pot. Don Chan gathered his papers in one hand and propped his weight on the cane.

She was in trouble. He was sure of it. He had to warn her. Trailing behind her, he recalled the long walks he used to take only to find that his teachers had canceled classes. There was no schooling, but he earned big calluses on the soles of his feet because he never wore the right shoe size.

Don Chan checked for his hat on his head. He was walking on Broadway. That intersected Quepasó. Where was she going? Dallas descended into the train station. Don Chan, afraid of tripping and falling, grabbed the railing. He forewent the turnstiles and walked through the side door that was open. Boys catcalled Dallas from across the platform. What if something happened to him? If he ended up bedridden, because of a sprained ankle, and never recovered? Any minor accident to remind his body that his time was up. He looked around at the strange faces. Where were they all going? Don Chan searched for Dallas on the crowded train. He held on tight to the pole, cold and greasy, infested with people's germs, people who picked their noses, asses, and ears. Thousands of germs seeping into his hands. He noticed he was on the red train. He pulled out his pad and wrote it down. What if he forgot? He said his name to himself many times. Don Chan Lee Colón de Juan Dolio. Don Chan Lee Colón de Juan Dolio. It calmed him.

—There she is, he told the man with the solemn face. Dallas bopped her head while reading the ads on the train. She must be going to school. He watched her slip off the train at Seventy-second Street and Broadway. He followed her. His leg fell asleep.

—Maldita sea, he said, dragging his leg against the pavement with most of his weight on the cane. He started walking closely behind her, afraid he would lose her in the crowd of humans rushing to their destinations, talking on their cell phones, lugging babies, shopping bags, briefcases, instruments, pets. Excuse me. Get out of my way. Sorry. What the fuck you looking at?

Dallas checked her reflection as she walked by all the store windows. Adjusting her ponytail, reapplying her lipstick. Where was she going? —Wait, Dallas, I have something to tell you, he said, lifting his cane and pressing his weight against it as he lifted his leg over uneven sidewalks, dog shit, and litter. Dallas, he said out to the crowd, his voice hoarse, like an old recording. Faint. From another time and place.

It was time for his nap. It was nine thirty AM. She couldn't hear him. She had her headphones on. *Guantanamera / Guajira Guantanamera.* She sang out loud. He knew that song. It used to come out of his small radio in D.R. His backyard, under the shade of their mango tree, roosters crowing, a cold Presidente beer on the back of his neck, and Celia Cruz cooing *Yo soy un hombre sincero . . . Ay, papá,* thought Don Chan, skipping a beat as he thought back to the days when he could still dance. *De donde crece la palma,* he sang to himself on Broadway, looking for the palm trees and El Malecón. And the sun beating down on his skin wasn't hot enough. Don Chan looked around at all the people rushing around him. Missing everything, every opportunity to live. —*Y antes de morirme quiero / Echar mis versos del alma.* It was from José Martí's poem. *Mi verso es de un verde claro / Y de un carmín encendido / Mi verso es un ciervo herido / Que busca en el monte amparo.* And now one hundred years later, Dallas sang Martí's words. *Con los pobres de la tierra / Quiero yo mi suerte echar: / El arroyo de la sierra / Me complace más que el mar.* What

would Martí think of that? Don Chan wanted to call up Martí and
tell him the news. Martí said, Before I die, let me sing from the soul.
He predicted carmine flames, his verses a wounded deer searching in
the mountains for protection. As a child, Don Chan's father made
him memorize that poem. How easy it was for Don Chan to recall
Martí's words.

Penny for your thoughts, a nickel for your kiss
A dime if you tell me that you love me
Guantanamera . . .

Wyclef and Celia Cruz mixed it up and Dallas sang along with them.
When she listened to the music while walking around the city, she
felt like she was in her own music video. Everything welcomed her.
Everyone glided along with her, the cars slid on freshly paved tar,
children smiled and bounced about without a worry in the world.
She was free to guantanamera anywhere she wanted. That was until
she saw the police officer, a cute one with platinum hair and eyes
like kiwis, sitting in his car, looking at her suspiciously.

Dallas pretended not to care that he was staring a hole into her
head. If she showed fear, she was screwed. She was almost a junior,
which meant that she could hook up her schedule and the cop
couldn't even start with her. Technically, because she was still fifteen,
if he wanted to mess with her, he could. And it was the end of the
month and the truancy cops had their eyes wide open. They had
quotas to meet.

She went to Tower Records on the corner of Sixty-sixth and
Broadway, a good place to spend some time. The cop looked bored
and wouldn't be going anywhere. She pulled off her sweater, tied it
around her waist. Checked her book bag so she was more comfortable to browse.

—Excuse me, miss, can I help you with something? A security
guard looked at Dallas as if he were about to interrogate her. —Are
you all right?

—Yeah, just looking for something.

Dallas didn't look at him so he wouldn't remember her face. Arcades and record stores took bravery. Freshmen hid there. But Dallas was not a freshman. She was almost a junior, wearing makeup. She could've easily been in college. She was in City College. That's right. Studying something. Undecided. That's what all the college guys who stepped up to her would say. Which made Dallas assume they must not be too bright.

She walked through the isles of rock, classical, and movie sound tracks, looking for a good spot to squat. She dashed over to the leather chair when she saw a woman getting up from reading a magazine. The chair had a listening station beside it. —You need to have the eye for it, her father would say about parking a car. Dallas believed it was the same for places to sit. She programmed the first CD, raised the volume, wore the headphones and listened while she read through the magazines someone had left on the floor. She watched people come and go. The line formed at the information counter, the guy with bad skin was having trouble with the computer. People moved around the store, none of them worried about the cop sitting outside. None of them having to go to school. She didn't want to think about her grades. It didn't matter how hard she worked, all semester she floated somewhere between a D and an F, the Doomed and the Fucked. The teachers wrote on her report cards that she wasn't working up to her full potential. All semester she leaned back on the F grade and then when she saw the semester closing in, she panicked at being left back. Dallas reached out to the D like a harp, reaching out to its beautiful round belly, believing that if she could just touch the other side of it, she would no longer be Fucked. Just Doomed. Which was better in the bigger scheme of things. Defiant, Devious, Dicked, Dwarfed, Deranged. Damaged, Desperate, Damned. She couldn't think of any beautiful words that started with D. Her report card would be filled with them, and her mother would be pissed. She had to get her mother to Macy's before Esperanza saw her grades. Dallas consoled herself by thinking that lots of successful folk didn't do well in school and still made it big. School was not the only way. She could work her way up. She could try for a job at Tower Records. That would get her mother off her back.

She smiled at the guy restocking CDs. The name tag said his

name was Peter. He looked like a white boy. Maybe he could hook me up with a job, she thought.

Don Chan entered the record store. At first, he thought it was a library. When he pulled out a CD from the shelf, he realized that they were those things Dallas and Bobby played music out of. Mini LPs. Digital, they said. You could change the songs with a remote control. They used words like *shuffle, rewind, fast forward, repeat.* Don Chan didn't understand how so much music could be stored in such a small object. He'd rather listen to music when he could see the needle play a song.

He went toward the escalators. Don Chan stepped on them and was startled by the speed at which they moved. He tried to get off, but he was already halfway up to the next floor. He anticipated stepping off of them, lifting his leg high up enough so his shoes wouldn't be eaten by the machine. —An invention for the lazy? he mumbled.

What was Dallas doing in a place like this? Shouldn't she be in school? He found her sitting on the chair. Her body bent over a magazine. Bopping her head to music. She was tapping her fingers against the magazine pages. Did she want to play? Santo played. Where was that piano of Santo's? Maybe he could fix it up and give it to her so she could play it? Maybe she wanted to sing like her father. *Sí, sí,* he knew exactly where it was in his bedroom, in a box on top of his wardrobe. Caridad had wrapped Santo's piano up real nice to save it from the humidity.

Don Chan started to leave the store to get it for her. He climbed on the moving stairs and walked out into the bright lights. He looked north and south on the busy street. The sign said Broadway. He lived a block away from Broadway. He looked at the sun to make sure he was walking in the right direction. Quepasó couldn't be too far off.

—Abuelo's missing, Bobby said as he ran into the apartment.

—What are you talking about?

Dallas was making dinner. Something experimental. Chicken

with pasta. Esperanza would be coming home that night from work. Dallas intended to juice her up so they could go to Macy's. Besides, Dallas was in celebration mode. She had met a boy. Peter. At Tower Records. He had a job. He was going to be a famous DJ and fall in love with her.

At first, Peter looked shy, but during his lunch break, he stepped up to her.

—Wanna eat upstairs? I got thirty minutes, he said, glancing at his watch.

—Do I know you?

—Don't act like you weren't checking me out. You smiled at me. Dallas's face turned beet red. —You have a big ego, man.

They had lunch. They talked. He knew people in the music business who would help him with his career. He rhymed for her.

—What you think?

—For a white boy? Not bad.

—I ain't white.

Dallas did a double check. —You look it.

—Gotta open your mind, girl. Get some information. Color is a concept that keeps us from transformation.

—You're always rhyming?

—It's the way I keep myself in shape. If I don't practice, I'll sound like an ape.

—That's pretty bad sounding already.

—I'm playing with you. 'Cause you're cute.

—You think I'm cute?

—I wouldn't be talking to you, would I?

Bobby checked all the rooms again. He called Esperanza at Mrs. Hernández's. She had already left.

—He's not here, next door, or at the luncheonette. The guys on the corner said they saw him going into the train station.

—Why would Abuelo do that?

—We need to go look for him. He could be in trouble. He's like a hundred years old. Maybe something happened to him?

Bobby's stomach twisted up. He was preoccupied with a thought that had never occurred to him before. With Don Chan gone, he would be the last of the Colón family. The end of the line. And he wasn't ready for it.

—Calm down, Bobby. He knows where we live.

—He forgets what day it is. You think he'll remember his address?

She couldn't be bothered with Don Chan's condition. That's what they called it, la condición: the condition of the fantasmas, where yesterday and today walk alongside each other. Sometimes it was funny, but recently Dallas had less patience for it. Especially when Don Chan left the house to meet Caridad, at Heaven's Gate, and she had to go get him. For Don Chan, Heaven's Gate was the corner of the roasted-chicken place where the smell of chicken was so strong, you felt like you had a full meal before putting anything in your mouth. Don Chan said heaven tasted like roasted chicken.

—We have to go out and look for him, Bobby said.

—That's what the cops are for. They will call if they find him.

—He doesn't talk to the cops. He thinks they're after him. Remember?

—Not all the time. Abuelo gets his wits when you push him a little. Let's give him some time. It's still early.

—Mami's gonna freak! Bobby paced in and out of the kitchen. He exhaled, but had trouble inhaling. He sat on Don Chan's recliner and rubbed the leather on the armrest. He scared himself with his own reflection in the mirror. Breathe. Bobby put his hand on his stomach to help him focus, to keep tragic thoughts away. Breathe deep, in and out of the belly. What if Don Chan was in the emergency room? What if no one could identify him? He hadn't realized how much Don Chan meant to him. How he was the last link to his father.

The police precinct told them they had to wait twenty-four hours before they could file a missing-person report.

Don Chan returned before sunset. They were all waiting at the kitchen table and stood up at the same time to grab him.

—Broadway is one long street, he said, looking over at them, and then headed straight into the bedroom.

—Pero, Don Chan, are you all right? Esperanza called after him. She examined his face and squeezed his hands and arms. Everything was in place.

—Abuelo, what happened? Bobby asked, relieved.

—Sí, sí, I'm fine. Why all the fuss? Went for a walk that's all.

That night, Don Chan lay on his twin bed with his clothes on. Every muscle melted into the mattress. He pulled his sheets up to his chin. He flexed each foot to feel them on his body. It was never warm enough in Nueva York. Not enough for his bones. Sleep terrified him when he was tired. If he shut his eyes, would it send him off to the other side? Every day he felt his spirit inching away from his body. It sat beside him, like a shadow. His body lagging behind in the physical world and his soul watching him and waiting for a good moment to depart.

He refused to close his eyes voluntarily. He waited until sleep took him. Sometimes it took a long time. He watched the shadows of passing cars race across his ceiling. Listened to the drunken loner outside his window slurring words to himself. The restless German lady with the hairy upper lip who lived above them paced throughout the night, moving chairs from one side of the room to the other. He listened to the soft squeaking of the mattress from the woman who lived alone, next door. She had a visitor that night. By the length of the squeak he could tell if the lover was stopping by or planning to stay with her.

Bobby heard that his old friend Ed was doing well. Working from home with his own clients. —Dime con quien tú andas y yo te diré quien tú eres, was his mother's refrain. And Bobby was convinced that if he hadn't been with Lalo and Arnold that day, he would not have gotten into the mess he did. He wanted to be around people who were doing something with their lives. Maybe something positive would rub off.

Ed lived alone. The dismembered computers in his apartment resembled a tragic automobile accident. The computer parts and all their colorful wires waited to be operated on and put back together. He had one lamp on his desk, a door propped over two file cabinets. A big television mounted on the corner, high up, near the ceiling. Two folding chairs for company. His fridge a collection of beer, cola, and Tupperware, brought over by Ed's mother so he made sure to eat. In his bedroom, he had a pile of clothes on a chair and the bed unmade, always in transition, implying he hardly slept. Ed had no phone, only an Internet connection and a cell phone for emergencies.

Bobby wanted that life. One where he never had to see people. Where no one told him what to do, and he worked when he felt like it. For Ed, when he was working, day or night was the same thing.

—Can I see? Bobby asked Ed about his computer.

—Do what you want, bro, Ed said and sat on the floor to roll a joint. —I need a couch and a table. He hunched over on the floor to handle the weed.

—I know this program. I learned some of it at juvie. Bobby looked into the computer screen. Rolled around the mouse and got excited from it.

—If you wanna learn some more, I got the tutorials right here.

Ed bounced up to pull a crate out of his kitchen cabinet filled with CDs and books.

—Every time you learn one of these programs, you become more valuable. Sometimes I clock a hundred an hour, Ed said. —You can come over when you want, bro. I won't sweat it. 'Sides, I got myself a freelance gig at night . . . so I give you the keys, you go crazy.

—For real? Bobby wondered, if once Ed lost his high, he would change his mind.

—It's no biggie. We got to help each other out. You know what I mean? Been trying to get some of the fuckers on the corner to learn something so they could make some money, but you know how it is. People want shit easy. He took a drag from the joint rolled tight and thin: delicate. —You want some?

Ed passed the joint to Bobby. If he turned it down, would he break their agreement? Bobby hadn't smoked anything but cigarettes. He was afraid weed would scramble his brain. It was hard enough for him to keep his thoughts straight. He took a hit and let the smoke fill his lungs.

—Smooth, no? Your friend Lalo manufactures this shit in his apartment. It keeps me straight, you know what I mean?

Bobby returned home in the early morning when everyone was sleeping. He was floating. Everything looked the same but different. Exaggerated, colorful, animated. He went to the kitchen to check out what his mother had left him on the stove. Popped the dish into the microwave while he contemplated a beer. Soon I'll have my own place, Bobby thought, looking around the kitchen where nothing got thrown away. His apartment would be empty space.

Hush gasped when she saw Bobby sitting by the window. She hadn't planned on staying over, but since Esperanza was working that night, Dallas told her she could sleep over if she wanted to.

—Don't she have a house? Esperanza had asked once, when she noticed that Hush was another mouth to feed.

—Who are you? Bobby checked Hush out. He wasn't sure if it was the weed or if a real person was actually before him. He squinted and bent forward to take a better look. There was a stranger in his kitchen. Bobby looked away and then back. He reached out to touch her. He felt off balance. His body felt heavy, his arms ached as if he had been carrying weights. The microwave beeped. He sat down.

—I'm Dallas's friend. She let me crash here. Hush noticed that Bobby's T-shirt stuck to his pecs from the sweat. —I was just getting some water.

—Where's everybody? he asked, recognizing Hush as the same girl who stayed at their house back in the day before prison. She was with Dallas when he got arrested.

—Sleeping. It's like three in the morning.

Hush had grown. Had she always had those eyes? He opened the refrigerator door to do something with himself. The refrigerator light revealed her in small parts. Eyes like big chocolate almonds. Her nipples poked out from under her tank top; he imagined they looked like Hershey's kisses. His mother had to have some chocolate hidden somewhere.

—You're Bobby, she said, remembering her crush on him. —I heard you were back, but I hadn't seen you around.

—I'm just avoiding people. Can't be outside without folk bothering me. I don't want to get myself in trouble, that's all.

—It's gotten pretty bad since you were last here. It's called Operation Clean-up. The cops are everywhere, undercover.

—Worse? Been having cops feeling me up since I was eleven years old, waiting for me to fuck up. Where you going, son? Got no business standing around, son, and now you telling me it's worse? I guess they gots to find peops for all those prisons they're building.

Bobby walked over to the fridge to get something to drink, forgetting he already had a beer opened on the table. He started to laugh at himself. He was so out of it. He handed it over to her so she could take a swig.

—It's only good when it's cold, she said.

—You too young to be drinking?

—Who says? Besides, if you're gonna give me a hard time, why did you offer? Hush curled up on the chair at the table. Pulled out the dish from the microwave for Bobby. —Eat, you look hungry.

—You're funny, he said and his cheeks hurt from all the smiling he was doing. Hush was a bad idea. She was Dallas's friend. Dallas's age. Fifteen years old. His stomach turned with the thought.

—You shouldn't drink around men, they can take advantage of you.

—You're not a man, you're Dallas's brother.

—Got a dick like any other man, especially the way you dressed; I'd be more careful.

—Don't that dick have a brain?

Hush slipped on Esperanza's housedress, hanging on a hook by the sink. She wrapped it around her.

—That's more like it, Bobby said, nodding and smiling.

—It's a hundred degrees in here and I gotta cover up 'cause you don't trust your own dick. I thought you were a different kind of man, Bobby.

—You talk like a woman, Bobby said.

—What?

—You don't talk like a girl, you talk like a woman.

Hush assumed it was because he had been incarcerated so long that he had lost touch with things.

—Well, I'm surprised you talk so much. I heard juvie ate your tongue.

—My mother told you that? She be starting rumors.

Hush tucked wisps falling into her face behind her ear. Hid her smile away from him.

—Nah, your mom is cool.

Hush held the beer in her mouth before swallowing. The aftertaste was sour and made her tongue numb. Bobby took a bite of steak, being careful not to make funny noises. He could hear himself chew.

—Well, when you spend so much time without anyone to talk to, you realize that the word is often wasted on bullshit. I rather keep to myself.

He washed the food down with the beer, licking his lips and making them shiny.

—So why you talking to me if you like being so private?

—I don't know. He watched her pull her hair out of a knot and shake it loose around her head. She yawned and looked at the time.

—If I don't sleep, I'll never get to school on time tomorrow.

—It's good to learn things. Bobby pointed at his head and raised his eyebrows. He pretended he wasn't staring at her as she walked into his bedroom. She was probably sleeping on his bed. Smelling up his sheets. Shedding her hair all over his pillow.

Dallas sneaked up on Peter. He waited for her outside school, leaning against the parking meter. She pulled off his baseball cap. He turned around to hit her and when he saw who it was, he grabbed her under his arm. They walked toward his father's place, not too far from school.

She was nervous. Peter was in college and had probably had sex with plenty of girls before. This was the first time they'd be alone. She had met him a few times at work. But he took off from work so they could spend *quality* time together. He wore a Puerto Rican flag around his neck because his father was stationed in Puerto Rico when he was born.

—I was born in Puerto Rico too, Dallas said. —I was there seven months. My moms went there after D.R., before New York.

—Oh yeah? Peter wasn't listening. He was checking her out. According to Peter, Dallas had talent. That's what him and his friends called it when a girl had big breasts: talent.

Peter pushed open the door with his foot and held it so Dallas could walk in front of him.

His father's apartment was a one-bedroom. Peter slept on the couch when he stayed with his dad, but since his dad wasn't home, Peter walked Dallas to the bedroom and left her there while he turned on the radio. It smelled like dirty socks and sweat. It was a male smell that Dallas knew all too well, from sharing a room with Bobby.

—Wanna drink something? he asked as he peeled off one layer.

—Why not? she said and he disappeared again to the kitchen. He didn't bother to turn on the lights, so Dallas didn't either. There was enough light coming in from the windows. She sat back on his father's pillows. They hadn't been washed in a long time. They smelled like morning breath.

Dallas opened the bedstand drawer. Condoms and lubricants. One had been used. By his father, she hoped, and wondered if she was in way over her head with Peter. She closed the drawer and smiled over at Peter, who had a glass of orange juice in each hand. He handed one over to her, but there was nowhere she could place it. She inched away from the drawer with the used condom, the dirty pillows and tried not to look repelled. His father's room was filled with little papers and business cards. His floor a mess of shoes and clothes, stacks of newspapers and magazines.

Peter was in his first year of college, so he wasn't that different from the seniors in her high school. Dallas forgave him for being an undecided major, because he had a dream of becoming a DJ. —You can't major in music in a community college, he said, putting some of the clothes on the bed over on a chair. He awkwardly leaned on one side of the bed, over rumpled sheets. She had made out with guys in parks, under the stairwell at school. She had even fooled around with guys while Hush waited outside the door. But Peter and Dallas were alone. Alone. No one knew where she was, and no one was waiting for her.

He pulled her hair out of her ponytail. The masses of thick curls fell down to her shoulders. He curled one in his finger.

—They are like waves, he said. —Big ocean waves.

His kiss was wet and sticky from the orange juice. His tongue slathered her face and neck.

It wasn't what he said that made her like him. It was what he didn't say.

—Who made you? he asked, touching her skin with the back of his hand. Pressing his fingers on her lips. —They're so full.

When his hand moved south, Dallas moved it away from her breast.

—Slow down, Peter.

—Can I at least see them? I promise I won't touch, just look at them, promise.

—Fine, but no touching. Dallas went under her shirt and unclasped her bra and stood up from the bed to show them to him. She was ready for this. She had shaved her legs, armpits. She had borrowed some of her mother's scented lotion and rubbed her entire body with it. She was ready to go the next step with Peter. They had met a few times and they had kissed. Long kisses. In the stockroom of Tower Records. She lifted her T-shirt, looking everywhere else but at him, two hands on each side for a clear viewing. Peter sat on the edge of the bed and pulled her by her hips and licked one breast. And then the other.

—They're so brown, he said. —I love the color of your skin, and pressed his pale hand on her belly, making her feel uncomfortable.

—And? She was pissed off but not sure why. —You promised no touching, she said. His hands felt good but strange. As if her breast were not part of her body. His lips were cold.

—I'm not touching.

He extended his arms and sucked her nipples.

Dallas pushed his forehead away from her. And put her shirt back on.

—Happy? she said, with an eerie feeling that her father was watching her. She could hide from her mother. But her father could be anywhere.

—What's the matter with you? Peter said. —They're beautiful.

—Can we slow down a little?

—So what do you want to do? He looked irritated.

—We can dance? Like people do when they are alone, in the movies. You know the man, he dims the lights, and turns on some music. And he says, *Can I get you anything?* And the woman says, *Something to drink would be fine.* And they toast to something silly like life, money, health. And he pulls her to him and dances with her before he kisses her. And she moves away and gets very shy with him only to grab him and give him a passionate kiss.

—Are you for real?

Dallas pulled him off the bed and turned up the radio. Without all his layers of clothing, Peter had a strange body. His shoulders were big and wide and the rest of him was bony and narrow.

—C'mon. Please.

Dallas tugged at Peter's hands that were clammy and cold. The music was hard rock, while she was thinking *bachata*. Peter grabbed her waist. He'd had a shot of whiskey before meeting Dallas and was wishing he had some left. He grabbed her hand and placed it over his heart. He pulled her in tighter so she could feel his erection come through his pants, against her pelvis. He hated to dance, but girls were complicated. They needed lots of foreplay.

—You do this with all the girls, don't you? Dallas accused him. He smelled like a blend of underarm odor and detergent.

—Never.

—You want to trick me into sleeping with you.

—You're bugging, he said and jumped back on the bed thinking Dallas wasn't going to put out like he'd hoped. He grabbed a lighter from among his father's things. —The problem with you girls is that you watch all that TV and you expect life to be one romantic thing after another. But you don't realize that in the movie, they pack a two-year relationship into two hours and edit out all the dead time.

—Lay with me. Peter extended his arm toward Dallas. She tried not to touch the pillows.

—Your father needs to clean in here, she said.

—He works a lot. He just crashes and showers here and then leaves. It gets worse sometimes.

Peter put Dallas's hand on his erection.

—I like when you touch me, he said.

She placed her hand over his pants and rubbed.

He unzipped his pants.

—Don't! Dallas jumped.

—What's the big deal? If you don't want to be with me, say it.

Peter sat up and looked down at her.

—I do want to be with you. It's just that . . . She didn't know how to explain to him that she wasn't ready to fool around with him all alone like that. And his place was a mess. It smelled bad.

And if he would at least throw out that used condom. Couldn't he see any of that? And what if he couldn't control himself? What if he didn't know when to stop? What if she screamed for help, who would hear her?

—I took the day off and everything to be with you.

—I'm sorry, Peter, I have to go. Maybe we can meet next week or something.

Dallas gathered her things, looked into the mirror and fixed her hair. He walked her over to the door and waited until she was outside the apartment.

—Hey, Dallas.

—What, Peter?

—Don't call me anymore, he said.

—But I thought you were going to hook me up with a job at Tower Records.

—Don't count on it.

Esperanza was waiting for Dallas at the kitchen table, holding a slip of paper, fanning herself frantically. Dallas turned back toward the door to get away. All the lights were on in the kitchen and the foyer. The rest of the apartment wore a heavy darkness that provided no escape. Esperanza made eye contact and Dallas was her captive. Esperanza pointed for her to sit down at the table. Dallas sat on the farthest chair, keeping her eyes alive, prepared for her mother's attack.

—You're just like your grandfather, the way you sweeten words and lie.

Dallas was immune to her mother's accusations.

—Your poor father must be turning in his grave seeing you waste your life the way you are. I didn't risk my life to end up in *this place*.

When Dallas dared to look up at the angry Esperanza, she noticed her mother looked haggard.

—Malcriada, Esperanza said, making that face with pursed lips, her eyebrows lifting, meeting her hairline. Malcriada was the word for girls who disrespected their mothers by speaking their minds. It was the word that made Dallas feel like she had committed the ultimate betrayal, as if disrespecting her one more time could get her shipped back to the campo in D.R. to live without a TV, a CD player, or new clothes.

Dallas noted all the things that hadn't been done: the pile of laundry on the floor by the washing machine. The chicken they were having for dinner was still defrosting in the sink.

—Don't you see? All I want is a better life for us. If we all work together, one day we can leave this place, she said to Dallas. —Your dad might not be with us, but he expects certain things from you.

Dallas wanted to put a plug in her mother's mouth. The pitch of her voice went up high when she went off in Spanish. At least in English, she stumbled over words and couldn't keep up with her thoughts. In Spanish, Esperanza's voice was a drill.

—That's why I work so hard. That's why I expect so much from you, Dallas, because so much was sacrificed for us to have a better life. And then I come home to find this. What's this? Esperanza yelled some more, waving the slip of paper. With her free hand, she leaned over and grabbed Dallas's chin and squeezed it tight enough to leave an impression.

—You want me to end up like you, working for some stupid jerk who makes you stay up all night cleaning his ass? For what? Dallas said under her breath, quick enough in English so that her mother couldn't decipher what she was saying. Dallas looked at her short nails. She had tried everything to stop biting them. But she only stopped when she bit too deep and the hangnail bled. And once it healed, she bit them again.

Dallas looked away. She counted to twenty-four in her head because that was the day of her birthday. There went her jacket. She wished that Bobby or her grandfather would walk in. Dallas didn't know how she would get out of this one. She could say the machine at school was broken and people got notes even when they didn't cut class. Or that when she arrived at school late, they sent notes home because the computers didn't mark the difference between being late or absent.

—You're a disgrace to your father's memory. Esperanza was now teary eyed.

It wasn't like Dallas was getting left back. Esperanza would never understand what her life was like. She took everything her children did personally: Esperanza should feel lucky that Dallas didn't report her to the authorities for abuse. Hit me, Mami, Dallas wanted to say. I'll get the camera and tell on your ass.

—What do you want from me, Dallas? I don't know what to do with you anymore!

All Dallas wanted was to have the same freedom Bobby had. He came and went as he pleased. Even before juvie, no one asked him shit.

—Bobby goes to jail and you have me making him dinner. You got me making his dinner and washing his clothes. Why don't you make him do something around here?

—He's a man. You know a man can only use one burner at a time or else they burn the entire house down.

—It's the nineties, . . . feminism . . . have you heard of the concept?

—What am I going to do with you? Esperanza got up. She slapped the slip of paper against Dallas's head. —You're so hard-headed. Just like ese abuelo tuyo.

Dallas rolled her eyes. She tried to remember the lyrics from a song she had heard that morning. The water running, her mother sighing. Dallas was glad that she didn't inherit her mother's hair. The way it stuck out of the ponytail holder. It didn't grow. And no matter how hard Esperanza tried to cover her black roots with red hair dye, her roots exposed her. Maybe it was because she resisted. Maybe if she left her hair all natural, it would look beautiful. But Esperanza tried to control everything, even her hair. Dallas dug her hand inside her own mass of hair. The curls fell over her face. She looked over at the mirror by the table and spread her hair evenly around her head so one couldn't tell the front of her head from the back. Her hair was thick like her father's.

—Dallas, don't put your hair on your face like that, it scares me.

Dallas twirled her hair with her fingers.

—Dallas!

—I hate my name! Don't say it out loud. It makes me want to barf.

—What's wrong with a name like Dallas?

—It's a freaking city, Mom.

Esperanza looked horrified. That mouth.

—Dallas, you be quiet right now, because you're crossing the line. I've put up with enough of you.

Dallas covered her face with her hair again. Inside her hair, she was no longer visible. You couldn't tell if she was coming or going. She closed her eyes and saw bloody red.

—Dallas! Why won't you listen to me?

Esperanza's words blended together as if they were one long piano note.

Esperanza got up and gathered her things. She was late for Mr. Hernández.

—If you get left back, I swear, Dallas, I'll ship your ass to D.R. so quick.

Dallas looked up at her mother through her locks. Esperanza was looking down at her, holding a pair of scissors. Dallas imagined her mother stabbing her or even stabbing herself.

—So that means you ain't buying me my jacket?

—You kids son mal agradecidos. All you say is, *Mami can I have this? And why don't you get me that?* You act like money grows on trees.

—You promised.

—You promised to go to school.

—I do go to school, Dallas said and got up to walk away from her.

—I'm not finished with you.

Dallas kept walking. Forget her. She didn't need her help anyway. She was going to get a job and move the hell out.

—Dallas, come back right now, Esperanza said, standing at the table. How could she turn her back on me? If she allowed Dallas to do what she pleased, Esperanza would lose her. Like all the other girls she saw getting pregnant, messing up their lives. She couldn't watch her twenty-four hours a day. And now she wasn't going to school. How long had this been happening? She had found the note in Don Chan's things. How long had he been hiding this from her? Was everyone working against her?

Esperanza went to Dallas's room, scissors in hand. After she had gone through thirteen hours of labor she had a brat who treated her like nothing—I'm your mother! Esperanza grabbed Dallas's chin and Dallas rolled her eyes to the side. Her mascara was running.

Dallas no longer cared what her mother thought. Caring about what other people thought was a trap. Dallas gnawed at the inside of her cheek softly. Tapped her foot waiting for Esperanza to leave her alone.

—Look at me.

—Leave me alone!

Esperanza grabbed a chunk of Dallas's hair from the crown of her head and chopped it from the root. She took the strand of hair and balled it up in her fist, putting it up to Dallas's face.

—I made you and I can destroy you if I feel like it, even if it means I have to go to prison my entire life. You won't disrespect me again. Are you listening to me now?

Esperanza grabbed the hair left on Dallas's head and curled it with her fist. —Don't try me, Dallas. I'm tired of your shit. If I find out you miss school one more time, I will shave your head bald.

Dallas wanted to get up and look in the mirror but was afraid to move. Her mother was holding on to the scissors, the same ones she used for sewing, the sacred scissors that were not to be used on anything else because it would blunt them and then butcher fabric.

—You're crazy, Dallas whispered to her. —That's my hair.

—I'll show you crazy, she said. —Keep it up and you'll see how crazy I am.

Dallas waited for Esperanza to leave the apartment to look at the damage. Ever since she could remember, Dallas had had long hair. To grow it all again would take a decade. Her mother had lost her mind. She was grateful that she hadn't cut a wad of hair on the sides. Dallas would've been forced to cut it all off. Now Dallas had a one-inch chunk of hair on the crown of her head. In a ponytail, the damage was unnoticeable. She would have to wear scarves, and braids, to cover it up for the next ten years. —Bitch, Dallas whispered.

She went to Esperanza's room to take something, to destroy something precious of hers. She looked through her closet. Dallas pulled out boxes of things, looked through her mother's clothes. But couldn't find anything Esperanza would miss. She went to her dresser. She popped open a cookie tin. Inside it was filled with loose bills. Fives and ones. —And she lied to me, Dallas said, quickly closing her mother's bedroom door and then putting the tin on her lap to count just how much her mother had stashed. —You said you didn't have enough money to buy me a quinceañera present? Bullshit! Dallas said. Dallas counted 150 dollars and tucked it into her jeans pocket. With it she would buy her jacket at Macy's.

When the Colón family heard the doorbell, no one rushed to answer it. Especially on the weekends. Esperanza never knew how to turn away the nice people who knocked on her door to preach sermons, or the man who worked for the gas company and came around to check the meter, and never gave her enough time to remove the cans of beans she put on the meter, to help lower the gas bill.

—Dallas! Bobby! Open the door! Esperanza yelled as she scrambled on a chair to remove the cans.

—Dallas, open the door! Bobby yelled as he flipped through channels.

—Why doesn't Abuelo ever get it? Dallas yelled from her room.

—'Cause he's old. You fucking princess!

—Well, the princess needs to go to the bathroom. Dallas had been on strike and would be until she received an official apology from her mother.

Bobby went for the door. The same girl he had been jerking off to, since the night they'd met in the kitchen, a few months ago, was standing before him. Hush. There was something different about her. She wasn't well. Bobby waved her to come inside.

—Hush, he said in disbelief. Looking her over, remembering her scent of sawdust and lilacs.

—Where've you been? Bobby said, trying to act like she was just any other girl and that he didn't notice that she had been knocked up by some guy from around the way, forever to have ruined her life. But that smell she had, of fresh furniture and flowery soap, invaded every orifice of his body. He couldn't pretend not to care. And the way she looked at him for help, he couldn't help but crack open.

Hush walked in, and when he pulled out a chair for her, she cried on his shoulder. Wiping her face with his shirt, Bobby put the box of tissues within her reach.

—Qué pasó? Esperanza said, rushing over. Hush's belly was small but noticeable.

—I tried to stop him, but I couldn't. Hush lost her voice to an outburst of tears.

When her belly had started to show, her mother asked her to leave.

—Don't cry, Bobby said, handing her more tissue.

—What happened? Dallas rushed over to Hush to hold her. Bobby didn't let go of Hush's grasp. Dallas tried to comb Hush's hair back from her face. —I've been calling you and you never called me back.

—What's all this yelling about? Don Chan said.

—It's la amiga de Dallas . . . Esperanza started to explain.

—Is she pregnant? Don Chan lifted a finger to help him remember Hush's stepfather's name. —Where's Oswaldo?

Hush burst into a loud wail at the mention of his name.

—Leave her alone. Bobby waved all of them away and held Hush closer to him.

—Is it yours? Esperanza asked.

—Why didn't you tell me you were sleeping with Bobby? All this time I thought you were getting fat, Dallas said, wondering how Hush had kept it from her. How long had it been going on? Bobby had only been back three, or was it four months? Agh! She had sex with her brother. Gross. Slut, bitch, cunt, Dallas thought.

—But, Dallas, I thought she was your friend. What does this have to do with Bobby? Don Chan asked.

—She's not my friend anymore. Dallas stormed away, slamming her bedroom door behind her.

—Can everyone just be quiet? My goodness, we're going crazy here for no reason. This is a girl expecting a child. She could be like Mary. And Bobby, Joseph. And she came knocking and as a Christian family, we must do what we can for her, Esperanza said.

Hush stopped crying to listen.

—Bobby, like Joseph? Don Chan asked, wondering if Esperanza had lost her mind. She always complained when Hush slept over.

—Can everyone just shut up? This isn't my baby, Bobby said. He did like Hush, but she was under eighteen. And he wouldn't go back to jail, not even for her.

—It's not? Dallas whispered to herself, elated. She watched her family from her bedroom door, but with the turn of events she slipped out and hovered around the door.

—Thank you, God, Esperanza said and clapped her hands with joy.

—Stop talking about God, Don Chan said. —It makes me nervous.

—Whose baby is it then? Esperanza asked Hush, who had swollen eyes and beet red cheeks from all the crying. —Why did you come here?

—I've nowhere else to go, Hush said and started crying all over again.

—She could have my room and I could sleep in Dallas's room, Don Chan said.

—You're giving her my room? Dallas couldn't believe it. Her mother chopped off her hair for cutting class, and now Don Chan was offering Hush a room of her own.

—She's pregnant, Esperanza said.

—I'm bald! Dallas said, patting the baseball cap she wore, to cover the nub on the crown of her head. She pulled off her hat to show Hush how crazy her mother was.

—Your hair? Hush said. —It was so pretty.

—It's not that bad, it'll grow back, Esperanza said, wondering for the first time if she'd gone too far. When Dallas had a daughter, she'd understand.

—No, Abuelo, Hush could sleep on my bed and I can crash on the sofa, Bobby volunteered.

—Yeah, let Bobby sleep on the sofa, Dallas said.

—My goodness, you're all so generous, Hush said. —But no, I'll sleep on the sofa. Please don't change anything for me. I promise, I'll pretend I'm not even here.

—Bueno, you can stay here until you figure things out, Esperanza said. —What else can we do? All God's children are our children.

—There she goes with God again, Don Chan said.

Esperanza was relieved that it wasn't either of her children in such trouble. She crossed herself, kissing the air.

—C'mon, Hush, let's go into my room so you can rest, Dallas said, anxious to hear all the details.

Meanwhile, Bobby wondered what had led Hush to his doorway. He didn't care to think that Hush was actually looking for Dallas. He could only think of the ray of light she encompassed, which he so desperately needed and had not realized he was missing.

6

¡Rompamos las alambradas
y las empalizadas
la tierra de quisqueya
para el que la trabaja!
—Dominican laborer's chant

La Zona Franca
1997

Miraluz crammed into the buses with hundreds of other women, six days a week, to work at the underwear factory in La Zona Franca. She sewed a sleeve, a bra strap, a seam of a crotch, wondering what all the pieces she put together looked like as a whole. She had tried to organize the women to better their working conditions. But when she found a gang of union breakers tormenting her sons in front of her house she realized that she too should lay low for a while.

But Miraluz was never one to sit still. Even after 1965, when many of the Invisible Ones fled the country or became too disillusioned to fight for anything but themselves, Miraluz stood in front of the American tanks that rolled through her streets, refusing to believe that it could be that easy to be defeated by them. —Why aren't you on our side, she yelled out to the Yanqui who looked past her.

Twenty years later, insults, ideas, anger raged inside of her and made her body swell up. Soon the seat at the sewing machine started to feel smaller, her clothes tighter. Her feet pushed up against the leather of her shoes. She had heard that feet expanded with time. But why had she not felt the difference before? Nothing was fitting her right. The crotch on her jeans was riding up on her and the shirts sent to her from abroad stained quickly at the armpits. Her clothes were rebelling against her.

Miraluz was convinced that the factory was also shrinking. Some said that Miraluz's preoccupation was making her bigger, or that the piles of bras on her sewing table were getting higher, or maybe the ceiling was gradually descending due to rain that didn't cease or the weight of the fluorescent lights. Maybe the manufacturer was hiring more people, adding more sewing machines, and thus the space was more crowded, so that the perception of shrinkage made sense. All of those reasons would have rung true if everyone had agreed that the factory was indeed shrinking, but it was only Miraluz who insisted. And she was having a hard time breathing and it wasn't just the lint in the air.

Her colleagues thought Miraluz was using the shrinking as a metaphor for the oppressive factory environment, but when they saw her shoulders slump over, her head dip on her way into the room, they began to worry. Miraluz didn't need them to understand. She knew that the space had become too small for her; and soon would be too small for all of them. If she didn't find a way out of there soon, she'd be another stalk in the cane field, cut, refined, and devoured, with only the cavity as proof of her existence.

Miraluz sewed her last pile of bras and thought about the land in Los Llanos. Why couldn't she return and live there with her relentless abuela, María Magdalena de Jesús? To move back to Los Llanos would be crazy. She wouldn't have a way to survive. Yes, she could attempt to live off the land. They had done it successfully in the sixties, but the land needed a lot of work and she would need people to join her. It was an impossible situation, because if she sold her plot, like many others had, the foreigners would turn the land into a plantation. It would go against everything the Invisible Ones had fought for. But then again, what use was it to have land that so few people lived on?

Miraluz stitched labels onto seams, day after day. Piece after piece.

Piles of Victoria's Secret labels, waiting to add their signature to a bra, a panty, a camisole.

—Victoria, Miraluz said to herself, was like victory, —*Victoria Secret*. Must be like a secreto. Victoria Secreto.

It was a strange name for a bra. Who was Victoria? What secret did she have? El Secreto de Victoria sounded like the name of a soap opera. Or was it el Secreto de la Victoria?

The secret of victory?

The blood rushed up to her face, warming her cheeks as she said the words over and over, as she sewed hundreds of labels to the tiny pieces of fabric. As the sweat beads piled up against her skin, the machines' trill roared without pause, making her eardrums tremble in agony. El Secreto de la Victoria, she said, the voice in her head loud and full.

Miraluz stood up to stop everyone from what they were doing to announce her discovery. All those years after they had lost the hope of living in a true democracy, she and Don Chan would contemplate where was the secret of victory. And all along it was staring at her every day. She looked at the women in the factory, stuffed like sardines, without elbow room, backs hunched over, one beside another, under artificial light, the machine trilling and churning without ceasing. The overseer yelling, —Rápido, rápido. Women squeezing balls of fabric in between their legs, while they trembled because they were afraid to ask for permission to go again to the bathroom. —El Secreto de la Victoria, Miraluz whispered. She tucked one of the labels in her fist and raised her hand as a symbol. No one looked up at her, they were too busy filling their quota or they would get fired. Miraluz tucked the label in her shirt pocket, making sure no one saw her. The women were known to snitch on each other for small bribes by the overseer. She couldn't afford to lose her job. Not yet.

At lunch, she shared her discovery with some of her comadres who had joined her in trying to organize a union. —I found the answer, she said at lunchtime, remembering the year the Invisible Ones took to the streets in the name of democracy. El Secreto de la Victoria. It was as if someone had turned on the light in the factory with small windows. The threads floating in the factory choked many of the women and the warmth made them so drowsy that some of them sewed their fingers right into the lace. But not Miraluz. She was awake and ready.

—Don't you see, mujeres? The reason we can't get our union is because if we all get fired, there are hundreds of women just like us willing to take this job. The owners have all the power. Who gave the power to the factories? The owners of the companies. When we unionize, we try to get the owners to care about us. But they don't.

—That's because the people still buy their clothes. Miraluz, we've been through this a million times at the union meetings. Shit is never going to change. Estamos jodidas, said one.

The women were leaning in, forming a circle around Miraluz.

—You think gringos who buy these bras don't know that we get paid five dollars a day? They don't care about us, said another.

—People who have money buy what they want. I would if I was them, another added.

—How could they not know that we're jodiéndonos la vida while they buy their fur coats and diamonds? Don't you see them on television? They don't care about anything but themselves.

The overseer glared at them and waved his hand, motioning them to end their lunchtime. The bells went off and the women went back to their stations.

Miraluz rushed home that night to make a plan. The younger women had no idea what she meant when she spoke of victory. All their lives they knew only one way to live. Some women had been working in la Zona Franca since they'd dropped their first period. They were happy to have a job that paid them at least a minimum wage, unlike many of their friends who worked as trabajadoras for pennies a day. They had fallen into the rhythm of the machines. The machines' loud trill and the steamers' deep suction, a steady breathing, day in and day out, had paralyzed their imagination. They needed to think bigger than getting paid three or four dollars more a day.

When Miraluz saw her sons playing with a ball and stick on the street, she called out to them,

—Muchachos, come inside. You two are making dinner tonight, I have work to do.

—We don't cook, her eldest said.

—You better learn or we'll all go hungry.

She ordered her son to heat up the water so she could soak her feet, which ached from working the sewing machine pedals. That night, they ate burned rice, unsalted beans, and fried plátanos with avocado.

It was too great a risk for Miraluz to talk about her ideas to the women at the factory. She invited them for a birthday party at her house, the same way Don Chan had organized parties to lure people into the Invisible Ones.

—Should we bring something? one woman asked.

—Sure, if you want.

—I can make a cake, another said.

—Maravilloso, Miraluz said, wondering if the young women would show up at all. Most of them were half her age. Miraluz knew that was to her advantage.

The women arrived at Miraluz's small home dressed in their Sunday best on a sunny afternoon. They gathered around, surprised that there weren't any men besides Miraluz's sons, and complimented each other on how glamorous they appeared outside work.

—I wanted you here to talk about the factory. Miraluz tried to remain calm.

—But I made a cake.

—I hope this is not a union meeting. Is it? one woman said. —I want no trouble with those unions.

—Well, I'm sure it's someone's birthday here. We can't let the cake go to waste.

—You mean this isn't a party?

—Mine is in two weeks. Does that count?

—Mujeres, please . . . I'm very serious. We don't have much time.

—Time for what?

—Ay, mujer, it's Sunday. I don't want to go back home and deal with shit. Take all the time you want.

—All of us know how to sew, right? Miraluz asked. It was always good to start with the positive.

—No, I only know how to put the pieces together, one said.

—It's true. I can make a pocket and collars, but to sew? I wouldn't say I sew that well, another said.

—Okay . . . shall we say that together, we can make a T-shirt, a panty, a pair of shorts?

The women started nodding and looking at each other. One third of the women from the factory had shown up. But yes, it was possible that together, they could manage to make something to wear.

—But we don't have the machines, said one. —Without a machine I can't make nothing. My fingers are too thick to sew by hand.

The gaze from the young women in her living room made Miraluz feel silly. They had no money, no machines, nothing. She stood up. It was hot and the fan was blowing more hot air on their faces. The ice had melted in their cups filled with water. The women were becoming restless.

—What if we could find a way to work for ourselves? Miraluz said as she fanned herself with a piece of paper she planned to use as a sign-up sheet. —Start our own company.

—We don't have the money to buy fabric.

—And why would anyone buy clothing made by us?

Maybe starting their own business was too much for them to do. For years it was the unions that bettered the lives of the workers. But how much better? People still depended on the mercy of the companies that exploited them. No, no . . . she couldn't do all that work, only to find that the lives of the people remained the same. She was tired of working for others. How many jobs had she had in her life? Too many.

—I know this woman who sold fish in Boca Chica, working for

this man, and little by little she saved enough to buy her own casita fish stand. And now she makes three times as much as before, one woman said.

—I don't make enough to save. My children haven't had a piece of meat in two weeks. They need notebooks for school.

—I'm not saying it's going to be easy, Miraluz said.

—But when has our life been easy? one woman said.

—That's true, another agreed.

—Who has family in the States? Miraluz asked.

All the women except one raised their hands.

—Okay, maybe from the money being sent to us we can put some aside and start a pool from which we can build our company.

One woman laughed. —Compañía? You're ambitious!

—Besides, the money my sister sends me is for medicine. I have high blood pressure and I can't breathe without an inhaler.

—If you didn't work in the factory, you wouldn't need the inhaler, another woman said, annoyed that no one was cooperating. Maybe Miraluz was on to something.

—You mean like we would be paying taxes, but to ourselves, form our own collective?

—Yes, a collective, Miraluz said, liking the word very much.

—But how do we know we could trust each other? Who holds the money?

—I'm not giving anyone my money, said another.

—Mujeres, please . . . this is a conversation. I know we won't find the solution right away.

—And on hungry stomachs, no less, one woman said, eyeing the cake. She shifted her weight in the plastic seat Miraluz had provided. The sun was hiding behind the clouds, the small living room lights dimmed. Miraluz turned on the lightbulb hanging from the ceiling.

—Do you know the story of the child blowing bubbles in India? Miraluz lit a candle on the table. The living room took on a warm glow that livened the colors of their bright shirts.

The woman looked at Miraluz with anticipation.

—The boy started blowing bubbles toward the arid fields. At first he was alone. But soon, more children blew bubbles in the same direction. On the other side of the fields, the farmers prayed for rain so they could grow their crops. Every day they prayed. Then one day, they woke up and there was rain. The children thought it was their bubbles. The farmers thought it was their prayers.

—Are you asking us to pray? one woman asked. —Weren't we talking about starting a business together?

—No. I'm saying, for those of you who want to work with me on starting something, I welcome you to my house every Sunday and we can work toward that goal. For the others who can't or won't, for whatever reason, I respect you and ask you to pray that we succeed. Regardless, if we think with similar intentions, together we will be victorious.

One woman clapped and soon the others followed. Embarrassed, Miraluz stood up to serve the cake and unwrap the other dishes the women had brought.

—Let's eat, she said, and they all bustled around the food. In their own heads, they debated if they would return next Sunday. What if Miraluz was right? Maybe one of them couldn't save enough money, but together they might be able to do something.

The next Sunday, Miraluz didn't expect such an audience. The women dressed casually, each with their own food offering placed on the backyard table. They collectively joked about how their husbands didn't like that they were going over to Miraluz's. Soon after, wives were asking their husbands to make their own meals and their sons were doing their own laundry. In weeks, Miraluz had a regular group of women who started addressing immediate concerns. Who would babysit for their children? Who would cook? Who would take care of the viejos? Who would take care of all the things the women had to do after they got off work? And in weeks, they started a bartering system that inspired even the most skeptical to want to join El Secreto de la Victoria. For years, people had been hoarding the little they had, but something was changing in the women and how they treated each other, that for Miraluz was reminiscent of the days when the garden of Los Llanos was abundant and the people were feasting. Women volunteered to babysit. They shared their fruits and vegetables from their yards and the clothes and other supplies they received from their families in New York City. The young men, including Miraluz's sons, were called to duty, fetching the women water, delivering food to the elders who were left alone for days because their daughters were working at the factory. Optimism had taken over Miraluz's community in San Pedro de Macorís, and like an unexplained outbreak, it was difficult to contain. With time, even the ones who preferred to pray put money in the small donation box that Miraluz kept in a safe at the bank.

In no time, Miraluz's living room was equipped to make three hundred panties in a day. Three hundred panties in thirty days was nine thousand panties at ten dollars a panty, which amounted to ninety thousand dollars. Money that they would divide among all the women who made them.

—Even if we could make these panties, who will buy them?

—The same people who buy Victoria's Secret? said another.

—We can start a campaign: Don't buy Victoria's Secret, buy El Secreto de la Victoria. A person who works the land should own the land, Miraluz said, excited.

—What land?

Miraluz was too overjoyed to explain that Don Chan had been right. If they work at the factory, they should own the factory. Same concept that he had about the land.

—Mujeres, we must get in touch with all our family members and find out who buys Victoria's Secret and see if they will buy from us. We must involve them in this movement. If the money that our families send us makes up about half of our economy, then what they choose to buy can affect the conditions of the women in these factories? You'll see, a part of the money will go to building up our community. Better schools, better clinics.

—But then the bosses will know it is us, and we will get fired from la Zona Franca.

—We won't need the job once we start to sell the panties. Yes, at first we will take a big risk, but if we call our families and ask each of them for thirty dollars, there are twenty of us here. That would be six hundred dollars between all of us. That means that maybe four of us can take one to two months off to work on El Secreto de la Victoria.

—But what about the other women who need jobs in la Zona Franca? What if the factory goes to Mexico or Thailand, then what?

—Mujeres, don't you see, we have to stop thinking like that. They want us to be scared. We have to think, what if for every label a woman at a sweatshop has to sew, there is a revolutionary label to compete with it? What if those who have the money to shop, shop from the companies owned by women like us?

7

Nueva York
1998

Don Chan sat at the kitchen table, organizing his newspaper clippings. He stapled them together by day, paper-clipped them by week, rubber-banded them by month, and boxed them by year. Seven boxes piled up in a corner in his bedroom. The eighth one on the floor by the kitchen table as he sorted out the last few weeks. He was falling behind. Sometimes he forgot to clip the headlines and had six days for one week. So he had to look through the dates and make sure they were all in order. It helped him sleep to know that the weeks were complete, and if not, he would put a note that one day was missing to fill in for the lost day.

—What are you saving them all for? Hush walked into the kitchen and sat down. She was seven months big and the baby was pressing against her bladder.

—Who are you? Don Chan kept counting the days. —Seven, he said and stapled them at the ends, making sure they all lined up on one side. The clippings were different sizes, from biggest to smallest.

—La Virgen, Hush kidded and rubbed her belly, wondering what it would be like to have a child outside her body. What would she do with it?

Don Chan laughed. —So you're a comedian?

—Only during the day. At night, I guard the sofa in the living room so no one will steal it.

Don Chan continued to count the clippings. When he held a month in his hand, he became overwhelmed by all the information in them. When he dug his hand in the boxes from years before, he reassured himself of the passage of time. Each piece of paper made his days count.

—Can I make you some café? Hush asked Don Chan. She wanted to make herself helpful.

The way she said it shook Don Chan in a way that threw off his count and had him start all over again. —Caridad, don't you know I don't drink coffee at this hour?

—Oh, sorry, she said. He had called her Caridad before.

—And why aren't you helping me? We must get to work. He gave her the box of clippings. —I know the answer is hidden in here somewhere, he said and started laying out the days on the table in rows.

—Sorry. Hush laid out clippings, cleaning up the uneven edges. Pulling out the words. *Transfer. Women. Stock. Reshape. Power. Building. Bomb. Biological. Fire.*

Don Chan loved to spend his days alone with his Caridad. Watching her read books while she sat on the sofa. Her stomach growing each day. Him reading his newspapers. It was just them, their unborn child, and the trees. Except there were no trees inside the apartment, just some sad-looking plants and lots of boxes filled with things to send one day to D.R.

—I should water the plants, Don Chan said and poured water in a glass. He placed it on the table and then forgot about the plants and started reading his headlines again. Don Chan was waiting for his son to be born. But he already had a son. What was his son's name? Don Chan looked at his newspapers for guidance. His son's name? Coño, maldito nombre. And where was he? They had much to do.

That's right, his wife Caridad gave birth right on the table where they slaughtered the pigs. There was a lot of blood. His wife nearly died giving birth. She was supposed to die. The woman who knew about such things said that his wife was on borrowed time.

—Who are you? Don Chan asked Hush, who was diligently laying out his headlines neatly just like when she worked with him at the luncheonette. She started to read them aloud.

ALREADY STRUGGLING DOMINICANS
SINK DEEPER INTO POVERTY
DOMINICANS MAY ALLOW VOTING ABROAD: IMMIGRANTS
IN NEW YORK WOULD GAIN INFLUENCE

—Ay, mi Caridad, Don Chan said. —I've put you through so much.

Hush became worried. The side of his face had dropped a little. She had noticed it before. His eye was lower on one side of his face.

—Are you okay, Señor Don Chan?

The way she said señor made him realize that Caridad was gone. Don Chan noticed his old hands near Hush's cheek and saw the passage of time in such a way that he was ashamed of himself.

—Ay, Miraluz, I'm sorry . . . when you get here?

—I'm not Miraluz.

—I've been wanting to tell you something.

—Tell me, Viejo, I'll make sure to let her know.

He patted her hand and her head. Touched her knee. His hands trembled when he wasn't holding on to something. His wrinkles, like canyons riding up and down his face.

—Touch your belly button, go ahead, see how it feels, Don Chan said.

To please him, Hush put her finger over her belly button, which was pushing out against her T-shirt. Don Chan put his hand over her hand, pressing on her belly with hesitation.

—Your belly button is the place that connects your child to you, you to your mother, her to her mother, and on and on back to when people were connected to the earth because they had no other choice.

Don Chan paused for so long, Hush wondered if he had fallen asleep with his eyes open. His breath sounded funny. She was tempted to check his pulse. He hated being fussed over, so she pretended not to worry.

Finally, he said, —Bodies don't lie. Our minds can mess with us, but the body provides an ancestral knowledge. That's the real purpose of the umbilical cord. Everything you do, the body remembers it and passes it on.

Hush looked around her for a piece of paper so she could write everything down. Maybe these were his last words and he was excavating wisdom from long ago. What if she forgot? Belly button, connection to mother, the purpose of the cord is the connection to her ancestors.

Don Chan tightened his grip on her hands. He cleared his throat. He looked at Hush with such intensity, she got goose bumps.

—It's important you know this.

—I'm listening. Hush straightened herself. His voice was low and weary.

—Men have made such a mess of things. Man thinks his dick is enough. He cuts his mother's cord and shoots off with the other, Don Chan said, letting go of her hand. Lacing his fingers, putting his head down. His palms holding his forehead.

—It's up to you women to help men remember what history has taught us. You understand?

—Sí, Hush said. But she didn't. She just knew that men couldn't have children and their belly button didn't feed anyone. Men only get fed by their mothers. That is why they make so many mistakes. They forget to tap into their belly buttons for advice.

—If you dig deep inside yourself, you'll know more than any book could ever tell. You know the history of the emotions and the spirit. Don't let anyone make you think different. If you learn anything from me, learn this . . .

Hush waited for the one piece of knowledge that could change her life. That would help her make sense of things. She was waiting to find out more about this inner power that she possessed as a woman. She looked over at more headlines.

PANEL DIVIDED ON POLICING OF SWEATSHOPS
MONEY STARTS TO SHOW ON INTERNET SHOPPING APPAREL

—What's going on? Dallas walked into the apartment and found
Don Chan with his hands on Hush's belly.

—Nothing, Hush said.

Don Chan looked at both of them. —Who are you?

Hush's presence had Bobby beside himself.

—I can help you with that, he said as Hush tried to prop up some pillows to make herself more comfortable on the sofa. She was reading.

—Is he for real? Dallas teased.

—Shut up, stupid.

Bobby tousled Dallas's hair.

—If you hit me again, Bobby, I'll tell Mami.

Bobby pushed Dallas away.

—Mami! Dallas yelled.

—I'm sorry, Hush, my sister is a brat sometimes.

—It's okay.

—You're taking his side, Hush?

Esperanza rushed into the living room to see what was going on.

—Hush, are you all right?

—Sí, señora. Everything is fine.

—It's just Dallas being stupid, Bobby said.

—I'm being stupid? Bobby hit me for no reason.

—Ay, Dallas, calm down and come help me fix dinner. Hush must be exhausted.

—I hate you. I hate you all.

All those years, Hush had always done well in school, prompting Esperanza to say things like, —Why can't you be more like Hush? Why can't you win awards like her? And now Esperanza's idea of the perfect child was pregnant at sixteen. Even Hush's mother turned her away because she thought Hush was possessed by the devil and all that evil should walk the earth alone. When had Esperanza become so generous? Dallas wondered.

—You should start reading like Hush does, instead of listening to that CD player all the time. You'll never do well in school, listening to esos tígres.

—You rather me get pregnant, sit around all day, and read books?

—Shut your mouth, Dallas Colón. I've had enough of you talking back to me.

—I can return those books for you at the library, on my way to work, Bobby offered Hush.

—But they're way overdue.

—So what? I'll take care of it.

—Can you get me some more? Hush asked him.

—Which ones?

—I like stories, mostly. Something to help me escape.

Hush refused to leave the house because she didn't want people to stare at her. She felt safe in the Colón household, sitting under the lamplight, watching the Colóns enter and exit.

—Sit on the floor, Dallas. Hush pulled on her arm to get her to sit in between her legs. Hush pulled off the bandanna Dallas wore to cover up the nub.

—What the hell are you doing? It took me forever to get it on right.

—Relax . . . I'm gonna make it look cute. You'll see. Hush combed her fingers through Dallas's hair. She tugged gently at the roots. Dallas liked the way it felt. She reached out for the remote control and flicked on the television. She changed channels, but wasn't watching anything.

—If I braid it, it will grow faster. Hush took some of the oil she was rubbing on her belly and combed it into Dallas's hair. —Your mother must've been mad at you.

—Whatever, Dallas said, still pissed because she was being punished when everyone else was messing up.

—Imagine if she had caught you with Peter. She would've shaved your eyebrows off or something.

—Don't even mention his name. Wack wanna-be DJ who gonna be working in Tower Records all his life because he's so stupid.

—Damn, Dallas. You liked him a minute ago. Hush laughed. She understood how it went. Sometimes guys went ugly fast, especially when they messed up.

—I hate my life. I got nothing, Hush. No boyfriend, no summer job, no hair.

—You've got a family. You should be grateful for that. Hush wove in small strands of Dallas's hair inside the longer strands.

—It's 'cause you're not related to them, Dallas said, envious because it was so easy for Hush to be around them. They weren't in Hush's way. Hush wasn't in theirs. Everyone catered to her.

—What does it feel like? To have a baby inside of you that will love you? Dallas felt Hush's belly on the back of her neck. It was warm and lumpy.

—She might not love me. Look at you and your mother. I don't even want to think of my mother, who took Oswaldo's side. I swear, I would never take a man's side. Especially not over my kid.

—What about me and my mother? Dallas defended herself. She was mad at her. But it wasn't like she didn't love her. —Do you think you'll ever talk to your mother again?

—Not unless she leaves Oswaldo.

—Does it hurt, making a baby?

—It feels like what it is. Uncomfortable, I guess.

—But it's also like you'll have something that is yours alone. And no one could tell you what to do with it, because it's yours.

—You buggin', Dallas. I should've had an abortion. But I waited too long. And then I could've gone to college like I planned. You lucky, you could do anything you want with your life. Now I'm stuck with this.

Hush sighed and adjusted the pillow on her back, raising her swollen feet on the coffee table. Dallas wrapped her arms under Hush's legs. She was the only one allowed to put her feet on the coffee table. Esperanza said that to deny a pregnant woman what she wants will mark the child with patches of desire all over its body.

—Give me skinny braids.

—Relax, you'll be so cute, you'll be like, Peter who? And he'll come chasing after you and you'll be waving him away. Spitting on the ground and watching him swim in your spit.

Bobby no longer asked Hush about her books. He took the books piled on her left to the library and piled the books she was about to read on her right. He didn't ask her what she wanted to read. He fed her books in exchange for seeing her thank him with a half smile, as if to smile completely would break her.

Bobby did notice that the book piles he brought home became heavier than the ones he returned. He didn't understand why. He had never looked into the books before. He took them out at random from the new-books section then returned them. And with time, the weight had such a discrepancy, he wondered if books became lighter after they had been read. The idea seemed feasible. Since a reader did take something away from a book: knowledge, ideas, a story they could tell. Could one reader make all that difference? Would it mean that if enough people read a book, it would have no weight to it at all? That it would cease to exist, or maybe its existence relied on the memories of its readers? At first, this theory satisfied Bobby's curiosity, but even Bobby knew that he wasn't a philosopher, that he was a man of matter, of real, physical-world things, and there must be a better reason.

On a clumsy day, Bobby dropped the pile of books on his way to the library, and as he picked them up, he noticed they were missing pages. The books were faulty. People didn't respect public property on Quepasó Street, why would they take care of books? So he carefully inspected each book when he borrowed them. How frustrating to read passages and have pages missing like that. And when he picked up the pile to return it, he inspected the books, to find that pages were missing. Random pages had been torn out. He didn't know how to approach Hush about it. As it was, he didn't know how to approach Hush, because every time he looked at her, his tongue curled itself under and stuck to the roof of his mouth. So he decided to watch her while she read, when she didn't think anyone was looking.

Hush curled up on the sofa, her belly large compared to her small frame, but it was only the size of a basketball. She read the book, and when she reached the end, she went through the pages skimming passages she liked. She didn't always read books from beginning to end. She felt books had their own time, and if she didn't get lost in them, they were wrong for her at that moment. But there were passages that she didn't want to forget. When she found them, she ripped the page out, held the page in her hand, and carefully tore it in sections, putting each piece in her mouth. She chewed it slowly and swallowed. The blandness of the paper comforted the slight nausea she had been told would go away, but hadn't.

Esperanza had complained that Hush wasn't eating. She worried that while Hush appeared healthy and was gaining weight as the months progressed, she hadn't eaten the food she served her. Esperanza asked Bobby and Dallas if she craved anything in particular. Did she ever complain about the meals? She wondered why her plates were left untouched and how Hush kept growing without any proper nutrition. No one else admitted to feeding her.

Should Bobby keep Hush's secret? As it was, the family never talked about her pregnancy. They never talked about the father of the baby. They treated Hush like a guest who was visiting for an indefinite amount of time. Why did he have to tell anyone she ate paper?

—I'll bring you books if you take the vitamins. Deal?

Hush grabbed the glass of water and took the vitamins Bobby bought her. And for a number of months, Hush continued to devour passages of books, while the Colón family fluttered around her. Don Chan spent his afternoons telling Hush about Los Llanos while he waited for Santo to come home. Esperanza watched reruns of *Dallas* with Hush every other day, when she was off from work, and made sure that Hush filled her in on what she missed when she worked at Mrs. Hernández's house. Dallas tried outfits on for Hush and, without telling her she had 150 dollars stashed in her room, she debated with Hush for hours whether buying something with stolen money would bring her bad luck.

So much time passed with Hush sitting in their living room, no one remembered when she was supposed to deliver.

—We should take her to the hospital. I mean, she should've had that baby weeks ago, no? Esperanza asked Bobby.

—It wouldn't hurt to get her checked.

On a Saturday, when everyone in the Colón family was home, with all their strength and abilities of coercion, they convinced Hush to go to the emergency room. At Hush's request, Dallas disguised Hush's face with big sunglasses and a scarf wrapped around her head. They stood around her when the nosy old neighbor opened her door to find out what the commotion was. They went around the block, avoiding Broadway, the luncheonette.

It had been five years since they had visited the emergency room as a family. That's when it hit Dallas, Esperanza, and Bobby that Santo's death had been long ago enough that it wasn't as painful, that they had moved on, and become a family without him.

Esperanza told the nurse she was Hush's mother, and she went in with Hush as the doctors performed a sonogram. This must be a good job, Esperanza said. Maybe I should take a class, amazed by the small black screen with the impression of the baby inside Hush.

—Is it a boy or girl? Esperanza asked.

—Do you want to know, Hush? the nurse asked.

Hush shrugged, busy reading the patient's rights, taped to the wall.

—Hush is having a girl, the doctor said and looked over at Hush, who looked disinterested about the child who was keeping her from leaving for college as planned.

Esperanza asked the doctor to take some tests, to find out if Hush was healthy, because she wasn't eating and her pregnancy had been going on for so long. When did she expect the baby?

—She's fine, the doctor said. —Any day now, the baby should come. Maybe a few weeks. It always feels like the last few months take forever. I often believe the baby comes out when it knows its mama is ready.

Esperanza didn't want to admit it, but she was looking forward to having a baby in the house. She liked the spark Hush ignited in Bobby. She actually caught him smiling, and the coldness from juvie in his eyes was no longer threatening. For once, the Colón family was together in the living room, joking and talking, fighting and playing as Hush propped herself in the sofa's corner, reading anything she could put her hands on.

—Hush? Bobby tried to talk with her but his tongue was tied.

—Yes, Bobby?

He was afraid he would make her cry, scream, or that she'd get bored with anything he had to say. He assumed she was a bit fearful of men after what she'd gone through with Oswaldo.

—What is it, Bobby? His cheeks were flushed. He wasn't breathing right. He had never cared about anyone in that way before.

—What you reading? he asked, feeling stupid.

—Sit, I'll read you some. Bobby sat next to her, awkwardly spreading his legs to touch her knees. Her legs were crossed and the book propped on her belly. —Well, I'm toward the end . . . you see, it's about this man who is being taken care of by a young nurse in an abandoned building, in Italy after the war. She is so dedicated to him, as if by caring for him she has a reason to stay alive. Caring for him reminds her that she exists, that watching so many men die, didn't kill her.

—Do you want to go there?

—To Italy? Hush said. —But it depends why. I don't want to go and look at it like people look at me.

—What do you mean?

—People don't see me, you know . . . they look at me. Their gaze hurts, Bobby. They don't have to say anything, but it's as if I expose them and they hate me for it.

—Do you see me like that?

—No, you're my angel of books, she said and punched his arm.—Why you always so nice to me?

He was tempted to caress her. To feel her skin. He had never thought of such things, like Italy, war, caring for someone before, but from her lips it all sounded interesting.

—And what else happens? —Does the nurse fall in love with him? Does he fall in love with her?

—Well, there's a man who deactivates bombs. And they fall in love. But he is Indian. And she is English. And while they're in that strange place in the middle of nowhere, it's okay for them to make love. It's like they could love each other in this bubble that exists away from everything they know. But when the U.S. bombs Japan, something explodes in him. He realizes he's on the wrong side of the war. That the enemy he was helping could have easily killed him.

That day, Bobby didn't tell her he loved her, but he silently committed to her.

Don Chan was up at four in the morning when Bobby walked into the apartment. The murmur from upstairs kept him company. The old German lady was losing her hearing. Often, she fell asleep watching the television.

—Where've you been? Don Chan asked, cloaked in the night, revealing his hand as he reached for his cigar. Don Chan had been waiting for him so they could leave la capital. The Trujillistas from across the way had released Santo with a warning. And now he was disappearing in the night again to find himself in more trouble. Don Chan couldn't watch one more person get hurt. It didn't matter who won that war, the rich enemies and allies, both alike, sat around a table and negotiated deals and watched more poor hungry men fight and die for them.

—Santo, gather your things. We gotta leave before the sun is up.

Bobby went to the refrigerator and drank from the carton of orange juice, wiping his mouth with his shirt cuff. He sat down on the stool holding Don Chan's calf as he waited for him to finish his lecture. Pobre viejo, thought Bobby. He noticed Don Chan's tremors. The way the end of the cigar shook. Bobby held his arms close to himself. He grabbed his biceps and noticed how small his arms felt since he had stopped lifting weights. A few feet away from Bobby, Hush was sleeping on the sofa. Don Chan leaned back to extend his legs, revealing more of himself. He tugged at the curtain to let the streetlight pour into the kitchen.

—I worry about you, you know, Don Chan said.

—You don't have to worry.

All Esperanza did was complain and talk about Bobby in the third person. —Bobby is lost to the streets. It's too late for him. If only Santo were around.

—You show up at four in the morning and you gonna tell me not to worry.

Let them think what they will, Bobby thought, fearing that the more he disclosed about the computer work he was doing with Ed, the less likely his dreams would become real. People who talk have nothing. It's the quiet ones who move ahead. And Bobby was keeping quiet about his ideas. To marry Hush in a church, her in white, him in a tux, him carrying her through a doorway to a two-family house. They would live on the income they earned from the other tenants who would rent from them. He had already looked at the prices of some property up in Castle Hill, in the Bronx, and how much a mortgage would cost him. He figured they'd have a small yard so Hush's baby could swim in one of those plastic pools, and they could barbecue in the summer. The Colón family could visit them on weekends. They would set up the extra bedroom for his mother's visits. He was waiting until Hush turned eighteen, until she had the baby, until she was ready to kiss him with those bee-stung lips of hers. My sweet little Hush. He wasn't going to hurt her like her stepfather or any other man had.

—It's that Esperanza who got you crazy, Santo. She already has you working for her father.

Don Chan held the cigar in his mouth, enjoying the taste of the tobacco.—When one man knows what another man is hungry for, he's got you by the balls.

—You hungry? Don Chan waited for Bobby to answer. Bobby was busy looking over at the sofa in the living room and pretending not to listen.

—No, I'm not. I ate something before I came here.

—Hunger makes men do crazy things. But we haven't lost yet . . . , Don Chan said.

—Lost what?

—Our country, mijo. You're working for the wrong man. He's

selling us away. And because they're starving us to death, we sell ourselves. If we don't stop them, we'll spend our lives scratching a güiro on beaches to entertain them.

—That's why I'm working for myself.

Don Chan and his mother thought he was dealing. But it wasn't the night to try and convince Don Chan otherwise. Not at four in the morning. He had spent eight hours in front of a computer screen.

—So why are you hanging on the corner? Coming home late at night?

—I don't hang on the corner.

—Yes you do, Don Chan said. —I see you there every day.

—It's not what you think.

—Let them assume, let them think what they want, Bobby mumbled under his breath as he grabbed a beer from the fridge. Bobby wasn't sleepy. He hardly ever slept anymore. When he went to bed, all he could think about was the fact that Hush was close to him. He spent most nights contemplating kissing her. What would she do? Would she be mad? When would it be the right time to approach her? Did she already know how he felt about her?

—Abuelo . . . I think I should go to bed, it's late.

—Late? We can't sleep. Because that's when they get us.

—No disrespect, Abuelo, but you're confused. We're in New York. I'm your grandson, Bobby. Look at me, Abuelo. No one is after us.

Don Chan didn't want to look at him. If this was Bobby, then where was Santo?

Bobby let the silence hang for a while.

—You know, Abuelo, I hope you don't go dying anytime soon, so you can see what my plans are. Bobby nearly burst out laughing, because the idea of being with Hush brought him so much joy. He couldn't believe how corny and ridiculous he must've sounded, but he felt it deep inside him, like warm bathwater on his skin.

—What's so funny? Don Chan asked. He was trying to have a serious conversation with him.

—Nothing, Abuelo. I'm mad tired. I'm going to bed. He left Don Chan alone in the dark.

Esperanza was tired. She was tired of getting up every morning and taking the train crowded with people. She was tired of spilling out of the train and into the streets where more hurried people rushed to their jobs, classes. People stomping all over her, too busy looking at their watches, clutching their newspapers, stomping their rubber soles onto the pavement and never once did they look left or right, just forward. She was tired of thinking about her next paycheck and seeing it disappear into her bills. Had she already paid for the electricity last month or was it the phone bill? Was she supposed to call the doctor for Don Chan's appointment, or was it Hush's appointment? She was tired. And what for? Now the agency required her to travel downtown and take a seminar to prevent injuries in health aides while lifting and working with disabled patients. Did her work ever end?

Esperanza read the ads over people's heads as she rode the train. Ads for lawsuits, for doctors for bunions, for condoms. She tried not to make eye contact. And when she did, the disgruntled and tired faces on people belonging to the business suits, the young, anxious faces heading to school with their backpacks clutched in between their legs, men and women heading to work made her more tired. Many of them struggling to keep their own eyes open in the morning and their heads falling over onto the stranger's shoulder next to them.

Then she noticed a tall white man getting on the train, holding his paper.

Esperanza blinked hard, lifting her eyebrows, leaning forward to get a better look. She knew that man. Yes, she did know him after watching him for so many years.

It was the haircut. The beady eyes. The can't-do-no-wrong Bobby Ewing.

She tugged at the woman next to her, reading the Bible.

Bobby Ewing was on the train! In her train! Going in her direction!

—This is a sign, Esperanza said to the churchgoing, hat-wearing lady.

—Who's Bobby?

—He's like the richest man in Texas! Esperanza said. No one seemed to care or notice. She had to speak to him. It was no coincidence that it was happening to her at that moment. She went into her purse to look for a photograph of Bobby and Dallas to show him how he was partly responsible for everything that had happened in her life. That he owed something to her after she had made such a long trip.

She got up and stood next to him. Grabbing the pole, trying to look interested in the subway map next to his head. She didn't want to scare him. He read the *New York Times,* folding it in quarters.

—Excuse me, she said, and he looked up at her. He looked so old in person, nothing like he did on television. He waited for her to speak. She didn't know where to begin. Should she tell him about la Loca's TV or the yola, or when Dallas was born? He was waiting and she wasn't prepared. She didn't have a camera on her. Oh my, she thought. He will think I'm crazy if I don't say anything.

—Excuse me, Bobby, she said.

—My name is Patrick.

—Are you sure? Bobby Ewing from la televisión, no?

—I did play Bobby, but—

—Yo lo sabía, she said and looked around to show people how right she was. And why didn't they look excited?

—I have photos of my children. Aquí está Dallas, and mi hijo, Bobby. I named him after you, well, actually, his real name is Roberto María, after his great-uncle who saved like a hundred people, but in America nobody cares about Roberto María, so I told my son, you want to be an important man like Bobby Ewing, you have to have an important name like Bobby Ewing. Patrick pulled his shirt collar away from his neck.

—Please, my name is Patrick Duffy. Bobby was a fictional character.

—What's that?

Esperanza didn't know that English word.

—Make-believe, not real.

—But Bobby's a much better name for you. I prefer Bobby, if you don't mind.

—But it's not my name. He looked over her head. She had him cornered.

—Let the lady call you Bobby, the big man standing by the door said.

Patrick Duffy tucked his newspaper under his arm. The train stopped between stations.

—I can give you an autograph. He pulled out a pen from his jacket.

—On a check, Esperanza teased.

The man standing by the door chuckled.

—So what do you want from me?

—Want? Nothing. Just to tell you about my kids.

Why was he so upset? Esperanza turned around and noticed that everyone was staring. Esperanza wanted to touch his face. The skin was so pale and blotchy. Was he really the man she saw on TV? Had he ever ridden on a horse?

—A man like you should wear moisturizer, she said and the churchgoing lady laughed with Esperanza.

—What?

The train moved again.

—All that horseback riding is chafing your skin. It's the wind, you know. White people like you get chafing right around the cheeks.

She wished one of her kids was there to see him. No one would believe her. Maybe she should get the autograph as proof.

—Give me something of yours.

—Are you insane?

—I don't know that word, she lied.

—Insane, Patrick said and twirled his finger around his ear.

—Why would you say such a thing? I just wanted something of yours to show my children. Like a business card. I came from D.R. to go to Dallas. And now I find you in New York City. My children will never believe it.

—I live in California.

—But I thought you lived in Dallas.

—Lady, that was make-believe. The show was about Dallas but I live in California.

—No me digas. But if it was in California, why didn't the Ewings live on the beach? He was lying to her, but she didn't care. He had to protect himself. He was an important man and couldn't talk to every stranger who recognized him. She might've known him throughout the years, but this was his first time seeing her.

—So the rancho is in California?

—No, the ranch on *Dallas* is in Dallas. But I live in California.

—But why do they trick me like that?

—It's no trick, lady. Television's not real.

—But . . . that should be against the law.

Patrick faked a smile at her as if to hurry her along.

—I'm trying to read, he said and put the newspaper over his face.

—You should give me something. Something for tricking me that way. The least you could've done is to show on the TV that you ride the train like everybody else so maybe I wouldn't feel so deceived. All this time I assumed men like you didn't ride the train. You were supposed to be the sweet one. It was your brother who was the un-kind one. Now I see you're also unkind.

—Miss, please.

—They should've shot you. They should've shot all of you for lying to people, making it look so easy. And look at you, you're a nothing, like me, on a train, like me, you live like me, but on TV, you pretend that you're something else and I believed in you.

—What do you want from me, lady? Please calm down.

—I want to go to Dallas. Esperanza felt stupid. —I want to live in a house like yours with horses and chandeliers and crystal glasses.

—I'm sorry, lady.

—Not even Pamela . . . she doesn't live in Dallas either?

When the subway doors opened and Patrick Duffy rushed out with the crowds on the train, Esperanza watched his back.

—Bye, Bobby! Thank you for nothing.

She sat back down next to the churchgoing lady reading the Bible. The corners of Esperanza's lips sank into her cheeks. All along she was dreaming about Dallas when she should've been aiming for California.

—Envy slays the simple—Job five, verse two, said the lady.

—What are you saying?

—I'm saying the Lord's words, the lady said, licking her lips and spreading her lipstick evenly around her mouth.

—But I don't envy nobody.

—I saw your eyes wide open, as if that white man was handing you salvation.

Esperanza looked around for another seat. But the train was full of new faces. She wasn't sure who on that train had witnessed her meeting Bobby Ewing. She wondered if Bobby was single. She regretted not having gone to the salon. If she had more time, she could better explain to him what a miracle their meeting was. Important men like him got nervous around strangers.

—Matthew twenty-two, verses thirty-seven to thirty-eight. The lady looked up from her Bible. —Love the Lord your God with all your heart, soul, and mind. This is the first and greatest commandment.

—I do love God.

—And the second is, You shall love your neighbor as yourself.

—If you met my neighbors, you would know they are hard to love. They blast the music and piss in the elevators. It's hard to love people like that.

—Do not judge and you will not be judged. That white man is not your neighbor. You don't judge him, but you judge the people around you.

—I'm not judging.

—Second Corinthians five, verse seven. We know things are true by believing, not by seeing. God bless you, child, she said to Esperanza as she exited the train.

We know what's true by believing, not by seeing. What did that mean? Esperanza did see Bobby Ewing. But no one would believe her.

Maybe Bobby Ewing had been on the train before and she hadn't looked up to notice.

Who were her neighbors? Did she judge them? She noticed a woman with the look of new love, smiling to herself, feasting on a recent memory. And she envied that look of anticipation and longing. Why hadn't she seen that before? She envied the children looking up at the signs, captivated by any new word or image. She envied the guy drinking his cup of coffee, listening to the small radio by his ear and laughing to himself. Why did she think that everyone around her was miserable? Maybe she was the one who was miserable. Maybe she was the one without hope. She should've taken the autograph from Patrick Duffy. Something to prove their meeting.

Bobby Ewing wasn't as handsome as Esperanza imagined. Seeing him changed everything. She wasn't going to Dallas, or California for that matter. Over sixteen years in Nueva York, hoping to live her dream, and suddenly someone turned on the lights and she was awake. What had she been waiting for? Did she really think a man like Bobby would knock on her door and sweep her off her feet? Or that she would wake up one day and Santo would be by her side again? If she didn't pay those damn credit cards, she wasn't ever going to own anything but the shoes on her feet. When Santo died, she had been warned by the financial adviser that it would take thirty years to pay off the cards. It had now been six years since then, and she had hardly made a dent.

Instead of going straight home, she went to the credit union.

—Señora Esperanza Colón, said the same man who had helped her before. He was no longer in college, but a professional with a degree, who recognized her from the building his mother lived in.

—You have to help me. If I don't pay these bills, I can't get a loan, I can't buy anything. I work and work. I have no retirement plan. I'm not getting any younger.

Esperanza was on the verge of tears.

—Calm down. Start from the beginning, he said. —Refresh my memory.

—I have these bills. Before Santo died. You have to help me.

—How much do you owe?

And he started to write down figures for her:

- Original bill, 2,000 dollars
- 40 dollars a month (30 in interest, 10 on principal)
- 18 percent interest

—To pay a bill of two thousand dollars, it will take thirty years. And you will have paid five thousand in interest and two thousand for your original purchase when you're finally done. You continue this way and you'll be paying for another twenty-two years.

Esperanza's eyes welled up. I would've spent seven thousand dollars? —I'll be dead before I see the end of it.

—Hopefully not. The young man started typing some numbers.

—You were smart to come here. But this time, you must follow my advice. First you have to find a way you can pay more than forty dollars a month. A big chunk, to lower the principal. Maybe you can sell something you don't use. There must be something you have of value.

She thought about the tin can she kept on her dresser. It had been over a year of savings. She had to have at least 365 dollars, but definitely more. —I have a little saved for a house.

The financial adviser passed her some tissue. People at the credit union were staring.

—It's not easy being alone. I lost my husband five years ago, she said. Why couldn't her children be professionals? Dallas was still young, but Bobby? She was afraid to ask Bobby for anything. What if he got himself into trouble again? No, he had just come home. It was too soon to ask him for help.

—Look, if you can find a chunk of money, three hundred to five hundred dollars, come to the credit union to get an account. I will help you refinance your debt, with one of our loans so you can start paying less interest. We'll make a plan. Don't worry, Ms. Colón, it's less scary than you think. Maybe we can clear up your debt and get you to start investing. If you had been putting forty dollars toward an investment fund with eight percent interest, instead of paying the minimum on those credit cards, you could've had fifteen thousand dollars by now, maybe even more.

—Really? Do you really think I have hope?

—More than hope.

Reality is like the moon. You know it's there, but you don't always see it. And if you do acknowledge it, it can only help and maybe even inspire, thought Esperanza. And she wanted to see the moon and jump over it. Something in her life had to change.

She rushed home to look in her tin can. She closed the door behind her and took it over to the bed. The tin was embossed with a nativity scene. Mrs. Hernández had given her the tin of cookies. Chocolate-mint ones.

Esperanza was nervous. Her hands clammy. At least three hundred, maybe five hundred. Even more, she thought and became proud of herself for waiting to dig into the tin for as long as she did. That alone merited a prize.

She opened the tin, spread the dollar bills on the bed, and started to count. It felt like less than what she had expected. Ten dollars. Thirty dollars. She piled the money in small stacks. Eighty dollars. Two hundred and twenty dollars. But she had put money in the tin every day. How could that be? Two hundred and twenty dollars? Her heart sank to her stomach. A pain shot to her head. There was money missing. Her throat swelled up, making it difficult to breathe. Bobby. She had seen him wearing some new things.

—Mom, I'm going to the store, do you need anything? Bobby said, knocking on her bedroom door. Esperanza's face was in her hands. —How could you? she said and threw herself against his chest.

—Yo, what's the matter with you? Bobby tried to control his mother's flailing arms. Dallas and Don Chan ran to the room.

—What happened? Don Chan said.

Dallas hid behind Don Chan.

—How could you? Esperanza yelled at Bobby. —Stealing from your own mother? She pounded on his chest.

—Wait a second, Esperanza. Calm down, Don Chan said.

—Bobby? Hush ran into the room and immediately felt a contraction that made it hard for her to speak.

—But I haven't done anything! Bobby tried to hold his mother to keep her from collapsing.

Dallas slipped into her bedroom to check to see if the money was still there. Rolled up inside a drawer inside the pocket of a T-shirt was 150 dollars.

—Bobby! Hush said again, tugging at his shirt.

—What!

Hush waddled out of the living area and Bobby ran after her.

—What's going on?

—The baby, Hush said, breathing deep and fast.

Without thinking twice, Bobby picked up Hush and told her to hold on to his neck. She was heavier than he expected.

—Where are you going? I'm not finished with you, Esperanza said and ran after them.

—Hold on, Hush. We're having our baby the right way, with a doctor. Bobby ran with Hush in his arms, and between contractions, Hush breathed in Bobby's skin of orange rinds and garlic. She breathed in the Bobby who fed her vitamins and brought her books. She breathed in Bobby and sucked his neck, leaving a hickie that stayed with him for a number of years.

—Wait for us, Don Chan yelled after him, grabbing his cane.

—Wait for us, he said, making sure Dallas gathered Hush's things.

Hush was ready. The baby was ready, and it was pressing against her bladder so hard that they couldn't wait to get a taxi. Bobby was going to walk as quickly as he could to that emergency room or else she was having that baby on the street. And as he walked, everyone looked out their window on Quepasó Street to see Bobby struggling to carry Hush, whose belly was now twice the size of a basketball, who didn't care who saw her, not caring about the gossip that would surface, not caring that Don Chan was struggling to keep up with them.

And Quepasó Street was all hush, whispering about the crazy Colón family who had housed Hush, for no other reason than that she had shown up at their door.

•••

Bobby arrived at the hospital and the attendants rushed Hush into the delivery room.

—Who'll fill out her papers? asked the nurse. —Does she have insurance?

Don Chan and Bobby looked at each other. And said, —Yes. —No.

—Are you the father? she asked Bobby.

—Yes, I'm the father. He begged them to take care of her any which way they could. He wore the thin blue paper gown with pride. Donned the gloves, wore the cap, and held Hush's hand and told her to push. —I love you, Hush, he said, not believing the words were coming out of his mouth. Not believing his tongue had found its place. —Push, woman, we're having a baby.

The Colón family stayed in the waiting room while Hush pushed the overdue baby out of her body.

—How long has it been? Esperanza asked.

—The doctors said seven hours. They say the baby is too big.

—Should we call her mother? Esperanza asked, wondering if Hush's mother cared.

—Let's wait, Don Chan said. We're her family now. And for once, Esperanza listened. She listened to Don Chan and sat, feeling worried, excited, and impatient all at the same time.

Eighteen hours had passed, Hush pushed and pushed, and Bobby was wide awake, pepped with coffee and cola, holding Hush's hand and telling her about their future house in Castle Hill. Telling her how hard he had been working and about the marvels of the Internet. —Imagine a new world called cyberspace, with super malls, lounges, clubs, schools. We'll never have to leave the house again. And that once she turned eighteen, they would get married, if she permitted it to be so.

—Will you marry me, Hush? The words were coming out of his mouth, pushing their way out with a certain desperation while he saw the blood drain from Hush's face as she pushed.

—Yes, Hush, said. —Yes! she screamed, pushing and crying.

And Hush admired Bobby's fine-looking face. The same face she had known from a very young age. And there he was, loving her, wanting to be with her forever. She thought about the way Bobby took care of her and let her do as she pleased without reprimanding her. The way he welcomed her into his home and was very decent to her.

—Yes, Bobby.

Bobby squeezed her hand. Or was Hush squeezing his? And the doctor told her to push one more time and then realized that no amount of pushing would make her child come out into the world. So they put her under.

—Are you sure about this? Bobby asked as the doctors hurried around Hush, in preparation for cutting her open.

Consuelo Colón was born on the night of a full moon. Hush never came out of her sleep. The doctors were baffled. The procedure had been simple. There was nothing unusual about their efforts. But Hush's breath stopped and her heart slowed down until it ceased.

Bobby was inconsolable in the emergency room. It no longer mattered that Esperanza had butchered Dallas's hair, that Esperanza had accused Bobby of stealing the money Dallas had stolen. A mother had died. A child was born and they were all responsible for it. Consuelo was born with her eyes wide open and a smile of mischievousness that made the Colón family afraid of what they had gotten themselves into.

After Consuelo's birth, Esperanza could no longer work the twenty-four-hour shifts at Mrs. Hernández's house. Bobby's heartbreak led him to stare at the computer he had built himself in his bedroom, where he worked and thought of nothing other than the needs of Consuelo.

—I need your help, Mami.

He explained to Esperanza that for the past year, he had been working with Ed, developing websites.

—But I thought—

—I'm sorry, Mami, I should've told you.

—But you could've helped me with the bills. What are you children thinking? All this time I was so worried . . .

—Help me with Consuelo, and I'll take care of you. I promise.

—But we can give Consuelo back to her family. You have no idea what it takes to raise a child.

—I'm her family, Bobby said. —Consuelo is mine.

Esperanza rehearsed how she would tell Mrs. Hernández that she could no longer take the trip to the Bronx at night. That the agency was already looking for a replacement. Although Mrs. Hernández wasn't always nice to Esperanza, she had become fond of the woman throughout the years and knew that while Mrs. Hernández didn't admit it, she looked forward to their conversations before going to work at the laundromat.

Esperanza used her keys to enter the apartment and noticed that the lights were dim and the candles of San Lázaro and San Miguel were on. Mrs. Hernández was still in her robe, smoking a cigarette. Esperanza was afraid of interrupting her. She was more afraid of walking into a problem. She couldn't handle any problems at the moment. She had been on very little sleep.

She had counted on an uneventful night with Mr. Hernández. But before she could turn around to take a breath, to prepare herself, Mrs. Hernández looked up and waved her to come closer. She didn't look at her. Esperanza studied the doilies on the table, which Mrs. Hernández crocheted while she watched the novelas. She said she could tell the passage of time with each loop caught with her hands. She didn't want time to pass without her making something of it. All over her house, her handiwork marked time, dressing her bureaus, lamps, tables.

—Ay, Esperanza, he didn't wake up this morning, Mrs. Hernández said.

—Did you call an ambulance? Have you called anyone?

—No.

—Do you want me to call?

—Not yet.

—That's fine, Mrs. Hernández. Why don't I make you some coffee? Esperanza said as if it were just another day. —Maybe we should call the laundromat and tell them you won't be going to work today, Esperanza said. —Let's open up the windows to let fresh air in, if you don't mind.

Mrs. Hernández sat at the table and didn't look up for what seemed like hours. She sat there and Esperanza sat with her, preparing fresh coffee and some warm bread with slices of cheese. She was relieved she didn't have to tell Mrs. Hernández that she was switching her assignment. And without expecting it, Esperanza felt a great sense of loss for the man who hardly said a word to her except for the occasional grunt.

—I woke up this morning and he wasn't breathing. It's the first thing I do. I did that with my sons, you know. Every morning, make sure they were breathing. Because no matter how healthy we are, a falling dream can take us and we won't know how to come back. So I always checked.

Esperanza nodded. She also checked in with her children at night and in the morning to make sure they were safe.

—I should call my son, Mrs. Hernández said and started tearing up again.

—I'm so sorry, Esperanza said, thinking about Hush. The impression of Hush's body on her sofa cushions was still there when she left the apartment. A baby left behind without a mother. Esperanza also began to cry.

—You're a good woman, Esperanza. Mrs. Hernández handed her a tissue.

—If I call my son, he'd want to come. But what could he do? He's so far away, you know. I didn't plan for this. I imagined this day, but I never planned for it.

Esperanza hadn't planned for Santo's death, either. She assumed there would always be time.

—What am I going to do all alone? He was my compañero for forty-five years. What will I do, Esperanza?

—You'll live as you always did. Esperanza wanted to tell her that, yes, she will live, but now she'll always have the feeling that she had forgotten to do something, and there will always be a void that nothing will fill. Thinking about it made Esperanza's eyes well up with tears once again. She didn't want to be reminded of the pain of her husband's death, and even though she knew very well what Mrs. Hernández was going through, she wanted to leave her and not deal with it. But what are experiences for, if not to make us stronger for others who have yet to live through such things? Mrs. Hernández needed her. As nasty as she had been sometimes, watching her cry, bent over at the table, poking her hands inside the eyelet of her tablecloth, she seemed like a good woman.

—My husband died too. Esperanza took a long sip of coffee, unsure if her story was appropriate. —When he died, I thought that was the end of my life. Then days went by and by, and now days pass and I'm only reminded of him by his photograph on my altar. And I hate myself for forgetting, but it's been so long now.

But there were still moments, like the day of his death, their anniversary, his birthday, when the loss of him hit her in a way so that she would lose herself again. How sometimes she caught Santo's scent of petroleum, burned wood, the wet earth and sea when she least expected it.

—At least Mr. Hernández lived the life he wanted. His soul will rest in peace.

—But he wanted to go to Cuba, and I didn't let him. I insisted we wait until Fidel died, because I was afraid. We didn't leave on the best of terms.

—I know perfectly. Esperanza held Mrs. Hernández, who broke out into bigger tears, louder cries. Esperanza pulled her toward her chest. —I'm so sorry, Esperanza said, mad at God for being so unfair. For giving people life and then taking it away. For allowing pain to penetrate good people. Mrs. Hernández wasn't so bad as to be left in a big apartment alone without her sons or a husband. At least I have my children, thought Esperanza. At least they would never leave me and go away to Russia like Mrs. Hernández's son had.

Esperanza fetched Mrs. Hernández a warm, damp towel. She cleaned up the makeup running from her eyes. She looked younger without all the makeup. She noticed that Mrs. Hernández didn't have any teeth. She must've forgotten to put them in. —Ay, Mrs. Hernández, Esperanza said, trying to remember what words had soothed her in her time of grief, knowing that nothing helped except for time. Esperanza went into the bedroom where Mr. Hernández's body lay. She closed his eyes. She took the sheet and covered his body. His skin yellow from dehydration, his lips cracked and skin flaky. She took the newspaper he liked to read off his bed and rested his hands with his palms down.

He liked the quiet, the newspaper, and a good hand massage. He didn't ask Esperanza for those things, he just stuck his hand out before his bedtime and she grabbed the lotion and pressed against his fingers, pushing the blood up, all the way down to his fingertips. — Ay, que dios te bendiga.

—Ya no más. You have tried your best to stay alive. Sleep in peace, Viejo, Esperanza said, as if he was her father. When her father was dying, she wasn't there to care for him. He was angry with her for marrying Santo, so she stayed away to not make him sicker than he already was. She wondered what Mr. Hernández must've been like when he had all his faculties. Esperanza looked up at the photo in the bedroom of the younger Hernández couple and wondered if they were in love when they got married, or if their marriage was one of convenience. And what convenience? Did they have any regrets? She didn't want to have regrets. I don't want to grow old and wonder, what if?

Esperanza called Russia and left their son a message to call his mother. She left Mrs. Hernández with a cooked meal, in case she got hungry. It would be difficult to eat when death was in the air. She called the ambulance, and then watched them take Mr. Hernández away. Mrs. Hernández chose to stay. There was no reason to go. She would deal with the paperwork tomorrow.

—I can stay with you, Esperanza said, although she didn't want to.

—No, it's fine. Mrs. Hernández stared out the same window her husband loved to look out from every day for hours on end.

—What do you think he saw when he looked out the window? Mrs. Hernández said.

—The same things we see, I guess. The pigeons, the people walking, the cars honking, the other windows in apartments. Stuff like that.

—I never asked him, you know? It's funny how we never ask people when they're around, and then when they're gone, all these questions surface.

—Are you sure you don't want me to stay with you?

—No, mija. You've done enough.

—I'll leave you my number in case of anything. And make sure you eat something. No point in making yourself sick.

Esperanza needed to take a walk and make her way home to care for Consuelo.

—I'm fine, Mrs. Hernández said, lighting another cigarette. My old friend and me are being reacquainted. It had been years since I lit up one of these. But I always kept a pack in the fridge, waiting. It helped to quit knowing I had a pack nearby whenever I needed it.

—Call me, Esperanza said, as she walked away from her. It was the last time Esperanza ever saw Mrs. Hernández, who was looking out the window, on the wooden chair. It was the last visit Esperanza made to Van Cortlandt. She had assumed she'd be invited to the funeral, but Mrs. Hernández never called.

Esperanza returned home. She opened the children's bedroom and found Bobby asleep on the bed with Consuelo next to him bundled tightly in a blanket. Don Chan was on his bed, the sheets soaked in tears. Esperanza pulled a blanket over Don Chan, and for the first time, he didn't resist her. —I want to go home, he said and grabbed her hand and wept for the unrequited dreams of all those he loved. She waited until he fell asleep and then retired to her room. The tin box was on her bed, waiting for her. Someone had moved it from the dresser. Inside it, she found a new wad of dollar bills, 150 dollars. It would never repair what had broken inside her. All those years she worked for her children, thinking that one day they would take care of her; instead they stole from her.

She held Santo's photo on her altar and kissed it. She looked at the boxes filled with the outgrown clothing of her children, Santo's belongings; all the things that waited to be sent to D.R. All the memories that crowded her home, that waited, that never changed; all the things that she accumulated to fill the void, the emptiness, to fill the absence.

—Está bien, Viejo, I'll take you home.

8

Boarding NYC—Sto. Dgo.
1999

The Colón family arrived in Dominican Republic when suddenly the new president had decided to push the hour forward. What better way to show his power than to darken the mornings and lengthen the nights? So what if the farmers who relied on the hens, who cockadoodled with the rise of the sun, were running late; and if children walked to school in the dark, in the early mornings. Everything was off the clock; flowers were late blooming, the cows were not milking, women's periods didn't come, creating a panic of pregnancy and a variety of screams that competed with the traffic jams on city corners.

But the Colón family was all too sore and hot from wearing heavy coats and carrying their bags to care about the hour changing. They didn't have the energy to notice that the sanitation contracts were corrupt. Bridges were built halfway, construction was put to a halt until the new president figured out how much money he could make off the government before the next government came in and did the same. To Don Chan and Esperanza, nothing much had changed since they left. Everyone vying for a coffee bean, a cane stalk, a grain of rice, to sell, to eat, to live on. No, the Colón family didn't care (at least not right away) about the strikes, the endangered flora and fauna, the below-living wages at American-owned factories in the free-trade zones. They had traveled like a family and together they got off the plane, each in their own heads, each with their own dreams and desires.

They were welcomed by anticipating Dominican faces and pushed out of the plane and airport by anxious Dominican Yorks, whose bodies were ornate with gold, lugging baggage dubbed los muertos. Esperanza was looking for los muertos, the large suitcases that resembled body bags as they slumped on the conveyor belt. Seventy-pound suitcases (plus or minus two pounds), which each passenger who had relatives in D.R. brought over. They were filled with secondhand clothes and things that nobody wanted anymore back in New York City: canned foods, candy and cereal, electronics and accessories.

Don Chan exited Las Américas Airport to be welcomed by a light drizzle and a rainbow that arched over the partly cloudy sky.

—Ay mi país, Don Chan said, looking around teary eyed. It had been eight years. He didn't carry a bag, only his Dominican passport. He had never become a U.S. citizen, always thinking his stay in New York City would be temporary. But as time passed, more and more of his comrades had died. Like he was dying. Like everything he knew to be true was dying.

—We're going home, he said, but no one was listening. And as they walked out of the airport and were greeted by the excited faces of strangers, the scent of the sea . . . oh the sea . . . Don Chan was compelled to see the sea.

—Where's the sea? he said and went up to a taxi driver and asked to be taken there.

Bobby ran after him and apologized to the taxi driver.

—Dáme un regalo, 'mano, the taxi driver said with a con-artist smile.

Bobby didn't smile back; he grabbed Don Chan by the arm, realizing how thin he was, how easily his bones could break and how careful he had to be with him.

—Come with me, Abuelo. Don't worry. We'll go to the sea.

—Did I ever tell you, Bobby, that before we were cane people, we were sea people?

—Sí, Abuelo, you did.

Don Chan could taste the sea, he could hear it. His ear full of water, his skin sticky to the touch, his veins on his arms, oh yes, look, the sea runs through my body, he told Dallas, who was looking over at the fast-food counters.

—Ah yes, my father didn't want us to grow up and serve tourists. Not his children. He wanted us to go to school and work for ourselves, like he did. He was a fish man, from a line of fish men, Don Chan continued talking, but no one was listening. Esperanza was anxious to put Santo to rest; by spreading his ashes she could once again sleep through the night without him whispering in her ear. Dallas, still buzzing from the rum they gave her at the airport, was holding on to Consuelo.

—Bobby, go get one of those guys with the vans. It doesn't matter which one. They're all thieves in this country. Puros ladrones!

—Dallas, don't take your eyes off the luggage. Give them a chance and they'll steal your clothes right off of your body, Esperanza said.

Dallas suspiciously looked at all the young men hovering around them, offering to help. She held Consuelo tighter against her.

—Ah! Don't listen to her. People only steal when you suspect them, Don Chan said. —If you trust people, you disarm all their bad intentions. Isn't that true, primo, Don Chan told one of the young men extending his hand. To Don Chan, every man could be a cousin.

Bobby returned with the driver.

—Whatever the driver said it cost, we pay half, Esperanza told Bobby and then pushed her way into the van. The heat was unbearable. —Don Chan, sit in the front, Esperanza yelled out to him. —Here's some water so you don't dehydrate. People can die from the heat.

Once the luggage was packed in the back, Bobby and Dallas climbed into the van with Consuelo. Bobby looked at the rubble, buildings in the midst of construction, big posters of future presidential candidates, piled palm leaves, broken bottles, tin barrels holding contained fires, kids fencing with branches, and stands selling fried fish and batata, close to the road to tempt drivers. Music blared out of car hutches; meat fried behind doors, luring the hungry who hovered around open windows.

—A year ago, you never saw the city so dirty. This government is robbing us of our money, the driver said.

—What else is new? Esperanza said. —No one ever follows the laws here.

—God, Mami . . . why you being so negative? Dallas said. Her mother had a different air about her. From the moment they landed, her mother was bossing everyone around and complaining.

—Me, negative? Esperanza looked out the car window to see the sea along the Avenida de las Américas.

—It's something else, Don Chan said, admiring the horizon, the sparse palm trees bent over as if they were bowing to the sun.

Esperanza had forgotten how beautiful it was. The familiarity of the sea smell, the dense air, the taste of salt on her lips. The muscles around her neck immediately began to relax.

—Sure does look pretty, Esperanza said and grabbed Consuelo so she could look out the window.

The traffic was slow moving. Don Chan noticed three large buses pass by.

—Los deportados, the driver said and sighed. —The U.S. turns our people into criminals and then sends them back to us so we have to suffer the consequences. Cabrones son.

—They were born criminals, Esperanza said, looking into a small mirror, frustrated that the humidity was making her mascara run.

Dallas was listening to her CD player, bopping her head, looking out the window. Damn, it was hot. She stuck her hand out of the car and let it ride the air.

—Look at those cabrones, the driver said, sighing again. —They might've been better off if they had never left.

Bobby took in the smell and sights of his childhood. But he couldn't find his childhood in la capital, which was lit with Mc-Donald's arches and Baskin-Robbins neon signs. On one strip, he saw KFCs, Häagen-Dazs, Burger King, Pizza Hut, Benetton. He saw six-story-high shopping centers and high-rise luxury build-ings. Behind the concrete structures were the small dirt roads, randomly paved, many littered with potholes that led into crowded streets, haphazard food markets, wooden houses, barefoot children. He was jolted when a man on a motocicleta banged on the car hood.

—Who are we staying with? Dallas asked.

—Your tía Pura. You're finally meeting some of your family, Dallas. It's also the house I grew up in.

—Does she have a toilet?

—Of course she has a toilet, Esperanza said.

—Does it work? Don Chan joked, knowing of the many Dominicans who had purely decorative toilet fixtures because they didn't have enough water for a flush.

—Does she have a phone line? Bobby asked. He had work he needed to send to New York City in a few days and needed to connect online.

—Yes, but don't worry, you're only here for a few days. I'm sure you'll manage, Esperanza said and was glad that her children would see that things here weren't as great as Don Chan had made them out to be. And if it were up to the Colóns, they would've been peddling candies on the street for pennies. And that was just the capital. Wait until they got to Los Llanos, her children would see what she saved them from.

—When we drop them off, I want you to take me to Los Llanos, Don Chan said to the driver.

—It'll be too late to go there tonight, Esperanza said.

—I want to go tonight. Don Chan slapped his hand on his knees and shook his head.

—It's only a two-hour drive from the capital. I don't mind, the driver said.

—Of course you don't mind, because you make the money, Esperanza snapped.

—Mami, be nice, Bobby said, holding Consuelo on his lap. Bouncing her to keep her from getting restless.

—It's decided. We drop off the women, and Bobby and I will go to Los Llanos. We'll have to stop by San Pedro de Macorís to pick up the keys.

—Why can't I go? Dallas asked.

—Trust me, you don't want to go there, Esperanza said. —Besides, who'll watch Consuelo while I distribute all the stuff we brought back for the family?

—We'll see you there tomorrow, to spread the ashes, Esperanza said. —Bright and early. I don't like traveling in that campo at night with all those small roads. They're an accident waiting to happen.

While Bobby and the driver unloaded the car, people from Pura's neighborhood gathered around them to see if they would get anything from the Dominican Yorks. Esperanza and Dallas stood in front of the small cement house. Its walls peeled open like burned skin.

—Hey, Pura, Esperanza yelled through the iron gates that locked Pura in. —Ya llegamos. Esperanza looked around to her street and across to the building that had once housed the clinic where she'd first seen Santo.

Dallas held Consuelo against her hip while Consuelo played with her hair.

—Qué linda! Y cuántos años tiene? a young woman asked Dallas, as she sashayed out from the house next door. Fanning herself with the daily paper. Her hair in a tight *tubi*, waiting to be set loose that evening for her night out.

—Un año, Dallas said and realized that the young woman assumed Consuelo was hers. The thought made her hold her with pride. She noticed how the men standing in front of the colmado across the street were staring at her like they would a full-fledged child-bearing woman.

—La llave, Pura yelled to her granddaughter, who had lived with her ever since her mother moved to San Pedro to work in la Zona Franca.

—Corre . . . que llegaron! Pura yelled in excitement and stood on the other side of the locked gate, extending her arms through the bars to touch the sister she hadn't seen in over a decade. Pura, who took care of her parents until their last days and who lived her entire life in the same house.

Bobby carried the large bags onto the front porch. He piled them on the corner, tearing off his long-sleeved shirt, leaving on his short-sleeved T-shirt and exposing his trim and muscular body.

—You're so tall, the young woman in the tubi said as she walked around him, as if studying a good slab of cow meat in the market.

—¡Vámonos! Don Chan slammed his hand against the hood of the car to get Bobby's attention. The clinic they'd worked out of in 1965 had been turned into a colmado. Pura's house brought too many painful memories to Don Chan. —Let's go now, he said.

—But don't they want to eat? I made so much food, Pura yelled out to the van. —Don Chan, qué sinvergüenza eres . . . , she yelled out to him, not offended that the old man was being aloof.

—Bobby! Don Chan yelled again.

—Bendición, Tía, Bobby said and gave Consuelo a long hug and kiss good-bye. It was the first time he had parted with her since her birth.

Dallas walked into the room she and Consuelo and her mother would sleep in. It was her cousin's room. She had to be careful not to flail her arms or she would hurt her knuckles on the ceiling fan. Inside the room, there were two small cots, a dilapidated bureau, a small window decorated in flowery curtains, facing the food market. Two folded towels. She recognized the sheets that her mother had sent, on the bed. At the end of the hallway, there was a small shower, sink, and toilet. The door was unhinged. A thin piece of white fabric divided the room. The door propped on the side.

—Ay, prima, if you want, I can show you how to climb out to the roof. You feel like the sky is yours alone up there, her cousin said and grabbed Dallas's arms and touched her necklace and earrings.

—Did you bring me earrings like those?

—I don't know, Dallas said, unsure what her mother had packed in the bags.

—Where will you sleep tonight? Dallas asked her cousin.

—With my mother.

Dallas felt like a giant in the tiny room. Consuelo was already making herself at home by touching everything she found. Dallas watched the ceiling fan turn and her insides turned along with it. The curtains danced to the soft breeze and the sun caressed her skin. The mosquitoes buzzed around her, landing on her and launching off.

Don Chan was anxious to arrive in Los Llanos. As if the longer he waited to get there, the more likely that his home would cease to exist. He had left it behind with a padlock. He had called Miraluz to warn her of their arrival. She assured him everything was fine.

—Are the graves still there? Don Chan asked her.

—The last hurricane killed some of the vegetation around them. But yes, they're there.

—Ay his wife, Caridad. Could she feel him in the country? He caught a glimpse of the sea as they drove toward San Pedro de Macorís. —All these years, he said, and felt his insides spin, his bladder coming loose from the anticipation of returning home. Don Chan was returning home. —Ay mi país! he said again.

For most of the trip, it was only the sounds of the old radio playing some popular songs and Don Chan's voice, which sounded as if he were talking out of a cordless phone with a low battery, that accompanied them. But no one was listening to either Don Chan or the radio.

—Stop the car, Don Chan told the driver.

—It'll be extra, the driver said.

—Can't you give the old man a break? Bobby said as the driver turned into the small opening on the road near the beach of Juan Dolio.

—Your grandmother found me here. Don Chan climbed out to find the exact place. Bobby walked out and looked around. He checked to make sure he still had his wallet, an extra stash of money in his pocket, and that he had taken off his gold necklace. He walked on the small strip of the highway that sped along the sea. On the other side was an expanse of flat, green land waiting to be developed. When the beach appeared, the tide nearby, there was a narrow, rough path for them to walk through. A watchman stopped them. He was a hungry-looking fellow, carrying a gun the length of his leg.

—Área privada, the watchman warned Don Chan.

Bobby lifted his hands up in the air to show he was unarmed. It was a reflex.

—If you want to walk on the beach, you have to get a hotel pass, the watchman said, pointing over to the pink-and-yellow building up a ways.

—I thought the beaches were public, Don Chan said, asserting his rights.

The watchman placed his hand on his rifle.

—Está bien, Bobby said and waved good-bye.

—And you want to give up so easily? Don Chan tugged at Bobby's shirt.

—Let's go, Abuelo. Miraluz is waiting.

—Ah, Miraluz, did I ever tell you she made the best bread pudding? Don Chan hurried into the car, forgetting about Juan Dolio. Bobby looked to the hotel strip, the wall that separated him from Don Chan's home, and realized that this place was far from where Don Chan had grown up. It was the home of tourists, not what Don Chan had described.

Soon after Juan Dolio, they arrived at the malecón of San Pedro de Macorís, where the navy had docked in the early 1900s. Where Don Chan first saw the city. Where his father decided that they would no longer be sea people in order to protect Don Chan. The rotunda looked over the malecón, filled with the heavy traffic of motocicletas, cramming in between the cars. The street vendors knocked on their windows, selling peanuts, cell phone carrying cases, and bags filled with peeled oranges.

—She lives by the movie theater, Don Chan said, looking around for it.

Santo had told Bobby stories about the old movie theater in San Pedro where he had first seen *King Kong*. But there were no movie theaters to be seen.

—You mean you don't have an address? The driver looked pissed off. He had to get home before his wife locked the doors on him.

—Who needs an address when I have my memory? Don Chan said and got out of the car and bid the driver farewell.

—Abuelo, why did you tell him to leave?

—We don't need him, Don Chan said and walked to the malecón, to sit by the sea.

—Did I ever tell you that before we were from the valley, we lived by the sea?

Bobby grabbed their two bags and propped them next to Don Chan.

—Stay here while I call Miraluz, Bobby told Don Chan, wondering if he would remember to stay put.

—Yes, sir, Don Chan said and saluted his son for taking control of the situation. Any minute now, they would be piling into cars to go to the capital and fight the marines. All their ammunition was packed tightly in their bags.

Bobby laughed and took the bag with the computer just in case. The laughter felt good. Ever since Bobby got off the plane, he'd rediscovered the muscles on his face that were numb from disuse since Hush died. The thought of Hush gave him a pang of separation anxiety from Consuelo. His greatest fear now was that something would happen where he couldn't see her again. He checked to see if he had Pura's number.

Bobby crossed the busy streets and noticed that some streets were paved and lined with mansion-style homes. A few steps away, he found himself walking on dirt roads, riddled with potholes, crowded with houses that were suffocating with people and swayed with a heavy wind.

The colmado was in plain view to Don Chan. Bobby was proud of him. It couldn't have been easy for him to stay in one place. Bobby ordered a Presidente beer to appease his thirst and asked the guy behind the counter if he knew where the old theater once was.

—Not too far from here, he said. But it closed ages ago. Before my kids were born.

—Oye, Miraluz, this kid is looking for the old theater.

Bobby turned around to see Miraluz, a woman wearing fitted orange pants and a black T-shirt, two long braids going down her back. Miraluz paused and took a closer look at the apparition before her eyes.

—Ay, ay, ay, no me digas, she said and walked right up to Bobby, who was sitting. She put her arms around him, her breast in his face.

—Ay, Santo, amor, cuánto tiempo. Look at that face, you haven't aged. It must be that Chinese skin. All these years and you look the same, she said, taking a swig from Bobby's beer. —You haven't changed a bit since you left for New York. Ay, dios mío. Santo Colón.

She was talking so fast, Bobby wasn't sure if he would ever be able to get a word in edgewise. She rubbed his back and pulled him close. He could smell her hairspray, her makeup spread on his T-shirt, but she kept hugging him, feeling his arms, his face, his neck despite the sweat. He needed a shower from all the traveling. She took the beer bottle and rubbed it against her neck, against his forehead.

—Ay, Santo, so much has changed since you left.

Bobby wanted to tell her that he was his father's son. His mother had told him many times how much he resembled his father, but to be mistaken for him? Besides, his father had left twenty years ago. Couldn't they tell how much time had passed?

Bobby looked around and New York City felt very far away, a long time ago.

Then the colmado's lights went out. —Se fue la luz, yelled the man behind the counter. How different could this place be from twenty years ago? Bobby didn't see a computer, cell phones were the only indication that he was not in the past. But aside from the Mc-Donald's advertisements, it was hard to tell what year it was.

—This is Don Chan's son, Santo Colón, she said to anyone who was listening.

Bobby tried to interject, but she covered his lips with her fingertips, rubbed his firm abs and grabbed his hair, tugging it in admiration.

Bobby had never met a woman like Miraluz. She was affectionate, comforting, and she had known his father. Maybe in ways his mother didn't know his father.

—Don Chan is waiting over there, Bobby said and pointed at the old man sitting on the edge of the malecón by the chimichurri stand.

Miraluz looked back at Bobby. She touched his face in disbelief.

—It's like you brought Santo back from the dead. Miraluz rushed across the street to Don Chan.

Esperanza had forgotten cold showers. Pura had boiled some water and placed it in the bucket by the tub, but the water was still cold enough to lift all the little hairs around her body. Pura didn't wear a stitch of makeup and her skin had a deep orange glow under the caramel color that Esperanza's clan was famous for. Pura never seemed hurried, as if every day was the same as the next. She kept her home in order in all its sparseness and had the percolator going all day, waiting for the next person to pass by to sit in her backyard for some gossip. Two sisters couldn't be more different. While Pura was seven years her elder, Esperanza didn't think twice about bossing Pura around.

—Pura, don't you have the towels I sent you? These towels don't dry.

—I gave those towels to Luisa, Pura said. Their other sister had moved to Santiago with her husband to raise goats that fed on oregano.

—Why do you give away what I send you? That's why Pura never progressed.

—You want some coffee? Pura went to sit in the backyard in the sun.

—The sun will give you cancer. Esperanza shaded her eyes.

—At my age, who cares? Pura shooed away the chicken that she hadn't had the heart to kill.

—Dallas, come help me separate all these clothes before the vultures get here, Esperanza said, looking at all the clothes she had packed. And piled the plastic garbage bags she planned to label with each family member's name.

—You're giving this away? Dallas pulled out a pair of jeans that her mother had bought her, but that were too small. —I might fit into these one day.

—Put it in your suitcase. But take it before everyone gets here. You have no idea how crazy it gets.

Esperanza remembered the joy she used to feel when someone returned from America with clothes for them to wear. And how they all fought over the newer pieces. This time she was the one giving things away. Maybe she hadn't accomplished what she had set out to do just yet, but when she looked at all the things she'd brought for her family, the history was there inside the clothes, she saw her labor. Every piece of clothing she had earned from her own sweat. Every hour of sweat was inside each garment. She picked up a dress she had worn when Santo was still alive. She had worn it once. How much did she pay for it? Was it forty dollars? Five hours of work for that dress. The thought made her want to take it back. The family would never appreciate that. No, they had no idea what she went through to buy all those things only to then lug them over, all the way from New York City.

—We have a lot of shit, Dallas said, looking through men's clothing with tags on it. —Were these Dad's? She lifted the shirt for Esperanza to see.

—I got that one for him for Christmas. But he never liked new shirts. I told him if he never wore them, how could they look worn? It was the funniest thing about your father. Sometimes I would wash his new clothes and hang them in his closet so he would wear them.

—It's such a waste, Dallas said, and sorted the clothes by size. Adult male. Adult female. Small female. Large female . . . —Imagine if we could return all this stuff to the store.

—The sad part is that most of it is still unpaid for. Besides, nothing is worth anything once it's used.

—You'd have mad money if you could take it back.

The idea made Esperanza overheat.

—Get your mama some cold water. Pura doesn't know anything about hospitality.

On Pura's living-room floor, Esperanza's purchases resembled a wasteland.

Miraluz grabbed Don Chan and picked him up from the floor. She had gotten fuller and he had gotten shorter.

—Maldita sea, mujer. A star has fallen in the middle of the day, Don Chan said and Bobby was surprised by how charming Don Chan could be.

Miraluz grabbed one of the bags and pulled him with her toward her house, a few steps away from the colmado. She led him through the small doorway.

—Ven, ven . . . , Miraluz said, pointing for Bobby to put their bags in her sons' bedroom. And then to follow her through to the dining-room area.

—What is up with all the sewing machines? Don Chan asked, seeing the colorful piles of lace and stacks of threads, and satin fabrics. There were two sewing machines facing each other. A large table with scissors and paper.

—I have so much to tell you, Viejo. And you, Bobby, make yourself at home. She got a pillow for Don Chan to prop behind his back on the rocking chair.

—Go to the cooler and get Don Chan a ginger ale, Bobby. I'm sure he's tired from his trip.

Don Chan didn't want to let go of Miraluz's hand. He cupped her face in his hands and looked at her as if for the first time. —I thought I was never going to see you again, he said. And she kissed his forehead.

—Bobby, get me some sandals from the boys' room.

—Your feet must be burning up in those shoes, Miraluz said, peeling off Don Chan's socks. Kissing each foot in jest. —I can't believe you're here, Viejo.

—And you, Bobby . . . My god, it hurts to look at you.

Bobby couldn't take his eyes off Miraluz. Her smile filled her face and her voice was raspy and low, making it hard to tell how old she was. She must be at least his mother's age. But she didn't look it.

It took a few bottles of beer and ginger ale for Miraluz to explain El Secreto de la Victoria.

—A revolutionary label? Don Chan said with a smile.

—I call it socially responsible capitalism for the people, where everyone can participate in the process. Those who want to buy can still buy, but without the guilt.

—But people don't feel guilty when they buy, Bobby said.

—We must make them feel guilty, Miraluz said. —It's the only way it will work. People have to become more conscious.

—A brilliant idea. We spent all those years trying to change the government and it's still as corrupt as it's ever been . . . it's too in-vested in its own power to help us. You were right about that from the beginning, Miraluz. The individual helping the individual.

Don Chan listened to her ideas and felt something melt inside him. His spirit was inching away from his body.

—We're almost done with the first batch of underwear. All we need to do is sell them. We want to start with the university students, in the United States. You know, Dominican Yorks who care about their fam-ilies back home. And of course, in time we can expand.

—We can sell them via the Internet, Bobby said, wanting to touch Miraluz but not in front of Don Chan. Every time she spoke about her idea, he felt the desire to kiss her.

—El tenete? Miraluz asked.

—No, el Internet. Bobby said it slowly, looking over to Don Chan, who was falling asleep in the rocking chair. It had been a long day.

—Bobby started his own business, Don Chan said, suddenly opening his eyes.

—Your own business?

—Inside a television, Don Chan said and fell asleep again.

—You're a movie star? Miraluz pictured Bobby starring on a show in television.

—No, no . . . I work with the Internet. It's computer work. Bobby laughed at all the misunderstandings.

—Let's put him to bed so you can show me, Miraluz said and felt a rise inside her.

—Put who to bed? I'm resting my eyes, that's all.

It was like the beginning of a horse race. Esperanza's relatives were outside Pura's gates, and Pura, with fear and anticipation, took her time opening her door. She hadn't had so much family visit her in years. But when someone arrives from New York, the word gets out, and Esperanza was about to pay her dues for leaving family behind. The cousins gawked at all the gold Esperanza wore around her neck, wrist, and hands, and pretended they could care less about what she had brought them. Each of them carried Consuelo and bounced her around, saying how much she looked like Dallas.

—She's not Dallas's child, Esperanza insisted. —Dallas has plenty of time to become a mother. She's going to the university.

—Education is good, they said, but what about los enamorados? They winked at Dallas, who blushed. Her cousin had already introduced her to some of the guys from around the way. Most of them were hicks, but there was one she liked called Jorge, who she wouldn't mind making out with.

Esperanza pulled out the bags and looked at the names she had painstakingly written in permanent marker. The bags held a mix of household items—used pots, silverware, sheets, outgrown and outdated clothes. Some bags were filled with sample lipsticks she had gotten at the stores, and medicines, unconsumed before their expiration date, by the clients she took care of.

—Ay, gracias, prima, one said after the other, pulling out the treasures, checking to see if the cousin or sister received something better.

—You always send Minerva jeans. Why not me? Soraida complained.

—My mother makes this bra in la Zona Franca. How much you paid for this, eh?

—And what about the watch I wrote you for? You never sent me that watch.

—I could really use some sneakers, prima. These have holes in them.

Esperanza didn't hear the thank-yous. Only the complaining. The sweat dripped off her body. The silk shirt she wore was stained under the armpits and all along her back. Her mascara was running again. Her lipstick bled onto her teeth.

—Dallas, get me a napkin, Esperanza demanded.

—No more napkins, Pura said.

—So get money from my purse and buy some.

Esperanza was frustrated. She was staying in Dominican Republic for a few days and they couldn't even buy her napkins, just in case she needed them.

—But we buy them as we need them, Pura said.

—Sí, tía, it's not like Nueva York here, one prima said. —Even the toilet paper is expensive.

—You'll never understand how hard it is in New York, Esperanza said, pulling out bags of used clothing. —They're like new. You know I wouldn't give anything that wasn't in good condition.

But they wouldn't know because Esperanza had never made the trip back. And when they called her to ask her for money or supplies, she sent things with friends.

She sat among the bags, her family crowded over them, and suddenly Esperanza wasn't feeling so well.

—Did you bring pictures of your house in New York City? one asked.

—No, I didn't.

—We don't have a house, we have an apartment. Dallas handed over the napkins to Esperanza.

Esperanza sneered at her. They didn't need to know.

—Everyone has an apartment in New York, Esperanza defended herself.

—I heard Nueva York's dangerous. Is that true, prima?

—How did they kill Santo again?

—And wasn't your son in jail? Is he out now?

Esperanza didn't answer. She methodically dug into the bag and called out the women's names who would then distribute the clothes to their husbands and children.

Dallas noticed her mother slowing down. She hadn't realized how big her family was, how much they counted on her mother.

—Leave her alone, Dallas said.

—But why is she crying?

Pura pulled Esperanza out of the crowd and took her to the bedroom, where Esperanza shed more tears.

Dallas looked at all of them in disgust. With Consuelo on her hip, the women respected her. She placed Consuelo at her feet and dug in her mother's bags and called out the foreign names that her mother knew so well. She might have been away from D.R., but Esperanza had kept up with every child born, every person married. Dallas grabbed the bags, some bigger, others smaller, and yelled the names. —Yrene, Patricia, Julia, Blanca, Aurelia. And when the name was called, there would be a gasp, or a jump, as if they had won a prize. By the time Esperanza returned, Dallas was done. The suitcases were collapsed into each other like Russian dolls for the return trip.

—You okay? Dallas asked her mother.

—Why don't we put some music on, it's like a funeral in here, Esperanza said and everyone became jovial and scattered their energies around the house and the yard.

—I'm proud of you, mijita, Esperanza said, noticing that Dallas's hair was growing out. When exactly did Dallas grow up? And why hadn't she noticed it before?

Don Chan fell asleep without a struggle. Miraluz and Bobby sneaked into the other bedroom where they could close the door and continue the conversation.

—Show me, she said, and pulled him toward her bedroom and sat him on the bed covered with a satin comforter. Bobby was nervous. As if he had never been alone with a woman. Maybe it was the way she touched him. Maybe it was that she'd confused him with his father at the colmado. Everything about Miraluz felt familiar. The smell of her home was like that of burning wood and wet zinc. The small taps on the tin roof, the howling dogs, the soft honking from cars on the main streets.

—The Internet?

—Sí, por qué no?

—We need to plug into a phone line.

—Explain to me then.

—It's difficult to explain. I'd need to show you. But imagine, with one button you can send information to thousands of people.

—For free?

—Yes, Bobby said, wanting to touch her but didn't want to scare her. It was the first time since Hush that he felt strong desire.

She turned on the small fan and closed the door. She left him alone in the room. Miraluz reappeared in the room wearing another shirt, a fresher face, with a beer wrapped in a napkin in each hand. She sat next to him and wiped his brow.

—How could it be free? she said and held his hand clumsily.

—It's new, so they haven't figured out how to control it. So for now it's free.

—What took you so long to return here? she asked and rubbed his back.

—I never thought about it. I left when I was just a kid.

She turned Bobby's face toward her. She touched his lips with her fingertips in amazement at the likeness to his father. And before he could say no to her, she kissed him. But she wasn't kissing Bobby. No, it was not an ordinary kiss. She was kissing her past. She was kissing him for all the years his father was away from her. And with a familiarity, as if she had done it many times before, she sat on top of him and wrapped her legs around him. Her plump body, her bulging flesh, her salty skin, her breasts sagging from feeding her children, pressed and rubbed against his taut skin. He grabbed her padded feet and hands. She was so small, so soft, like a cushion, so warm and salty. Bobby licked every inch of Miraluz. And his body was reawakened and reminded that he was still alive. He never did get to make love to Hush. He wanted to seal the agreement of his arrival, to enter home. And being careful not to break her, he entered Miraluz and made love to her. Made love to Hush. Made love to San Pedro de Macorís. Made love to Dominican Republic. And after he climaxed, he didn't want to leave that small room or Miraluz, who looked so beautiful once her hair curled up from the sweat and the makeup was gone. He didn't want to stop making love to the soft-spoken—Ay, Santo, which inspired every lick and touch. He fed on her, entered her from every orifice. He found himself in every crack that made her: between her toes, behind her legs, inside her thighs. He licked up her spine, on her shoulders, in the back of her neck. He dug deep inside her as she screamed, —Ay, Santo, que maravilla Santo, ven conmigo, Santo.

—Yes, he crooned along with her. —Yes, he said as he collapsed into her and fell into a long-awaited sleep.

Esperanza stopped in San Pedro to pick up Don Chan and Bobby. She, Dallas, and Consuelo all piled out of the car. Consuelo squealed when she saw them.

—Was she crying a lot? I missed you, little one, Bobby said while Miraluz watched him. Her hair was wet from a shower, her skin glowing, her smile stretched from ear to ear as she watched Bobby extend his arms with Consuelo in them, spinning her around in front of Miraluz's house.

—What took you so long? Don Chan said. He had been up before the roosters, anxious to arrive in Los Llanos. Doña Caridad was waiting for him.

Esperanza greeted Miraluz out of decency but pulled away in haste to hide in the car. Every time Esperanza looked at her, she became angry all over again. She knew about her affection for Santo.

—Can I hold her? Miraluz said, extending her arms. —Qué bella es! Consuelo grabbed Miraluz's necklace with her name on it.

—It's getting late, Esperanza said. —We don't have all day.

When Bobby tried to take Consuelo back, the baby cried. —I'm so sorry, she never acts this way.

—You're a wild spirit, aren't you? Miraluz said.

—Maybe she's hungry? Dallas said.

—But she just finished eating, Esperanza said. —Put her in the car and she'll shut up when she feels the car moving.

She didn't care to be around Miraluz one minute longer.

Don Chan was amazed by the sunlight falling on the blades of the palm leaves, the gleam off Dallas's earrings, the glimmer on the hood of the car. Light was bouncing off everything.

—Miraluz, ven con nosotros, Don Chan said.

—But she doesn't fit in the car, Esperanza protested.

—It's a short drive, c'mon, Bobby said.

They drove through the small roads and into an opening inside the lowest of the valleys, where all one could see was sky and miles and miles of skin-splitting cane. Among all the green, the Colón family of Juan Dolio had built themselves a house with a zinc roof and a wood stove. And after all those years, the house was still waiting, nestled in an abandoned landscape, with struggling avocado and cashew trees. The deceased Colóns de Juan Dolio were buried nearby, far enough not to disturb the living's sleep, but close enough for them to spot the tombstones. The small house was locked with a padlock. The names of all their ancestors carved on wild stones pressed against the ground. Despite the hurricanes, and the mild earthquakes, despite it all, the tombstones were as visible as day, to be read and respected.

The Colón family walked on the dirt, moist from a recent rain. The smell of latrine and wood burning filled the air.

—The land to the west of here was recently sold. I tried to convince them not to, but the price was right. Miraluz showed Don Chan as they walked around Los Llanos. She pointed to the newly grown sugarcane and sighed. They bring in the workers from Dajabón for short periods and treat them like cattle.

—How could our people sell the land if it wasn't theirs? Don Chan asked, mortified. He had bought all the land with the money he had found; he'd distributed the land evenly among all who joined the Invisible Ones movement, and together they created an agricultural system that worked toward Los Llanos being self-sufficient. Now, it had been mostly turned into sugarcane fields.

Field workers passed by and nodded. Dallas wiped the dirt off the windowsill and sat on its edge. She wondered what it would be like to live in such a place. She tried to imagine her grandfather as a young man hiding in all the green. His lean body exposed as he worked his days in the fields. She watched Miraluz in awe, her long, black hair braided and wrapped around her head.

Bobby pulled over a rusted folding chair and sat under a tree for shade with Consuelo and craved being with Miraluz again. He wanted to help her, and decided he would stay with her for a few extra days. He wanted her to spend time with Consuelo. He thought about Hush as he watched Consuelo stumble after a loose chicken. He feasted on the sun and imagined Sunday-afternoon barbecues with music blaring out of his surround-sound stereo system. He couldn't imagine a cloudy day in D.R. He could live in such a climate. As long as he could plug in, he would be happy to stay.

Esperanza paced around and tried to keep the sweat off her face. Her makeup melted off, revealing caramel skin under white powder. How much was the land worth? The cane, where the house was. Once Don Chan died, she'd sell the land and pay all her debt so she could be free. Maybe even start saving for a house to retire in. She'd keep the small section of land for the graves. But the rest was useless to her. It was part of a past she didn't care to remember. She paced and looked at her children and was taken aback by Bobby, who was smiling and pointing and carrying Consuelo around.

Bobby clapped with joy when she reached up to grab a bitter orange from a tree.

—Look at this. Where in New York City can you do this?

—The supermarket, Dallas said.

Esperanza sneaked off to spread Santo's ashes over the blossoming bleeding hearts near the graves. She was caught in the thick air feeling relieved. And when she was accosted by a strange bug or flying leaf, debating if she should use the latrine, or piss in the wild shrubbery, thirsty but afraid of the water in the well, Esperanza was sure that Los Llanos was never a place she could call home.

Dallas poked inside Don Chan's old house, studying the yellowed photos taped on a damaged mirror, all coated with dust. She looked at their ancestors in the photos. Esperanza had already taped a photo of Santo next to Doña Caridad. No matter how much the Colón family willed time to move faster, to keep in rhythm with their New

York City pace, D.R. resisted and time went along as it needed to go. They weren't like the president, who shortened and lengthened days. None of them had control of the sun that hovered over them in the late afternoon. Besides, willing time takes effort, and the familiar and not-so-familiar scenery kept their minds so busy they didn't notice when Don Chan walked into the cane fields with Miraluz.

—It's my time, Don Chan said, walking away from Miraluz. The mosquitoes nipped at Don Chan's arms and chest. The cane leaves sliced his face. He didn't feel the blood come down his left eye. He saw the bright blue, the blazing sun. His clothes stuck to his skin, the sweat ran down his body. It wasn't until he was far away that Bobby yelled after him, —Abuelo, where are you going? He tried to follow him, but the cane was tall, even taller than Bobby.

—Leave the old man alone, Miraluz said. —The cacique death of honor is when he doesn't fear it.

—What are you talking about? Bobby walked after him. Miraluz pulled him back.

The sun was falling. It didn't spread like the sunset spread in New York City, it stayed whole, the sun on one side of the sky, the moon on the other.

Don Chan thought back to the day when the land of Dominican Republic was new to him. When he was left with no choice but to study the journeys of the Chinese families who sailed to the Americas for a better life and a bit more freedom. With each fact he dug up from history books and campesinos' lips, he couldn't help but think that his poor old father was one of the unfortunate ones who had found himself indentured, trapped in a credit system where he worked forever to pay the landowners back. Perhaps his father died in the fields, like so many Chinese immigrants who worked the cane. Or maybe his father did the impossible and fled. That was Don Chan's favorite interpretation. That his father looked at his future, working in the fields of Cuba, and all he saw was misery. He imagined his father begging for work just so that he could provide his family with a few meals a day, so that his skin wouldn't stick to his bones and his family would have a roof over their heads. He was convinced that his poor old father found so much ill-paying work, he could no longer feel his hands, his body, his tongue. That's why his father had fled and never looked back, fearing that if he did, he'd get killed for it. He fled to the ocean, yes the ocean, because the ocean seems infinite, vast and cleansing. He found work on a big warship. And to his father, it was the most impressive ship he'd ever seen. It had a sail as tall as a palm tree, which ballooned out against the sky's canvas and sang a song, large conch seashells whistled into the ear. The ship had a calling to another place, an urgency to chase the song of the wind.

Don Chan told his father's story often. He sometimes forgot which stories came from people's lips, books, or his own imagination. To him, all his stories were true.

—And what about your mother? You never talk about her, his adopted mother, la señora Colón de Juan Dolio asked him one day.

That's when it occurred to Don Chan that not one single passage in the books he read contained a Chinese woman. So he was left with no other option but to imagine his mother dying from a fever that made her float right up to the heavens, like the Chinese woman he had heard about once who lived on the other side of his town. Who was so thin, she had pebbles sewn in the hem of her skirt so the wind wouldn't blow her away.

Don Chan continued to walk into the cane fields where he stood, finally, and looked at the blue and green blending. He sat down on the dirt because he was tired of walking. He couldn't see his house anymore. All the workers had left for the day. He was alone. Only the field mice sped across, chasing prey. The sun left the sky. He saw the sky turn a darker blue. He could hear his name in the wind. He felt the hold of a man at his elbow, but when he turned around to look there was no one there. He went to grab a piece of white fabric blossoming in the green stalk, only to find there was nothing there. He saw the shadow of a man running, but there was no man attached. He ducked at the flying machete, but there was nothing to fear; it disappeared as the night's breeze made the cane stalks sway. He saw a woman birthing, a child running, an old man eating the insides of a passion fruit, a man much like himself, when he ate in the fields, trying to hide from his father. Not his Chinese father, but his Dominican father. He walked away from the voices that called his name. He knew the farther he went into the green, the harder it was to get out. The dark blue was his blanket, the earth was his bed. He was listening for the first time in a long time to the songs of the earth. He was hearing names—Chan Lee, Hsu Hsu, Guacanagari, Olivorio, Ch'iu . . . Names whispered with the rustling, the chasing, the running, and then he wondered if his name was Chan Lee at all. That if he was born from the sea, his name could be any name, he could be any man who was lost to the sea.

The earth was asking him to surrender. He had learned that all he could do for the world was nourish the earth with his blood, with his skin. And as he fell into a deep sleep, he wondered if maybe the reason he didn't remember how he got to this land called República Dominicana was because it must have been a peaceful six years of his life. He imagined the ocean like a womb that nurtured him with its warmth.

Don Chan's hands dug into the earth. And as he dug, the earth cracked open and he fell into it, catching glimpses of women nursing their sons; men running, shooting, building machines to kill, to incarcerate; women setting themselves on fire. As he fell deeper into the earth, he saw women killing their children in rivers and crying; people making love; hurricanes, tornadoes, rainbows, and blocks of ice drifting in the sea; the insides of people's bodies, sprouting tobacco, sugar, and coffee. People being cut up with machetes and tossed into rivers; armies in white cloaks with burning crosses; women protecting their homes with swords; buildings collapsing into dust, burning like embers of a cigarette. He saw children, stomachs filled with air, as they struggled not to float away. Whips and chains; communities offering the sea fire, flowers, sweets, wishing for forbidden love, the resurrection of the dead, the return of the lost. Naked women displayed in store windows, for sale. Children buried in unmarked graves after their lungs gave out from working in the mines, children inhaling glue to appease their hunger; men hanging off trees with their cocks in their mouths. Castles. Blue ocean. People cutting off their own limbs out of desperation; children crying and laughing.

At the core of the earth, there was a woman with features that changed with the movement of the sun. She grabbed him. He was no longer frail, but small like a child and the woman who lived in the core of the earth threw his body up into the sky, and before he could blink, he was surrounded by hundreds of women in bright dresses grabbing at him, laughing with joy that his fall had not killed him.

Acknowledgments

This work of fiction was inspired by some historical facts, lots of cuentos from people's lips and from the memory our bodies carry. For that I want to thank the ancestors and the lineage of women I descended from. Throughout the journey in writing this novel, many generous spirits offered me their time, ideas, thoughts, books, and resources. A special thanks to Julia Kang, for your intelligent observations and continuous support as a writer and friend. Chris Heiser, your feedback was priceless. Nelly Rosario, just when I thought I didn't have any more energy left to finish this book, you reenergized me with your insight. Juan Aceves, I am indebted to you for your love and honesty. Gracias, Joanne Cruz, my dearest sister, who assisted me with translation and research. Adelina Anthony, it was you who invited me to Dallas seven years ago and inadvertently started me on my *Dallas* trip. Marta Lucía Vargas, it was during the many sleepless nights in organizing WILL with you that I gathered the seeds for this novel. And Paolo Piscitelli, you are a constant inspiration. Grazie. Also thank you to: Eugene Datta, Hector M. Graciano, Alba Hernández, Madhu Kaza, Lily Liy, Jeff Montero, Rosie Scott, and Lidia Torres.

My wonderful editor, Marysue Rucci, I thank you for all your thoughtful advice and dedication to this book. To my agent, Ellen Levine, your support and faith in my work is invaluable. To the assistants, Tara Parsons and Melissa Flashman, I truly appreciate all your help in this process.

I am grateful for the scholars who took the time to review my historical references: Professor Sintia Molina and Professor Silvio Torres-Saillánt. A very special thanks to Lenina Trinidad and her team of lawyer friends for making sure I got my facts straight. I also want to acknowledge Yaddo, the MacDowell Colony, the Ledig House International Writer's Colony, the Camargo Foundation, Fundación La Napoule, all of which provided me with financial support and a tranquil space, for significant amounts of time, to work on this novel. There were many books, videos, newspaper articles, and internet sites to inform this novel. Among them, *The Dominican Republic,* by Frank Moya Pons, and *Dominican Diary,* by Tad Szulc. Thank you, Alex Rivera and Bernardo Ruiz for your documentary, *The Sixth Section.* Your work documenting immigrant laborers taking action within their communities was extremely helpful in providing me with the imagination and energy to continue our struggle to make this world a fairer place. I would also like to acknowledge the helpful staff at the Archivo General in Santo Domingo, and my deepest gratitude for the resources of the Dominican Institute at CUNY City College.

Gracias, Madre mía, for sending me off every summer to live in Dominican Republic and for accompanying me there as an adult to revisit the places of your childhood. To mi querida abuela Leoncia Gomez and mi tío Luis Gomez, whose dedication to our family in Los Llanos inspired me to learn the history of the eastern part of the country. To the many family members from the Gomez, Cruz, Sosa tribe who shared their life stories and insights, including my cousins David, Ronald, Dre, Rolin, Manny, and Alex. I am especially grateful to my brother, Edwin Cruz, who gave up his laptop when mine broke down so I wouldn't lose a day of work.

About the Author

ANGIE CRUZ was born and raised in the Washington Heights section of New York City. She is a graduate of SUNY Binghamton and received her MFA from New York University. Her fiction and activist work have earned her the New York Foundation of the Arts Fellowship, the Barbara Deming Memorial Fund Award, and the Bronx Writers' Center Van Lier Literary Fellowship. Cruz lives in New York City. She is the author of *Soledad*.

Visit the author at www.angiecruz.com.